DANGEROUS
OUTSIDER

DANGEROUS OUTSIDER

Graeme Roe

CARROLL & GRAF PUBLISHERS
NEW YORK

Carroll & Graf Publishers
An imprint of Avalon Publishing Group, Inc.
245 W. 17th Street, 11th Floor
New York, NY 10011-5300
www.carrollandgraf.com

AVALON
publishing group incorporated

First published in the UK by Constable,
an imprint of Constable & Robinson Ltd 2007

First Carroll & Graf edition 2007

ISBN-13: 978-0-78671-959-4
ISBN-10: 0-7867-1959-1

Printed and bound in the EU

32903000239050

Acknowledgements

Trying to single out individuals who have helped me along the way to producing *Dangerous Outsider* is not easy. Many of them are the same people who made such important contributions to *A Touch of Vengeance* and *Odds on Death*.

Once again Richard Dunwoody, Mark Kershaw and Bob Champion have all given specific advice and encouragement. Adrian Pratt helped me with the insurance scam and the Willesley Equine Clinic assisted with some of the specifics concerning equine medical matters.

Racecourses up and down the country have welcomed and helped me. Racegoers and readers have also offered kind comments and support. Pauline Dawes battled with the draft and redraft of my manuscript with efficiency and cheerfulness. I am deeply grateful.

Lastly, it would be totally inappropriate to omit the encouragement, advice and friendship from my publisher, and in particular, Krystyna Green who has had the humour and patience to encourage me to keep writing.

To all of you, my deep felt thanks.

Author's Note

It is almost impossible to believe that a sport, which goes back to at least the days of King Charles II, should be the source of new and unexpected developments. Yet racing never ceases to intrigue and amaze me. Major changes take place as established racecourses like Ascot alter dramatically, and regrettably some of the smaller courses disappear. All-weather racing has become a significant part of the sport, providing not only new interest but much needed funds. Top horses like Ouija Board jet set around the world becoming sporting celebrities in their own right, and champion jockeys become household names not only in their own country but also in the international media. At one end of the scale, prize money escalates to millions, and at the other extreme, a winning horse at one of the minor tracks may pick up as little as £1,000.

Who could have believed that the Internet would have thrown up an entirely new system of betting? This online system has brought not only a new dimension for the individual punter to exploit, but has also become associated with serious concerns about race fixing and the integrity of some of the leading figures in the sport.

Against this ever-changing background, the sport remains glamorous, exciting, tragic, and above all unpredictable. From the multi-millionaire owner to the housewife who occasionally dabbles on the Derby and the Grand National, it provides an intriguing and exciting diversion.

There are many heroes in racing, the majority of whom are unsung. Amongst these heroes are the starting stall loaders, and the stable staff who cheerfully accept the drudgery of grooming, cleaning and exercising their charges, often in the most horrible of weather conditions. There are also villains and, like the heroes, they come in all shapes and sizes, from every walk of life. But above all there's one group of heroes without whom the sport would not exist and would certainly not have the glamour and the beauty that excites and intrigues – this is the thoroughbred racehorse.

I apologize if I inadvertently cause offence by using the name of a real person or horse. I hope that *Dangerous Outsider* reflects the great love and esteem I have for horse racing and the people involved in it. But above all, I must insist that this is a work of fiction. Neither the people nor events are real, although hopefully they will reflect at least some of the essence of this wonderful sport.

Prologue

The tall Oriental crosses the suite in the Shangri-la Hotel in Bangkok. He walks on to his balcony and looks down on the river – a kaleidoscope of colours and shapes, and still one of the most important means of communication and commerce in the city. He gazes at the boats of all sizes, at the teeming activity, walks back into the room and sits in a large chair in front of a coffee table. On it are two mobile phones. One has the number which is used by his senior employees and other privileged businessmen who are part of the vast international network which he controls.

The other has a number known only to two men. The two he's waiting to meet.

Each will ring from the lobby downstairs, the first at precisely ten o'clock and the second ten minutes later. They will mingle with the crowd and talk to no one. Both of them will melt into the background. To the casual observer each is just another businessman. Both are well known to the occupant of the suite. Both are on his payroll and are locked into his operation. Each also is involved in other operations, mainly as part of their cover to ensure they are in no way linked to him.

He is always immaculately but rather conservatively dressed. He oozes confidence, power and wealth. His charming manner hides a ruthlessness he is careful to conceal from all but his closest employees and those who are unwise enough to thwart his will, whether intentionally or not.

He only recognizes one code of law – his own.

At one minute to ten the phone rings. An Irish voice announces, 'I'm here.'

'Right,' is the one-word response.

Within minutes there's a knock at the door and the Oriental crosses his room and opens it. Kieran Hanagan is also conservatively dressed. He's a little above average height and slightly overweight. His manner is reserved and his speech and appearance suggest a lawyer or a banker. He is in fact a money man, a specialist in tax avoidance and money laundering. Like his employer, he is totally unscrupulous but he's meticulously honest with his clients. They know, however, that to cross him in any way would be dangerous and probably fatal.

They shake hands with respect rather than warmth. Hanagan accepts a glass of iced water and obeys the gesture to be seated. At almost exactly ten past ten the phone rings again and a similar brief conversation takes place. The Oriental replaces the phone, switching it off. He does the same with the other, and then walks across to open the door as it is knocked.

Michael Coleman is nearly six foot tall, suntanned, wiry and with greying hair in a close-cropped military style. He too shakes hands, accepts a glass of water and sits down.

The three of them are meeting to discuss the next stage in a plan they have been working on for several months. It is now March.

They are planning to undermine one of the largest racing establishments in Europe with a worldwide reputation.

The Oriental is the driving force and financier. He moves the money where it's needed and when, with complete secrecy. He is also responsible for ensuring that a specific figure in Irish racing is persuaded to become part of their plans and that, once in, he has no exit. If muscle is needed he knows who to use.

Coleman is English, an ex-flat trainer who had some success with the relatively small string of horses at his disposal. During the course of these activities his charm and encyclopedic knowledge of breeding led him to move into the bloodstock industry. It took him only a short time to build a reputation for shrewdness and skill. Unfortunately he made the mistake of allowing greed and carelessness to overtake him. He has narrowly escaped both the law and the taxman, and the racing authorities have made it clear he is no longer a welcome member of the now closely regulated industry. His reputation in England in tatters, he made his way to the Far East where racing flourishes. Here he has a number of contacts and a few friends who, for various reasons, find the grass greener than in Great Britain or Europe. They are prepared to overlook his past indiscretions as long as he performs as well for them as he did in his early days in Newmarket.

Like the Irishman he is largely funded by the Oriental, but has enough other clients to ensure that his business appears to be perfectly legitimate and in no way connected to the well-known but rather mysterious figure who has invited him to the Shangri-la.

The Oriental addresses Hanagan. 'Have you got your trainer tied up?'

'Absolutely. He is wildly ambitious, has a good reputation, but is in too much of a hurry to allow that to generate the size of operation he's determined to have. As you know, his father has no real money to talk of, and certainly not the ability to fund his son in the way we have in mind.'

'What's the timetable?'

'I have an option on the yard at Lambourn and anticipate completion by the middle of April. He will be tied up by then so I expect him to move to England at the end of that month or by the middle of May. I've allowed for a few weeks' delay in case there's more to be done to the yard and other facilities than we know of at the moment. If we reveal the extent of our plans too quickly, rumours will start flying before we're ready to show our hand fully.'

This is met by a nod of approval. Turning to the bloodstock man, the Oriental asks, 'So what's the news on your front?'

'Well, as you know, they've closed the US operation and are now concentrating on New Zealand, France and South Africa. France is definitely losing money and South Africa would be about break-even. On the other hand New Zealand is doing really well and is not only funding the other two operations but making a substantial contribution to the holding company's turnover and profit. They were very shrewd in the mares they bought. Their use of top-class stallions, some of which they own, has proved very fruitful already. Their reputation, particularly for jumpers, is sky-high and growing.'

'So what's your plan?'

'Initially I'm going to concentrate on New Zealand. I'll try and damage their profitability and at the same time, hopefully, erode their standing in the bloodstock industry.'

Again the Oriental nods approvingly.

They discuss a few further details and then the meeting is brought to an end. No further refreshment is offered. The Englishman leaves first, followed ten minutes later by the Irishman. The farewells are brief and curt.

As soon as he is alone, the Oriental switches on both his phones and walks across to the bar in the corner of the room. He pours himself a large measure of Johnnie Walker Black Label, adds a splash of plain water and sits down. A contented smile crosses his normally impassive face. The stock market is going up, his businesses are doing well, and one which he recently entered is proving profitable beyond his wildest expectations. A lot of people are going to get a lot of surprises. None of them good. His involvement in their catastrophes will never surface.

Yes, he thinks. Life is good.

Chapter One

On a beautiful early May morning the London Eye was turning in its slow majestic way on the South Bank of the Thames near Westminster Bridge. In one of the capsules was a family of three. Jason Jessop, universally known as Jay or JJ, was pointing out the features of the London skyline to Max, his seven-year-old son. Watching and listening to them, Eva, his wife, felt she could never be happier.

Jay was something of a celebrity in racing circles. After winning the Amateur National Hunt Jockeys Championship, he started to train, and had been champion trainer five times in the last seven years. The previous year had been a near thing – it was not until the last day of the Aintree meeting that he eventually tied it up.

Eva was the daughter of the late Max Botha, an immensely wealthy South African diamond merchant who had left his fortune to his only child. The legacy included a separate sum in a Swiss bank account to be invested in National Hunt racing, his passion since his days at Cambridge University.

Towards the end of Jay's riding career he had met Eva through a trainer called Fiona French for whom he had ridden many winners. Subsequently Eva and Fiona revealed that Eva was in fact Fiona's daughter by Max. They had never married because Max's wife was extremely ill and he refused to leave her. With him spending so much of his time in South Africa and Fiona being based in Lambourn, they agreed that there was no point changing their relationship, even after the death of his invalid wife. They had, however, remained friends and lovers to the end of his life.

Jay had become a very rich man in his own right. After leaving Cambridge he had founded a scientific publishing company. This flourished and eventually an American publishing house, headed by Hal Bancroft, made a huge offer for the business which Jay accepted. The financial independence allowed him to indulge in his lifelong dream of becoming a racehorse trainer. Hal and Jay's business compatibility developed into a close friendship, and eventually Hal, along with two of his American friends, had become a shareholder in Jay's training business.

At the same time Jay approached Howard Barrack for whom he had ridden many times. This association had resulted in a close friendship developing between him and Jed Larkin, Howard's trainer. When Jay outlined his plans, Howard immediately agreed to become a major investor and also to send horses to the new venture. This concerned Jay. He did not want to poach Jed's most important owner. However, almost simultaneously, Jed had confessed that his health was failing and he had been told to take it easy. The obvious solution was for Jed to join Jay's operation as assistant trainer. He and his wife Cathy happily moved to a cottage at the new training establishment, a converted airfield in the Cotswolds. By this time Eva and Jay had become lovers and she insisted on investing a substantial part of her father's racing bequest in County View, the name of the new racing complex.

The other main investor had been a man called Victor Rainsford who had a construction business which played a major role in developing the enterprise so successfully. Sadly it subsequently emerged that Victor was not the genuine investor they thought. In fact he was eventually arrested and given a long term in prison following his conviction for a wide range of criminal activities. Some of them he had financed in an effort to discredit Jay.

The other key figures in the County View venture were a young ex-City man called Roddy Clinton-Bowes, and Jerline, his beautiful Oriental wife. She was the daughter of a fabulously wealthy Hong Kong businessman called Hamish Tang. Hamish had also invested in County View and was now a director of the company.

As a result of Roddy's enthusiasm and Hamish's whole-hearted backing, County View had embarked upon buying or setting up a number of studs around the world, including France, South Africa, New Zealand and the USA. The venture in the USA had not been very successful and was eventually sold off. South Africa was beginning to make real progress, and New Zealand was doing extremely well. A number of highly promising young horses had already been sent to be trained by Jay. France was breaking even but was not proving as exciting as had been hoped.

The other director was Percy Cartwright, a Cambridge friend of Jay's, a big operator in the insurance industry.

Now, as they left the Eye, the Jessop family were watched by a nondescript middle-aged man sitting on a motorbike. He replaced his helmet and followed their taxi to Simpson's in the Strand. He had nearly completed a highly professional dossier on Jay, his staff, his horses and his fellow directors. It would soon be on its way to Singapore. At the restaurant Max could hardly believe the size of the piece of beef which was carved at their table. A huge fuss was made of the three Jessops by Peter, the head waiter, who had known Jay for years. Many of the important meetings during the planning of County View had been held there – particularly at breakfast.

After lunch, Eva drove her husband and son back to County View. As usual, Jay made a point of walking round the yard in the evening with Jed and Danny, his Head Man. Danny had been a top jockey before an injury had forced him into an early retirement which had led to drug addiction. He had nearly been killed by an Irish drugs baron known inappropriately as The Friend, who eventually wound up in an English jail charged with drug smuggling. Although he was indeed guilty of many crimes, this particular one had been manufactured by Jay and a friend of Howard's called Benny. Benny was an East Ender famous for his amazing network of connections throughout the criminal world. He was not a criminal in the true sense of the word but was not averse to sailing close to the wind. He had been an enormous help to Jay on a number of occasions.

Danny had kicked the drug habit and was now an essential part of the successful training team. Among the other key players was Freddy Kelly, the champion jockey, who had retired at the end of the previous season. He was now living in Ireland and had started his own bloodstock dealing agency. His replacement was Paul Jenkins who had joined Jay as an up-and-coming conditional jockey (the National Hunt term for an apprentice). He had developed into a top-class performer, first of all winning the Conditional Jockeys Championship, and then riding many winners including some very big races for County View. If Jay didn't need him for a particular race or meeting, he always encouraged the young jockey to take outside rides. Following Freddy's retirement, Jay told him that he would be taking over as the stable number one jockey.

Sitting down to supper after Max had gone to bed, Jay smiled at Eva and announced, 'I think I've got an idea that might appeal to you.' Eva raised a questioning eyebrow.

'How about if we take a six week break, go over to South Africa, visit the stud, and leave Max with your mother for a few weeks? We can then visit Hamish in Hong Kong, travel on to the New Zealand stud, return via Cape Town, pick up Max and be home in time for the beginning of the next season.'

Eva jumped up, ran round the table, and threw her arms round Jay's neck. 'I can think of nothing better,' she enthused, planting a kiss on his cheek. 'But what about County View?'

'Well, as you know I'm not too keen on summer jump racing. The going is often rather doubtful, although the courses do as good a job as the weather allows. Most of the horses have had a hard season, and we have a lot of young ones to back, get half fit and see if they can jump. It will be a change of pace for the staff, who deserve a break.'

'In that case I'll get started on the arrangements and call Mother.'

After Fiona had retired from training, she moved to South Africa where she had many friends, a house outside Johannesburg, a lodge on one of the big safari parks, and a large flat in Cape Town. Although she came to England frequently, both parents knew that Fiona would love to see more of her grandson. Jay felt it would be a wonderful opportunity to broaden his son's education and give Fiona and Max the opportunity to bond. It was readily agreed.

The next morning, after those horses not turned out for the summer had been exercised, Jay called Jed and Danny into his kitchen where most major discussions took place. Outlining his plan, he asked their views. Was he putting too much of a strain on them? 'Not at all,' was their unanimous answer. 'We can reach you on the phone, Howard's always available, and young Roddy is becoming both helpful and knowledgeable,' Jed reassured him.

Jay phoned Chris Langridge, the vet, who promised that he and his wife Amanda would come over once a week to check things out with Jed and Danny. Amanda had been a good amateur jockey and work rider. She was pregnant so had given up riding, and Eva rather missed this bubbly young woman's company on five or six mornings a week. They had remained close friends and normally had dinner once or twice a month.

Jay rang Howard who thought the trip was a great idea, and Roddy who was thrilled that Jay wanted to visit his father-in-law as part of his tour. He made a mental note to phone Hal later in the day when America was awake, and left Eva, who was also a director of the company and played an important role in the PR, to start handling the travel arrangements.

Lastly he called Percy Cartwright who felt the stud visits an excellent idea, and jokingly asked if he could carry their bags.

During their mid-morning coffee break Jed walked in and said, 'Have you seen the *Racing Post* today?'

'No. For once I haven't got around to looking at the papers at all.'

'Well, you might be interested in this.' The front-page story was that a highly successful young Irish trainer called Quentin O'Connor had bought one of the big training establishments at Lambourn and was moving from Ireland to the UK. A number of his successful horses were coming with him, and it appeared that most of his current owners were very supportive.

'What do you know about him, Jed?' asked Danny, who had followed the older man into the kitchen.

'Very little, apart from what I've read in the papers. His father was a very successful trainer in a small way, and Quentin started his working life with him. He then moved on to become assistant trainer at one of the big yards, and after a couple of years moved back to take over from his father who retired but continued to give him advice and the benefit of his experience. It seems from this article that he has some pretty substantial financial backing. He must be confident of getting a lot more horses than those that he's bringing over from Ireland. Why don't you phone Freddy and see what he can add to the background? If he's as good as the papers say, we could have a serious new competitor on our hands.'

'No sooner said than done,' replied Jay, and a few moments later he was talking to Freddy at his yard on the edge of the Curragh. But Freddy had little to add apart from the fact that he'd met Quentin a few times and found him charming and able, although he was said to have a short temper.

'I'll ask around a bit and come back to you with any extra information,' he promised.

The next two weeks flashed by as the team broke in the young horses that had not been raced. They also increased the workload of those that had had an easy season the year before, and the horses that loved fast ground and therefore needed to run in the early part of the season.

When County View had been set up, the original plan had been for nearly all the horses to be owned by the syndicate. This strategy had slowly been eroded as owners wanted to send top-class horses to the successful yard. This revised strategy worked incredibly well. One such horse, Splendid Warrior, had won two Gold Cups for Jay. Following this, a number of other top-class horses had come, mainly young animals from the flat. Jay had turned most of them into terrific hurdlers.

A couple of days before the three of them left for their trip, Freddy phoned from Ireland to say that he'd learnt very little more about Quentin. He was rumoured to have a very substantial backer and was likely to move into buying high class bloodstock, with money being no real object.

'Ah well,' said Jay, 'let's see what happens.'

On the day of their departure the Jessops were sent on their way with enthusiastic wishes for a good break from Jed and Danny and many of the stable staff who had been with Jay for a long while. The family were driven to Heathrow by Jack Doyle, their senior horsebox driver, who was going to take Jay's beloved Jaguar back to County View.

Max was beside himself with excitement as they boarded the plane and were taken upstairs to the first class compartment of the British Airways 747 which was flying them directly to Cape Town. Instantly recognized by the cabin crew, Jay was made welcome and the senior stewardess set out to spoil Max rotten on the journey.

'Six weeks without hassle,' enthused Eva. 'I can hardly believe it.' With that she finished her glass of champagne, switched to a video film she wanted to watch, and left Jay to entertain their son. They did a number of puzzles and played simple games like noughts and crosses until Jay started to think it was time to get Max settled down for the night. However, at that moment the stewardess asked if she could borrow Max for a while, giving Jay a big wink.

'That's a great idea,' he said. 'It would give me some peace and quiet.'

Max was led by the hand to the front of the plane where he was ushered into the cockpit and the captain explained in simple terms what he was doing. Fifteen minutes later an ecstatic Max was back, telling Jay all about it.

'Right, young man,' said his father, 'we're both going to get some rest now.' The excitement had the desired effect and in no time Max was fast asleep while Jay took the opportunity to glance through the papers. Soon he too was fast asleep, as was Eva who had nodded off well before the end of her film.

Chapter Two

At Cape Town airport the family were met by Fiona who was thrilled to see all of them but particularly her rapidly growing grandson. They were driven to her spacious flat on the Waterfront, unpacked and then relaxed. Fiona produced lunch, having refused to let Jay take them out.

'There'll be plenty of time for that tomorrow, and you must all be really tired. A quiet day relaxing in the flat is definitely in order.'

Even Max was happy to play quietly on the balcony and then have an early night. After supper the grown-ups settled down over a bottle of excellent South African red wine and brought each other up to date with their activities. They were just getting ready for bed when Jay's mobile rang. It was Jed.

'I'm really sorry to worry you, Jay, but thought you ought to know that Cool Customer has left the yard.' Cool Customer had won the Queen Mother Chase the previous year at the Cheltenham Festival.

'What do you mean?' asked Jay.

'Bill Smith, the owner, phoned up this morning and said that he had received an offer he couldn't turn down. He said a horsebox would be arriving to collect the horse and he would settle the outstanding training fees as soon as he received our bill. He was clearly embarrassed, and I asked if he would like to speak to you directly, but he said no, that could wait until you came back.'

'Well, that's extraordinary,' said Jay. 'Have you any idea where the horse is going?'

'None at all, and Bill wasn't forthcoming when I asked him.'

'Well, there's nothing we can do about it, but it's a real shame to lose the one horse that won a major race at last year's Festival.'

This was the first time that Jay had been confronted by such a situation and it had obviously upset him a great deal.

'No point worrying about it,' said Fiona. 'If you knew the number of times that happened to me, for no good reason, you'd be amazed. It's little comfort, but it's bound to happen to you again.' They finished the wine, Jay lit up one of his trademark Monte Cristo No. 3s, and Fiona produced a bottle of extremely old Armagnac which she insisted would help him sleep.

They were woken up at seven the next morning by an extremely excited Max who was jumping up and down on their bed.

'Granny's going to take me to meet penguins,' he said. 'Are you going to come too?'

Jay looked at Eva. 'I don't think we can miss that,' she said. After a quick breakfast they all got into Fiona's car and drove along the coast to Boulder. Max was in heaven watching dozens of the birds, so ungainly on the sand, play like acrobats in the ocean. It took Jay's mind off the events of the previous day. Fiona tactfully steered away from the subject as well, and that evening Jay took them out to a special fish restaurant on Camps Bay. They all agreed on another early night as Eva and Jay were flying on to Mauritius the next day, and Max was very excited that Granny was going to take him up to the top of Table Mountain.

Jay and Eva had decided to stop off at Mauritius on their way to Hong Kong. They'd been recommended the Tropical Hotel on the east coast, and as soon as they walked in they knew it was just what they were looking for. There was a grass apron in front of their room with steps leading down from the sea wall straight into the glass-like sea. The next six days they spent swimming, snorkelling, sleeping, and enjoying each other's company in an air of relaxation that they'd not really had since the very early days of County View.

The next stop was Hong Kong. They were surprised to be met by Hamish himself when they had expected a company car and driver. He whisked them off to his penthouse in a prime position in the famous Peak area. As a director, Hamish was fairly well in touch with what was going on in County View. He didn't get to every board meeting, but normally he was on a video link on these occasions, read the minutes with great interest, and nearly always made some valuable contribution to the discussion and decision-making. As soon as they had settled down, Jay told him about the loss of one of their top horses in inexplicable circumstances. Hamish made light of it and reassured Jay there was nothing to worry about. That night he took the two of them out to dinner to meet his sons, Fraser and Gavin.

Hamish had got his name as a result of his father being greatly helped by a Scotsman of that name when he started what was now a huge multinational business. Hamish had spent much time in Scotland, including a significant part of his education. He then followed in his father's footsteps and continued to expand the business to its now huge proportions. The two sons each had a major responsibility for about half of the business empire, and both were charming and highly attentive. Fraser, apparently, had little interest in horses, and, apart from working extremely hard, his main interests were sailing and water sports.

Gavin, on the other hand, had always been fascinated by horse racing. Off his own bat he had bought four horses that were trained locally, and he told Jay that he'd like to come over to England in a few months' time to see if there was an opportunity for him to have a couple of National Hunt horses at County View. The evening passed pleasantly, and Hamish, realizing that his guests must be pretty tired, ensured that they had an early night.

The next morning Jed rang again, sounding very worried indeed.

'Two more horses are leaving us,' he said, 'and I now know where they're going.' The two horses were both young and owned by the same man, Eric Hammond. All That Jazz had won two top class bumpers, one at Newbury and one at Sandown, and Winning Hand had won two novice chases, the second being a very important affair at Haydock Park. Again the reason given was that a huge sum of money had been offered. The owner insisted that when he was paid he would come and see Jay and try to replace them, but he felt that the offer was too good to miss.

'Well, where are they going?' queried Jay.

'They're going to Quentin O'Connor,' was the reply, 'and I now hear that Cool Customer is already there. The story is all over the racing pages, including the front page of the *Racing Post*. The phone hasn't stopped ringing. Every racing journalist wants to talk to you. I've explained that you're away and have made no comment on the reason they may be leaving. On each occasion I've said it's for the owner to comment on that, not me.'

'That's absolutely right,' agreed Jay. 'It's obvious that Mr O'Connor is hell-bent on buying ready-made horses rather than finding young ones and making them, as we did in our early days.'

'That certainly seems to be the case,' replied Jed.

'Is there anything else I ought to know?'

'No. As far as the rest of the horses are concerned everything is going well, and by the time you get back we'll be able to start making entries for the early season. The weather's been kind, so the grass gallops haven't dried out and we've been able to use them as well as the all-weather whenever we wanted to. One or two of the younger horses are looking particularly exciting, especially Hot to Trot. He's schooling over hurdles like an old handicapper, and Gentle Minx I think will be ready to go into novice chases as soon as you want her to.'

'Well, at least that's some good news,' replied Jay. 'Let me know if there's anything else that you feel I should know.'

He paused and added, 'You might give Percy a call for me, bring him and Howard up to date. I assume Roddy knows all about this?'

'Yes, but there's one other thing,' Jed went on. 'In no circumstances are you to cut your holiday short. There's nothing you can do about what's happened, and you not only deserve, but you really need a break before the next season starts in earnest.'

'Thanks for that,' replied Jay. 'I know I can rely on you and I think you know that.'

'I do,' said Jed. 'Give my love to Eva and say hi to Hamish for me.'

'I will,' promised Jay, and rang off.

Eva and Hamish had overheard the conversation, but Jay filled them in on the details. Eva looked worried, but Hamish was his normal calm self and pointed out it was hardly the end of the world, even though it was very annoying.

With that they changed the subject and started to discuss the stud operations that Hamish had been a major factor in building up in order to support his son-in-law. One of the reasons why he was so anxious that this side should succeed was that he wanted Roddy to be as successful in his area of activity as his two sons were in theirs.

Leaving Jay and Eva to have a quiet day and do some shopping, Hamish had arranged for them to go to Happy Valley Races the next day. Gavin would be joining them but Fraser had, as expected, declined.

Jay and Eva were very keen to see Happy Valley, which had a tremendous reputation even though it was flat racing. Going into what seemed like a huge arena, they were soon in a lift and whisked up to Hamish's luxurious box. This was full of well-dressed and voluble locals who were clearly excited and set on having a good time. They all sat down at a table laden with food, and almost immediately an immaculately dressed waiter was offering them every drink they had ever heard of and some they hadn't. Jay soon had a flute of Dom Perignon in his hand and Eva a glass of superb Chablis.

They were seated opposite each other, with one of Hamish's other guests and Gavin on either side of Eva, and Hamish next to Jay with another guest on his other side. The conversation flowed easily; a number of the other guests had more than a passing knowledge of County View and Jay's reputation in England.

Time flew past until the first race. The Jessops went on the balcony to watch it, and were immediately struck by the huge screen in the middle of the racecourse which showed the horses already on their way down to the start. The vast area for the public was teeming. The betting appeared frantic and the excitement was electric as the race took place. Flat racing had never really appealed to Jay, but the atmosphere and the excitement of the thousands watching the contest certainly struck a chord with him. The roar from the crowd rose to a deafening crescendo as the horses passed the winning post. Within seconds, betting slips were being thrown away, while the lucky few were making their way cheerfully to collect their winnings.

There was a great deal of animated conversation inside the box, and it was clear that many of these people had had a substantial interest in the race, including Gavin.

As the afternoon sped by, Eva and Jay were charmed by the attention paid to them. Jay declined to bet, explaining that he had no idea of the form of any of the horses, and he was thoroughly enjoying himself as a spectator. A number of their fellow guests offered him advice and some even insisted on giving him tips. Politely and firmly, but with a big grin, he stuck to his decision to keep his money in his pocket.

It soon became apparent to Jay that Gavin was gambling heavily, and this appeared to include side bets with some of the other guests. Hamish was watching his son but it was impossible to tell whether his expression was that of an indulgent father enjoying his son's relaxation, or a concerned parent wondering if his betting was getting out of hand.

Surprisingly quickly, the afternoon had come to an end

and Hamish insisted that everybody sat down and enjoyed at least a farewell drink as the crowds began to disperse. Looking down on the public areas, Jay was amazed at the sea of failed betting slips that had been left behind. Eventually Hamish started to escort his English guests out of the box, having a brief word with Gavin on the way out, and smiling and waving to those who lingered.

In the lift he announced, 'That's the hard core we've left behind. I expect they'll continue to give the bar a hammering, and I imagine it will be the early morning before any of them get home. I'm tempted to say that's the way of the young world, but as you can see a lot of them aren't young but probably feel they have to keep up with the pace just to prove they're still young at heart.'

With a grin, he shepherded them through the now diminishing crowd and outside the back of the grandstand to where his limousine was parked ready to get them home as quickly as the traffic would allow. That evening they had a quiet supper at a small local restaurant. Racing was hardly mentioned and Hamish kept them fascinated as he explained the economic and political changes which had followed the takeover of Hong Kong by China. He was concerned for the future and was moving his main office to Singapore. He also mentioned that he was using the banking facilities of the Cayman Islands more and more.

The next two days passed quietly with no more calls from the UK, several discussions about the County View stud interests, and some splendid meals. All too soon they were thanking Hamish, not only for his hospitality but also for the amount of time that he had lavished on them, as he shook their hands warmly and left them at the airport check-in gate.

On the flight to New Zealand Jay was deep in thought and Eva knew that this was probably a good time to leave him to think things out for himself. She knew he was upset because each of his horses was very special to him and represented so much hard work and loving attention by the staff as well as himself, Jed and Danny. This was the sort of situation that would have a very bad effect on morale, particularly on that of the grooms responsible for the horses concerned. To them it would be almost like losing a child.

Arriving in New Zealand they were met at the airport by Angus Stewart, the stud manager. With over twenty years' experience he had proved to be an absolute treasure. His advice on which mare to send to which stallion had paid off handsomely in over eighty per cent of the offspring, as had his advice on the purchase of several brood mares and one particular stallion. The New Zealand enterprise was both making money and providing County View with successful and highly valued horses, in particular Maori Warrior who had won two novice hurdles, The Haka who had won novice chases at Newbury and Wincanton, and Kiwi King who had been placed second in his two runs in high class bumper fields at Ascot and Chepstow.

Every morning, Jay and Eva rose early and went riding around the beautiful countryside with one of Angus's staff. In the afternoon Angus always had something interesting for them to do, including a visit to a rugby international between New Zealand and South Africa. The match was narrowly won by the Springboks, much to Eva's delight. It seemed no time at all when nearly five weeks had passed and they were on their way back to Cape Town to spend two days with Fiona and to collect young Max.

The pair were at the airport to greet them, and Max was so excited at what he had seen and done that he could hardly get the words out fast enough. Fiona was beaming, and quietly told her daughter that it had been one of the happiest times of her life.

After dinner that night, Jay told Fiona about the new setback at County View, and she reassured him that these things are likely to happen for a number of reasons. She pointed out that as trainers got bigger and more successful there were always some owners who felt they weren't getting the sort of treatment they deserved, and who extended this into feeling that their horses could do even better if they were given more individual attention.

'Well, that might be true if these horses hadn't all performed exceptionally well,' said Jay, 'but you can't do much better than win the Queen Mother Chase, can you?'

'Point taken,' replied Fiona with a wry smile, 'but you have a lot more ammunition in your yard.'

That evening, Jed phoned with more bad news. Two of last season's winners had gone to O'Connor from two different owners. Both had the same story about the size of the offer. Jay was now really put out and it took the combined efforts of wife and mother-in-law to calm him down.

For the next two days the four of them chilled out, although they did go up to see the vineyards in Stellenbosch and Jay took the opportunity to order some fine South African wines for shipment to County View. Three days after arriving in Cape Town they were back in the air, and this time Eva took the responsibility for entertaining Max, leaving Jay to his newspapers and books.

Jack Doyle met them at Heathrow and they were soon on their way back to County View. The security guard at the gate gave them an enthusiastic wave, and Jay felt the surge of pride and excitement that he always had on returning to his yard. Max had nodded off in the car, but Eva gave her husband a big smile and said, 'It's great to be home, isn't it?'

Chapter Three

The next day Jay slipped back into his normal routine of getting up early and finalizing the day's work plan for each horse which had been provisionally prepared the night before by Danny and Jed. He then mounted his wonderful old horse, The Conker. He was one of the horses owned by Howard that Jed had trained and moved with him to County View. Jay had won many races on him before retiring. The Conker was now his hack and the old horse was fighting fit though his racing days were long past. This partnership cantered up beside the gallop and stood next to the Land Rover in which Jed had preceded them. The first string went past in single file at half speed and Jay was delighted to see how well they all looked. He and Jed then separated those that would be racing early in the season and sent them back to the start of the gallop. This dozen then came up in pairs side by side at three-quarters racing speed.

Returning to the kitchen for his customary coffee, Jay had barely sat down when the telephone rang. It was obvious word had got out that he was back and the *Racing Post* was asking for his comment on the loss of his horses.

'I have no comment,' responded Jay. 'Horses belong to the owners – it is their decision to do with them what they wish.'

He had always had very good relations with nearly all the racing journalists, so although this particular reporter tried to be insistent they still parted on amicable terms. The call was repeated by racing correspondents from many of the national newspapers. All callers met with the same response and none of them was really surprised. One, however, did ask him what he knew about Quentin O'Connor. Jay's somewhat cryptic reply was, 'Only what I have read in the press.' There was a chuckle at the other end of the line.

For the rest of the morning Jay was left in peace by the media. He phoned Howard who said he was coming down the next day to have a chat. His call was followed by Roddy who rang to say he would like to come and catch up on the latest news from Hong Kong and Singapore. Then Percy Cartwright phoned. He also wanted to visit.

'It's going to be like Piccadilly Circus down here,' Jay told him. 'Are you sure you wouldn't prefer me to come up to London?'

'No,' said Percy, 'you must have a lot to catch up on and I could do with a day out of the office.'

Apart from being a director of County View he had three horses in training there. He was knowledgeable and had an impressive network of business connections, not only in Britain but around the world.

As expected, Howard arrived mid-morning. He immediately went to see The Conker, made a suitable fuss of him and fed him almost a whole packet of Polos. Next stop was Pewter Queen, his other star. She was now eleven and this would certainly be her last season. She had won a number of top races, and although past her best was still capable of winning the occasional good handicap. Howard was sad at the thought that this was going to be her last season, but excited at the prospect of breeding from her. After lunch at the nearby Shepherd's Rest pub, which was almost a County View club, Howard returned to London, having reassured Jay that the loss of a few horses was nothing to get too depressed about. He was looking forward to the first race of a young horse called Quietly Confident bought for him in Ireland by Jay. Quietly Confident had won two good point-to-points so was going straight over novice fences.

In keeping with the overriding policy of County View,

31

the directors only had one or two horses running in their own names; the rest of the home string ran in the name and colours of the stable.

Howard had barely left when Percy arrived. He was staying overnight with Eva and Jay. After a glass of wine, the two men sat down to talk while Eva prepared dinner.

'I had a very strange telephone call,' announced Percy. 'Quentin O'Connor rang to say he had an owner who would be interested in buying my horses.'

Percy had three very promising horses with Jay – Canada Square, a five-year-old who had won a good bumper the previous year, Cash Talks, a six-year-old, the winner of three novice hurdles, and Understated, another young horse who had won over hurdles the previous season and ended with a second in a good novice chase. Not having won, he was still a novice and was ready to run over fences early in the season.

'I assured him they were not for sale and he then, to my amazement, said would I consider moving them from County View to his yard. He clearly hadn't done his home-work and was put on the back foot when I said that, as a director of the company, I was hardly likely to do that. He had the grace to apologize and said perhaps he could buy me a drink sometime at the races. What I find extraordinary, Jay, is that not only is this fellow offering sky-high prices for horses, but it seems he is only interested in buying horses from County View.'

'The same thought had occurred to me,' said Jay. 'Freddy in Ireland tried to find out about him but basically all we know is what has been published in the *Racing Post* and the rest of the racing media.'

Pausing, he added that it was rumoured O'Connor had access to a huge amount of money from some unknown backer. The alterations that were being made to his yard in Lambourn were the talk of the town, plus the fact that several of Jay's horses had wound up there, supposedly for large sums of money.

'I think we should try to find out a lot more about this chap,' suggested Percy.

Jay agreed. 'Why don't we get Benny involved?'

'That's a very good idea. I'll get Marvin in on it too. They worked together very effectively finding out what Victor was about, and they seemed to get on well.'

Marvin was an Afro-Caribbean with a degree in languages. He was Percy's investigator. Like Benny, he had a wide range of contacts, particularly in the financial world within the UK and abroad.

'I agree,' said Jay. 'I'll come up to London next Monday and let's have a chat with them.'

'Let's have lunch in my office and we can brief them as fully as possible,' Percy proposed. This was soon settled.

The three of them had a relaxed evening, and after dinner, over brandy and cigars, the men amused Eva by recalling exploits from their Cambridge days. They also relived some of the highlights of County View's amazing racing record and by bedtime they were all feeling much more positive. The next morning Percy stayed long enough to see the first lot work. He was full of enthusiasm when he made his way back to what he always called his 'treadmill'. In fact, as Jay knew very well, he adored his work. The satisfaction of being excellent at his job, plus having built up such a fine reputation and first class team, gave him as much pleasure as his well-earned affluent lifestyle.

A little before lunch Roddy and his gorgeous wife Jerline arrived. The two girls always got on well, as did Jay and Roddy. Jay had been very suspicious of Roddy when he first met him. Later he discovered that his apparently aggressive style arose from a certain degree of insecurity, but even more from his desperation to become a member of the County View operation and to prove to his wife and father-in-law that he had real business ability and could be a success in his own right.

Jay brought him up to date with their activities in Hong Kong and said how kind and considerate Hamish and his two sons had been.

'I'm lucky to be part of that family,' Roddy enthused to Jay, 'particularly in having such a stunning wife.' But it was clear to all that Jerline was as devoted to her husband as he was to her.

After a light lunch the two men went into Jay's office to discuss the stud business. New Zealand was making real money and beginning to supply successful horses to County View. South Africa was at a break-even point, and only France was losing money, but not too much. Adding the three together, the stud operation was making a modest but still significant profit. Jay then asked Roddy for his view of the three managers. He could not have been more enthusiastic about Angus in New Zealand or Roger in South Africa.

'I do have my reservations about Jean-Paul, simply because he seems to be overcautious. If you want to succeed in any business you've got to take a certain amount of risk but I seem unable to convince him of this. However, he is technically extremely sound and knowledgeable and there is no doubt he is enthusiastic and loyal.' Roddy paused thoughtfully. 'Do you think it would be an idea if we got the three of them together, perhaps in South Africa, and let them exchange views? The more adventurous natures of the other two might rub off on Jean-Paul.'

'That's an excellent plan,' agreed Jay. 'Talk to all of them and see if we can get this set up in the next couple of months.'

They then turned their attention to the Quentin O'Connor affair. Jay briefed Roddy on all he knew and the decision that Percy and he had taken earlier that day.

'Let's not discuss O'Connor over dinner,' Jay said. 'Eva's already worried enough about it and there's no point in concerning Jerline too. Let's go out and have a relaxed evening – by the way I've invited Chris and Amanda to join us.'

A couple of hours later the six of them were settled at a corner table in the Shepherd's Rest, and the men could hardly get a word in edgeways as the women talked about

Amanda's pregnancy, Max's trip to his grandmother, the latest fashions in London, and the plays they all wanted to see. Jay quietly reflected how good it was that the whole County View team got on so well and obviously liked each other.

Roddy and Jerline had insisted on staying at the Shepherd's Rest but said they would be back at the yard early in the morning to watch the first lot exercise. Jay knew from previous experience that Jerline was just as enthusiastic as her husband. He remembered his surprise the first time they arrived as this elegant lady turned up at the gallops dressed in the most practical and sensible of clothes.

As Amanda and Chris left, the vet gave Jay a beckoning nod. Jay excused himself to the others, saying he had to make a telephone call to Hal in the States, then he joined Chris and Amanda in the car park. Chris couldn't contain himself any longer.

'What the hell's going on with these horses moving to this guy Quentin O'Connor?' he demanded.

'Search me,' was the reply, 'but he seems to have a lot of money behind him and for some reason he's targeting County View.'

'What do you know about him?' asked Amanda.

'Very little, but if you hear anything at all let us know because frankly it's beginning to get my rag up.'

With warm handshakes and hugs, they parted, Chris saying he'd be up the following day for some routine equine anti-flu jabs.

Just as they were having a nightcap at home, the phone rang. It was Fiona calling from South Africa. Having had a chat with Eva about life in general and her grandson in particular, she asked to speak to Jay.

'I have a favour to ask you,' she said. 'I've got a friend out here who I met years ago with Eva's father. His name is Jan Schmidt. I've kept in touch with him and see him and his wife Liza quite frequently since I've spent more time in South Africa. He has a commodity trading business, but the bulk of his turnover is in gold. His only son is also in the business and is going to spend at least a year working in their London office. I know the young man and I've seen him riding in amateur races, and also showjumping, and he's certainly got natural ability. He's desperate to continue riding in England, and in particular wants to ride in some National Hunt races. Is there any chance that you could let him come down and ride out with you as often as he can and see how he measures up to his ambition?'

'Of course,' was the instant reply. 'What's his name?'

'Hansie Schmidt. He's twenty-eight and very good-looking.'

'In that case I'll keep him away from Eva,' chuckled Jay.

Chapter Four

There were now only three weeks before Jay intended to have his first runners of the new campaign. As usual, these would be at Stratford-on-Avon. This was his favourite course for the beginning of the season. The ground was always kept in immaculate condition and the racecourse was an easy, short drive from County View. He and his staff were certain of a warm welcome: his very first winner as a trainer had been at Stratford and the racecourse had enjoyed a huge amount of positive publicity as a result. The Stratford runners were Canada Square, Percy's bumper winner, who was having his first run over hurdles in a two mile six furlong novice race, Maori Warrior who was owned by Cyril Hopkins, the New Zealand bred horse who had won the previous season and was now running in a handicap hurdle, and Jack the Lad who had won three moderate novice chases the previous year but had won them easily. He was also having his first run as a handicapper. Jay was confident that they would all acquit themselves very well. Obviously, without yet knowing what the other entries would be he was in no position to assess their chances. Jay was particularly interested in Jack the Lad. He was one of two horses owned by a rich but not very well-informed owner called Peter Lumsden. All three horses had worked well that morning. Jay was impressed with the confidence with which Paul presented his horses to their obstacles, instilling the same confidence in the horses themselves.

At the end of the morning Jay phoned Percy who confirmed the meeting for the following Monday with Benny and Marvin. After evening stables Jed and Jay sat down and mapped out the possible entries for later in September; as always they had at least two options for every horse in case the state of the ground did not suit, or unduly fierce competition was going to influence their decision. Jed left and went back to his nearby cottage and Jay was about to join Eva when there was a knock at the door. Paul Jenkins was standing outside.

'Come in, young man,' said Jay. 'I thought the schooling went particularly well this morning.'

'Yes, it did,' agreed Paul, but he looked distinctly uncomfortable.

'Well, what is it you want to say?' Jay demanded. 'Spit it out.'

'Well, I'm very sorry, Jay, but I'm handing in my resignation.'

Jay was flabbergasted. He had seen this young man ride his first winner at Plumpton, in fact beating Jay into second place. The trainer had taken a personal interest in him from that day, and once County View was up and running had employed him as his conditional jockey. Although there had been one or two mistakes in the early days, Jay and Freddy Kelly had groomed him so successfully that he won the Conditional Jockeys Championship. He not only rode a lot of Jay's best horses, but picked up many good outside rides with Jay's support and encouragement.

'What are you going to do?' asked Jay.

The young man looked even more embarrassed. 'I'm going to go and work for Quentin O'Connor.'

If Jay could have been more thunderstruck, he couldn't think in what circumstance.

'And why, may I ask you?'

'Well, I've been offered an extremely good retainer by him.'

'I don't know what that is,' snapped Jay, 'but I've already told you you're going to be this stable's number one jockey, so there's every reason why you should earn an extremely good living here. What's more, your future with

38

the yard is on the agenda for the next board meeting, and a retainer was certainly going to be considered.'

The young man looked even more uncomfortable. 'Well, there's another reason,' he said.

'And what's that?'

'It's all this bad publicity that the yard is getting.'

'A few stories in the *Racing Post* hardly herald the demise of County View.'

'Well, it's not just the press, it's what's being said in the weighing room,' Paul replied. 'They seem to think that you're on your way down, and frankly it's important for me at this stage in my career to be connected with a successful and high-profile yard.'

'Well, I'm not sure how you work that one out,' growled Jay. 'Quentin O'Connor may have been pretty successful in Ireland, but he's certainly unproven over here. He hasn't even had a runner yet.'

'Well, I'm afraid I've made up my mind,' said Paul, now looking extremely stubborn. 'I will, of course, give you a month's notice.'

'Thanks a bundle,' said Jay, rather sarcastically. 'Well, I guess there's nothing more to say. Goodnight.'

It was clear that Paul couldn't get out of the room fast enough. Slamming his office door behind him, Jay strode into the kitchen. Eva had heard the bang. One look at Jay told her that he was fuming.

'What on earth has happened?' she demanded.

'Paul Jenkins has just resigned and is going to join Quentin O'Connor.'

Eva was as staggered as Jay had been. Walking over to the bar she poured him a large scotch and said, 'I think you'd better drink this and cool down. What are you going to do?'

'My instinct is to get rid of him immediately rather than let him work his month's notice. The less up-to-date inside knowledge that O'Connor has the better.'

'I agree with you,' said Eva, 'but I think you ought to talk to Howard and Percy first.'

Jay finished his whisky and made the two telephone calls.

Howard could hardly believe his ears. 'The ungrateful little bugger,' he said. 'I agree with you, kick him out tonight.'

Percy was of the same opinion. He added, 'This gives even more pertinence to our meeting on Monday. Something very odd is going on.'

Having cooled down, Jay then rang Paul Jenkins. The young man had reached the cottage that he shared with three of Jay's other stable staff.

'Paul, I want you to come and see me before first lot tomorrow morning. I want you to pack your bags and be out of the yard by ten o'clock, and I'll have what money we owe you ready.'

There was a stunned silence at the other end. 'I thought I could leave on good terms with you, Jay, after all these years.'

'Well, you thought wrong,' and Jay finished the call.

Jay was sitting in his office after he and Eva had finished dinner. He was still thinking about Paul Jenkins when the phone rang.

'Is that Mr Jessop?' enquired a male voice with what Jay immediately recognized as a South African accent.

'Yes, it is.'

'I think that your mother-in-law may have called you. My name is Hansie Schmidt.'

'Oh yes, I was expecting your call,' replied Jay. 'I understand you would like to come down and ride out here with a view to possibly riding in a few races.'

'That's absolutely right, Mr Jessop.'

'Well,' said Jay, 'you'd need to be here by 7.30 in the morning, and if that's difficult in terms of driving from London, there's a very good pub nearby where a lot of our visitors stay. It would be easy for you to drive down after work and be on our doorstep the next morning.'

'That sounds a grand idea,' said the young man. 'When would it be convenient for me to start?'

'Whenever you want. How about the weekend after next?'

'Would the following Saturday be possible? I've got to settle in here.'

'Certainly,' was the reply. 'I'll give you the Shepherd's Rest's telephone number and then you can make your reservation. Have you got everything you need in the way of riding gear?'

'Absolutely. As soon as I knew you were going to be kind enough to let me ride I made sure I had everything, and even asked Fiona to check it for me.'

'Right,' said Jay, 'I look forward to seeing you.'

At least the next day's *Racing Post* didn't have Paul's departure on the front page, but it was the lead story on page five. Under the headline 'Another loss at County View', it explained that the extremely promising and successful young jockey, Paul Jenkins, had decided to leave County View to join Quentin O'Connor. O'Connor had commented that he was delighted such a talented young rider should have decided that he had a really great future with his yard and that Paul could count on Quentin's support in every way.

Paul was quoted as saying, 'I had a great time at County View and am very grateful to Mr Jessop. It was really brilliant to be part of the team that built up such a successful operation but I now feel the time has come to move on. Mr O'Connor's offer to be in at the ground floor of another exciting operation was too good an opportunity to miss, particularly as I'm going to be the stable's number one jockey.'

The *Post* had tried to speak to Jay a couple of times but, anticipating this likelihood, Eva had answered the phone all the previous day. As a result it was just stated that Jay Jessop had proved unavailable for comment.

Sunday followed the usual pattern, with a number of owners arriving to watch their horses work. Amongst them were Al and Maria Lambert, Amanda's parents, so of course she and Chris came over as well. Al knew all about the goings-on at County View and sympathetically asked

41

Jay what he thought was happening. Jay explained that he had no real idea but it did look as if there was some concerted effort to lure key horses and people away from the yard.

'Well, if there's anything I can do to help don't hesitate to contact me, and you know that my two horses are totally safe with you.'

The other key owner was Cyril Hopkins whose horse, Maori Warrior, was due to run at Stratford-on-Avon. He saw his horse have a gentle canter and school very successfully.

'What do you think his chances are?' he queried.

'At the moment I've no idea,' replied Jay, 'because I don't know what else is running, but the horse is very well and we know from last season he certainly has ability. As soon as I know the runners I'll give you my opinion.'

He knew that this particular owner liked to back his own horses, so he was always ultra cautious in forecasting the results.

Chris and Amanda took her parents home for lunch, and for once none of the other owners had accepted the normal open invitation to eat with the Jessops. Jay waved them all goodbye, and with a sigh of relief joined Eva in the kitchen where they had a simple salad.

To Jay's mild surprise but great delight Hal phoned that evening to say he'd decided to come over to England in a few weeks' time and was looking forward to spending some time with Jay and Eva. He was immediately invited to stay at County View, and he said he would love to for one or two nights. As he had a lot of business as well he'd be mainly based in London in his favourite hotel, the Dorchester.

After a long and exhausting weekend, both physically and emotionally, Jay and Eva climbed into bed, having checked that Max was fine, and soon joined him in a deep and welcome sleep.

*   *   *

On Monday morning Jay was up bright and early and was already in the yard as the horses were being groomed, tacked up and made ready for their exercise. The early season runners had all worked hard the day before so they were going out second lot for a long walk. Jay concentrated on a number of horses who were less advanced in their preparation. He was pleased with their progress. Leaving Jed and Danny to supervise the last lot, Jay returned to the house, changed, said goodbye to Eva and Max, and drove to London to meet Percy at his treadmill. At Canary Wharf, he left his car in the underground car park and took a lift to Percy's headquarters on the thirty-second floor. The company was also represented in the main Lloyd's building but Percy preferred to work from Canary Wharf.

Jay was shown into Percy's office by his long-standing PA, Moira, and was greeted effusively by Percy.

'Have a glass of champagne, my friend,' he said.

'I'm not sure I ought to – I've got to get my car back to Hays Mews after lunch.'

'Don't worry about that,' his friend replied. 'My driver, Francis, will take you back in your car. I'm not leaving until pretty late this evening. He can come back here by taxi.'

'In that case I'd love to,' replied Jay.

After a few minutes Benny and Marvin were ushered in and they got down to business immediately. Jay outlined all the incidents that had happened plus as much as he knew of Quentin O'Connor's background, which was still limited to what he had gleaned from the press and Freddy in Ireland. He also mentioned the rumour about a mysterious backer of the yard.

Benny looked thoughtful. 'It seems that whoever is behind this has an ulterior motive. The sort of prices he has been paying and offering for Jay's horses don't make any commercial sense.'

'I couldn't agree more,' said Percy, 'and that's why we're meeting today.'

Turning to Marvin he continued, 'What we'd like you to do is dig around and find out all you can about

O'Connor's finances. In particular we'd like to know where the money's coming from and who's behind it. Benny,' he went on, 'we'd like you to keep a close eye on O'Connor himself. Find out if he has an Achilles heel, any unusual connections, any skeletons in his cupboard.' Both investigators agreed.

'Right,' said Percy, 'let's go and have some lunch.'

The conversation over the meal was entertaining, as they recalled some of Benny's previous exploits. Benny and Marvin finished quickly and left while Percy and Jay had another cup of coffee.

Percy looked at his friend. 'There's one thing I think we should consider. So far all the publicity has gone pro O'Connor and anti County View. You've been quite right to make no comment on horses leaving your yard or even young Jenkins' treachery, but I think we should keep our eyes open for a chance to mount a counter-offensive.'

Jay pondered for a moment and then nodded his agreement. 'And, let's hope the opportunity comes sooner rather than later. This is really beginning to irritate me.'

'I can imagine that,' said Percy. 'Let's keep in touch.'

Jay went down to the front entrance of Canada Square where Francis had already retrieved his car from the underground car park and was ready to drive him to his small London flat. Lately he had been considering moving. It had been ideal when he was a bachelor, and indeed when it was just Eva and himself. However, Max was growing up quickly, and with only one bedroom it was hardly ideal for the lad to be on a put-you-up in the living room. He made a mental note to discuss this with Eva.

He rang Howard and brought him up to date with the conversation at Percy's office and the decisions made. Howard was enthusiastically in favour of the action plan and then, as an afterthought, asked, 'If you're in London tonight, are you doing anything?'

'No plans at the moment.'

'Right, I'll come up and take you out to dinner. It's a long time since we had a chat by ourselves, and I'd really enjoy that.'

'So would I. Where do you want to meet?'

'I fancy some good Indian food,' said Howard. 'Why don't we go to Amaya?'

'We'd be lucky if we get in.'

'Don't you worry,' said Howard, 'I'm a mate of the owners.'

Jay had a shower, changed and strolled down to the Turf Club just behind Pall Mall. He knew he was bound to be quizzed on what was happening but thought it was better to get it over sooner rather than later. As with the press, he played a straight bat, but to two or three of his closer friends he admitted that he was extremely angry as well as being at a loss to know what was behind it all. Time passed pleasantly enough, and then he set off to meet Howard at the fabulous Indian restaurant a stone's throw from Belgrave Square.

Howard was already in the bar and it was quite clear he was well known to the staff, as well as a number of the diners. When they were seated at an excellent table, Howard ordered a range of dishes which all proved to be delicious. The two men barely mentioned the current problems, having discussed them at length on the phone that afternoon. This was just a pleasant evening with two old friends – relaxed in each other's company – reviewing the prospects for County View in the forthcoming season, plus the overall progress being made on the stud side. Howard was very enthusiastic at the idea of getting the stud managers together in South Africa and agreed with Jay that Roddy seemed to be doing a very good job in building this side of the business. The evening flew by and it was late when they eventually called it a day. Howard was driven home to Surrey, and Jay decided to walk back to his pad. He still planned to make a very early start to be back at County View in time to see the horses being exercised.

Having left Hays Mews just after 5 a.m., Jay was back at County View in time to have a cup of coffee with Eva before work started for the day.

Chapter Five

A few days after his trip to Canary Wharf, Jay was sitting in his office just before lunch making a number of routine telephone calls. Eva opened the door and stood there with a rather worried look on her face.

'There are two policemen here to see you, Jay.'

'Well, bring them in.'

Two men in plain clothes entered. The older of the two addressed him. 'Mr Jessop?'

'Yes,' replied Jay.

'I'm Detective Sergeant Morgan, and this is Constable Michaelson.' Both policemen showed their identity cards.

'Please sit down,' said Jay. 'What can I do for you?'

'Can you tell us where you were last night?' the sergeant asked in a rather challenging manner.

'Well, it depends on the time,' was the reply. 'Up until 7.30 I was here. My wife and I then went to the Shepherd's Rest for dinner, and we returned here. May I ask why you're interested?'

The sergeant ignored the question. 'Do you have any witnesses other than your wife?'

'Well, a number of members of the staff would confirm I was here until 7.30, and the manager and a number of people in the bar could confirm I was at the Shepherd's Rest.'

'And what time would that be?'

'We left just after half past ten.'

'You came straight back here?'

'Yes. We start early so we seldom have a late night.'

'And you didn't go out again last night?'

'Not at all.' Jay was adamant.

'In that case, Mr Jessop, can you explain why your Land Rover was seen leaving Lambourn just after two o'clock this morning?'

Jay looked genuinely stunned. 'It couldn't have been.'

'Am I right in thinking that it's a blue Land Rover and the registration number is LYX 772?'

'That's correct. I'm still awaiting a reply to my question, why do you want to know?'

The sergeant paused for a moment. 'You know where Mr Quentin O'Connor's yard is?'

Jay nodded. 'I've been there in the past but not since Mr O'Connor took up residence there. I still want to know what's behind this questioning.'

'Well,' replied the sergeant, 'early this morning an intruder tried to get into at least one of Mr O'Connor's stables. He was disturbed by the Head Man and ran off dropping a plastic carrier bag behind him. Shortly before 2.30 this morning we had a telephone call that a blue Land Rover matching the description of yours was seen driving fast and erratically from the direction of Mr O'Connor's yard. The caller took the licence number. He assumed that it was a drunken driver and phoned the police believing that the vehicle was a danger to other road users. Can we see the Land Rover?'

Jay laughed. 'Well, certainly. Would you like to accompany me?'

'Where to?' the policeman asked.

'To a garage at the bottom of the hill. I believe that may answer all your questions.'

With that Jay marched out of his office and jumped into his Jaguar. The police, following him, looked rather bemused but got into their vehicle and waved for him to proceed. He drove out of County View, turned left and made his way down the hill. Right at the bottom on the crossroad was a large garage with a smart sign announcing it belonged to Jack Bailey. Turning into the forecourt, Jay stopped his car and waited for the policemen.

'Please follow me,' he said.

Walking towards the large workshop, he stopped at a small office where a wiry man with steel grey hair was working behind his desk.

'Good morning, Jack,' Jay greeted him. 'These two gentlemen would like to ask you some questions.'

The sergeant showed his identity and looked at the garage owner.

'Do you know anything about a dark blue Land Rover with the registration number LYX 772?'

'I certainly do,' was the reply. 'It belongs to Mr Jessop there.'

'When did you last see it?'

'Every day for the last four days. Do you want to see it? It's here now.' And with that Jack walked out of the office and strode purposefully into the main part of the workshop. Stopping in front of a ramp, he pointed to a vehicle above him. There was a dark blue Land Rover with the registration number LYX 772.

'And how long's that been here?' the sergeant demanded.

'It's been here non-stop for the last four days. As you can see it's not in the first flush of youth and the gear box was beginning to play up significantly. It's not that easy to get these gear boxes immediately. We've taken the old one out and we're waiting for the arrival of the new one which should be here the day after tomorrow.'

'Can anyone other than you confirm that?'

Jack made a sweeping gesture with his arm, taking in five men all working on different vehicles. 'Any or all of them.'

The officer thought for a moment. 'May we go back into your office?'

Following the owner, Jay and the two policemen walked back in.

'I've no reason to believe that you're not telling the truth,' the sergeant said, 'but I'd be grateful if you could give me your name and telephone number, and also the names of your mechanics.'

Jack sat down behind his desk, and finding a clean sheet

of paper wrote down the requested information. 'Is there anything else?'

'No, that's all. Would you mind coming outside and having a word with us,' the sergeant said to Jay in a rather more friendly manner.

Jay followed them into the courtyard.

'Well, what's all this about? Frankly I'm at a loss.'

'Well,' replied the sergeant. 'I'm interested in racing myself and it's commonly thought you and Mr O'Connor are not exactly bosom friends. As I said, an intruder attempted to enter at least one of Mr O'Connor's stables last night. When he was disturbed he ran off and dropped a plastic bag. In it was a syringe and a bottle of what was labelled phenylbutazone. I believe that this is a drug commonly used in treating horses but prohibited for use on horses who are about to run.'

'That's broadly correct,' Jay agreed. 'It's commonly called Bute and is used as an anti-inflammatory. It can be used, but there must be no traces of it by the time the horse runs.'

'So a horse which ran and was found to have this in its system would be disqualified?'

'It most certainly would, and the trainer would be in some difficulty with the racing authorities. But the doper would need to know the right horse or horses and the immediate entries.'

'Mr O'Connor explained that to us, but he pointed out that all the horses have their names on their boxes and the entries are published in the racing papers four days in advance and again the day before.'

'That's true, but it would still need someone with some knowledge of injecting horses.'

'Mr O'Connor mentioned that, too. Now can you think of any reason why somebody should go to the trouble of using a Land Rover which was carrying a copy of your number plate? It would also appear that the driver was deliberately drawing attention to himself so that the vehicle would be seen and reported.'

'I have no idea. It's a mystery to me,' Jay replied. 'Have you traced the Land Rover?'

'No, but we've put out an announcement on local radio and it will be on the local television station tonight as well.

'I'm sure you can understand why we visited you,' the sergeant continued in a more conciliatory manner. 'I'll keep you informed of any development.'

'Needless to say, I'll be more than interested,' Jay said. 'May I go now?'

'Of course, and thank you for your help, Mr Jessop. I'm sorry to have troubled you.'

Jay returned to County View and told the very concerned Eva the story.

'How extraordinary,' she said. 'It looks as if somebody tried to frame you.'

'I know,' agreed Jay, 'but I wasn't going to suggest that to the police. They can work it out for themselves.'

A few moments later Jed walked in wanting to know what had happened. Jay quickly filled him in on the details.

'This looks mighty suspicious to me,' the older man said. 'Do you think O'Connor was trying to get you into trouble?'

'It looks like it,' said Jay, 'but it's almost too obvious to be true. Anyway it'll be interesting to see what, if anything, the police find.'

He phoned Howard, Roddy and Percy to let them know the very strange new development. It was Percy who took it most seriously.

'Jay, this is no longer remotely amusing,' he said. 'I think we should have a board meeting and have it really quickly. Can you do tomorrow?'

'Well, we don't have any racing tomorrow so the answer is yes, as long as Howard and Roddy can make it.'

'You've got plenty on your plate,' Percy commented. 'I'll get in touch with both of them and, if they can, we'll make it late morning here. Does that suit you?'

'Absolutely,' replied Jay. 'If it goes ahead we should let

Hamish know. He'll probably want to set up a video conference facility if he doesn't mind the rather unearthly hour it will be for him.'

'I'll be in touch,' Percy promised, and rang off.

Less than an hour later he phoned to say all was arranged and Roddy had phoned his father-in-law who promised he'd make every effort to be in touch via the telephone video link.

After watching first lot the following morning, Jay and Eva drove to London. Eva had taken Max to school and Cathy had agreed to pick him up as it was unlikely they'd be back in time.

Shortly before eleven they were ushered into one of Percy's meeting rooms. Roddy was already there and Moira brought in a tray of freshly brewed coffee which they savoured as they waited for Howard. Soon the door opened and he bustled in with his normal beaming smile and cheerful greeting.

'Right,' said Percy. 'Let's check that the video connection is working.' Moira came in and made a few adjustments to a TV screen in the corner and mysteriously, thousands of miles away in his new centre in Singapore, Hamish was virtually sitting in their room. He greeted his fellow directors, but true to form didn't beat around the bush.

'Roddy has filled me in on the recent strange events at O'Connor's yard, but this, along with the poaching of horses and Paul Jenkins' departure, obviously gives us all cause for concern.'

Percy reviewed the information they had about O'Connor. There was now a growing body of rumours suggesting that he had financial backing from someone in the Far East. On Jay's suggestion he had spoken to Freddy Kelly who had also heard this but had not set too much store by it. He also explained that they had Marvin and Benny working on O'Connor's background. Marvin had called that morning to say that he had discovered a good lead into the financial background of O'Connor and it did seem almost certain that Far East money was involved.

Hamish paused and took this in.

'Well, I've got a number of sources here myself. I'll talk to them. The man I'd most like to work on this is a cousin of mine called Johnny Tang. He does a considerable amount of investigative work for two of the large banks here, one of which is my company's main bank. He has also worked for me.'

Nods of approval went round the table. Then Eva spoke up.

'So far we've been on the back foot in all of this. It seems to me that even if O'Connor isn't making many friends, he's getting a lot of publicity and you know what they say, all publicity is good publicity. Up to now his behaviour may not be what we call playing cricket, but he's actually done nothing wrong. He hasn't really even sailed particularly close to the wind. Nevertheless I feel that we should make a gesture. Any opportunities that Jay has to register less than approval would be fine as long as it doesn't look spiteful.'

'My view exactly,' interrupted Percy. 'Jay knows this.'

Eva continued. 'That's fine but we should do more. The real idea I've got is for us to have an open day for the press. Although we've had a lot of journalist visitors at County View, we haven't had a real show since our opening, and we all know how successful that was.'

Howard immediately jumped in. 'That's a splendid idea. How soon can we do it?'

'Well, it won't take me any time at all to set it up,' Eva replied. 'Two weeks at the outside, though a lot depends on if we're racing on a Sunday, and also if there are any big local meetings that day.'

'Hang on a moment,' said Jay, and opened his briefcase. Taking out his desk diary, he thumbed through it. 'The third Sunday from now would seem fine,' he said. 'The nearest National Hunt meeting to us on that day is Fakenham, and there's not a major flat meeting either. It also gives us plenty of time to get invitations out. Are you sure you can handle this in time?' he asked his wife.

'No problem.'

'Right,' said Percy. 'Let's agree that. Anybody got a different view?'

Roddy was as enthusiastic as Howard, and then Hamish spoke.

'I'm going to come too,' he announced. 'I was going to be in London later that week so it's no great hardship for me to juggle things a bit at this end, and I'd love to be there.'

'That's settled then,' said Percy, who had taken the lead at this meeting, although not formally the chairman. In fact they never felt there was a need for anybody to assume that particular title.

'Is there any other business?' asked Hamish.

'Nothing that can't wait till you come over,' Jay replied, 'and I'm sure that Roddy's been keeping you informed about the stud side of the business?'

'He most certainly has,' affirmed Hamish. 'Well, if you don't mind, I'll say goodbye to you all now and keep my fingers crossed that there aren't any more unfortunate episodes.'

He'd clearly turned his connection off as the screen went blank. The UK members of the board turned to each other.

'Well, I don't think there is any other business,' said Jay, 'unless any of you have something to raise?'

Negative shakes of the head brought the meeting to an end.

'Who can have lunch?' Percy asked. 'I've got a cold buffet set up next door so I hope you can make it.'

They all cheerfully accepted his invitation and moved next door. As always when Percy entertained, everything looked perfect and the wines were excellent. Eva declined any alcohol, whispering quietly to Jay. 'It's a shame for you to miss the opportunity for two or three glasses of really good wine. I'll settle for mineral water and I'll drive home.'

A very pleasant forty minutes passed. The positive

things about County View were discussed and the negatives forgotten.

Back in the Cotswolds that evening, Jay phoned Hal in New York to update him on the latest developments and the board meeting. Hal was fascinated, but again reassured Jay that the loss of a few horses was not the end of the world. He did, however, agree that it was beginning to look like some sort of conspiracy. He would let Jay know as soon as his London visit was finalized.

Chapter Six

Monday morning, just before he went out to help organize the first lot, Jay was surprised to see Danny walk into the kitchen looking deeply concerned with a copy of the *Daily Mirror* in his hand. It was already folded back to one of the early inside pages. He put it on the table in front of Jay. 'Read this.'

The headline was 'Suspected Murderer Escapes'.

The story went on to explain that the previous day Liam Ahearne, generally known as The Friend, was being transported from England to Dublin, where he was due to face trial in connection with the murder of a bookmaker some time before. The wheels of justice had ground rather slowly, but eventually he was being moved from the English jail where he was serving a term of imprisonment for drug smuggling. On arriving at Dublin airport, he had been met by two uniformed prison officers. The English handcuffs had been exchanged for Irish ones, and he'd been marched off to a waiting Garda car. The English officers saw him safely in the back of the car, and went off to have some food before flying straight back to England.

It seems, however, that the two Irish prison officers and the Garda escorts were in fact bogus. The police car and its escort had been stopped at what had appeared to be a major accident on the way to the airport. Six masked men had grabbed all four policemen and bundled them in the back of a waiting van which drove off. At the airport, The Friend had been driven off at high speed along with the two uniformed impostors and one of the party from the fake accident. After a while they left the road and went down a deserted country lane where the car was abandoned and all concerned were transferred to a waiting vehicle. The captives in the back of the van eventually managed to escape by attracting the attention of a passer-by. This was over half an hour later and The Friend was clearly well away.

A major manhunt was under way but so far nothing had been discovered. All The Friend's known accomplices in Ireland were being questioned, including those at large and those serving jail sentences for a wide range of crimes, most of them drug-related.

Jay looked at Danny, who was clearly shaken.

'I don't think you've got anything to worry about,' he reassured his Head Man.

'I do,' the ex-jockey insisted. 'I've dropped my fake name since I've been working with you, and it wouldn't be difficult for The Friend to have found out what I'm up to. What's more, he's clearly aware of the fact that those drugs were planted on him, and whatever else he is, he's not stupid. Even if he can't prove that we were involved, he'd have a pretty deep suspicion. You can be quite sure that his cronies in Ireland would have been digging around to see if there was a vendetta against him over there, and we know they're likely to have come up with a blank. He'd also know that I'm aware of what he was doing, and he could well be worried about any information I might give to the Irish police. Even if not strictly relevant to the murder, it could point to his possible involvement and would in itself be enough to help convict him for separate drugs-related activities in Ireland.'

Danny hesitated. 'Do you think he set up the O'Connor incident?'

Jay frowned thoughtfully. 'Well, if he did, at least he didn't attack you personally. We'll get our friend Benny and his brothers to do a bit of digging around here and in Ireland. Don't go worrying too much, Danny. It's all conjecture at the moment. Let's see what happens. You can be sure there'll be a massive manhunt on the other side of the Irish Sea.'

Danny nodded without a great deal of conviction. 'The sooner that bastard is back behind bars, the better I'll like it,' he growled. 'Anyway, I'd better get on with the work in the yard.'

'I'll be right out,' said Jay.

He rang Benny, who'd already seen the papers.

'Don't say anything to Danny,' he told Jay, 'but I wouldn't put it past Ahearne. He'd have built up a good network in prison, and although it's highly unlikely that any of his close friends would have taken the chance of being seen with him on visiting days over here, there's every chance that he'd connect you and Danny with his arrest. He wouldn't be a man to take that lying down. Anyway, I'll start putting feelers out and come back to you as soon as I've got any information. I'll be in touch.'

The next few days passed relatively quietly, with Jay and Danny going to the races, sometimes to separate courses, and Jed holding the fort at home. As nothing unusual happened, Danny seemed to relax a little, but Jay knew that underneath the apparently calm exterior the young man was still very concerned.

Maori Warrior, Jack the Lad and Canada Square were now going through their final preparations for Stratford, and Jay was giving serious consideration to jockeys. He had a few ideas himself but thought that input from Freddy in Ireland would be useful.

'Well,' said Freddy, 'there's one young man I would certainly recommend and that's David Sparrow.'

Jay certainly knew of Sparrow. He had been the champion conditional jockey the season before last. Since then he had ridden a number of good-class horses, particularly in handicaps, with a high degree of success. He worked for Harry Kenyon, one of the smaller trainers, who had about thirty-five horses in his care. For the last two or three seasons Kenyon had punched well above his weight. As a matter of courtesy Jay called him before speaking to David.

'Well, I've got to admit, Jay, I'm not surprised you called me. He's a very good young man and of course he can ride for you at Stratford. I'll be honest with you. If it turns out that you're really satisfied with him and the chemistry's right, I wouldn't feel put out if you hired him full-time. I like him, I think he's got a lot of talent. It's only a matter of time before he goes to a bigger yard than mine. I'd just as soon it was yours as anyone else's.'

Jay thanked him profusely and then phoned David Sparrow's agent. As soon as he knew that the trainer had agreed to it, he immediately booked the young man for Jay's three runners.

Two days later Hamish called to say he was in London and was delighted to accept Jay's invitation to join them at Stratford-on-Avon the following Monday. Needless to say, Roddy and Jerline were also in the party. With Percy, Peter Lumsden, Cyril Hopkins and Eva, there was going to be a large County View presence. On Monday the yard was brimming with excitement. Eva had booked a large table in the very comfortable owners' and trainers' dining room. Jay, Jed and Danny arrived in good time and concentrated on their charges. Apart from the runners, the racecourse had agreed that Jay could take along one of his young horses who had not yet run. After racing she would be led round the paddock to get used to the crowd. This was a tactic that Jay had employed with many of his young horses since he first started training. It was particularly useful with nervous horses like this one.

The previous day the entries had been published and speculation was rife in the press and Jay's yard. Quentin O'Connor was having his first runner. No Killjoy was one of the successful horses he had brought over from Ireland and was due to run against Jack the Lad, Peter Lumsden's steeplechaser. Prior to that Maori Warrior was running in the two mile six furlong handicap hurdle. That morning the *Racing Post* and most of the other racing columns were agog at the impending confrontation. Looking at the opposition Jay felt pretty confident that all his runners would acquit themselves well. The one doubt he had was just how good O'Connor's horse was. It had won novice hurdles in Ireland but it was hard to equate that form on very different ground to that of his own horse.

Eva met the County View team in the owners' and trainers' bar. When everyone had arrived she led them into the dining room, where she was greeted warmly by Theresa, the stunning and highly efficient restaurant manager. Their window table had a good view of the TV monitor which would show all the races and replays as the afternoon progressed.

Jay bumped into Cyril Hopkins, who again wanted to know his horse's chances. 'I'll be disappointed if we're not in the first three,' replied Jay, 'but I know very little about some of the opposition. If you're going to have a bet I'd be cautious and I don't think we'll be a particularly long price anyway.'

The owner nodded and hurried off.

It was nearly time for the first race and Jay went off to the weighing room. He found David Sparrow and took him outside to a quiet corner. Jay gave him his instructions and the young man seemed to understand – he had apparently done his homework.

'The long distance hurdle is the one you're going to need to watch particularly,' said Jay. 'Chances are they will go much too fast at the start. Don't get left too far behind, but don't go mad over the first mile. Once they leave the back straight for the second time, start to make up ground steadily.' The young jockey nodded his understanding and walked back into the weighing room to get ready.

The first of Jay's runners was Maori Warrior in the handicap hurdle race. Sparrow rode to instructions and there were no fallers in the early stages. He was fourth leaving the back straight and remained in that position about five lengths behind the leader until they entered the finishing straight. Approaching the second last hurdle, he encouraged his mount up to second place with a slap on the neck and jumped the obstacle about two lengths behind the leader. Both the jockeys now started to ride in earnest but Jay's horse was making no inroads on the leader. Approaching the last fence the leader's jockey checked his horse momentarily to ensure that he cleared it safely. David decided it was now or never and asked Jay's horse to take off a stride early. The horse responded magnificently and landed half a length in the lead. Both jockeys were now riding hell for leather, but Jay's horse passed the winning post with a neck to spare.

Everybody was delighted, not least Cyril who had placed a substantial bet in spite of Jay's caution. To start the season with a winner was a huge tonic for both Jay and the yard. Photographs were quickly taken of the winning connections with their horse, and Sparrow rushed off to get ready to weigh out for his next ride. There was one race between the novice hurdle that had just taken place and the novice chase in which Jack the Lad was County View's runner. Jay glanced at the horses in the pre-parade ring and noticed a rather striking figure leaning on the rails. About six foot tall and athletically built, he was very bronzed. He wore a beautifully tailored tweed jacket and gaberdine trousers and was making notes as the horses went round. He occasionally spoke into a small hand-held dictating machine.

He must be a journalist, thought Jay, and gave it no further thought. Soon it was time for Jay's runner to be saddled, and standing in the middle of the parade ring waiting for the jockeys Jay noticed the same man still making notes and speaking into his recorder. Suddenly he turned on his heel, walked over towards the bookmakers, and Jay lost sight of him. The jockeys were in the ring and Jay introduced Sparrow to Peter Lumsden who was clearly nervous and excited and asked the jockey how he was going to ride him.

'As the guv'nor has instructed me,' was the sensible reply.

'And how's that?' asked Lumsden.

'Not to go too fast at the beginning, or to lose too much ground, and try and come with a good run at the end. That's how your horse has won its novice races.'

The owner nodded in wise agreement and Jay couldn't help smiling to himself.

For the first time he saw Quentin O'Connor, whom he recognized from photographs in the racing pages. He also, of course, recognized Paul who was riding O'Connor's horse, and studiously avoided eye contact with either of them.

O'Connor had that special brand of Irish good looks which so often proves fatally attractive to women. A shade under six foot, he had the build of a middle-weight boxer and still looked like a man who kept himself in good trim. Black, slightly wavy hair crowned an intelligent face bronzed from his outdoor life. His eyes were large, laughing, and that deep blue which seemed peculiar to the Irish. He had a dazzling smile which displayed a set of perfect white teeth. He was in every sense what Freddy had described to him as 'a real ladies' man'.

Apart from his looks, he was clearly intelligent, and his soft Irish accent went hand in glove with a vivid sense of humour which he used to charm men and women of all ages and backgrounds. It was not at all surprising he had been so successful in Ireland, not just because of his charm and good looks, but because he had shown he really could train horses.

He did, however, have a reputation for being quick-tempered, with an ability to make enemies almost as easily as he did friends. Beneath that smiling exterior it seemed there was a significant degree of ruthlessness.

No Killjoy, the O'Connor horse, was a striking-looking animal and in very good condition, but on the other hand, Jay reassured himself, so was his.

As soon as the horses left the ring, Jay strode out quickly to avoid meeting O'Connor who was at the other end of the paddock. He positioned himself in his favourite place on the stand and watched the race by himself, as he preferred to do unless Howard, Percy or Jed happened to be with him. Although two of them were there, they stayed with the rest of the party to allow Jay to concentrate on the race.

The tape went up and, as Jay had expected, they set off at a scorching gallop. It was clear that Paul had similar instructions to those of David Sparrow as, entering the back straight for the first time, they were both in the middle of the pack. There were no incidents and both Jack the Lad and No Killjoy were jumping well. With twenty runners in the race, they were well strung out going down the back straight for the second time. Paul had moved O'Connor's horse up to third place. Sparrow was sitting some five lengths behind and was riding his horse patiently. Going round the long Stratford bend, Paul made rapid progress on the two horses in front of him and took the lead entering the home straight. Sparrow was creeping up but doing nothing dramatic. Nevertheless, jumping the second last fence he moved into second place but was still four lengths behind O'Connor's horse. Paul now asked for an extra effort from his horse, which at first seemed to work as he gained an extra half length on Jack the Lad, but the effort was too much and too soon. Jack the Lad made rapid headway on the short run between the two fences and was side by side jumping the last. One slap on the neck and Jay's horse shot away from his rival, and with no further encouragement won by a clear two lengths. The owner was absolutely delighted, as were all the County View connections. Waiting for his horse and jockey in the winners' enclosure with Danny and Peter Lumsden, Jay was the first to congratulate his jockey on an excellent ride. At that moment, Paul came in and jumped off the second horse, to be greeted by a scowling Quentin O'Connor. It was clear he made some very critical remarks to Paul before striding away. Paul looked amazed and angry and ran off to the weighing room. Danny looked at Jay and grinned.

'Well, that looks like a short honeymoon,' he quipped, and with a chuckle Jay nodded his agreement.

Everybody went for a celebratory drink while they waited for Percy's runner in the last race. Percy went with Jay and Danny to watch his horse saddled and followed her into the parade ring.

This time Jay's instructions had been different.

'Canada Square doesn't have a very fast finish, but she is an out and out stayer as she showed in her bumpers, so I want you up there with the two or three leaders the whole time. As soon as you come off the crown of the bend on the second circuit, make your way for home as hard as you can, but don't be overhard on her. She is completely genuine and is still a youngster.'

Sparrow nodded his understanding, was legged up and soon on his way to the start. A couple of the less experienced horses played up, and one broke the tape which resulted in a short delay. Next time all was well and they started at a really competitive gallop. Sparrow had Canada Square in fourth place, and soon the first four had drawn away from the other nine runners. Going down the back straight, the third horse started to falter and Sparrow moved up confidently into third place. He stayed there, turning for home on the crown of the bend, and then asked his mare for an extra effort. She willingly responded, and entering the home straight was in the lead. However, she had not shaken off the other two. As she cleared the second last, she still had a length and a half in hand, but the second horse was going very easily. Jumping the last, the lead was down to half a length, and the second horse still looked to be going easily. This proved to be the case. It quickly caught Percy's horse and passed the winning post with a length and a half to spare. The third horse had also made a valiant effort, but as soon as it got up to Canada Square she responded gamely and held on to second place by half a length.

Jay greeted the young jockey in the winners' enclosure, saying, 'Well ridden, young man.'

'You don't think I should have won then?' he asked.

'No, you rode exactly as I told you. You just had one too good for yours on the day. She probably needs a little further than this, and perhaps on slightly more testing ground.'

Percy was slightly disappointed but realistic and agreed his mare should probably try a longer trip next time.

Hamish, who had kept Eva company all afternoon, was full of enthusiasm. 'Well, that should show your critics a thing or two. I told you not to worry.'

Jay made sure that he said goodbye to Cyril Hopkins and Peter Lumsden. Understandably, both were very happy with the results of their races. Checking the horses were all fine, Jay left Danny to supervise the young horse's introduction to the parade ring. Although still brooding on The Friend's escape, he seemed at last to have put it to the back of his mind. Along with Eva and Hamish, Jay left the racecourse to return to County View, with Roddy and his wife following them. Cathy, Jed's wife, had prepared a wonderful dinner of smoked salmon, roast leg of lamb, stilton and a tasty cheddar which was washed down with some of the excellent South African wines Jay had bought a couple of months earlier. Hamish was staying with Jay, but Roddy and his wife were lodging at the Shepherd's Rest. It turned out to be a rather later night than normal – but it's not every day that the season starts with two winners and a second.

Chapter Seven

The following morning Jay went into the yard and checked that the previous day's runners were well. All were in fine shape, had eaten up the night before and were now tucking heartily into their breakfast. He had a quick word with Jed and Danny, saw the papers arrive, and for once rushed in to see them and grabbed the *Racing Post*. He wasn't front page news, but a major story inside described what a storming start he'd had to the season. There was also mention of the fact that Paul Jenkins had been beaten on O'Connor's horse. The other papers were all equally enthusiastic about Jay's achievement. He had always been very popular with the racing journalists and it clearly showed.

Giving Eva the good news, he rushed out, jumped on The Conker, and was soon cantering up the gallop in time to see the first lot go up for the second time. The following Saturday he planned to have two runners at Sandown. These were Gambler's Dream and Victory Roll. Both looked in splendid shape as they passed him neck and neck at full working speed.

Hamish had accompanied Jed to the gallops and shortly afterwards Roddy and Jerline arrived. After watching the horses work they went back to the house, collected Hamish's bag, and Roddy drove his father-in-law and Jerline back to London.

After the gallops, Jay and Jed walked over to watch a schooling session which involved a young stable lad with the nickname of Ali. Watching the young man, whose real name was Vijay Hasan, Jed turned to Jay and said, 'This lad really is rather good.'

'He certainly is,' agreed Jay, 'and my goodness he's worked hard to become as competent as he is.'

The lad had arrived at County View some months earlier asking for work experience. Although he had never ridden he had clearly studied National Hunt racing in general, and County View in particular. For a complete novice his knowledge and enthusiasm had impressed Jay enough to take him on. At the end of a few weeks he asked Vijay if he'd like a full-time job. The response was a huge grin and a violent nodding of the head. He worked extremely hard in the yard. His horses and their boxes were always immaculate and he was popular with the rest of the staff.

After a couple of months Jay put him under Danny's tender care and he started to learn to ride. One day Vijay asked Danny if there was a local boxing club. Danny knew from his days at Lambourn that there was one at Swindon and took him over there one evening. He was interested to see that the lad had all the correct equipment. Introducing him to one of the coaches, Danny sat and watched the proceedings. First of all the coach put him through various exercises, including a session on the punch bag. He was then put into the ring with a lad about his own age and they sparred for three rounds. At the end of this the coach told him to go and shower and get changed. Walking over to Danny he said, 'This lad has real ability. That was the county champion he was sparring with. He more than held his own.' On the way back Danny asked him where he'd learnt. Vijay explained that his father had been a good amateur boxer and encouraged him from a very early age. 'Well, I'll check out trains for you,' Danny said, 'but I think you ought to be able to get to Swindon and back in an evening without any difficulty.'

The next morning Danny relayed the previous evening's activities to Jay and Jed. 'Why don't we enter him in the stable lads' championships?' suggested Jed. 'If he's that good, he might go a little way.' This was done and in due course to the yard's delight Vijay won his weight division of the championships. From then on he was known as Ali after his hero Muhammad Ali.

'I think we ought to encourage him to have his first race-ride,' Jay announced.

'I agree,' said Jed, 'but we ought to give him as much schooling practice as we can between now and then. I suggest we don't say anything to him until a couple of days before the race. Otherwise I can see him getting over-excited and perhaps very nervous.'

'Well, I'll start looking around for a suitable race for him, and we'd better think about who he's going to ride.'

'I'll give it some thought,' said Jed, 'and make my suggestions in the morning.'

Jay went back to the office to look at entries and do the enormous amount of paperwork that went with running a large racing yard. As soon as he settled, he had more calls of congratulation from many of his owners as well as other racing friends. It was obvious that they considered him a far from spent force. A little later David Sparrow called to enquire how the horses were.

'They're all in fine fettle,' said Jay, 'and I've two horses I'd like you to ride on Saturday if that's all right with your guv'nor?'

'I'll check with him, but I'm pretty sure he has no runners anywhere. I'll phone you back and confirm it, and then perhaps you could be kind enough to let my agent know.'

'Of course,' replied Jay, 'and well done about yesterday.'

Next morning, after exercise had been completed, Jed, Danny and Jay sat down to discuss the Ali situation. 'I've looked through the possible entries,' said Jay, 'and a two mile apprentice novice handicap hurdle at Worcester seems to be the first possibly suitable race. I know it's only a novice, but we have several young horses who are very confident and pretty experienced, so I don't think it would be too much of a challenge for his first outing.'

Jed thought for a moment before suggesting, 'What about Hyde Hill? He's genuine, doesn't pull too hard, and there's no doubt that he jumps so well it won't be long before he's going over fences.'

'That's a good idea,' agreed Jay. 'What do you think, Danny?'

'Well, he's a pretty safe ride, but what about Country Cousin? I know he's currently jumping fences, but he's never actually won a novice hurdle, although he was placed several times. He's in such good form at the moment, he might even run into a place in a race like this, and he shouldn't be too heavily weighted.'

'That's another good idea,' Jay responded.

'Well,' suggested Jed, 'why don't we give the lad two or three days of riding and schooling both of them to see which he gets on with best? If you enter both he could make his own choice a couple of days before we declare.'

'That's a good old English compromise,' chuckled Jay, 'but it does make a lot of sense. Let's work to that plan.'

With that they turned their attention to the next day's racing, which was at Towcester. Sparrow had been engaged for all three races. The Northampton course was extremely tough but a number of County View's horses had run particularly well there. Part of this Jed put down to the fact that most of the gallops at County View were very stiff and so their horses had no problem in dealing with the steep and long uphill finish which was almost infamous for its test of stamina. They had already made the decision which three horses would be entered this time. Wild Sultan would run in the two and a half mile novice hurdle, Gentle Minx in a novice chase over the same distance, and Understated in the three mile chase. Although the plan had been for Sparrow to ride in all three races, Jay had decided he needed to have another jockey in reserve for the rest of the season. He wanted one he knew he could count on for days when they had horses running at more than one course. In the old days the races had been split between Freddy and Paul, but that was no longer an option. Harry Solomons was Jay's main rival but a good friend. He had an extremely good conditional jockey called

Brian Phelps who had come second in the previous year's conditional jockeys championship. Jay had given Harry a call and early that morning found to his delight that he had a runner at the meeting but not in any of Jay's races. He was more than delighted to make his young jockey available, adding that riding different horses from different yards would be good experience for the young man. 'As far as I'm concerned, Jay, you can have him whenever he's available.'

'That's very helpful. I'll buy you a large drink at the course,' promised Jay.

When he told Jed and Danny the outcome of the call, Jed nodded enthusiastically. 'That will give us the option of taking a few pounds off our horses' backs if we ever feel that it would make a significant difference. A few more winners and young Sparrow will have lost his allowance. Also I've noticed that the lad rides as confidently over fences as he does over hurdles, but of course you'd expect anyone from Harry's yard to be as well schooled as his horses always are.'

Back at the house the phone rang and Eva, putting her hand over the receiver, whispered, 'It's Channel 4 Racing Television.'

Jay picked up the phone. 'Hello.' It was Gus Try, a man whom Jay had known and trusted for ten years.

'Jay, I'd very much like to have you interviewed before racing at Sandown next Saturday. We'd like it to be a frank discussion about what's happened at County View in the last few weeks. Obviously there is added piquancy to the situation with you having such a good day at Stratford and beating O'Connor's horse ridden by your ex-rider.'

'I'd be more than happy to,' promised Jay. 'Can we make it well before the first race as I've got two runners that afternoon?'

'Of course,' replied Try. 'The interview will probably be conducted by Angela West.' Angela was not only very attractive but also extremely knowledgeable, having come from a racing family, and she always did her homework.

She and Jay got on very well, and he couldn't be more pleased at the choice.

He told Eva the news and she said, 'Now's a chance for your first fight-back.'

'Absolutely,' replied her husband, and with a broad grin he went out into the yard to talk about the second lot and to tell Jed and Danny the good news.

'The yard's in great form today,' Jed announced. 'The morale is sky-high after Stratford and I have to tell you they're particularly thrilled we beat Paul and O'Connor. Paul is definitely *persona non grata* with our lot. This by the way includes Annie, the stable girl, who he had been going out with.'

Later that morning Jay explained the riding arrangements to David Sparrow, who took the loss of one riding fee in his stride and showed his mature understanding of the situation.

The incident at O'Connor's yard had faded from Jay's mind as he became increasingly busy with the now almost constant stream of runners which accompanied the season getting into full swing. It therefore came as a mild surprise when he received a message from Eva that the police had called and would he phone back at his convenience.

Going into his office, Jay dialled the number and was immediately put through to Detective Sergeant Morgan.

'We've got some information for you,' the sergeant told him. 'The vehicle has been located. It was at a very respectable dealers in Newbury. The owner heard our request for information on local radio and went out to his yard. He had a similar model and he checked the mileage on it against the recorded mileage after the last test drive and found that there was getting on for a hundred extra. He asked his staff who all vehemently denied any knowledge of it, so he phoned the local police. They in turn came up and interviewed the five people who work for him and then ran this through their computer. Guess what? Not only did one of them have a criminal record, but he'd also worked for you, Mr Jessop.'

'Good God,' exclaimed Jay. 'Who the hell was it?'

'Does the name Billy Dean mean anything to you?'

'It certainly does,' Jay told him. 'He was involved in an attempt to kidnap one of my horses some time ago but was caught and sent to jail.'

'Well, obviously we were suspicious of him, but even under intense questioning he refused to admit anything. However, one of the other employees eventually broke and admitted that he had helped Dean that evening. He wasn't quite sure what was going on, but had agreed to wait for Dean while he went into O'Connor's yard. As soon as Dean came out he was to drive off quickly. Evidently they changed places a little way down the road and it was Dean who was driving in a deliberately erratic manner.

'The accomplice also told us that Dean had said he was doing something to get even with some guy who "shafted him a few years earlier". We've done a bit of digging around and found that Dean had attempted to get employment in racing stables at Lambourn but without any success because of his record. However, he managed to persuade the owner, Mr Butcher, to take him on with false references. Evidently he was fairly efficient as a mechanic – which he learned while in jail – and he also worked pretty diligently.'

'That would figure,' Jay agreed. 'He worked hard with us and if he'd only been straight he could have made a thoroughly efficient groom and he might even have got a conditional licence, although he was probably too old for that by the time he came to me.'

'Well, both the culprits have been charged and will appear in a magistrates court tomorrow. I imagine that Dean will get quite a stiff sentence with his record, but the younger guy will probably be treated more leniently. He was clearly only an accomplice and has otherwise got a clean sheet. I'll let you know what happens.'

'Very kind of you. I wonder if you could let me have Mr

Butcher's telephone number?' Jay asked. 'I'd like to thank him for his assistance.'

The sergeant gave Jay the information and he rang Butcher straight away, explained who he was and thanked him for his action.

'It's a pleasure,' Butcher replied, 'particularly when I found out that it was you who was under suspicion. Being a Newbury man you can imagine I take a real interest in racing with the course here and Lambourn a stone's throw away. I've watched your progress over the last few years with great interest and not a little admiration.'

Jay paused. 'Do you enjoy a day at the races?' he asked.

'I do indeed,' replied the car dealer.

'Well, as soon as you've got a free day and you see that I've got runners, give me a call and you'll be my guest along with anyone else you'd like to bring.'

'My wife's as interested in a day at the races as I am, and to tell you the truth she's a bit more of a punter than I am.'

'Well, you're on,' promised Jay. 'Thanks again, and I look forward to meeting you.'

Jay told Eva the news and then phoned Howard, Roddy and Percy, who were delighted the incident had been settled with no possible blame on Jay or County View. He then walked into the yard and beckoned to Danny. He told him about Billy Dean and could see that Danny was not particularly surprised. 'Well, at least that rules The Friend out of that incident,' he told Danny.

'How? They may well have met in prison, and even if they didn't there was enough publicity about Billy Dean and County View for The Friend to know he might well be up to helping out, particularly if there was money in it for that little sod.'

'I doubt it,' replied his boss, but seeing the young Irishman was not open to persuasion went back to his office and decided to call Percy and Howard again, and this time Benny as well. They could all see Danny's point, although Howard was less concerned than the other two.

'You ought to call Jackson,' Percy suggested. 'He'll be able to find out if Dean and Ahearne could have met.'

Harvey Jackson was a high-ranking member of the police force who had been deeply involved in uncovering the Victor Rainsford plot and had excellent contacts with the police in just about every European country as well as all the English-speaking forces. He and Jay had become friendly, if not bosom pals, and subsequently Jackson started to take a more than passing interest in the horse-racing industry. What was more the two men trusted each other.

Harvey was almost as sceptical as Jay but agreed it was worth checking. 'I'm not sure it will get us much further even if it proves to be the case,' he thought aloud. 'Anyway, I'll let you know.'

Chapter Eight

The weather at Towcester was bright and sunny, with the early winter crispness that follows a light frost. Danny and Jay were having a cup of coffee before racing started, when Percy breezed into the owners' and trainers' bar. 'So you managed to get away from the old treadmill,' observed Jay.

'I really needed a break,' his Cambridge friend said with feeling. 'I thought Howard was coming?'

'He is. He phoned a few minutes ago to say he was running a bit late but would definitely be in time for our first runner which is in the second race.'

'How's my horse?' enquired the Lloyd's man. Understated was one of his favourites and was running in the chase.

'He's on top form. We schooled him yesterday, and as always he was immaculate. It's a tough old contest, but I'll be very disappointed if he's not in the frame.'

'What about the other two?'

'Much the same,' Jay replied, 'and it'll be interesting to see how Harry's young jockey gets on with Gentle Minx.'

'What's the thinking behind using him when Sparrow's here already?'

Jay explained the advantages of having another jockey whom he knew well and who would usually be able to sit on any of his horses a day or two before a race if County View had runners at two meetings on the same day. He also pointed out that Sparrow would soon lose his weight allowance.

'That certainly makes sense to me,' agreed Percy.

'What's more, the lad's as good over fences as he is over hurdles so it really does give us a second string to our bow,' added Danny, echoing Jed's comment from the previous day.

Percy fetched himself a cup of coffee and sat down. They chatted about racing generally until it was time to saddle the first horse. The two friends carefully avoided any conversation about the current mysterious events, or any reference to O'Connor or The Friend. Jay didn't want the stable staff, even senior people like Jed and Danny, worried about matters over which they had no control. At this moment Howard hove into view and went with them to the saddling boxes. Jay and Danny together did the honours, and soon Wild Sultan was being led round the parade ring. Jay's horses always looked a picture, and he was delighted when Polly, the horse's groom, won £50 for the best turned out horse. It was a pity that Philip Farr, the owner, was abroad due to business but he had insisted his horse should run if he had half a chance.

David Sparrow joined them in the parade ring and chatted amiably to the three men, waiting for the moment when the mounting bell would ring. He and Jay had already agreed that he'd ride a waiting race on the horse. It was very seldom that a horse ran prominently in the early stages of a race at Towcester and still made it up the final incline.

The field of fifteen was at the start and soon on their way to the first hurdle. Sparrow had his mount settled comfortably in eighth position, with the seven horses in front of him bunched up, running two or three abreast. The pace was generous but not extravagant, and passing the stands for the first time Wild Sultan was moving very easily and clearly enjoying himself. He reached the crest of the bend and started the downhill descent towards the next hurdle. One of the two leaders got far too close, hit it and fell, interfering with the two behind him, leaving his companion with a lead of three or four lengths. Sparrow had avoided the disruption and was now lying fifth and closing on the second, third and fourth horses. The young jockey remained calm, quietly following them and letting the leader maintain his three or four lengths' advantage. All of them jumped the flights down the back straight fluently and soon turned for home. Approaching the last hurdle before the home straight, it was obvious that the leader was now struggling, as indeed was the horse in fourth position. Seeing this develop, Jay's young jockey encouraged his horse to go into third place. Wild Sultan and the second horse both started to close down on the leader as they approached the second last hurdle. They both jumped past the now rapidly tiring leading horse, and David waited patiently a length behind the new leader as they approached the last hurdle. Both horses cleared it cleanly, and Jay was beginning to wonder if the first horse was going to hold on. However, Sparrow had timed his run perfectly, and with one slap behind the saddle Wild Sultan increased his pace enough to gradually draw level and then pass his rival with thirty yards to go. Riding with only hands and heels, Sparrow passed the winning post with a comfortable length and a half in hand.

The whole County View team were delighted to start the afternoon with such a success, and congratulated the young jockey on a very mature ride.

The group of friends returned to the bar. They all had a glass of champagne, at Percy's expense, while watching the next race. Quentin O'Connor's horse was ridden by Paul Jenkins and won a ding-dong battle over the last hundred yards to win by a head in a photograph.

'Well, you couldn't fault young Paul on that,' commented Percy.

'I wouldn't have thought so, but it seems that our Irish friend is very difficult to please.'

However, a television screen soon showed him grinning happily in the winners' enclosure and patting Paul on the back.

'I think they had a few pounds on that horse,' commented Howard. 'It was twelve to one in the papers this morning, and I see that it started at nine to two. By the way, I've noticed one or two of his horses had been heavily backed recently, and not all of them have won.'

'That would probably explain the grin,' Percy suggested wryly.

It was time to saddle Howard's horse Gentle Minx. This they did a little early to allow Jay time to talk to Harry Solomons' young jockey, Brian Phelps. He explained that the mare would undoubtedly stay the trip but didn't have a particularly fast finish. Jay instructed Phelps to keep the mare handy, in third or fourth place, and make his move as soon as he turned for home.

'Don't do anything dramatic, but increase the tempo and don't be afraid to jump the last two fences in the lead. Once you've jumped the last, go hell for leather for home and hope that nothing behind you turns out to be faster.'

'Don't hit her too hard,' cautioned Howard. 'I don't agree with it.' Phelps nodded his understanding.

The field was soon on its way and this time there were no early fallers and no serious mistakes. By the time they were halfway down the back straight for the second time the horses were well spread out with Gentle Minx in second place and beginning to cut down the leader's two lengths' advantage. Howard was getting very vocal in his excitement. Turning for home his horse had gained the lead, and with hands and heels Phelps urged her to move away from the field. He succeeded to an extent, but the third horse was moving steadily up into second place. The rival jockey sat patiently behind Howard's mare as she jumped the second last. He stayed there as Gentle Minx cleared the last. Young Phelps now administered two sharp slaps behind the saddle. The Minx immediately responded, increasing her tempo, but as Jay had expected there was no sprint finish. The second horse waited until they were a hundred yards from the winning post, then its jockey also gave his horse a couple of cracks. There was an instant response, and with significant acceleration it swept past the Minx to win the race by two and a half lengths. However, the County View horse plugged on gamely and resisted a challenge from the third horse and kept second place by half a length.

Howard was slightly disappointed at the result, but as always delighted to have been placed and to see his horse return unscathed.

Congratulating Brian Phelps on riding to orders, Jay spotted Harry Solomons and thanked him warmly, adding that he'd certainly use the lad again if that was all right with Harry. Solomons nodded his agreement, as Jay promised 'A glass of champagne after our next runner. Win or lose,' he added.

'You know me,' smiled Harry. 'You're on.'

Jay rushed off to the weighing room where David Sparrow was waiting for him. The two of them joined Danny, Howard and Percy who were already at the saddling box. Moments later Understated was quickly saddled and on his way to the parade ring. Jay knew from past experience that Percy was extremely good at hiding his emotions, but he could see that there was an undercurrent of excitement running through his old friend. Howard was, of course, his normal enthusiastic self about any County View runners, irrespective of whether he was directly involved with them or not. He was still delighted with Gentle Minx's performance.

Over the last couple of years the original rule that most horses would run in the County View colours had been gradually eroded as outside owners brought high class horses to the yard. This had led to Howard having a number of horses running in his own name, as did Eva, Roddy, Percy and Hamish. However, all horses wore the County View paddock sheets of indigo blue with white edging and the white County View logo in the bottom corner. Likewise, the jockeys' colours had County View across the front as the board had taken the decision not to accept any outside sponsorship, with the exception of the manufacturers of the horse feed which was specially made for them. The suppliers of this feed had their name and logo on the County View horseboxes and on the yard's helicopter. This had replaced the one which, in the early days, had been hired on an ad hoc basis from one of Howard's business friends.

Walking back to the stand, Jay saw the note-taking bronzed man. He had seen him several times now and took little real notice, assuming he was just another of the mixed crowd which made up the regular racegoers.

In a three mile chase Percy's horse Understated would be able to exploit his undoubted stamina, but he was also blessed with a good turn of hoof at the end of even a three and a half mile race. O'Connor had entered Cork County King, ridden by Paul Jenkins. This horse had useful form in Ireland and was favourite as they made their way to the start.

Sparrow had been instructed to keep Understated out of the way of two horses that had a habit of falling, though they both had real ability. With clear rounds either could be a danger. To be on the safe side, over the first three fences Sparrow stayed on the outside in sixth place of the field of twelve. The first circuit was incident-free, but by the time they had passed the winning post for the second time the field was more or less in single file, with Percy's horse now lying close up in fourth position. 'It's a strong gallop but not mad,' Jay remarked to his old Cambridge friend, who nodded as he watched with fixed attention through his binoculars.

At the first fence in the back straight on the second circuit, one of the two inconsistent horses lived up to its reputation and took a crashing fall when lying in second place. However, because the field was in single file, neither the faller nor the jockey caused any problems to the rest of the field. The runners approached the second of three fences almost in a straight line. Sparrow had moved Percy's horse up to third position. There was an 'Ooh' from the crowd and a great intake of breath from Percy as his horse cleared the fence, slipped on landing, and Sparrow finished up round his neck. Luckily, his balance was great and he managed to get himself back in the saddle. The blunder had, however, cost him a place, and he dropped back to fourth. Nevertheless, he was still in good contact with the three horses ahead of him, and bided his time. Sparrow let his horse regain his smooth rhythm. At the next fence down the back straight, he took a slight pull on the reins approaching the obstacle to ensure that the horse didn't have to make a massive leap. Understated duly obliged and jumped the fence easily in a confidence-restoring manner and repeated this fluent performance jumping the fence round the bend. At this stage Sparrow decided to start using his horse's stamina, and gradually quickened the pace, moving into second place approaching the second last as they entered the finishing straight. Paul now had O'Connor's horse in the lead. Both Understated and Cork County King cleared the last fence fluently, and now Sparrow went in serious pursuit of Paul's mount. Two back-handers, and Understated responded, but so did the leader. Percy's horse closed the gap until Sparrow and Paul were riding stirrup to stirrup. With fifty yards to go Percy's horse inched ahead and Jay, Percy and Howard were screaming encouragement. The Irish horse was not done for, and in the closing strides got up to push his head in front. All of them were disappointed, particularly as the winner was Quentin O'Connor's horse.

'Well, he ran a blinder, and I've got no argument with how Sparrow rode him,' announced Percy, 'but it's a shame that if we had to get beaten it would be Paul and O'Connor who did it.'

'I agree,' said Jay, 'but I'm not sure it's all over yet.'

'What the hell do you mean?' queried his friend, and Howard was equally bemused.

'Well, I think that we got seriously bumped by O'Connor's horse as they landed. I wouldn't be surprised if there's a stewards' enquiry.'

No sooner had he spoken than the public address system announced a stewards' enquiry. Jay hurried off to the weighing room in case he was needed to give evidence. Sparrow, who had just weighed in, was waiting to know if the stewards wanted to interview him and Paul Jenkins. 'What do you think?' asked Jay.

'Well, I've got to be honest, guv'nor. He gave me a bit of

a bump but I think it probably affected the other horse as much as us. He might have even won by a length instead of a neck if the incident hadn't happened. What should I say if I'm asked to give evidence?'

'Tell the truth,' was Jay's prompt reply. 'When we win races we want to win them fairly.'

They waited tensely for a few moments before an announcement was made. 'Places remain unchanged' was broadcast over the public address system. Jay gave the young man a sympathetic pat on his back and went back to join his friends who were already having what had turned out to be a consolation glass of champagne.

At the other end of the bar Quentin O'Connor was talking to two men, presumably the owners, who were also celebrating but rather more loudly and ostentatiously than would have been the case if Jay's party had won. O'Connor gave Jay a smug smile and raised his glass ironically. Jay nodded back but made no other gesture.

'Do you think it was a fair result?' Percy asked.

'Yes, I do, but let's be honest, O'Connor's horse is a good one with more experience than ours and we've lost very little in defeat. We're still well handicapped, and coming second is hardly likely to result in us getting a significant rise in weights for our next race. We may even escape with no extra penalty.'

'Well, let's keep our fingers crossed and hope the horses are fine.'

A little later Danny came in to say that all was well. All they needed now was for all three runners to be as sound in the morning as they appeared to be after their exertions of the afternoon.

Chapter Nine

The next day Jay went to Ascot Sales. He had been told
there were three well-bred horses to be sold by the ex-
ecutors of a prominent National Hunt owner who had
recently died. He had a good look at them but was not
impressed enough to stay and bid. After a chat with a
few friends, he drove back to County View and arrived
halfway through evening stables. He was met by a
concerned-looking Jed.

'Two of the horses have got runny noses,' he told Jay.
'I'm not very happy about them.'

Jay went to have a look and saw that there was indeed
a significant discharge from their nostrils.

'I'll phone the vet. You get them moved to the isolation
boxes.'

'I'll be over first thing in the morning,' Chris promised
as soon as Jay told him the news.

Jay spent the early part of the evening helping Max with
his homework, and then they watched some cartoons on a
DVD before it was the youngster's bedtime. He rang
Roddy, Percy and Howard with the worrying news and
promised a second call after the vet had been. It had been
a long day. Jay unwound with a large brandy and a Monte
Cristo No. 3, while Eva read one of her favourite books
of poetry.

So much had been going on that Jay was almost surprised when Benny phoned to tell him that he'd done
some research into the two women who were Quentin's
constant companions.

Pippa Hansen was an upper-crust, tall blonde with a

model-like figure. Her father, who had been a highly successful financier in the City, had been killed in the 9/11 terrorist attack in New York. Following his death, his widow sold the very grand house they had in St Leonard's Terrace, Chelsea, and moved to a smaller but still luxurious converted Georgian farmhouse in Sussex. The father had also left Pippa, his only child, a substantial sum under trust which would ensure that she could continue living in her pampered style. She promptly bought herself a flat in Walpole Street, also in Chelsea.

'She's clearly well connected,' said Benny, 'and loves the social scene. In particular she likes racing which I guess is her connection with Quentin. She drinks pretty heavily, but as far as I can find out she's not into drugs. Incidentally, she's not exactly a one-man woman. In the words of my brother Angel, who's been following her a fair bit in the evening, she certainly doesn't let the grass grow between her legs.' Jay roared with laughter at this remark.

'I think it might be worthwhile trying to get a bit closer to her,' continued Benny. 'I've got a feeling that she might not be too discreet with a couple of drinks under her belt.'

'I'll leave that to you,' said Jay. 'I'm sure you'll manage something.'

'Now the other one's a totally different kettle of fish,' Benny went on. 'Her name is Gina Corelli, and she's Italian. Unlike Pippa Hansen whose Scandinavian looks are probably inherited from her grandparents, Gina is medium height, extremely voluptuous, with a dark complexion and almost black hair. She is a pretty successful artist specializing in horses and dogs, mainly on commission, but she also has two exhibitions a year where she shows portraits of well-known horses.'

'Oh, I've met her,' interrupted Jay. 'She's painted a number of our horses including Splendid Warrior, the Gold Cup winner, and she's done two for Howard – The Conker and Pewter Queen. I must say she seems very pleasant, and I love her work.'

'Well, she certainly seems very different to Pippa. She

does have a number of friends but she's certainly not into the wild parties which Pippa attends frequently. She's more for a quiet dinner with three or four other people. However, she's clearly not short of money and lives in a very nice house near Portobello Road. Her studio is also there. Like Pippa, she often stays with Quentin O'Connor, but it seems she's more likely to cook dinner there. He and Pippa always seem to eat out. The odd thing is all of us have got the impression that neither of the girls know about the other one. We're just guessing of course.'

'Thanks a lot for that. Keep me up to date with anything else you find out.'

'Sure thing, guv'nor,' and Benny hung up.

Jay mulled over Benny's news and, in the interests of keeping his partners in the picture, rang Howard. He had a chuckle at Angel's description of Pippa's amorous activities and remembered Gina from when she'd painted his two horses.

'I'd have thought she was a pretty straightforward girl,' commented Howard.

'I agree,' said Jay, 'but we'll find out, I'm sure.'

Next he phoned Percy and told him Benny's news. There was a pause at the other end of the line, then Percy said, 'You know, it might be interesting to try and get somebody to take young Pippa out a few times.'

'Funny you should say that,' replied Jay. 'Benny agrees, but I can't think of anybody we can toss into that particular lioness's den.'

'Leave it with me,' said Percy, 'I'll give it some thought.'

Later that evening Chris called to say he had the blood results. 'So far it looks encouraging,' he reported. 'The two horses with discharges are definitely showing signs of some virus and only time will tell how serious it is, but on the other hand I've had much worse results than this so let's hope it's fairly mild. The only other horse that seems to be affected is Lucky for Some.'

'That makes sense,' said Jay. 'He's right next door to those two.'

'Well, I suggest you isolate him as well,' Chris continued. 'As far as your other horses are concerned, carry on normally and let me know if any more show a discharge or cough. I'll come over in a week's time and check again. If the white blood cell levels are significantly up it usually indicates a recovery phase as these are the cells that fight infection.'

'Thanks a lot,' a somewhat relieved Jay said. 'I really appreciate the speedy results.'

'That's my job,' the vet commented, and added with a chuckle, 'After all, you are my biggest paying client.'

Jay went out to arrange for the other infected horse to be moved up to the isolation area, then he returned to the house and poured himself a large glass of red wine which he drank slowly as Eva again buried herself in her book.

Well, at least something seems a bit better than I thought, he mused to himself.

Over the next few days the three infected horses began to recover, and Jay had runners at Exeter, Worcester and Plumpton. All of them performed well. He had two seconds and three thirds out of a total of eight runners. None of them, however, managed to pass the winning post first.

The following Saturday was Sandown, and County View still had two runners.

Jed was taking Really a Rascal and Forget Me Not to Warwick. It was only a short drive but Jay had insisted that Des Fallon, one of the senior work riders, should drive him and Cathy. Both runners had a real chance and were racing in County View colours so there was no outside owner to worry about.

Jay had opted to take the helicopter to Sandown where he and Eva were meeting Al Lambert and his wife Maria. Amanda was joining them in the helicopter but Chris was working that afternoon as he had an emergency operation to perform. Roddy and Jerline would also be there. Gambler's Dream was running in a novice handicap hurdle, and Al's horse, Victory Roll, was running in the main race of the afternoon, a two and a half mile handicap chase with a little over £20,000 for the winner. Gambler's Dream had been one of Jay's best young horses the previous season and as it ran in County View's name and colours it had not been targeted by O'Connor. He was very hopeful that they both had a good chance, and had settled on David Sparrow to ride.

Arriving at Sandown, Jay checked that the horses were OK, then went with Eva and Amanda to the owners' and trainers' bar where the Lamberts, Roddy and Jerline, were waiting. Amanda greeted her parents enthusiastically and sat down with them to have a soft drink.

Jay went off to find the television crew and Angela West.

'You'll be on in ten minutes,' she assured him, having given him a friendly kiss on the cheek. Jay leant on a nearby rail and waited for the time to tick by. Angela was talking to the camera crew. Then she started setting the scene for the viewers. She beckoned to Jay.

'I need hardly introduce Jay Jessop to you,' she announced to the camera, 'and it's a great pleasure to have you here.' She smiled at him. 'How do you feel about your runners?'

'Well, all our horses seem to be very well at the moment,' he replied, ignoring the three which had showed worrying signs.

'What about your runners today?'

'I think they both have a good chance of being in the shake-up, but the big race is a very competitive one, as I'm sure you understand.'

'Of course.'

She then asked him to comment on some of his main opponents, but as always Jay was very guarded in talking about other people's horses.

'You've had your fair amount of excitement in the yard, haven't you?' she declared.

Jay smiled. 'Well, it's the sort of excitement we could well do without.' He grinned wryly at her.

'And what about your relationship with Quentin O'Connor?' she pressed him.

'To be perfectly truthful I don't have a relationship with Quentin O'Connor. I've seen him at the races a few times but have never met the man other than to nod at him across the parade ring and possibly in one of the race-course bars.'

'Surely, you must be worried about his raid on your owners and their horses?'

'That's beyond my control, isn't it? The horses that have left belong to the owners and it's their decision. Of course I'm sad, particularly with a horse like Cool Customer, but it's no good worrying about something you can't influence.'

'Well, how do you feel about him taking horses from you?' she persisted.

'Well,' said Jay, 'it's not the way I've ever operated. Of course, from time to time people have moved horses to me – that's part of the game. But if you recall, County View built its reputation by acquiring young horses and building them up into good or even, in many cases, first-rate performers. It seems that Mr O'Connor is in a greater hurry than we were, but I'm not sure that's a good policy. If his proven horses do well, it doesn't really do much for the credit of the trainer. After all, they've been made by somebody else. On the other hand, if they don't perform to the same high level it makes him look less than adequate. In my view it's a very risky game to play and one I certainly wouldn't countenance.'

'So you think he's making a mistake?'

'I didn't say that, but let's say it's not a way of doing business that I admire and, I suspect, a large proportion of the informed racing public would also have their reservations about Mr O'Connor's modus operandi. He's new in this country and I would have thought that making friends was probably more useful than alienating other trainers and probably a large proportion of owners as well.'

'Well, thank you very much,' Angela finished, 'and good luck this afternoon.'

'Thank you too, Angela,' Jay concluded, and with a big smile walked away.

Angela had gone off air, and she gave him a quiet call and beckoned him back. Looking down at him from the steps, she gave him a broad smile.

'Well, you certainly didn't pull any punches there,' she said. 'Thanks for a splendid interview.'

'I just answered your questions,' was the almost coy response.

'And some.' She laughed and, giving him another peck on the cheek, turned back to her camera crew.

Jay walked back to his party, who had watched the interview on the bar television. They all clapped, and Eva, giving him a big kiss on his lips, chortled, 'Well, you certainly gave it to him then, darling.'

Jay took a good drink at the glass of champagne which Al had placed in his hand and said, 'That's enough of that. We've got to get down to work this afternoon.'

It was time for the hurdle, and both jockey and Gambler's Dream acquitted themselves extremely well, being beaten by only half a length by the hot favourite which had already won three races that season. Jay's party were all cheerful in spite of being narrowly beaten. They retired to the bar, and Jay was able to indulge in another glass of champagne as he was not responsible for the transport home. Roddy and Jerline tactfully left to see friends. Al and Maria's excitement rose as the big race drew closer, and they accompanied Jay and Amanda when they made their way across the parade ring and into the saddling area where, with Amanda's help, they soon had Victory Roll ready to start his walk round the parade ring where they waited for their jockey. Minutes later David Sparrow was touching his cap to Al and Maria as well as Jay, Eva and Amanda, and waiting for any last-minute instructions. He had already been briefed to drop the horse out towards the rear of the field, as Jay anticipated it would be a pretty strong gallop in the early part of the race with two well-known front runners in the field. What's more, the Sandown uphill fences took some getting, particularly on the run to the finish.

The race started bang on time. One of the front-running horses, pulling like mad for his head, completely missed out the first fence and took a crashing fall. None of the other runners were inconvenienced by this and, happily, both horse and jockey were almost immediately on their feet. The jockey grabbed the horse's reins and prevented it from being a riderless potential hazard to other runners.

Passing the stand the first time the field was already fairly well strung out, and Victory Roll and David Sparrow were now lying seventh of the eleven remaining runners. The positions were unchanged rounding the bend away from the stands, as the field all safely jumped the downhill fence. Entering the back straight with the famous railway fences, they all cleared these without more incident. Five of the horses at the back were beginning to be dropped, and Al's horse had now moved into fifth position. It was making significant headway and was now only about seven lengths behind the leader which was still galloping strongly. Jumping the pond fence the last time the third horse made a slight mistake and lost his momentum allowing those behind to move up closer to the leader. By now David had moved Victory Roll to third position and was moving sweetly. The second horse was travelling just as well, but the long-time leader was beginning to labour. Jumping the first in the home straight, the second horse and Al's horse made ground and moved past the early leader. Victory Roll now joined the new leader and both jockeys started to ask for added effort. Without changing places, they both moved quickly away from the penultimate fence, leaving the now struggling erstwhile leader a good ten lengths behind. Approaching the last, Sparrow had his mount within half a length of the leader and both of them cleared the obstacle fluently. Now it was hell for leather for the winning post. Victory Roll gradually inched past his remaining rival to go three-quarters of a length up. However, the other horse was not done for yet and gamely fought back to get on level terms again. In a few strides they both flashed past the winning post.

'Photograph,' the public address system announced.

'Did we win, did we win?' demanded an excited Al, who had been joined equally vocally by his wife and daughter as the County View horse had fought it out from the last fence.

'I really can't tell from here,' said Jay. 'Let's go and talk to David.'

They rushed off the stand and down to the chute where the horses left the track, and walked alongside Al's horse as it made its way up the famous Rhododendron Walk.

'What do you think?' Jay asked the young jockey.

'It was very close, guv,' the young man replied breathlessly. 'It was certainly a little ahead of me two or three strides before the winning post, but I don't know whether or not I got it on the line.'

There was an unaccustomed long pause before the result was announced.

'It must be very close,' Jay suggested. 'The judge may well have asked for another print.'

As they approached the winners' enclosure the public address system finally announced the result: 'A dead heat between number three, Victory Roll, and number five, Just Call.' The Lamberts were as excited as if they had won outright.

Having got over the initial delight at his horse having won, if only in a dead heat, Al turned to Jay. 'So what happens now?'

'Well, both jockeys weigh in, and as long as they both pass the scales and there are no objections everything proceeds as normal. I can't see any reason why things should be any different in this case.'

'So what about the prize money?'

'Well, the first and second prizes are added together and then split in half,' explained Jay. 'As far as the future is concerned, the win will count as a win for both horses so there's always the question of penalties for a win. Also how much their ratings change will be in the hands of

the handicapper when he assesses not only their performance against each other but also the quality of the field
they beat. In this situation it was a valuable race and there
were some reasonable horses behind us so I don't expect
him to be too generous in how much he raises your
horse's rating.'

'Ah well,' was Al's philosophical retort, 'if you win races
you must expect the weight to go up and of course the
odds to probably shorten next time.'

'Very true,' agreed Jay. 'Now let's go and have a celebratory drink.'

After a thoroughly enjoyable interlude, Al suggested
that he and Maria should be on their way before the
last race.

'We've got traffic to contend with,' he pointed out,
'whereas you don't – helicopter owners don't have that
sort of problem,' he joked.

Amanda gave both her parents a hug and a kiss. As they
left to go to the car park, she, Eva and Jay walked across
to the helicopter.

'I can't tell you how much Father's enjoying his racing,'
she told Jay, 'and Mother's delighted too. It keeps his mind
off his work and gives him another real interest. I suspect
when he retires he'll probably invest in a couple more
horses and you'll probably be fed up with seeing him at
the races.'

'You know he's always more than welcome,' Jay reassured her. 'I like both your parents and can't imagine how
they produced such a miserable daughter.' With a hearty
laugh, she punched him in the ribs and did up her seatbelt
ready for take-off.

During the flight Jay got up and said something to the
pilot before sitting back down next to Amanda. Eva was
reading an evening paper she had bought at the racecourse. As they approached Cirencester the helicopter
started to lose height. Amanda looked at Jay questioningly.
'What's happening?' she asked.

'Relax,' he replied. 'We're going to drop you in one of

Chris's paddocks, as long as we can see one without horses too close.'

'That shouldn't be a problem,' she assured him. 'We've only got three turned out at the moment and they're in at night anyway.'

A few minutes later they were descending the last couple of hundred feet and landed gently about two hundred yards from the house. Chris had come out to see what the noise was, and with a big grin trotted across to welcome his wife and ask Jay how the afternoon had gone. Jay quickly related the results but left Amanda to fill her husband in with more of the detail. Five minutes later Jay was at County View and walking across to meet an excited Max who had been to a birthday party. He almost immediately got a call from Jed who was able to give him the relatively good tidings that both his other horses had been placed, one second and one third. Forget Me Not had come second in the novice chase, and Really a Rascal third in the handicap hurdle.

'Really a Rascal was involved in a pile-up three out, and never got a fair chance to land a telling blow. He would probably have won,' he explained. 'Both of them finished unscathed.' Jed was clearly delighted at their performances and had had an enjoyable afternoon catching up with some of his old racing friends.

Chapter Ten

A few days later Eva was preparing supper and Jay was strolling round the yard just to relax. Max was with him, having had his supper, and Jay was chatting to him about his day at school. Suddenly Eva came rushing from the house, yelling.

'Jay, come quickly. It's Jack Doyle on the phone. There's a problem.'

Jay ran in and grabbed the receiver. 'What's happened, Jack?'

A clearly very worried driver answered. 'The horsebox has been stolen, guv. I'm really sorry. It's my fault.'

'What the hell happened?'

'Heather wanted to use the toilet so I went with her into the service area to get us both a cup of coffee. While I was collecting the coffee a nice-looking man came up to me and said, "Excuse me. Are you driving the horsebox?" I admitted I was. "Oh," he said. "I just wanted you to know I'm a great fan of Mr Jessop's and I follow your horses religiously. I'm not a big gambler but if I ever have a punt it's nearly always on one of your horses." He kept me chatting until Heather arrived. He asked if he and his wife could visit County View. I said I didn't know but he'd have to ask you. Then he asked where we were going. I told him Ayr. I didn't think there was any harm in this. He thanked me for my time, and Heather and I went out to the lorry park. The box was gone. At first I thought I'd mistaken where I'd parked it but Heather assured me I hadn't. I rushed to the phone and called the police, and now I've just called you.'

'How the hell did they steal the box?' demanded Jay. 'You didn't leave the keys in it, did you?'

'No, guv'nor, I didn't. They're still in my pocket.'

Jay thought for a moment. 'Well, you'd better stay where you are, phone the police again and ask them to call me here. Then I'll tell you what to do.' He explained to Eva what had happened and called Jed. He came over and the three of them sat there, not really knowing what to do.

'It must have been very well planned,' Jed suggested. 'Clearly somebody knew how to get a horsebox started without the ignition keys and I don't suppose for one moment Jack thought of locking the cab door.'

They were speculating about what had happened, when the phone rang again. This time it was the Lancashire police. 'I'm very sorry to hear your news, Mr Jessop,' the policeman said, introducing himself as Superintendent Cosgrove. 'We've got a general alert out, and I'll let you know any news as soon as I can. Have you got another line I can use in case yours is engaged as I imagine you'll be needing to talk to a number of people.' Jay gave him his mobile phone number, and just for good measure Eva's as well. He then phoned his fellow directors, more from the point of view of giving himself something to do than really thinking anything constructive would come out of his effort.

Roddy and Howard were appalled. Howard's comment was, 'My God, I didn't think lightning would strike twice.' Something very similar nearly happened with The Conker, he reminded Jay.

'I know,' replied the trainer, 'but at least that time we knew in advance.'

'Don't worry,' Howard reassured him. 'It'll all work out.'

Percy was much more constructive in his reaction. 'I think you should phone Giles Sinclair at the HRA and then get on to the media.'

'That's a hell of a good idea. I'll do so immediately.'

'What does the poor owner think? They're both Jane Cheveley's, aren't they?' queried Percy.

'Oh my God. I forgot her altogether,' said Jay. 'I'll call her straight away.'

'Where are they, by the way?' asked Percy.

'Jack and Heather are at the Lancaster service station. It's a few miles south of Lancaster on the M6. God knows where the horses are.'

'All right. I won't take up any more of your time,' said Percy. 'Keep me informed.'

While Jay phoned Jane Cheveley, Jed sat down and was clearly giving the situation very serious thought.

'Jane, I've got some really worrying news for you.' Jane Cheveley, who lived in Edinburgh, owned both the horses that had been on their way to Ayr. This was one of the main reasons why the trip to Scotland had been scheduled. She was clearly upset, but also sympathetic to the dreadful experience suffered by Jack and Heather.

'Please give them my best wishes and make sure they don't think I blame them at all,' she insisted.

Jay thanked her and outlined the action he was taking, including the media contacts.

'I suppose a lot of my friends will be on the phone in the morning, won't they? What should I say?'

'All you can do is tell them the police are giving this high priority and you will let them know of any developments. Of course, I'll let you have any news the minute I get it,' he assured her.

'Of course you will, and please tell that lovely wife of yours not to worry too much. Easier said than done, I know, but you look after yourself, Jay. Goodnight and God bless.'

He reported the conversation to Jed and Eva, who was not at all surprised. 'She's such a dear. I know we're having a rough patch but we do have some great friends.'

Jed broke his silence. 'Who the hell would want to do this?'

'Well, Run for Ever has a very fair chance, and The Despot is a hot favourite for Ayr's First Season novice chase,' Jay commented.

'Has O'Connor got a runner in it?'

'As a matter of fact I noticed he hasn't got any runners at Ayr tomorrow.'

'What the hell do you think we should do?' Jed asked.

'Well, the police have now got it in hand and I'm sure they'll let us know of any developments. I'm going to call Giles Sinclair and alert him to the situation. Then I'll phone Luke Harvey and see if he could mention it on the racing news on BBC Radio 5 Live tomorrow morning, and I'll phone Alan Brazil and ask if he could mention it on Talk Sport radio. At least then we can have a lot of people looking for the horsebox. It's pretty distinctive with our sponsor's name on the side.'

'I guess that's all we can do,' said Jed. 'Is it OK if I go now?'

'Of course,' replied his boss.

Jay made his calls and then poured himself a stiff whisky. 'God, will anything ever go smoothly?' he demanded.

As soon as he sat down, the phone rang. It was the police calling from Lancaster again. They'd checked Jack's story, and also the description of the horsebox, and assured Jay that all the police in the area had been notified of the missing vehicle.

Giles Sinclair phoned him back. 'I've sent out an email to all the racing editors,' he said. 'I'm sure you'll get a number of telephone calls. I'll get off the line now.'

Twenty minutes later the phone started to ring. A number of the nationals said it would miss their first editions but promised to give the story prominence in their later editions. Remembering that County View didn't receive the later editions of the national papers, he phoned Howard and asked him to get every national newspaper the next day and report back to him what coverage, if any, they'd received.

In all the excitement Max had sat quietly in the corner, when Eva suddenly realized it was way past his bedtime. Hugging his son, Jay sent him upstairs accompanied by his mother. Turning, Max gave his father a very serious look and said, 'I hope you find them safely, Dad.'

'Thanks a lot, Max,' was the reply. 'I'm sure we will.'

Jay sat down without the same conviction he'd conveyed to his son. Taking a good slug of his whisky, he tried to figure out what was behind all this. Eva came down and sat on the arm of his chair and put her arm around him.

'They can't be planning to steal them,' she thought aloud. 'They couldn't race them, they couldn't sell them, and they're of no value to them dead. I can't believe even our worst enemies would try something like that for spite. The risks are too great.'

'Well, whatever the reason, it was clearly well planned,' Jay retorted. 'You go to bed. I'll sit up for another hour just in case anything comes through.' At half past midnight he gave up and went into a spare bedroom so as not to disturb Eva. He set his alarm for 5.30. It seemed he had barely gone to bed when it went off. Getting up immediately, he had a quick shower and shave, dressing in the clothes he'd worn the day before, and went downstairs to make himself some coffee.

Just after six he was in the yard and joined Jed and Danny, who now knew the news.

'Well, are you going to go to Ayr?' asked Danny. 'The helicopter's all ready to fly you up at half past nine.'

'I don't see there's much point,' Jay responded. 'I'd sooner be here where I can be contacted by telephone, but I will phone the racecourse to say that obviously the two runners are not going to participate. Even if we did find them in time, they won't be in a fit state to run. The whole point of sending them up yesterday afternoon was to give them a chance to rest and have proper food.'

Pausing, he added, 'I'm going to miss out watching the exercise this morning. I'd sooner be near the phone.'

Danny looked at him with a grim expression. 'It's The Friend,' he stated. On top of all the worry, this speculation was the last thing Jay needed.

'How the hell do you make that out?' he snapped. 'Just cool it, Danny. You're getting paranoid.' He saw the real fear on Danny's face and changed his tone. 'I know you're worried and I do understand why, but nothing really links any of this to him yet so let's not panic about possibilities.'

He put his arm around the Irishman's shoulders. 'Come on, let's get on with the work. We've lots of races to win.'

By the time he got in Eva was up and preparing breakfast for young Max. Jay accepted another cup of coffee, but declined anything to eat. As promised, Howard phoned. It was front page news in the *Sun* and the *Mirror*, and all the other nationals had given it prominent coverage on the news pages. Unfortunately it had missed the *Racing Post*.

Luke Harvey rang to promise that he'd mention it on BBC Radio 5 Live. Luke also got a detailed description of the box, and of the two horses. Jay thanked him profusely and turned the radio on. He switched to Talk Sport radio and Alan Brazil was as good as his word the night before. He explained the whole incident to his listeners and, like Luke Harvey, gave a detailed description of the horsebox and the two horses.

Shortly after, Percy phoned to say that he'd seen the news in the papers and had heard it on the BBC.

'God, I'm so sorry,' apologized Jay. 'With everything that went on last night I completely forgot to phone you and let you know.'

'Oh, don't be ridiculous,' replied his friend. 'I can imagine it was absolute pandemonium down there. Have you any news?'

'None yet,' replied Jay, 'but I'm hoping that the broadcast and media coverage generally will turn up something. Obviously I'll keep you informed as soon as I know anything.'

'Please do,' came the reply. 'Now I'll get out of your hair.'

As soon as the first lot was over, Danny came in looking grave. 'I'm sorry, guv,' he said, 'but I'm sure it's The Friend. I just know it.'

'Come on, Danny. Why the hell would he do that? There's easier ways to get even with us.'

'I'm sure he'll have guessed we were involved in his arrest. He's got so many contacts.'

'Just relax. He's in Ireland, he's on the run, and this looks like a really well-planned local operation.' Jay put his arm around his Head Man's shoulders. 'Let's not get worried about who did it. We'll cross that bridge when, hopefully, the horses are back safely.'

The phone kept ringing and a number of commiserating calls came through. Jay was extremely grateful, but asked them to keep it brief as he was hoping for some positive news from another source or, with luck, the police.

Just after ten, Giles Sinclair phoned.

'I've got some information for you,' he said. 'There's been a lot of money for Harry Solomons' horse which was backed down from six to one to threes yesterday afternoon. The one thing we can be sure of is that Harry's not behind this, and it appears there was no great volume on your horse. If it's anything to do with betting, it would seem likely that it's connected with the big bets on Harry's horse and the abductors are banking on the fact that without your runner his horse will win. So far we haven't heard of any big wagers. I've had a word with Harry. He can throw no light on the situation either.'

Jay then phoned Benny to see if he could call some of his contacts who had their ears close to the bookmakers' ground. Within minutes, Harry Solomons himself was on the phone, commiserating with Jay and reiterating what Giles Sinclair had said. He just couldn't think that his yard was in any way connected. 'I'm sure that's right,' said Jay, 'it would never have crossed my mind.'

'I really do hope things work out,' replied his rival, albeit a very friendly one.

The day dragged by and Jay found it very difficult to concentrate. He was going around evening stables with Jed and a still subdued Danny when an excited Eva rushed out.

'They've found them!' she shouted.

The police were on the phone. They'd had a tip from someone who said he'd heard about the incident on Talk Sport radio. He'd seen the box in the yard of a derelict farm outside Conder Green as he and his son were driving past. He went in and could hear horses inside so he immediately phoned the police on his mobile.

The police had gone there, opened the box and taken the horses out. They'd found them some water and let them have some grass while they phoned for a nearby vet to come and examine them. The vet was looking at the horses at that moment and would phone Jay as soon as he'd finished. Jay thanked them very much, and asked if they could arrange for his box driver and groom to be transported to them as soon as possible. The police readily agreed to this.

Ten minutes later Jay's phone rang and the caller identified himself as Harry Donaldson, a Lancaster vet.

'I'm not an equine specialist, but I know enough to tell if horses are in good health or not. These two seem to be totally unhurt and little the worse for their adventures,' he said. 'Obviously you'll want them well looked at when they get back. By the way,' he added, 'I see there's some horse feed in the box and I suggest they're given a small feed before they travel. They must be starving, having been locked up for that length of time.'

Jay thanked him profusely, and asked him to send the bill through to County View.

'No need for that,' was the reply. 'By helping out the police, you never know when they might be of assistance to me in the future. I have been known to speed a bit,' he added with a chuckle.

Forty minutes later Jack phoned to say that the police had delivered Heather and him to the box. As far as he could see the two horses were in fine fettle. He was full of apologies for the incident and was clearly not looking forward to meeting his boss on his return. Jay sought to reassure him.

'It's hardly your fault it happened, but perhaps we have learned that in future there should always be one person left in the box, though whether or not this would have stopped such a well-planned operation is hard to tell. Right. Let's stop talking and get them on their way home.'

'I won't be able to contact you unless I stop because I'm

talking to you at the moment on a police phone,' Jack informed him.

'Don't bother to stop,' said Jay. 'Just come back as quickly as you can, but don't take any risks. One of us will be up when you get here, which I guess won't be much before ten o'clock.'

'Thanks, boss,' came the reply. 'See you as soon as I sensibly can.'

Shortly after, Benny phoned to say that he'd not come up with anything significant, but it seemed that there was very little money on Harry's horse in the southern part of England.

'Incidentally,' he informed Jay, 'Harry's horse won, and started as two to one favourite.'

Giles rang to give him roughly the same information. 'The money seems to have been mainly placed in Glasgow and Edinburgh, but the police have arranged for undercover people to be in the betting shops where some fairly substantial bets were placed, but none of these was more than a few hundred pounds, certainly not enough to change the odds as much as they had. Clearly the money was placed off-course and this will probably take longer to trace.'

'Well, this ties in with what Benny said,' Jay informed him. 'None of the abductors spoke to either Jack or Heather, but he was pretty sure that one of them spoke to a colleague in what sounded like a Scots accent.'

'Well, thank God the horses are on their way back to you, and I'll keep you informed if we hear anything else,' added Giles.

Jay and Eva had a rather happier dinner that night, after he'd called Jane Cheveley to give her the good news and promised to let her know how they both were in the morning.

Max, who had been watching television after his supper, came in and gave his father a big goodnight hug. 'I knew they'd be all right, Dad, and I hope they catch the crooks,' he added, looking very sternly at his father.

'So do I,' Jay assured him, with more than a little feeling.

Sitting and mulling over the recent incidents, he made a snap decision and phoned Harvey Jackson, saying that there were a few things he would like to discuss with him.

'I'm overdue a couple of days' leave,' Jackson told him. 'Why don't I come down to County View? I always enjoy looking at the horses and listening to your update on their racing plans.'

'Done,' said Jay. 'You name the day.'

It was agreed that Harvey would come down three days later and stay in the Shepherd's Rest before being on the gallops first thing the next morning. Jay pressed him to stay at County View but he politely declined. 'Well, what about at least having dinner with us at home,' said Jay. 'I can talk to you in complete confidence there, which might not be quite so easy in the Shepherd's Rest.'

'That seems like a very good deal indeed,' said Jackson. 'I look forward to it.'

Chapter Eleven

At precisely a quarter past seven the following Saturday morning, a yellow Ferrari edged its cautious way up to the house. Eva heard the growl of the engine, went out to meet the driver and directed him to Jay's office where the day's work programme for each horse was being finalized by Jay and Jed.

'Hi, you must be Hansie,' Jay greeted the young man. 'This is my assistant trainer, Jed, who you'll get to know well if you come here frequently.'

'Nice to meet you,' said Jed, giving the young man's hand a very firm shake. 'Are you ready to ride?'

'I certainly am.'

'Right,' said Jed. 'Come with me and I'll introduce you to your mount.' He and Jay had already decided that Pegasus would be the best horse for the young man to ride on his first morning. He'd been a bit above average as a racehorse but was now retired and was used as an excellent schoolmaster for both other horses and young jockeys learning their skills. He was as safe as houses over both hurdles and fences, and a really valuable member of the County View team.

Within minutes, the young man was mounted and riding out in the string with Danny alongside him. At that moment Eva came into the yard and said, 'I want to watch this too. I'll get the third degree from Mum about him.' She joined Jed and Jay in the Land Rover which parked as usual about three-quarters of the way up the gallops. All of them had binoculars trained on the South African as he rode up alongside Danny.

'Well,' commented Jed, 'he looks balanced enough but we're going to have to get him riding a little bit shorter than that if he wants to race.'

'Agreed,' said Jay, 'but he did seem to have good hands and didn't pull the horse around at all.'

Danny led the young man over to where the three of them were sitting in the Land Rover. 'How was that?' enquired Eva, after she'd introduced herself properly to him.

'Oh, it was fantastic, Mrs Jessop,' was the enthusiastic reply.

'I'm delighted,' said Eva.

'So am I,' said Jay, 'but we all call each other by our first names round here. So you go back with Danny and then come into the kitchen and we'll have a cup of coffee.'

Later that morning, sitting at the kitchen table, Hansie was still enthusing about his ride before he changed the subject.

'I understand Percy Cartwright is one of your directors.'

'That's absolutely right,' said Jay. 'He and I go back to our Cambridge days together.'

'Well, he's a friend and business contact of my father's and I thought I'd get in touch with him.'

'He'll be delighted to see you,' replied Jay. 'Give him a call and I'm sure you'll get a good dinner out of him. He'll also introduce you to a few interesting people.'

'You're on. Now, if you don't mind I'm going back to the pub. I brought a briefcase load of work with me and I'll crack on with that.'

'OK – but we're racing at Warwick this afternoon. If you'd like to come with us you'd be most welcome. We're leaving at noon.'

'That sounds great,' the young South African said with a grin.

'By the way,' said Jay, 'I suggest you bring that lovely car of yours here and leave it until you're ready to go back tomorrow evening. We can lend you an old Ford to get back to the pub, but I'm not sure it's a good idea to leave a car like that in the rather open car park at the Shepherd's Rest.'

'That's very kind, I'll take you up on that.' Hansie smiled as he got up to leave. 'I'll be back here at twelve.'

After he had left, Jay was watching a schooling session when his mobile phone rang. It was Frank Malone, his bookmaking owner.

'Jay, I see from the *Racing Post* that you have declared a horse to run at Plumpton tomorrow. It's not often you have Sunday runners except in big races. Are you going?'

Jay confirmed he was.

'I'll be there and I would like to have a few minutes' quiet conversation with you. I've got some information which I think is relevant to what happened to your horses on the way to Ayr. I see the first race is at two o'clock. Do you think you could be there by 12.45 and we could have a bite of lunch while I tell you what's going on?'

'I'm intrigued,' Jay admitted.

'I think you'll be even more so when we talk tomorrow.'

Jay said nothing to Jed or Danny but when he got back for lunch he told Eva.

'Frankly, I hadn't intended to go tomorrow as we've only Star Attraction running in his first race over hurdles, and I was going to get somebody to drive Jed there because he does like being in that area, so close to where he used to train.'

'Well, why don't you take him with you?' suggested Eva. 'Danny's perfectly capable of organizing the yard in the afternoon – it won't be the first time. You'll still be able to see the first two lots before you have to be on your way.'

'Hardly two lots,' he said, 'but I can certainly see the main work and then be on my way. I'll see how Jed feels.'

Halfway through his light lunch, he suddenly looked at her. 'I don't think that's going to work. Frank wants to talk to me about the hijacking and we're going to do it over lunch. I'm not sure he wants to talk in front of anyone else, and I can hardly tell Jed to get lost.'

Eva nodded her agreement. 'Perhaps it's best if you do

go by yourself, and we're pretty busy with runners in the next week to ten days so Jed will probably be just as happy here helping Danny supervise it all. By the way, how is Danny?'

'Well, he's not talking about The Friend any more but I'm sure he's still really worried. I guess the busier we keep him the better.'

Eva nodded. 'I agree, but let's not make it too obvious or that will worry him just as much.'

Finishing his lunch, Jay went back to his office to attack the paperwork and the never-ending need to plan possible entries.

It was Howard who had introduced Frank Malone to Jay with the comment, 'He may be a bit noisy but he's a diamond geezer. You couldn't want a better friend but you certainly wouldn't want him as an enemy. You look after him, Jay, and he'll look after you.'

He now had two horses with Jay, and although deeply involved in racing he didn't have any pretensions to understanding anything about the training side. He left it all to Jay and didn't get upset if his horses didn't win. The first time one of his horses ran, Benny had noticed the name of the owner. He had phoned Jay.

'You've certainly got a character there,' he told the trainer. 'I assume you know that he's a seriously big bookmaker?'

Jay grunted in the affirmative.

'Well, there's something else you ought to know. He's a hard man. He has a group of real toughies working for him. A few of them full-time, but another dozen he can call on at any time. If you're ever in a tight corner you could rely on him.'

'I thought that's what I had you for?' laughed Jay.

'I'm small-time compared with him,' Benny assured him. 'He's got a real army backing him if he needs it. You don't keep Frank Malone waiting for his money – not if you want to stay healthy. On the other hand he always pays up on the dot. You bear that in mind but let me know before you decide to use him. He's a mate and I can trust him, and if necessary I know we could work together.'

'I hear you,' Jay had responded, 'but let's hope it's not necessary.'

On Sunday morning Jay watched the first lot work and some of the schooling session, before leaving for Plumpton in his much-loved Jaguar. He had made sure Hansie knew he was welcome.

A little over two hours later he was pulling into the owners' and trainers' car park. Walking towards the stands he saw Phil, Star Attraction's groom, leaving the weighing room. The lad saw him too and turned to meet him.

'Everything's fine, guv,' he said. 'I've just declared him. He travelled good as gold.'

'That's great. I've got some business to do before racing, so I'll see you in the saddling box twenty minutes before the race.'

'OK, boss,' said the lad, and hurried off back in the direction of the stable yard.

'Don't forget to have some lunch,' Jay called after him.

The lad turned round and grinned at him. 'Never one to miss my grub, guv'nor.'

As he made his way to the restaurant overlooking the course, Jay spotted Frank talking to two other men in his usual cheerful way. Seeing Jay, he excused himself and walked across. He gave him a hearty handshake and, putting an arm round his shoulder, he guided him to a table with a reserved sign on it.

'What will you have to drink?' he asked.

'I'll wait till we eat and have a glass of wine then, but I've got to go easy as I'm driving myself.'

Frank nodded. 'We'll have a bottle anyway. I don't have to do the driving,' he added cheerfully.

A waitress came over, took their order, and disappeared.

'Well, I guess you want to know what this is all about?' the big man asked. 'When I heard about your horses being hijacked, it looked to me as if chances were it was

107

something to do with a gamble. Checking into the betting pattern, it soon became clear someone felt that your favourite was not going to win. As you know, the money went on Harry Solomons' horse which cut the odds in half. There was a bit of betting shop money, but when I made enquiries it was clear this wasn't enough to shift the price like that, so I put out some feelers.

'One of my long-standing friends has a substantial business in Scotland, both on course and off. I gave him a call and he told me that there had been two substantial bets on Harry's horse – one late the day before the incident, and another that afternoon. Putting two and two together, it seems to me that the first was put on when the hijack was planned, and the second when it was known that it had been successful. Thinking about it, I phoned him back and asked him if he knew who'd put the money on. I half expected him to say it was confidential, but we're good mates and he told me what he knew. The money had been put on by a professional who often places large bets for well-known people who don't particularly want their identities disclosed. He stuck to his normal policy of not saying who it was, but he did say that this man was known for putting on substantial sums on behalf of contacts he had in Ireland. That's all I know but I wondered if it would be helpful.'

Jay gave him a hard look. 'It might be very helpful indeed,' he said. 'I'm very grateful to you.' He immediately thought of Danny's comments.

With that, they went back to talking generally about racing, and Frank wanted to know what sort of chance Jay's horse had that afternoon.

'Well, it's his first time over hurdles, but he was a fairly useful bumper horse, one second and one third out of three runs. He's not a world-beater, though he ought to do himself credit this afternoon. To be honest, I'd be very pleasantly surprised if he wins. There are, after all, a couple of hurdle winners in the race, and two or three who've been placed.'

Frank nodded. 'So I shouldn't expect any big money on him?'

'Well, if there is, I don't know on what grounds anyone would be placing it.'

They soon finished their meal, and Frank wanted to get off to his pitch. He refused Jay's offer to pay for the lunch, or even his own half, pointing out that he'd been entertained more than once at County View.

'Well, good luck in the race,' he said encouragingly, and was on his way.

Looking at his watch, Jay saw he had a good ten minutes before he was due to meet Phil, so found himself a quiet spot near the stable block and phoned Giles Sinclair. The HRA man was fascinated to hear Frank's news, and said he would put feelers out. Jay then phoned Benny, who said that so far he'd found nothing, but this might help him. By the time he'd filled Howard and Percy in on this latest development, it was time to saddle his horse, and he decided to pass the information on to the police when he was on his way home. He had extremely good hands-free mobile phone equipment in his car, so there was no problem from that point of view.

As was normally the case now, David Sparrow was riding Star Attraction, who was running in the two mile novice hurdle. Showing his inexperience, the horse dwelt at the start and was last of the fifteen runners as they passed the stands the first time with a circuit to go. He managed to creep up to be twelfth as they jumped the hurdle on the bend, and was still twelfth as they started the downhill run to the first hurdle in the back straight. He jumped each hurdle with considerable fluency considering his lack of racing experience, and moved up to sixth halfway round the final bend. Straightening for home, he crept up to fifth, but a clumsy jump at the second last cost him momentum as well as a good deal of ground. By the time Sparrow had got him moving smoothly again there was no chance of him getting in the first four, let alone the first three.

To Jay's pleasure, the young jockey sat quietly on his

horse and let him finish with hands and heels but without giving the horse an unnecessarily hard time. Jay certainly didn't want his jockey knocking the horse around on the off-chance it might be fourth, but equally he didn't want the stewards accusing him of running a non-trier. He was quite satisfied that the performance, particularly in view of the mistake, would not fall into this category. Star Attraction was a County View horse, so there were no owners to discuss the race with or to look after. Telling his young jockey that he'd used his brains, he went to the stable yard to check all was well with the horse. He was being washed down by the time Jay got there, but as far as he could see he was none the worse for his baptism. Giving Phil an encouraging pat on the back, he waved to Jack Doyle, the box driver.

Before going to the car park he walked to the front of the stands and found Frank Malone. 'Well, you were right,' the cheerful bookie informed him. 'Hardly more than a few quid on your horse.'

Jay thanked him for the information and promised to phone as soon as he had definite plans for either of the bookmaker's horses to run. He then strolled across to his car and started his journey back to County View where he was due to have dinner with Harvey Jackson.

Arriving home, he was greeted by Eva who wanted to know all the news. He gave her a quick summary of the afternoon's conversation with Frank Malone. Jed had reported all the horses well and settled down. It seemed that Danny was a little subdued but was still performing his duties in his normal professional manner.

The table was set and dinner would take five minutes to serve. First would be wild smoked Scottish salmon. This was an annual present from Jane Cheveley who was almost as enthusiastic about fishing as she was about National Hunt racing. This was being followed by Eva's special shepherd's pie which they had discovered over the years was one of Harvey's favourites, particularly when he was allowed to half-drown it in Worcestershire sauce. Locally grown broccoli and carrots would accompany it, and the whole meal would be rounded off with local cheeses from Somerset and Gloucestershire.

Promptly at seven Harvey drove up in his black Rover, telling them he'd already dropped his bag at the Shepherd's Rest. Max was very excited about the prospect of meeting a real live senior detective. He wanted to know why he wasn't in uniform and where his gun was. Harvey played along by explaining that he was 'undercover' and the gun was in a secret compartment in his car that he wasn't allowed to show to anybody. Suitably mystified, but certain to relate the incident in a somewhat embellished way next day at school, Max very reluctantly agreed to go to bed.

'You two are not going to talk business until after dinner,' Eva laid down the law. 'It has received considerable attention during the preparations and I expect it to receive the same in the eating. Now, would you mind doing something to earn your keep, Jay, and pour out the wine.'

This prompted Jay to say, 'You'd better leave your car here, Harvey. We'll get Steve Gray to have you picked up tonight, and I'll collect you in the morning. We hardly want you limited to two glasses of wine, and it wouldn't do for some overenthusiastic local policeman to stop you on the way back.'

Dinner zipped past as Harvey entertained them with some of the funny incidents which had occurred since they'd last met socially. He also expressed considerable concern at the growing problem which drugs were presenting in the inner cities generally, and his London patch in particular.

'It's not just the inner cities,' Jay commented. 'There's a fair amount of it around here.'

'I know, but much of the problem emanates from big dealers in the cities and it spreads out through their networks to the smaller towns.'

After their meal they settled down to brandies and cigars. Eva started to clear up but promised she'd join them when she'd finished.

111

With their cigars lit, Jay gave Harvey full chapter and verse of the O'Connor poaching, the incident at his stables, and then the hijack on the way to Ayr. He listed everyone who was aware of the situation, including the directors, Benny and his brothers, Frank Malone, Freddy Kelly, and the policemen who had been involved in one way or another. He explained that Danny was still convinced that The Friend was involved. Harvey knew from their previous conversation about the possibility of The Friend and Billy Dean having met inside.

Jackson took copious notes and puffed thoughtfully on his cigar before making any comment. 'It does seem strangely coincidental that Dean should target O'Connor's yard, although there is some logic. The Irish betting would also point to some involvement from Ahearne, but I don't really get the Singapore money connection. That's not to say there isn't one. I've seen too many strange coincidences to discount what would appear to be totally unrelated incidents.

'As you know, I've developed excellent relations in Ireland and I'll have O'Connor and his associates carefully checked for you. Quite apart from Dean, it would be interesting to see who The Friend was in jail with, and any connections they might have with Ireland or the Far East. Frankly I don't think there's much further we can go tonight.'

Jay smiled his understanding and Eva, who'd joined them a few minutes earlier, sat next to him on the sofa and held his hand. 'Harvey, we know how busy you are, and in a way I know we're trading on our friendship, but frankly we're worried sick.'

'I understand,' he replied. 'This really is a serious situation. It's bad enough as it is, but if it did escalate it would take up a lot more police time than it will if we can nip it in the bud now. Anyway, you know how much I enjoy spending time with you and Jay, though obviously I'd prefer it to be in happier circumstances. By the way,' he went on, 'how's Danny taking this?'

'Not well,' Eva responded. 'Not well at all. He's even more worried than we are but trying to hide it.'

'Let's hope we can sort it out for him as swiftly as possible. You know I'll do my best,' he concluded.

Eva smiled and gave him a kiss on the cheek. 'I know, Harvey. Now let's finish on a rather more cheerful note.'

Much to their relief, Harvey started to ask about certain horses in the yard, when they were running and how well they were. Although far from being an expert, he now took a lively interest in National Hunt racing, and in particular the County View runners. 'Come on,' Eva eventually said. 'It's late and we've all got our normal early start.' She phoned Steve Gray and five minutes later they saw headlights coming up the drive from the security gate. Steve's wife, Jenny, was driving, and bidding a cheery goodnight to Jay and Eva, whisked Harvey off into the dark.

The next morning Jay grabbed a cup of coffee and collected Harvey from the Shepherd's Rest. By mutual consent they avoided the previous night's conversation until they got out of the car and were walking towards the yard.

'I can't avoid explaining to Danny why I'm here,' Jackson said, 'but I'll try and reassure him if I can.'

'Good luck,' was the response, with little conviction.

Jed spotted Harvey and hurried across to greet him. Jay saw that Danny had also noticed the policeman, but was more reticent in coming forward. Jed, as always, saw the concern in his boss's eyes. 'Don't worry,' he said. 'I'll take Harvey across to look at some of the horses and we'll talk to Danny in as casual a way as possible.'

Not surprisingly, Jed took Harvey to the stable stars, and Danny set about preparing Jack the Lad for a schooling session he was going to ride himself.

'I see your friend's in the news again,' Harvey said to Danny, deciding that there was no point in beating about the bush. Danny nodded.

'Well, I wouldn't worry too much,' Harvey continued. 'My Irish friends tell me that they're already getting tip-offs and although Ahearne has a lot of cronies over there, remember there'll be just as many competitors who won't be at all happy he's on the loose. I've already promised your boss that I'll let him know the minute I hear anything.'

Danny actually looked relieved and gave the policeman something approaching a smile. 'Well, the best present I could have would be for that bastard to be back behind bars.'

'I know, Danny, and you're not the only one. Now, come on, are you going to show me you can still ride a horse or stand here nattering all day?'

Danny gave him a grin. He led Jack out, jumped up with a spring in his step and took the first lot up to the gallops.

'That was brilliant, Harvey. I haven't seen him look like that since the news first broke,' Jay told the policeman.

'That's for sure,' Jed added. 'Now, come on, let's go and watch some horses work.'

An hour later Harvey was on his way back to work with some questions on his mind, not all of which he had discussed with Jay.

Chapter Twelve

The morning of Ali's first race at Worcester dawned rather dull and with a very light drizzle. However, walking into the stable yard Jay could see that even really bad weather would not have dampened the young man's enthusiasm, or indeed that of the yard as a whole. Ali was extremely popular with his workmates, and the fact that he'd brought County View some boxing glory had added to his popularity. Jed was very fond of the young man but Danny had almost adopted him as his personal protégé, having been responsible for introducing him to the boxing club in Swindon. In fact he often went with Ali to the club and seldom missed one of his bouts unless he was racing too far away to get back in time. After a great deal of discussion, eventually the decision had been for Ali to ride Country Cousin. This wasn't so much because the horse had experience of racing over fences as well as hurdles, but that he was well down in the handicap and there was a real possibility that he could win, and an even better chance of Ali riding into a place.

Jay consciously made no reference to the race as he walked round and looked at the horse that Ali was going to ride on the gallops that morning. He was quite sure the young man was already bubbling with excitement and felt it was better to behave as normally as possible until at least they were on their way to Worcester. Jay was certain that the young rider would already have checked the runners in his race and would know they included Keep Coming, the horse with the best form.

Jay and Jed had decided that Ali would only ride first lot

and that he would then go with the horse. From Jay's point of view it was excellent that he was in the first race which meant he wouldn't be sitting around the racecourse getting more and more nervous. Danny would check that Ali had everything he needed with him, including the smallest set of County View colours so that he would look smart and not in anything borrowed.

Jay had intended to run Remote Control at Worcester that afternoon, but Norman Barnes, the owner, was unable to be there, and also it had turned out to be a surprisingly hot contest for a not very large prize, so he had decided to run just Ali's horse.

The race was going to be televised on *At the Races*, so Jay knew there would be a large audience sitting in the stable canteen watching the young man's progress. There would also be support at the course as Des Fallon had hired a minibus and was taking a dozen of Ali's particular friends to watch the race. This had already been cleared with Jed, and as Ali was riding in the first race there was no reason why they couldn't get back in time to carry out their duties at evening stables.

Arriving at Worcester with Eva, Jay checked that all was well with both the horse and the declaration. He learnt from Johnny Hampshire, the valet, that Danny and his protégé were out walking the course. As the going was officially good to soft, Jay knew that Country Cousin would be well suited by it. He and Eva grabbed a sandwich, and he had a glass of wine while Eva settled for a sparking mineral water.

'In case we've got something to really celebrate, I'll drive home,' she told him.

Eventually the time came. Jay chatted away to Ali, avoiding repeating the instructions which had already been given more than once. In doing his best to hide his mixture of excitement and apprehension, the lad nodded vigorously at everything Jay said. Danny, standing behind him, was wearing a broad smile and occasionally gave Jay a long and deliberate wink. The bell rang and Jay let Danny leg Ali up. Danny walked alongside the horse and jockey as they made their final circuit of the parade ring and walked out on to the racecourse. As it was a two mile race, the horses turned right and cantered past the grandstand before turning and making their way back to the start. This ensured most of the crowd would see them before the race. As had been anticipated, Country Cousin behaved like an old campaigner and gave Ali no trouble.

While the runners were circling at the start, Danny and Jay, side by side on the stands, watched their young jockey intently. All went well and the starter walked across to his rostrum and called them in. The flag went down, the tape sprang back and they were on their way to the first hurdle. As instructed, Ali had Country Cousin in the middle of the fourteen runners and tucked in on the rails. The plan was for him always to be in the first half of the field and to stay on the inside until at least the end of the back straight. They would then have the long Worcester bend to give him a chance to make ground and move up to third or fourth by the time they entered the finishing straight with three hurdles in front of them.

Everything went exactly to plan and the County View horse jumped beautifully, showing the experience which he'd gained from over twenty previous races. Jay was delighted to see that Ali was riding him on a long rein and was letting his experienced mount measure himself up to each obstacle. This he did without any hesitation, giving Danny and Jay no cause for concern. Leaving the back straight in seventh place, Ali left the rails for the first time and moved out to start overtaking the horses in front of him. Although for a moment or two he was boxed in, one of the two horses immediately in front of him suddenly made a forward move which gave Ali the chance to pass the slower one, and follow the other horse as it gained steadily on the leading quartet and moved into the lead. By the time they entered the finishing straight Ali, following the same horse a length or so behind, was in second position. Jay looked for the favourite and saw that Keep Coming had now moved into third place but was still three to four lengths behind Ali.

Ali was unaware of this but, to Jay's relief, did not look behind him. Between the third last and the penultimate hurdle, with only minor encouragement from Ali, Country Cousin moved up and challenged the leader as they jumped the obstacle. Ali now moved into a clear lead approaching the last, and Danny and Jay were beginning to get really excited. Eva, who was standing behind them, was probably outdoing the two of them combined in the volume of her support. As they jumped the last hurdle, Ali had moved to three lengths in the lead and the favourite had closed up to a half a length behind the now weakening previous leader. At that moment the weakening horse jumped violently to the right. As it more or less clambered over the obstacle it seriously interfered with the favourite. However, the young jockey sat still and gave his horse a chance to recover. He then gave it three hard whacks behind the saddle which brought an instant response from his mount. He continued to hit the horse in a way that would certainly have earned Jay's disapproval if he'd been riding for him. However, it was having the desired effect, and the favourite rapidly closed on Ali. Rather than risk unbalancing himself and not being experienced in the use of the whip, Ali very sensibly rode out with hands and heels, and with fifty yards to go still had a neck lead over the favourite. However, the other horse, with just a little extra in hand, got up to pass the County View horse with only a few strides left to the post.

Danny looked at Jay. 'What do you think, guv?'

'I think the lad rode extremely well, and I certainly haven't got any criticisms.'

They hurried to greet their young rider as he trotted back to the exit from the racecourse to be led into the winners' enclosure. Jay, Eva and Danny waited there for him, and the grin on the young rider's face stretched from ear to ear.

'Sorry I didn't quite make it, guv,' he greeted Jay.

'You gave him a damn good ride,' responded Jay. 'You were just beaten by a better horse. And well done in not trying to knock him around. He gave you all he'd got.'

The lad jumped off the horse and started to undo his girth under the watchful eye of Danny. 'You go and weigh in,' Jay told him, 'and meet me in the owners' and trainers' bar when you've changed.' Danny walked off with Ali to make sure the final formalities were properly concluded. Jay and Eva walked into the bar and Jay ordered a bottle of champagne.

'I didn't think Ali drank, particularly during the boxing season,' she said to her husband as he returned with a bottle and four glasses.

'I think he might make a bit of an exception today, and if he insists on having an orange juice there's all the more for the rest of us,' he chuckled. A few moments later Danny joined them and picked up his glass, grinning with the same sort of pleasure he used to have when he was riding winners in the days before he was injured.

'Got a bit of news for you, guv,' he said. 'That young lad who won is in front of the stewards.'

'I half expected it,' said Jay. 'I thought the number of times he hit that horse was totally out of order.' Eva and Danny nodded their agreement. At that moment Ali came in and was obviously brimming with the excitement of what he'd achieved. Jay passed him a glass.

'Before you say anything,' he addressed the young man, 'this is a very special occasion. I've only given you half a glass but you're more than welcome to fill up if you feel like it. I just wanted you to know that we're all delighted with how you performed today and I'll certainly give you another couple of rides at least before the season's over.' Ali visibly puffed up with pride and pleasure, politely refused the alcohol and asked for a Coke. He then looked at the three key figures in the County View operation and lowered his voice.

'Young Martin's in trouble with the stewards,' he confided in them. 'I think he's got five days' suspension for overuse of the whip.'

'I'm not at all surprised,' Jay told him. 'We all felt that he was completely wrong. I know in the excitement of a finish, particularly if you think you can win, it's difficult to control yourself, but that's part of the job, and as you know we don't tolerate our horses being unduly knocked around. The first three smacks that lad gave his horse would have been quite enough, and I don't believe the additional dose made any difference to the outcome. Anyway, enough of that. Congratulations, and we're all thrilled for you.'

'I'll never forget this day,' the young man told him. 'My mum and dad are here so do you mind if I go and join them?'

'Not at all,' replied Jay. 'Are you sure they wouldn't like to join us?'

'Leave the lad alone,' Eva insisted. 'I'm sure this is a time when his parents would like to have him to themselves. They don't see him very often as it is.'

Jay remembered that they lived in Bradford so it had been a fair old trip down for them, and they probably wouldn't be staying that late anyway. 'All right, off you go,' he agreed. 'Be sure you tell them how pleased I am,' he added as the lad hurried off.

'Did you see our gang of supporters?' asked Danny.

'I didn't, to be honest,' replied Jay.

'They were down near the last hurdle on the inside of the track, and were going mad as Ali went past the leader. They managed to get on the track to congratulate him as he came back from the finish, but I think they're now on their way back to County View for evening stables.'

'Well, I think it's been a thoroughly satisfactory afternoon for all concerned. Are you coming back with us, or in the horsebox?'

'I think I'll stay and go back with the lad,' said Danny. 'He'll probably want to relive the race half a dozen times.'

'Well, I'll tell you what.' Jay got out his wallet. 'Here's twenty-five quid. Get a copy of the race tape and give it to him when you're in the horsebox.'

'He'll treasure that for the rest of his life,' said Danny. 'I know he'll appreciate it.' And with that, he finished his glass of champagne and hurried out of the bar.

Eva turned to her husband. 'See, we still have some really lovely moments, even if O'Connor and The Friend give us plenty to worry about.'

'I know,' said Jay. 'I just hope this lad carries on improving and doesn't turn out to be as ungrateful and silly as young Paul Jenkins.'

'I think that's highly unlikely,' his wife reassured him and, picking up the bottle, poured most of what was left into Jay's glass and just a couple of sips for her. 'Here's to Ali. Let's hope he has a successful and largely injury-free career.'

Jay raised his glass to the toast, drained the contents, and, putting his arm round her, guided her to the owners' and trainers' car park from where they made their way back to County View.

The following morning after breakfast, Jed walked into the kitchen. He thrust the *Racing Post* into Jay's hand. 'Read this,' he insisted. 'Harry will be fuming. I wouldn't want to be in his yard today,' the older man commented. 'See you soon,' and he walked out.

Taking the paper, Jay was intrigued to see that Harry Solomons had made the front page. Two of his top-class horses had been sold to an unknown buyer and then moved to Quentin O'Connor's yard. Reading the headline and the gist of the article to Eva, he said, 'Well, perhaps we were getting a bit oversensitive about being targeted.'

'That's a possibility,' said Eva, 'but perhaps all this publicity is beginning to work in a way for O'Connor.'

'Well, we'll see what happens,' said Jay. 'It is interesting.'

A little later Roddy called. He had spotted the item about Harry Solomons' horses and wanted to know if there was any more news. Jay assured him there wasn't but before he could end the call Roddy interrupted. 'By the way, Hamish phoned Jerline to say he won't be able to get to the Open Day after all. He sends his apologies but something big needs his attention. Needless to say

Jerline is sad but we all know what her father's schedule is like.'

Jay assured him he did.

Later that evening Jay and Eva were on their way towards Cirencester where they'd been invited to a dinner party hosted by Chris and Amanda. Jay's phone rang. Because he wasn't using his hands-free equipment, Eva was carrying the phone.

'It's Harry Solomons for you,' she told him. 'He says it's rather important.'

'Ask him to hang on for a moment,' said Jay. 'I'll pull over before we get to Chris's.'

A quarter of a mile down the road he found a spot where he could move off the road, and picked up the phone.

'Hi, Harry. What can I do for you?'

'I suppose you've seen today's news.'

'Yes, I'm sorry.'

'Well, now I know how you feel. Have you had a call from Alan Fenton?'

'No,' Jay told him. 'Why, should I?'

Alan Fenton was a trainer of some twenty years' standing. He was not particularly fashionable but rather like Jed in his training days he was well thought of. He normally had one or two good horses in his yard but seldom anything reaching top flight.

'Well,' continued Harry, 'he's called me to say that he and a number of other National Hunt trainers are very concerned about O'Connor's activities. It's not just our owners who are being seduced by way over market prices – there's a knock-on effect. It seems that he and a number of other trainers have been approached by some of their owners and asked to send their horses to the forthcoming Doncaster Sales. Apparently even owners with only moderately successful horses have suddenly got it in their minds that they can make unrealistic profits on their animals if they've won one or two half decent races. He assures me that this has been confirmed by Doncaster who say they have been surprised that an unusual number

122

of this type of horse have been entered for their forth-coming sales.

'The trainers are all extremely angry. While accepting that owners have every right to sell their horses, this group believe that O'Connor's activities are leading to an unset-tling situation across a lot of National Hunt yards. It's their intention to send an open letter to the *Racing Post* stating this and they wanted me to sign it. Although I'm very sympathetic to their situation and indeed their response, I declined.'

'Why's that?' queried Jay.

'Well, because it's now known that I've been targeted in the same way that you have, it occurred to me that this would look like a case of sour grapes, particularly as you have been so restrained.'

Jay paused before answering.

'I haven't been approached yet, but on the other hand I feel you're right. The man is a complete pain in the bum, but I think that if I am approached I'll take the same stance as you.'

'OK,' Harry replied, 'but at least I thought you ought to know.'

'Thanks. It's always just as well to know if something like this is brewing, and it'll give me a chance to be as sympathetic as possible.'

'It'll be interesting to see how the *Racing Post* handles it,' Harry continued. 'It's quite a good story for them and I'll be surprised if they don't give it decent coverage.'

Jay agreed with him, and then after a few pleasantries were exchanged he rang off and drove on to Chris's home.

There Jay and Eva had a relaxed evening in the company of a number of Chris's clients. Needless to say, all of them had horses. A few were avid point-to-point owners, and one couple had three very good show jumpers.

As was their custom, Eva and Jay excused themselves shortly after half past ten, explaining that as always they had a really early start in the morning. On the way back to County View they chatted about Harry's news and their fellow guests at the dinner.

Walking into the kitchen they found Cathy sitting doing a rather complicated piece of embroidery, while Jed was watching television in the other room. They reported that their babysitting duties had been uneventful. Max was sleeping like a log and had not moved the whole time they were out.

'Oh, by the way, Jay,' Cathy said. 'There were a couple of telephone calls for you but as the answerphone was on I thought it was just as well to let you deal with them when you got in.'

'Thanks so much, both of you,' Eva said.

'Ah well, you know, it's always a pleasure,' Cathy assured her. 'Any time.'

'See you in the morning,' said Jed, as he shepherded his wife out of the door.

Jay walked over to the answerphone and switched it on. The first message was from Alan Fenton asking Jay to call him, and the second from a reporter at the *Racing Post* also wanting to talk. Jay made a note to phone them both after exercise the next day, and he and Eva went up to bed.

In the morning Alan Fenton explained to Jay the action he and a number of other trainers proposed taking. Jay let him know that Harry had told him of this the night before, and sympathetically but firmly said that he was of the same view as Harry. While agreeing with their point of view, he felt it would look slightly churlish for him to directly associate himself with the letter. He did, however, tell the trainer that, if asked by the *Racing Post*, he would support their view without being seen as an instigator.

Wanting to make sure that he was not misquoted, Jay called the editor of the *Post* and explained his situation.

'I'm very happy for you to say that I'm sympathetic to their concerns,' he repeated, 'but I feel that to be seen as an instigator could be misinterpreted.'

The editor completely understood Jay's point of view and promised that he would quote Jay in that context.

'By the way,' he added. 'I also agree with what they're saying and I'm going to give the story a decent amount of exposure.'

'Good for you,' said Jay. 'I really do think this is damaging for the sport, and particularly for the small and medium-sized trainer.'

'I'll be running it in tomorrow's paper,' the editor told him, 'so you can see what you think of it.'

'Thanks a lot,' concluded Jay. 'I'll see you racing sometime soon.'

'You bet,' was the reply, 'and let's hope the whole of this comes to an end very quickly.'

The following day he proved as good as his word. A strongly written article made the point that this was bad for racing generally and for a few trainers in particular. Jay's earlier comments about not improving young horses were repeated, and Harry made the point that O'Connor seemed reluctant to let his horses take on any of the really top horses irrespective of who trained them. The article finished by revealing that O'Connor had made no comment other than saying it was up to owners where their horses went and who trained them. He refused to be drawn on the question of where the money came from.

Chapter Thirteen

By now it was only a few days to the Open Day and Eva, with a lot of help from Amanda, completely immersed herself in the preparations. The response from journalists was excellent and nearly every one of the papers Eva contacted had accepted the invitation. In most cases it was their leading racing correspondent who was coming. Jay, Jed and Danny organized the day like a military operation. They brought in a local contractor to touch up the paintwork where necessary, including all the gallop markers. The gallops would be mowed the day before the event, but the all weather surfaces would be chain harrowed on the morning.

The night before the big day the team went round the horses and checked the gallops and the yard, while Eva and Amanda made sure that the marquee was correctly set up.

The caterers were arriving at eight the next morning with tables, cutlery and glasses, and the food and drink were being delivered at half past eleven.

All looked as well as it possibly could and the weather forecast was for a clear and not too cold day. As it was mid-November, they had arranged for heaters to be installed in the morning and for them to be turned on a good hour before the guests were due to arrive.

They all settled for an early night, and even though Eva was a little nervous she managed to get a good night's sleep.

Jay was suddenly awake as he heard a fire bell ringing urgently. Grabbing tracksuit bottoms and a top, he careered downstairs, pausing in the kitchen to put them on, and rushed out of the back door. He was horrified to see the marquee was ablaze, but as far as he could see there was no problem in the yard. At that moment Vince Rudge, the senior security guard, ran up to him. 'I've already phoned for the fire engine,' he said breathlessly.

They could hear the sirens wailing as the emergency services climbed up the nearby hill. Two fire engines came speeding into the area followed by an ambulance. Without waiting to speak to Jay and Vince, who had by now run across to where the vehicles were parked, they got their equipment ready and were soon treating the still raging marquee. At that moment the senior fire officer walked across, and recognizing Jay, asked, 'Do you know how this happened?'

Before Jay could answer, Vince butted in. 'A dark four-wheel-drive vehicle smashed its way through the barrier, went straight up to the marquee, threw two or three objects, and left flat out. They had their lights off so I didn't get a chance to read even part of the number plate, I'm afraid.'

'Let's have a quick look at the rest of the property,' the officer suggested, and they all trotted across to the yard. By now Jed and Danny had also appeared, and had very sensibly checked the boxes and the hay barns. Happily it seemed that the marquee was too far away to have endangered any of the permanent buildings, and the wind was blowing in exactly the opposite direction. While all this was going on, Eva appeared holding a very excited Max by the hand. He clearly didn't understand the seriousness of the situation and was much more excited by the sight of the fire engines and their hoses playing on to the now dying flames.

'What on earth happened?' Eva demanded. 'We didn't even have any heaters in there.'

Jay explained what Vince had said. 'Well, that buggers up tomorrow. It's going to be one hell of a job letting everybody know in time.'

Eva gave him a hard look. 'Don't be ridiculous,' she

said. 'I know that Maurice Gardiner will do all he can to get us out of this hole. It shouldn't take him too long to put up a replacement marquee, even if it's not quite as grand as this one was. I'm going to phone him now.'

'For God's sake, Eva. It's three o'clock in the morning.'

'I'm fully aware of it,' she responded rather tartly, 'but Maurice is a businessman. He's also a friend. He'll understand. The more time he's got to think things through and get them organized first thing in the morning, the better for all concerned.'

Put firmly in his place, her husband grinned, gave her a hug, and let her go back to the house. Danny looked ashen. 'It's that bastard again,' he said. Although Jay by now was beginning to share his view, he wasn't prepared to add fuel to Danny's already considerable worries.

'Hell, Danny. We've got no idea who it is. Let's just cool it, get a bit of rest, and we'd better start at five. The very least we can do is to get the staff clearing up the burnt area and decide exactly where we want the new marquee to go as soon as we know its dimensions.'

Slowly Danny and Jed walked across to the yard, with Jed clearly trying to reassure the young Irishman.

Going into his office, Jay used his mobile phone to call the local police station and tell them what had happened. He assured the duty sergeant there was nothing that could really be done now, and it was probably better anyway to wait until there was some light. Vince would still be there the following morning, although he'd be relieved around ten thirty.

Walking into the kitchen to make himself some coffee, Jay found Eva still chatting away on the phone. She nodded vigorously as he pointed to the percolator. He fetched two mugs while she finished chatting to Maurice and thanked him profusely. Coming to sit at the kitchen table, she answered Jay's enquiring look.

'All's under control,' she assured him. 'He'll get the erectors in as close to six o'clock as it takes them to be there. They'll get everything loaded and be here as soon as it's light. He's quite convinced he'll have the replacement marquee up by half past ten. I'll wait till eight o'clock to phone the caterers and let them know. Now let's finish our coffee and have two hours' lie-down upstairs, even if we don't get any sleep.'

Seeing the wisdom of her suggestion, Jay drained his mug, and patting her bottom affectionately, followed her upstairs.

The next morning Jay kept out of her way and concentrated on making sure that the horses were got ready. The few that were being exercised were going up the all-weather gallop, and Jay put Danny in charge to try and keep his mind off the events of the previous night.

As soon as the exercise was over, the horses were washed down and put on the horse-walkers to dry off before they took their turn in being groomed within an inch of their lives. The all-weather gallop was then chain harrowed. Ensuring that all was well outside, he asked Jed to make sure everybody had a proper breakfast break, and joined Eva. Max was still sleeping after his disturbed but exciting night. By now it was after eight, so Jay phoned the directors and alerted them to what had happened. They were all horrified and insisted on getting there earlier than planned in case there was anything they could do to help.

Hansie, who had stayed the previous night at the Shepherd's Rest, was appalled when he came in and saw what had happened. He immediately put himself at Jed's disposal, and having ridden two horses was now helping with the grooming.

Once all this was completed, Jay decided it was sensible to phone Harvey Jackson, who was clearly taken aback by the news. 'I was going to play golf today,' he said, 'but I shall cancel it. I want to get down there as fast as possible and talk to the local police. This is now getting very serious, Jay.'

'Don't I know it,' was the terse reply. 'Are you sure about coming down?'

'I'm absolutely certain. Now get off the phone and do what you've got to and let me get on my way.'

Shortly after nine o'clock a police car drew up. To Jay's amazement, Colin Evans, the county's Chief Constable, got out. 'This was reported to me an hour or so ago,' he informed Jay. 'We take arson very seriously, and particularly if human or valuable animal life is likely to be involved. Now tell me all about it.'

'Go in the kitchen and get Eva to give you a cup of coffee,' Jay told him. 'I'll just get Vince over. He actually saw what happened, and it's best you get it from him first-hand. By the way, Harvey Jackson's on his way.'

Evans looked surprised and perhaps a little put out, Jay felt. 'And why would that be?' he asked. Jay quickly explained their long-standing association, and added that he felt it better if he and Jackson spoke directly to each other. Evans nodded agreement and walked into the kitchen. Jay grabbed one of the nearby stable lads and asked him to run over and get Vince. 'If his relief's not here yet, tell him not to worry. I think with the fire people and the police we've got enough to frighten off any unwanted intruders,' Jay told the lad, with the nearest thing to a smile he'd managed that morning.

Jay walked into the kitchen and gratefully attacked his third mug of coffee that morning, plus the toasted bacon sandwich which Eva had put next to it. Evans had politely but firmly refused one for himself, explaining he'd already had breakfast at home.

Vince came in and related all he could about the previous evening's events. Evans took notes, but there really wasn't very much for him to record. 'What time do you expect Jackson to arrive?' he asked Jay.

'Well, he's about an hour and a half from here, and we spoke nearly an hour ago,' Jay replied. 'He should be here in thirty minutes.'

Finishing his coffee, the Chief Constable stood up. 'I'll have a look round if you don't mind. Any time now the forensic people should be here, if they're not already. I'll also make a few calls from the car and alert all our patrols to keep their eyes open for an abandoned vehicle matching the description provided by Vince. If they were

130

professional I can't imagine they will have kept it for very long.' With that he marched out of the kitchen.

There was so much to do that Jay couldn't believe that half an hour had passed when Harvey's car drew up in front of his house. He pointed out Colin Evans who was now standing talking to two men dressed in white overalls who'd arrived in an unmarked van which Jay assumed contained their equipment. 'Do you want me to be with you?' he asked his friend.

'No, there may be a bit of a territorial issue here,' Harvey responded, 'so I think I'll have a friendly chat with him by myself.'

'Well, I won't be far away,' Jay promised him, and turned and walked over to the yard.

By half past ten the new marquee had arrived, and an extremely efficient team was erecting it about twenty yards from the site of its burnt-out predecessor. Tables and chairs were being unloaded, and it was clear that Maurice Gardiner had brought in a regular army of helpers to ensure everything was ready in time. While all this was going on, the directors arrived and made it plain that they were there to help if possible but did not want to get in the way.

Evans came over looking far more relaxed than he had before he'd had his chat with Harvey. 'I understand why Jackson is involved,' he informed Jay. 'I'll let you know as soon as I have any information, but our forensic boys are pretty sure that it was started by three different devices which probably ignited on contact. The Fire Chief is in agreement with their views.

'As I get any more news of any sort, I'll obviously let you know and I've also agreed to keep Jackson in the loop as well. I'm really sorry this happened, and I hope your day is still a great success.' Shaking Jay warmly by the hand, he turned, jumped into the back of the police car and was driven off at a smart but sensible rate.

Harvey joined Jay soon after and confirmed that he and Evans had parted perfectly amicably. 'I don't think there's much else I can do here today, so I'll be on my way.' Jay urged him to stay for the reception, but his friend was politely firm in his refusal. 'I don't see the wife very often for Sunday lunch, so I think I'll make an exception and let her know I'll be back, albeit a little late.'

Percy, Howard, Roddy and Jerline had all arrived but, after greeting Jay, the men had attached themselves to Jed and Danny, and Jerline to Eva. They helped where they could but everything was largely under control.

By now the journalists should be approaching County View. A number of them were coming under their own steam but most had accepted the transport provided by County View. Luxury coaches had been arranged to pick them up in Waterloo Place just off Pall Mall next to the Institute of Directors or opposite Reading station. When they arrived, they were to be met by the directors. Percy was still full of speculation about who was behind the arson as the journalists started to arrive.

'Well, let's not worry about it now,' Jay sighed. 'We need this to go really well.' Percy nodded and went off to help welcome the guests. Jay was about to join him when the phone rang. The Chief Constable was at the other end.

'We've found the vehicle,' he announced. 'It was abandoned in a small lane just outside Cirencester. We've also found out that it was stolen six days ago so it's probably going to turn out a bit of a dead end. At the moment forensics are going over it with a fine-tooth comb. I'll keep you informed of developments.'

'Thanks a lot. It's much appreciated, but I must rush. The journalists have started to arrive.'

After the initial greeting, the journalists were ushered towards the stables. Nearby was a small parade ring which Jay had installed when County View had first been built. This allowed the young horses to become accustomed to walking round such a facility in readiness for when they first visited a racecourse. It was also ideal for days like this when he wanted to show off horses to potential owners or journalists. On the way they couldn't fail to notice the burnt-out remains of the marquee. Questions came thick and fast as notebooks appeared and pens and pencils worked overtime.

Jay told them he had no idea who was responsible, or why, and kept his suspicions strictly to himself. Inevitably parallels were drawn with the attempted drug attack on Quentin O'Connor's yard and the hijacking of the County View box on the way to Ayr.

Making no comment on the Ayr incident, Jay did, however, point out that there were now two men in custody in connection with the drug attack. As quickly as he could, he moved them on and soon his horses were being paraded. The great majority were already known by name to this very knowledgeable group. Jed stood in the middle with a microphone and commented briefly on each horse as it went round, eventually finishing with the unraced horses and explaining their origins, their breeding and the likely date of their first run. There were some sensible questions from this informed audience, before Jay told them that they were welcome to watch six of his horses do a real piece of work and then follow two of them as they were schooled afterwards. The four horses working were Punter's Friend, True Tryer, The Peeler and Weapon of Choice, and the two who were also going to be schooled were Kiwi King and Jack the Lad. All six horses had a swinging canter for six furlongs before trotting back to the beginning of the gallops. The two who were going to be schooled then made their way quietly to the schooling hurdles and fences, while the other four worked in pairs at racing speed. Appreciative murmurs greeted the way in which they all performed, and again notes were made of the four horses' names and their likely forthcoming engagements. Walking over to the schooling area, two or three journalists, including the editor of the *Racing Post*, enquired about the background of young Ali, whom Jay had decided to allow to perform in public.

As Jay had hoped, there was considerable interest in Ali, particularly when he related his performance at Worcester. This was recalled by the editor of the *Racing Post* who asked Jay if it would be possible to have an interview with

Ali before he left. He added that it was the sort of human interest story his readers enjoyed, and he felt that a short profile would catch his readers' eye and not do the young man any harm. This was exactly what Jay had secretly hoped for, so he was delighted at the turn of events. The schooling went particularly well and the young boxing jockey did himself no harm in the eyes of this experienced audience. Soon they were on their way back to the marquee where pre-lunch drinks were served, and the directors, plus Jed and a still rather subdued Danny, made their way from table to table answering more questions and ensuring that everybody felt well cared for.

Those who had been to the opening gathering, or had visited County View since then, complimented their hosts on the still almost pristine appearance of the yard and facilities, as well as the immaculate condition of the horses. The food and service were all Eva could personally have hoped for, even if the fire had not taken place. A number of questions were asked towards the end of the afternoon when Jay got up to thank them all for coming and said he was open to any other questions. There was great deal of interest in his opinion about the likely outcome of the Trainers Championship. He confessed that he had no idea at this stage, but was sure it was going to be another close call between him and Harry Solomons.

'And what about Quentin O'Connor?' asked the racing correspondent of the *Sun*.

'Well, you'd better ask him, and in particular how many more top horses he's intending to buy. Will any of last year's Cheltenham winners be left in their current yards?' he questioned with a grin. 'And what about the first three in last year's Grand National?'

This was greeted with hearty laughter.

'Is that remark off the record?' the same questioner asked.

'Not at all,' was the prompt reply. 'And what's more, if it was I doubt if many of you would respect my confidence in this particular situation.'

There was more laughter. A few more serious questions

were asked. Jay then shook each visitor by the hand as they left County View. As the last guest boarded the coach Jay sat down at one of the now empty tables and invited his fellow directors plus Jerline, Hansie, Jed and Danny to join him. Eva waved to one of the waitresses and soon there were a couple of bottles of champagne in front of them. The group had been abstemious all afternoon as they were on parade. With the relief of a successful event being snatched from the jaws of a potential disaster, they all felt they could relax among friends. As Jay and Percy lit cigars, Roddy held up his hand.

'We're not going to have another bonfire, are we?' he joked. 'Are you sure this is responsible?'

'Absolutely,' was Percy's immediate response. 'As certain as I am that there's a bottom asking to be kicked.'

A ripple of good-natured laughter went round the table, joined by Roddy himself. Not forgetting their normal duties, Danny and Jed got up to go round evening stables, and this time the whole party bowled along behind them. At the end of the tour, Jed and Danny politely excused themselves, knowing that it would be pretty cosy in Jay's sitting room with the directors and Jerline, without them adding to the party. Jay thanked everyone for their work that afternoon and, led by Howard, gave them a heartfelt clap as they left. The group sat down to review the day, and the next couple of hours sped by, helped by Howard's insistence that some of the big moments of County View's triumphs should be replayed on the video. Although everyone had seen them before, the pleasure of reliving these great moments never seemed to pall, and Howard in particular got so excited over The Conker's and Pewter Queen's triumphs that you'd almost have thought he was seeing them for the first time.

At eight o'clock they all went to the Shepherd's Rest, driven by two of the stable lads who were getting a handsome tip for their chauffeuring services.

Jay noticed that ever since he'd ridden that morning, Hansie had been rather quiet.

'Have you got something on your mind?' he enquired quietly.

'Well, to be honest, I have,' replied the young South African.

'Well, what is it?'

'I was wondering if you thought I was ready for a ride yet – in a race, I mean, of course?'

'You're pretty close to it,' said Jay, 'but we've got a problem about which horse you're going to ride. To be honest, I can't put you on any of our good and experienced horses until you've had at least a couple of rides in public. It just wouldn't be fair on the owners, and that, I have to say, includes the County View horses.'

'Well, what's the answer? What do I have to do?'

'I think we're going to have to buy you a horse especially for this job. I don't suppose money's a problem, is it?'

'I wouldn't have thought so, but how much do you think?'

'Well, I would suggest something with winning form but coming towards the end of its career. Not over the top and still good enough to win an amateur race, particularly a handicap. You seem to have lost a fair bit of weight since you've been here. What do you weigh now?'

'Ten stone twelve,' was the instant reply, 'and I could easily lose another two or three pounds.'

'I don't think that should be necessary,' Jay reassured him, 'but if we start looking for something in the fifteen to twenty thousand pounds bracket, would that be OK?'

'Absolutely,' was the instantaneous response, 'and I think my father would be happy for two at that price.'

'Come on,' laughed Jay, 'let's settle on one to begin with. I'll start putting out feelers tomorrow.'

The next morning the telephone never stopped ringing with messages of thanks and positive comments. Towards lunchtime the Chief Constable got through.

'We've done some preliminary work on the stolen vehicle,' he announced, 'and have one interesting lead. As far as we can tell, the perpetrators had gloves on, as the only fingerprints we could find belonged to the previous owner, and it's clear that the steering wheel and handles had been wiped clean. However, when we searched the vehicle carefully we found a bus ticket crumpled up under the front seat. It's from Dublin and it's dated the day before the vehicle was stolen.'

'Good heavens,' Jay exclaimed. 'Why on earth should the Irish be involved?'

'I don't want to jump the gun,' continued Evans, 'but I'm a bit of a racing enthusiast and I'm aware that there has been a certain amount of ill will between you and this new Irish trainer in Lambourn.'

'Good God,' said Jay. 'I know we're far from bosom friends, but I can hardly believe he'd get involved in something like this.'

'Well, we've got no proof at the moment,' the Chief Constable said, 'but it's certainly an avenue we'll be examining. By the way, I'd like you to keep that to yourself.'

'Of course,' said Jay, 'but can I tell my board of directors?'

The policeman thought carefully before replying. 'Yes, on the clear understanding that they too keep it to themselves.'

'You have my word on it,' promised Jay.

'I'll make sure Jackson is in the loop,' the Chief Constable added as he finished the conversation.

Jay phoned Percy, Howard and Roddy. Howard agreed with Jay that it was highly unlikely O'Connor would be involved, but Percy was far less certain.

'Can't we get Marvin and Benny to do a bit of digging along these lines?' he asked.

'I really don't think so,' was the reply. 'I've given my word, so let the police get on with it for a day or two. If they don't turn anything up I'll ask if we can spread the information on a strictly limited basis. Anyway, Harvey will probably take that on himself.'

The next few days passed relatively quietly, with Jay and Danny going to the races, sometimes to separate courses, and Jed holding the fort at home. Danny seemed a little less tense, but Jay was fairly certain that underneath the apparently calm exterior the young man was still very concerned. There was no news from Benny, the police or Ireland, although Harvey had phoned to say he'd been in touch with his counterparts in Ireland and they were taking the bus ticket clue seriously. Fingerprints had been found on the crumpled paper and these had been transmitted to Dublin.

Then Harvey phoned again. The fingerprints had been traced to a man called Daly who was a known violent criminal. He very rarely used that name and had a number of very good false identities backed up with fake passports and driving licences. A hunt was on for him.

Chapter Fourteen

Jay returned to County View after a not particularly successful afternoon where he had had three runners at Exeter. One had come third, one had fallen, and the other had just run surprisingly badly, jumping so deliberately that eventually David Sparrow had pulled it up, concerned that there was something wrong. Walking into the kitchen, he was greeted by Eva and Gina Corelli who were sitting at the table sharing a pot of tea. Gina was to paint Jack the Lad for Peter Lumsden and, as always, the work was beginning to look absolutely splendid. 'Hi, gorgeous,' he greeted her, then leant down and kissed her on the cheek.

'I've asked Gina to stay the night,' Eva told him. 'She thinks she should finish her work here tomorrow, and it seemed silly for her to go all the way back to London and then return here in the morning.'

'Couldn't agree more,' her husband enthused, 'and after all what man would turn down the opportunity to have not one but two charming ladies to join him for dinner.'

The artist flashed him a grateful smile. 'You know how much I enjoy being here, and Max and I have struck up a great friendship. I've promised to do a sketch for him after he's finished his homework.'

'I'm just going to have a walk round the yard, touch base with Jed, and then perhaps we can all have a glass of champagne before dinner.'

'I've already put a bottle in the fridge,' his wife admitted. 'So we look forward to you joining us.'

Gina got up. 'Would you mind if I walk round with you?

I've been standing and sitting all day, and you know how much I love looking at the horses.'

'It will be my pleasure,' Jay replied, and Gina followed him out of the door. Jay had a quick word with Jed and then walked round the yard with his guest. He paused at each stable and briefly commented on each horse. A number of them she was familiar with, as part of her job was to know what was going on in racing. She read the racing pages regularly, and was an avid reader of *Pacemaker*, a magazine that often featured her work. On the way back to the house she paused and gently took Jay's arm.

'You know that I have seen quite a lot of Quentin O'Connor?' she said. Jay nodded. 'Well, I thought you ought to know that I'm not seeing him any more.' Jay raised one eyebrow quizzically but said nothing. 'Frankly, he has stopped being the fun he was. When I first met him he could lose his temper but it was soon over, and I have to say it was very seldom that I was at the wrong end of it. But now he explodes at the drop of a hat, and frankly I can do without it.'

'Well, I'm sorry to hear that in one sense,' Jay commented, 'but I'm sure you realize I've got little love for our handsome and charming Irish friend.'

She gave a decidedly girlish giggle. 'The final straw came when he received a telephone call the other evening just as I put dinner on the table. He left the room but I could hear a very heated conversation and he returned in a seriously angry mood. Over the meal this degenerated into a deep depression and he refused to discuss the problem with me. After dinner he drank so heavily and became so aggressive that I decided to get out. He went into his office to make another telephone call which also sounded heated, so I grabbed my overnight bag, which fortunately I hadn't unpacked, jumped in my car and drove into Newbury where I stayed at the Chequers. I had a surprisingly good night's sleep and drove home early the next morning. Interestingly enough, I haven't heard a word from him since, so I'm not sure if he's angry with me or rather embarrassed about how the evening turned out. Anyway, I thought you ought to know.'

'I appreciate your confidence, but as far as I'm concerned it's strictly between you and him. Subject closed.'

With that he put his arm round her shoulder and led her into the kitchen where he gave Eva a big wink as he walked over to the fridge and took out the bottle of champagne. They were soon chatting happily about the prospects of Jay's runners in the next few days. Max came in and, as promised, Gina sat him down and very quickly did a sketch of his profile. The lad was enchanted with it and insisted on running over to show it to Jed and Cathy. As he scampered out of the kitchen door, Eva turned to the artist and said, 'Well, you've certainly made a conquest there.'

Before she left the next afternoon, Gina found her host in the tack room chatting to some of his staff. 'I'm off,' she announced.

'I'll see you to your car,' Jay said. 'I'd better get back to work in the office instead of enjoying myself here.' He turned to the grooms. 'You mustn't think we don't appreciate all your hard work. It's just that sometimes in the rush we forget to show it.' He was greeted with rewarding grins.

Gina took him by the arm. 'I know you don't really want to talk about Quentin, but I do want to be fair. I know that he sets huge store on winning and being successful but he's not a nasty man. He may seem different to you but until recently he has been fun and a gentleman.'

'I'll take your word for it.' He pecked her on the cheek, opened her car door and waved cheerily as she drove off.

Was she asked to say that or was it just her honest opinion, he wondered as he walked back to the house.

Next morning Jay was sitting next to Jed in the Land Rover watching a schooling session when his mobile phone rang.

'Have you got a moment to chat? It's Frank here.'

'Of course,' replied Jay, not really needing his ebullient bookmaking owner to reveal his identity. He had a very

141

memorable voice, particularly on the telephone. Jay was expecting some more news about the Ayr betting and was totally surprised by the next question.

'Would you have three spare boxes?'

Jay hesitated. 'Probably. Why?'

'Well, I know that you're very particular about the horses you train but a friend of mine was in a spot of bother so I bought his three horses and I'd just like you to have a look at them. If they're no good we'll send them to the sales, but if they're worth hanging on to I wouldn't mind adding them to my string.'

'That's fine by me. When should I expect them to arrive?'

'Sometime tomorrow afternoon. Is that OK?'

'Certainly. It so happens that I'll be here tomorrow afternoon so I'll have a look at them and let you know my initial reaction. Have they been running recently?'

'Oh yes, I think so.'

'Have you had them vetted?'

There was a silence for a moment. 'Hadn't thought of that.'

'Well, I'll get Chris over to look at them too. This is all a bit sudden, isn't it, Frank?'

'You know what an impetuous fellow I am, Jay. Anyway, I'll make arrangements, and give me a call when they arrive.'

'Certainly. I'm rather intrigued to see them. What are their names, by the way?'

'You'll see from their passports,' Frank said. 'Sorry, Jay, but I've got to rush.'

Jay turned in his seat and brought Jed up to date with the rather unusual conversation.

'Well, we've always known he's a bit of a character,' the older man responded. 'I'll get the boxes organized. Where do you want them?'

'Just to be on the safe side let's put them in the isolation yard. We'll get Chris to blood-test them when he gives them a look-over, and then we can put them in more permanent quarters if we decide to keep any of them.' With that they turned their attention back to the horses that were working in front of them and no more was said on the subject.

Jay reported Frank's news to Eva over lunch, who smiled and said, 'I hope he hasn't been taken for a ride.'

'That I think is highly unlikely,' her husband commented.

The rest of the day passed quietly, and Jed and Danny popped in for a quick drink after the three of them had done evening stables. Danny told Jay that the three boxes were ready. His boss thanked him and then laughed.

'Well, it's the first time we've had one horse arrive that we know nothing about, let alone three, but I suppose there's a first time for everything. What does puzzle me is Frank's vagueness over the names of the animals and what they've done. Perhaps he's a bit embarrassed about the whole thing? After all he did explain that he'd done it to help out a friend.'

'OK, see you in the morning,' said Danny, and he and Jed left Jay to a family evening with Eva and Max.

By now the hectic Christmas period was approaching, and Jed and Jay sat down the following morning after exercise to plan their entries. 'We haven't got anything for the King George, that's for sure,' Jay commented, 'but we ought to be able to run Maori Warrior in the two mile hurdle, and Understated in the two and a half mile novice chase. Percy would love that. What do you think about running Jack the Lad in the Welsh Grand National?' he asked Jed.

Jay had been particularly successful in this race, beginning with The Conker, and he'd won it twice since then with Tobago Song, one of Eva's horses, who unhappily had broken down and been retired. After being sent to the Moorcroft Rehabilitation Centre, he was now enjoying life as a hack in the New Forest.

'Well, he's not that experienced, of course, but he is an incredibly sound jumper. We know he stays for ever and he's going to be pretty low in the weights. I certainly think it's worth entering him and having a look at the field and also obviously the going,' his right-hand man reacted.

They pencilled in more possibilities, including as far as the New Year's Day meeting at Cheltenham. 'Let's hope the weather's kind to us and we can keep them really fit without them going over the top,' was Jed's cautious comment.

'I agree,' the trainer responded. 'I think a lot of them can go for nice long hacks and I'll speak to Norman about using that forty-acre field of his.'

Norman was a neighbour with a two thousand-acre farm. He and Jay had become firm friends. Norman was very interested in racing, but as he still rode in point-to-points he concentrated on that sport rather than having horses under rules. He did, however, allow Jay to use this particular stretch of land from time to time. It was old sheep-grazing pasture and in excellent condition. It made a nice change for horses that needed to do a reasonable amount of work without the same routine of going up and down the County View gallops several times a week.

Jay was so engrossed in his paperwork after lunch, and in plans for the Christmas period, he'd completely forgotten about his conversation with Frank Malone until he heard the rumble of a heavy vehicle going past his house towards the stable block. He went out and saw a smart horsebox with the name of a very well-known public horse-transport company. Walking over, he recognized the driver but didn't know his name.

'Good afternoon, Mr Jessop. I've got three nice animals here for you.'

'I'm delighted,' said Jay. 'We'd better have a look at them.'

'We'll get them out and then I'll give you the passports. Come on, Freddy,' he barked at the young man sitting next to him in the cab. 'We've got work to do.'

As they lowered the ramp, Jed and Danny arrived on the scene with head-collars and leading ropes. Ali was with them.

Freddy led the first animal carefully down the ramp. The driver brought the second and handed the rope to Danny so that the third could also be unloaded. Jay looked at the three horses with amazement. They were all in fantastic condition and he knew all three. 'Bloody hell!' exclaimed Jed. 'I can't believe it!'

'Neither can I,' said Jay.

Danny turned from the grey horse he was holding. 'God, this'll cause some comment,' he announced. 'Do we still put them in the isolation area?'

'Absolutely,' said Jay. 'Get them bedded down and then come into the office. We'd better put our heads together.'

Slightly stunned, he walked back into the house, and then looked at Eva and roared with laughter. 'I don't know what the hell Frank Malone's up to,' he said. 'We've just had three horses delivered here.'

'I know, I could see that,' replied his wife. 'So what's so amazing about them?'

'Well, they are Rampant Raider, My Sweet Colleen and Double or Quits,' her husband informed her. 'They're probably the three best horses that O'Connor brought over from Ireland.'

'How on earth did Frank get hold of them?'

'I'm going to try and find that out right now,' Jay assured her. 'Send the boys into the office when they come in.' He phoned Frank immediately. 'They've arrived,' he informed the bookmaker.

There was a hearty chuckle at the other end. 'What do you think of them? Think they might win a race between them?'

'You know bloody well how good they are. How the hell did you come by them? By the way, O'Connor will go bloody mad.'

'Well, it's a long story,' Frank began. 'Fergus Mallory has been a bookmaking friend of mine in Ireland for many years. He's no spring chicken and recently he suffered a minor heart attack and just isn't feeling that wonderful so he decided to retire. He asked if I might be interested in buying his Irish operation, and during the course of our conversations he mentioned he owned these three horses and had decided he wanted to get rid of them too. He asked me if I might know anybody who'd be interested.

145

Frankly, Jay, the horses I've got with you are fun but they're not exactly top class.'

Jay murmured his agreement.

'So I did a great deal with Fergus. They will be really good flagships for my company, and what's more it's one in the eye for your friend Quentin, isn't it? On the other hand,' he added quickly, 'that wasn't my main reason for getting them. It's just jam on the bread.'

'Well, it's certainly jam for us,' Jay assured him, 'but I'll still stick to the plan we had. I'll have them vetted and blood-tested tomorrow. They all look extremely fit and they've all run in the last two or three weeks if my memory serves me right, so there's no reason we shouldn't enter them over the Christmas and New Year period.'

'That's what I was hoping,' Frank replied. 'Do I get a quantity discount now that I've got a string with you?'

'No, you bloody well don't,' Jay laughed with him. 'Who's ever heard of a bookmaker who needs a helping hand from a poor racehorse trainer like myself?'

Frank roared with laughter. 'Well, it was worth a try. Let me know what the vet thinks of them and where they might run as soon as you can.'

'Absolutely,' Jay promised him, 'and thank you so much. You've really put a charge into the yard.' With that he rang off.

Almost as soon as he'd put the phone down it rang again. 'I've just thought that we'd better let the press know. We don't want O'Connor putting out some cock and bull story. Do you want to do it or shall I?'

Jay thought for a moment. 'It would probably be best if you did it. I don't want it to sound as if it's some vendetta that I'm having with O'Connor. Nevertheless there's bound to be some comment along those lines.'

'Right,' said Frank. 'Then you better stand by for a deluge of telephone calls. It will be interesting to see if O'Connor phones you.'

'I very much doubt that he will. He wouldn't want to give me the chance to gloat.'

'You're right,' agreed the bookmaker. 'By the way, he

nearly went mad when Fergus phoned him and told him that he'd sold the horses to me and that I'd be collecting them today. He didn't know where they were going, of course. He'll probably burst a blood vessel when he finds out.'

'Couldn't happen to a nicer guy,' was Jay's totally insincere reply.

'I know, so let's sit back and wait for the fireworks.'

Almost as soon as Danny and Jed came in, the phone started to ring. The media were having a field day. Questions covered a wide range of topics. How good were they? When were they going to run? How did they come to Jay? Was this him getting his own back? In his normal tactful way he reminded them that Frank was an established owner with him and he understood that Frank had bought the horses from an Irish business friend. He knew nothing else about the background to their arrival, and any further questions they should address to the horses' new owner. He vehemently denied there was any question of getting his own back on Quentin O'Connor, and assured the journalists that it was a complete surprise to him when the horses had arrived in his yard that afternoon. 'A very pleasant one,' he added.

Once the barrage of calls had died down, the three of them sat down and looked up the horses' records both in Ireland and England. 'Well, you know it looks as if Rampant Raider might be good enough to run in the King George,' Jed suggested. 'He's performed better each time he's run, and that win at Sandown three weeks ago was a top-class performance.'

'I know,' Jay agreed. 'I was there if you remember and have to say I was impressed with the way the horse moved and his jumping. He's not another Warrior, but he's definitely top class.'

'What about Double or Quits?' Danny asked. 'He looks to be a pretty sharp two mile chaser.'

'I agree,' said Jay, 'but I don't think he's in quite the same league as Cool Customer. I think we'll try and avoid our champion, but we may have to take him on before the end of the season if this fellow improves.'

'Then there's My Sweet Colleen, the novice hurdler. She also looks to be a very useful animal, but might be difficult to place,' suggested Jed.

'Yes. She's going to be far too high in novice handicaps, so I think we're going to have to look for equal weight novice hurdles or put her up into the handicap hurdle company. I'd probably want to give her a run before we make any decision, but the other two appear to be a bit more straightforward. We won't do anything with them till Chris has seen them. They can have an easy day or two to settle in. Then if all goes well they can be back in full work.' His two key men nodded in approval and the trio went off to do evening stables. As if drawn by magnets, they all made their way to the three new horses when they'd completed their routine rounds with the rest, and went into each box one at a time.

After all three had been examined and made a fuss of, the County View team stood outside. 'Well,' announced Danny. 'Quentin O'Connor might be a bastard, and we may hate his guts, but he certainly turns his horses out looking a picture.'

'That's true,' Jay agreed rather reluctantly. They made their way back to the yard, each thinking about the way in which these three horses could bring extra glory to County View. Jay stopped and turned to the other two. 'There is one big problem presented by these three horses,' he said. His colleagues looked puzzled. 'I've been telling the press and the world in general how O'Connor will have egg on his face if the horses he's poached don't perform at least as well as when they joined him. Now we're in the same situation and won't he gloat if they don't live up to the high standards they set in his yard.' With that sobering thought, Jay went in to ponder what the reaction would be the following day.

Frank had released the story early enough for his comments and Jay's subsequent remarks to be quoted in the racing press. The *Racing Post* headline was typical: 'Top

Trio Leave O'Connor'. Not surprisingly, all the papers referred to the fact that O'Connor had poached a number of Jay's top horses and now it seemed that the traffic was going in the opposite direction. Most of them gave Jay's comments a fair hearing and only one or two suggested that there was any element of gloating in Jay's attitude towards his very aggressive Irish rival.

Percy, Howard and Roddy were jubilant, and Percy in particular felt that Jay could have been a little more triumphant. He was quickly reminded of the dangers of high-profile horses not performing when they moved yards. As Jay told Percy, he didn't want to put anything on the record that could come back to haunt him.

As the morning progressed one or two friendly trainers phoned Jay to congratulate him. In particular, Alan Fenton, who'd led the small trainers' attack on Quentin's activity, sounded delighted. Harry Solomons phoned expressing much the same feelings as the other trainers. He, however, was particularly aware of the possible pitfalls awaiting Jay if these three new horses failed to perform to the highest of standards.

Later that day Marvin rang Percy to say he'd now had some firm information on the O'Connor money. He arranged to come in that afternoon.

He arrived at Canary Wharf just before six and was shown into Percy's office by Moira. They greeted each other warmly. They'd worked together for over five years and had formed a high regard for each other, as well as a trusting friendship.

The young Afro-Caribbean looked particularly striking, thought Percy. He was wearing an immaculately cut charcoal grey suit and a dazzling white shirt, with a discreet claret Hermes tie.

'Well, what's the news?' Percy enquired.

'I've made a fair amount of progress. O'Connor receives about £40,000 per month from a Swiss bank. It's a small private bank in Zurich where, happily, Jeremy Glover, one of my university friends, is the under-manager.' Marvin had studied languages at Oxford. These included Chinese and Russian, but he also spoke good Arabic, French, German and Spanish. 'The money comes from a private account in Singapore. It's in the name of a syndicate which has the rather mundane name of QBQ Trading Partners. Unfortunately he has not been able to get any more information on the members of the syndicate and it doesn't seem to coincide with any well-known operations out there. He'll keep digging and has a very useful local contact called Lewis Rees who is helping him.'

Percy thought for a moment. 'Well, that sum of money would finance about fifteen horses a month, including training fees, entries et cetera, but it obviously wouldn't pay for the purchases.'

'No, but Jeremy also discovered there have been some very large additional transfers of sums between £100,000 and £200,000.'

'Ah, that would be paying for the horses,' Percy assumed.

'Interestingly enough there was one for £250,000. I imagine that was for Cool Customer.'

'Agreed. It would probably have needed all of that to buy the Queen Mother's Champion Chase winner. Well done. Let's have a drink. By the way, have you spoken to Benny recently?'

'No, but I'm having dinner with him tonight,' his investigator replied, 'so we'll be able to keep each other informed. I'm sure if anything new comes up on his front he'll let Jay know, who'll pass it on to you.'

With that Percy walked across to the cabinet where he kept a wide selection of drinks, poured himself a large scotch and a Jack Daniels for Marvin. Forgetting about work for a while, they turned their attention to the forthcoming test series between England and the West Indies in the Caribbean.

Chapter Fifteen

Benny rang just before lunch next day.

'Do you remember showing me photographs you took when you were in Singapore and Hong Kong? Some of them were with Hamish and his two sons. In particular you took quite a lot of the party at the races.'

'Yes,' replied Jay, 'I do indeed.'

'Well,' said Benny, 'you know I've got a pretty good memory for faces, and I'm fairly sure I saw one of the brothers in a chauffeur-driven car at the traffic lights on the Hogarth roundabout. I was going out to meet one of my friends at the airport and pulled up alongside this car at a red light and just looked casually into it.'

'Do you know which one it was?' asked Jay, slightly surprised at the news and that he hadn't heard from whoever it was.

'I don't,' replied Benny, 'but this guy was Oriental-looking and very well dressed. A rather handsome man with a very pronounced widow's peak.'

'Well, that does sound like Gavin,' agreed Jay. 'Are you going to be in London tomorrow?'

'Yes.'

'Well, I'm going to be up for a National Trainers Federation meeting so I'll bring some copies of the photographs with me and you can have a look. I'm very surprised I haven't heard from him if it was Gavin, but of course he may contact me yet.' They arranged to meet mid-afternoon at Jay's favourite bar in the Dorchester Hotel.

The next day's meeting at the Trainers Federation was rather routine, with no burning issues to discuss, although

151

one or two friendly trainers commented on O'Connor's activities and asked Jay what he knew about the man's background. Jay played it cool and gave the same response he had to the media.

After the meeting Harry Solomons came up to him and suggested a drink.

'I'm sorry, I can't at the moment,' said Jay, 'as I'm meeting somebody in half an hour.'

'Well, let's go round the corner and have a coffee,' said Harry. Sitting down, he got straight to the point.

'I seem to be losing some more of my best horses to this damned Irishman,' he said, 'and I know you were the first to suffer. Do you have any idea what's going on?'

'None at all,' confessed Jay. 'Until he picked up those horses from you I thought it was some sort of vendetta aimed specifically at me, but this seems to give a lie to that theory.'

Harry nodded in agreement.

'Well, I guess there's not a lot we can do apart from sit back and see what happens.'

Harry nodded again. 'You know, good competition is something I've never had a problem with,' he said. 'You and I have certainly been head to head for the last few years, but neither of us has played this sort of game, and I don't think any of our other main rivals would consider it either. By the way, I've heard O'Connor's is not a happy yard. Have you?'

'No,' Jay replied. 'As you said earlier, let's wait and see what happens, but keep in touch.'

With that they shook hands and Jay walked briskly round to the Dorchester bar where his normal table was reserved. Benny was already sitting there. 'Sorry to keep you waiting,' apologized Jay, 'but I got held up for a few minutes by Harry Solomons.' He repeated his conversation for Benny's benefit.

'It's interesting O'Connor's casting his net a bit wider,' said Benny. 'I didn't know he was after more of Harry's horses.'

'Neither did I until Harry mentioned it,' said Jay, 'so it

seems that he's just trying to build up a string of top-class horses and I happened to be the first he hit on.'

'Well, it's no less irritating for that,' the East Ender commented. 'Now, let's have a look at those photographs.' As soon as Jay spread them in front of him, he pointed and exclaimed, 'That's the one – the one on the left. I've no hesitation at all. That's the one.'

'You're completely sure?' asked Jay.

'Certain.'

'Well, I could imagine his brother Fraser not contacting me because he's just not into racing, but I find Gavin's failure to at least give me a ring very surprising. Still, as I said yesterday, there may still be time.'

'I think it might be worth my while keeping an eye on him,' said Benny. 'Can I keep this photograph?'

'Of course,' replied Jay. 'Where do you think he was going when you came up beside him?'

'Well, he was taking the road towards Richmond and Twickenham, so we'll start off by checking the decent hotels in that neck of the woods. There aren't that many, so it shouldn't be too difficult unless he has hired himself a house or an apartment.'

'Well, do whatever you can,' said Jay. 'I find this rather intriguing.'

'So do I,' agreed Benny, 'particularly with this rumour that the money's coming from the Far East. By the way, I'll see if I can find out anything about the O'Connor yard being an unhappy one.' With a cheery 'Keep smiling', he finished his drink and left.

The next day Jay found an excuse to phone Roddy about business, and then enquired about his family. 'Any likelihood that any of them will be coming over in the near future?' he asked. 'Although I know Jerline is really happy here, she's always excited when her father or one of her brothers comes.'

'Not at the moment,' said Roddy. 'I spoke to Hamish last night and he's tied up with a number of AGMs coming up, as indeed is Fraser, but Gavin is pursuing some new potential activities in China.'

'Ah well, you know they're always welcome here when they're over.'

'Sure,' said Roddy, 'I'll see you soon. When are you racing next?'

Jay told him the plans for the next week, and Roddy said he'd certainly try to get to at least one of the meetings.

Eventually Benny phoned. 'We've tracked him down. He's staying at the Runnymede Hotel and he's having meetings there with some guys from the New Oriental and Bank of Korea.'

'Never heard of them,' said Jay.

'Well, I bet your friend Percy has.'

'Thanks a lot. I'll keep in touch with you, Benny,' the trainer promised, and hung up. He phoned Percy and told him the news.

'Well, I can tell you that it's a very big bank and has a small branch here. It seems to do a lot of business with New Finance Capitals which specializes in takeovers and providing venture capital. They're relatively small but they have a reputation for doing very big deals.'

'What do you think I should do?'

'Nothing at the moment, but if you want to flush it out the next time you see Roddy and Jerline I should just say that you were having a drink in the Runnymede with a few friends. You saw Gavin. He was obviously busy with a couple of other men as they hurried to the lifts, so you didn't bother him.'

'I suppose so,' agreed Jay, 'but I'm reluctant not to tell Roddy the truth.'

'I can understand that, but let's not put the cat among the pigeons before we know a bit more.'

'OK. I'll keep you informed.'

On Saturday, Roddy and Jerline joined Jay at Ascot where he had two runners. Rodborough Way finished third in a good novice handicap chase, and Am I a Star won the handicap hurdle under a splendid ride from David Sparrow. The race had been highly competitive and run at a breakneck speed. The jockey nursed the horse near the back of the pack and then started to creep up as they turned for home. The long, uphill finish at Newbury catches out a lot of horses. Races often change dramatically in the last furlong, or even half-furlong. Jumping the second last, Sparrow was sixth, about three lengths behind the leader, Magnus My Man, trained by Quentin O'Connor. The Irishman's horse moved into the lead under Paul Jenkins, but he'd got there easily without the sudden injection of pace which was sometimes his jockey's Achilles heel. Approaching the last, Am I a Star had crept up to third place only a length and a half behind O'Connor's horse, and Sparrow gave him a sharp slap on the shoulder. With a hundred yards to go, he hit the front but Paul refused to give up, and giving his mount three or four hefty cracks behind the saddle, drew alongside. Jay's horse, however, was as game as they come and responded to the challenge, drawing away to win by a comfortable neck. As O'Connor had won one of the previous races, they were all square on the day, but from the look the Irishman gave Jay in the winners' enclosure, it was quite clear that he felt pretty antagonistic towards him and his horses. He also seemed less than pleased with Paul's performance, although in all honesty Jay couldn't fault it.

Praising his jockey on a well-timed race, Jay patted the horse, congratulated the stable girl, and made his way to the bar where he joined Roddy and Jerline. They chatted about the afternoon's activities and a few other business matters, then Jay casually mentioned his sighting of Gavin at the Runnymede. As always, he felt distinctly uncomfortable when telling anything other than the truth. If Roddy was surprised, Jerline was thunderstruck. She and her brother had always been particularly close and she couldn't understand why Gavin would be in London, or at least that close to London, without at least calling her. 'Ah, he's probably only just got here,' Roddy excused his brother-in-law. 'I'm sure you'll hear from him.' After a little more chatter about the racing and the studs they parted and Jay drove back to County View.

The next day he received a call from a clearly concerned Hamish.

'Are you absolutely certain it was Gavin?'

'Well, although I was probably fifteen to twenty yards away from him, I'm as positive as I can be without actually having spoken to him,' Jay assured Roddy's father-in-law, feeling even more uncomfortable. It emerged that Jerline had phoned him with mixed emotions of anger and hurt. Hamish had assured her that Gavin had been in China but was on his way back to Singapore at that very moment. He promised to let Jerline know the situation if it was different.

The next night Hamish phoned Jay again. He had tackled Gavin on his return and at first he had denied everything. He then admitted that he was involved in a major business deal to take over a company which made small, fast ocean-going boats. These were widely used by the services and the coastguards, as well as a number of big international companies.

The company was owned by an elderly man who wanted to retire. Gavin had seen an opportunity for this organization to make a significant profit contribution to his group of companies, and also felt that these boats could be valuable for a number of companies in the Tang empire. He had kept it secret because he didn't want to raise anyone's hopes and then for it to fall through. Somewhat reluctantly he admitted that he did not want the negotiations to go wrong and for him to be seen as a failure by his brother. Although he and Fraser always got on well, there was an intense rivalry between them when it came to business activities.

'So that's it in a nutshell,' explained Hamish. 'I told him in future to at least discuss these things with me, even if he wanted to keep it all under his hat until the deal had been successfully negotiated. I knew they were rivals but I didn't realize it was quite that intense. Incidentally, it looks as if the deal will go through and I think Gavin has done a really good job in landing this one.'

'OK, I'm delighted,' Jay replied. 'I was worried that I might have caused some sort of family upset.'

'Not at all,' insisted Hamish. 'By the way, I hope to be

156

over in two or three weeks' time and I look forward to going racing with you and having my usual visit down to County View.'

'You know you're always welcome. We shall look forward to seeing you.'

Jay reported the conversation to Howard, Percy and Benny.

'Well, at least it explains the somewhat disturbing implications of Gavin's behaviour,' commented Percy, 'but it gets us no further forward in finding out who's bankrolling this bloody Irishman.'

'Howard said almost the same thing,' Jay replied. 'So what do we do now?'

'Well, I think we keep Marvin and Benny on the case and see what else they can turn up. By the way, I had dinner with young Hansie last night and took him into my confidence about our concerns over O'Connor. I whetted his appetite about our blonde bombshell, Miss Hansen, and asked him whether or not, if I arranged an introduction, he'd be prepared to see if she had anything interesting to say on the subject of Quentin after she'd had a drink or two. He leapt at the chance, and I'm taking him to a party I'm sure she'll be at tomorrow night.'

'This is getting to be real cloak and dagger stuff,' laughed Jay. 'I'm not at all sure I want to know any more about your nefarious activities.'

'Nothing nefarious about them! I'm just carrying out my responsibilities as a director of County View.'

'If I may say so,' suggested Jay, 'I think you're taking a rather broad view of the duties that come with being a director. I'm not sure they fall within the tightest guidelines of corporate governance.'

'God, sometimes you can be a boring old fart,' chuckled Percy. 'All right, I'll tell you no more, but I suppose I better let you know if anything interesting emerges.'

'The information will always be welcome, but I think I prefer not to know how it was obtained,' Jay declared.

'Agreed,' laughed Percy, 'I'll talk to you soon.'

'What was all that about?' asked Eva, who had been in

the room whilst the conversation took place. Jay explained Percy's strategies.

'Well, as far as I'm concerned anything that can throw a light on this matter, and better still help us draw a line under it, will have my complete backing,' she informed her husband. 'As long as it's not illegal.'

A few days later Benny joined Jay for an afternoon's racing at Hereford. This was one of Jay's favourite smaller courses as he'd had many successes there, both as a jockey and a trainer. What's more, although the downhill run to the finishing straight was tricky, the course was very professionally run and the facilities had been improved out of all recognition in the last ten to fifteen years. The management team was excellent and the course was one of a number owned by a company.

Standing in the middle of the parade ring with Benny, he again noticed the rather well-dressed man with the notebook and the dictating machine.

'I've seen him around a lot,' Jay told Benny, pointing him out discreetly. Benny looked hard and then turned his back.

'Well, I've seen him too and funnily enough it was when we were keeping an eye on Gavin. I'm pretty sure that he was watching Gavin as well. I also think he was part of a team of two or three who had your Oriental friend under almost continuous surveillance.'

'That's extraordinary!' exclaimed Jay. 'Let me think about it.'

As a matter of principle, he phoned Howard and Percy to pass on this new information. Howard was fairly relaxed about it.

'I really don't see how it affects us. Whatever he was doing is obviously of interest to someone else, but of course if Benny does find out anything it might bear thinking about.'

Percy was altogether more interested.

'This smacks of our friend Gavin being in something fairly deep. There may be more to this than just the boat company.'

A few days after the party, Percy and Hansie were having a quiet drink in the American Bar at the Savoy. They chatted generally about how Hansie was settling in and whether he was enjoying working in London. Hansie's response was very enthusiastic. He had managed to pull off a couple of deals that had his father's approval, which was obviously something the young man set considerable store by. He also seemed to be getting on very well with the other members of the London office. Inevitably, the subject turned to racing and he told Percy how much he was enjoying riding out at County View and hoped it wouldn't be too long before he was actually having his first ride under rules.

Percy eventually steered him round to his social life, and in particular the gorgeous Pippa. Hansie blushed slightly, but admitted that he had spent the previous evening with her, and in fact quite a lot of evenings.

'I won't embarrass you by asking what time you left this morning,' Percy chuckled, 'but what is she like?'

'Well, to be honest,' said Hansie, 'I think she's really quite a nice woman. From my point of view she's ideal as she's attractive, really enjoys bed, and doesn't seem to want any commitment. You were, however, right in that she does drink a lot and gets drunk quite easily.'

'Has she said anything that might be relevant to our concerns about our friend Quentin?'

'She seems to think that he's good company and pretty easygoing. She did, however, say that the last couple of times she's seen him he's seemed rather worried and not his normal carefree self. She evidently asked him if there was anything wrong, and he assured her there was nothing in a rather short-tempered manner. That's about all.'

'Well, if anything else occurs do let me know.'

'I will,' promised Hansie, 'but I must say I feel a little bit uncomfortable in this spy role. She seems to trust me and she does give me a good time.'

'I do understand,' Percy assured him, 'and we've got nothing against her as far as we know. However, O'Connor does seem to be a serious threat to County View, so

159

anything that you can find out would be enormously helpful.'

'You know, Percy, I'm going to have to be a bit careful in the questions I ask Pippa about Quentin and his activities.'

'Oh, and why's that?'

'I think she's getting a bit suspicious. The other evening when I enquired where his horses were running next she gave me a hard look and asked if I was more interested in her or in Quentin's affairs. She said I'm always harping on what he's doing. Well, I explained that of course I was interested, because I ride at County View and there's a healthy rivalry between the two establishments. So then she told me Quentin had noticed I'd asked a lot of questions about him and his horses. He doesn't like it.'

Percy looked thoughtful. 'Well, perhaps you'd better go easy for a bit,' he said. 'Still see her if you want to, but be careful what you say.'

Chapter Sixteen

Jay had just returned from supervising a schooling session with Danny, David Sparrow and Hansie, who was coming on at a rate of knots. He was riding out every Saturday and Sunday, plus two other mornings most weeks. Fiona was right, the young man did have natural ability and was certainly applying himself with enthusiasm to the job in hand. The telephone rang and it was a highly agitated Percy.

'Something very odd has happened in New Zealand,' he announced. 'Have you heard from your New Zealand manager?'

'No, but I know he tried to get me and left a message last night for me to call him urgently. I couldn't get through but I'm planning to try again at a decent hour at his end.'

'Well, you better have a word with Roddy, but evidently a few weeks ago a syndicate bought four of your young horses, two yearlings and two two-year-olds. They were immediately insured for a total of US$700,000. My Far East office has just had a claim for the whole lot, saying they're all dead. This is highly suspicious, although I gather a vet's certificate was attached. Can you phone New Zealand and find out what the hell's going on?'

'Of course,' agreed Jay, 'I'll come back to you as soon as I've got some news.'

Jay waited impatiently until he was able to phone New Zealand and was quickly put through to a seriously worried Angus.

'What's going on?' Jay demanded.

'God knows,' was the reply. 'A Singapore bloodstock

agent arrived a few weeks ago and looked at all our young horses other than those earmarked for County View. He singled out four of them and announced that he would be having them vetted in the next few days. Sure enough, a vet arrived from Australia, but one I'd never met before. He seemed competent, put them through their paces, and then discussed the insurance situation. He said that he would be signing the insurance certificate on behalf of his client who, he said, was the bloodstock agent.

'The bloodstock agent phoned to say that the deal was now finalized and that a bank draft would be sent to us within the next two days. This duly arrived. He also said that he'd like to leave the horses with us for a couple of months, and we agreed the weekly charge. We also agreed they would be turned out during the day and brought in at night. We separated the four of them and put them in a paddock together. There were no problems and they seemed fine. They were checked when they were turned out and again when they were brought in. The paddock is some little way from the yard, but it is flat, well fenced and with a large field shelter. Three days ago two of my grooms went out to get the four horses in for the night and were completely shattered to find all four dead. I got our vet in immediately. His initial reaction was they had all been poisoned but he wouldn't know for certain by what until he'd conducted an autopsy. The four bodies were taken to his clinic where he discovered they had all been injected with Somolose. This, as you probably know, is one of the lethal injections used to put horses down humanely. That's all we know. I phoned the bloodstock agent who professed horror, but frankly, he wasn't as gutted as I expected him to be.'

'How much did you sell them for?' asked Jay

'The four of them went for US$200,000, which was a pretty good deal from the buyer's point of view, but I gave him a discount because he was buying four.'

'That seems very reasonable,' said Jay, 'but the four of them were insured for a total of US$700,000.'

'Bloody hell,' was the response. 'This looks like a real scam.'

'Can you phone the agent and ask him the name of the buyer and call me back as soon as possible? You'd better inform the police as well.'

'Done.'

Half an hour later the phone rang. It was New Zealand on the line.

'I've spoken to the agent. He said that the horses were bought by a syndicate. He didn't meet them, but the purchase price was paid into his bank account the day after the vet had cleared them.'

'What's this agent's name, and can you give me the name of the syndicate and the bank?'

'Surely,' replied Angus. 'The agent's name is Michael Coleman, the syndicate is called QBQ Trading Partners. Coleman advised me that he'd never heard of them before, and denied all knowledge of who or what the syndicate was. As far as he was concerned, the money had been paid and the deal was fine by him. By the way, the police are on the way and have already spoken to our vet.'

'Thanks,' said Jay. 'If you think of anything else please let me know, and I'll let you know of anything we find out at this end.'

Jay phoned Percy with the information. There was a pause.

'I'll get Marvin on to this. That's the second time this QBQ name has surfaced. It seems they are involved in financing O'Connor. Let's see if we can dig into this a bit further. I've talked to my office and it seems that under the circumstances we may have no option but to pay out. We'll hold on for a while to see what we can unearth. It sounds more and more fishy. Talk to you soon.'

A little later Hal Bancroft rang Jay from New York. 'What's new?' he enquired cheerfully. He listened attentively as Jay brought him up to date.

'There's certainly a lot going on you could do without,' the American commented. 'Remember, you've a great team, and with Benny and Jackson on your side there's no shortage of the right people to find out what this is all about.'

Jay agreed without any great enthusiasm.

Hal continued. 'The real reason I phoned was to say I'll be over in a few weeks' time. Do you have any travel plans?'

'Not at the moment, and frankly I don't see me going further than the race tracks until this is all sorted out.'

'Right. As soon as I can see a clear week I'll let you know. Take care and love to Eva and Max.'

County View had two runners at Haydock Park the following day. Haydock is one of the premier racecourses in Britain and enjoys high class flat racing as well as very competitive and well-rewarded National Hunt fixtures.

Hot to Trot, the first of their runners, was in a handicap hurdle worth £8,000 to the winner. The horse was owned by Philip Kerr, as was Wild Sultan who was running in a later race. Both horses would be ridden by David Sparrow. Hot to Trot had been placed second and third in his two previous races; Jay was fairly confident that he would be in the frame and was hopeful that he would in fact win as he was carrying a very low weight. With sixteen runners in the race, David had been told to settle him in mid-division and keep him out of trouble for the first mile. He had a fast finish at the end of the race so the jockey was instructed to creep up to second or third between the last two and then go hell for leather once he'd jumped the last. There was a long run in at Haydock so he would have plenty of time to use Hot to Trot's acceleration.

Jay, Philip and Eva were standing in the ring, a rare treat for Eva since she became a mother. Max was on a school outing, so Eva had a chance to enjoy a day's racing. Again Jay noticed the man with his notebook and tape recorder.

Jumping the third down the back straight, young Sparrow had the horse in exactly the right place. However, suddenly pandemonium broke out. The leading horse fell and brought down the second. This resulted in another horse swerving violently to avoid the two prostrate fallers and jockeys. In so doing, it carried the County View runner across to the outside of the track, and it was with great difficulty that Sparrow got him straightened up and back in line to jump the next hurdle. By this time he had gone from being handily placed to well over twenty lengths behind the three closely bunched leaders. The jockey kept his head, didn't hurry the horse too much, and gradually made up ground turning for home round the final bend. Jumping the last, Hot to Trot produced a sudden injection of pace and left his two closest rivals well behind. This was when Sparrow made his push and, as anticipated, his effort produced a blistering turn of foot. Cutting down the seven lengths with every stride, for a moment Hot to Trot looked as if he would land the spoils. However, the leader hung on gamely and won by three quarters of a length.

Turning to Philip, Jay said, 'Well, that was tough luck. There's no doubt he'd have won but for that incident.'

The owner smiled a little wryly. 'We can hardly blame him for that,' was his philosophical comment.

'It certainly shows we've got every chance of winning with him before the end of the season, that's for sure. Now, if you'll excuse me, I've got to go and saddle your runner in the next.'

This was a two and a half mile novice hurdle over small brush fences which were at normal hurdle height. These had originated in France and were like small steeplechase fences but qualified as hurdles. They were ideal preparation for young horses before they moved from standard timber hurdles to real fences.

Jay's runner was his Towcester winner, Wild Sultan. The horse had already been schooled over fences at home, and it was clear that he was destined to be a chaser in the near future. This was set to be another duel between O'Connor and Jay. The ex-Irish trainer had Galway Galaxy, a previous winner, running and it was favourite in the morning papers with Sultan next in the betting.

Sparrow had ridden and schooled the horse many times

at home over hurdles and fences, and knew that he could be confident of the horse's jumping ability.

The start was approximately halfway down the back straight, with a slightly downhill run to the first hurdle. As instructed, the horse was kept in mid-division for the early part of the race and was lying sixth out of the seventeen runners as they entered the long home straight with three hurdles ahead of them before they passed the winning post for the first time. Travelling easily round the bend and still in sixth place, Sultan jumped the three brush hurdles with the ease and confidence which came from having been schooled over fences. Fortunately the horse was not jumping them too big. This was always a danger when they'd been schooled over full-size fences at home. Jumping the last down the back straight, the field was now strung out, and the County View horse had moved into fourth position some four or five lengths behind Galway Galaxy. Sparrow sat quietly on him until three from the home straight. Still lying fourth, Sultan started to make further steady progress on the long run to the second last. This time the horse put in a spectacular leap which took him to within a length of the leader. He gradually crept up, and jumping the last landed neck and neck with O'Connor's horse. Sparrow gave his mount two sharp reminders. He drew a length and a half to the good and looked like staying there, but with less than a couple of hundred yards to the winning post Paul Jenkins brought the O'Connor horse up to dispute the lead again. Neck and neck, they fought their way every inch to the winning post. From where he was standing Jay couldn't tell which had won. Almost immediately, the public address system announced a photo finish. Hurrying to meet horse and jockey on their walk to the winners' enclosure, Jay gave David a questioning look.

'I honestly don't know,' was the response to the unspoken question. 'It was so close it might even be a dead heat.'

As they entered the winners' enclosure, both the jockeys paused, reluctant to commit themselves to the place reserved for the winner. Almost immediately it was announced that O'Connor's horse had won.

'Tough luck,' said Jay.

'D'you think I went a bit early?'

'Perhaps,' said Jay, 'but you still gave the horse a good ride, and we all make errors of judgement from time to time. Don't worry about it. I'm just sorry that we wound up with two seconds – it could so easily have been two wins.'

A slightly disconsolate jockey walked back to the weighing room to weigh in.

'Do you think he went too soon?' asked Philip.

'Possibly, and he asked me the same question,' Jay answered. 'But it was a good horse that beat us. After all, we know that O'Connor paid £80,000 for it.'

'Well, we lost nothing really in defeat, did we?' the owner said philosophically.

'Nothing, indeed,' replied Jay, 'and I think he can go straight into novices chases now.'

'Great,' Philip said with delight. 'You know I've always wanted a half-decent chaser. Now, if you don't mind I've got to rush. It's a shame we didn't get a win but both horses showed that they have what it takes. Be in touch,' and with a cheery grin he hurried off to the car park.

As Jay was leaving the winners' enclosure he almost ran into O'Connor who gave him a gloating, triumphant grin. Jay ignored it and continued on his way to check the two horses in the stable yard before joining Eva in the owners' and trainers' bar. She had run into a couple of other trainers' wives with whom she had been friendly for several years now. Declining a drink, Jay lit up a Monte Cristo and chatted amiably to the small group, which was soon joined by the husbands. They both commiserated with Jay for his two seconds, and he wished them good luck in the last race where they were competing against each other.

At that moment a young and fairly new lady trainer called Vicky Benson walked up. Smiling rather apologetically at Eva, she said, 'Excuse me interrupting, but would you mind if I had a word with Jay?'

Eva smiled back. 'Of course not.'

Vicky turned and walked out of the bar, clearly wishing to speak to Jay in private. He knew her reasonably well as she'd been a more than adequate amateur lady jockey towards the end of his riding career. She had continued riding until three seasons ago and had attracted a number of owners from the point-to-point circuit who'd given her a few horses to train under rules. She was a keen supporter of Liverpool and watched their home games as often as she could, making the short journey from her yard in Cheshire to the famous ground. As a result of this one or two of the players had also sent her horses. In all she had about twenty-five in her yard when she started and had done pretty well since. In a stroke of luck she'd bought Fateful Meeting, a mile and a half handicapper off the flat who had taken to hurdling like the proverbial duck to water. Although not winning anything very big she did have some success with the horse, which had resulted in favourable comments in the racing press. This, along with her good looks and very pleasant personality, had seen her yard grow to about thirty-five horses at the beginning of the current season.

She looked worried as she turned to Jay. 'I've had a rather frightening telephone call,' she confided to him. 'A man phoned last night and told me I was not to run Fateful Meeting at Doncaster the day after tomorrow. Frankly I think he's got a cracking chance and I would expect him to be in the first two or three.'

Jay thought. 'And who would be your main rivals?'

'Well, Harry Solomons has Stop Press News but frankly with the weight it's got I still think we'd have its measure. Quentin O'Connor has Positive Attitude and that's the one I'd be really worried about. His horses seem to have struck a good vein and I'm only getting two pounds from it.'

'What did the caller actually say?'

'Well, he was very specific about not running at Doncaster, and said I'd regret it if I did. He also went on to say that if the horse wasn't declared there would be a nice little present for me. Frankly nothing like this has ever

168

happened to me before, and to be honest I've never heard of it in racing.'

'I have,' Jay replied, 'but it's pretty rare, thank goodness. What have you done, if anything?'

'Well, I'm so worried I haven't done anything. What do you think I should do?'

'Don't waste any more time,' he said. 'Phone Giles Sinclair at the HRA and tell him exactly what's happened. I'm sure he will not only advise you to phone the police, but he'll almost certainly know the most senior man in your area who you should report this to.'

'Should I still run the horse?' she persisted.

'That's up to you. I certainly would, but Giles and your local police can probably give you better advice than me. Was there anything unusual about the man's voice?' he added.

'Well, I think it was deliberately muffled in some way, but I had a feeling there was a foreign accent involved. It might have been Irish but I'm not sure. I may well be associating it with the fact that O'Connor's horse was in my mind.'

Jay made no comment. 'I still think my advice is the best course of action you can take,' he assured her, 'but if you want to talk to me again don't hesitate to phone.' Getting out his wallet he gave her his card. 'Good luck,' he smiled, 'and don't let it worry you too much.' Giving her an encouraging grin, he turned and walked back to Eva and her friends. She looked at him enquiringly but said nothing.

Jay turned to her. 'Are you happy to be on your way so we can miss the rush at the end of the afternoon?'

'Absolutely,' she replied. Kissing her girlfriends goodbye, she joined Jay and as they walked off hand in hand towards their car he told her what had happened.

Eva drove while Jay got out his mobile, dialled Harvey Jackson and told him about his conversation with Vicky.

'Well, it wouldn't be the first time this sort of threat has been made,' Harvey reminded Jay. 'But I think it is somewhat suspicious that O'Connor has got what appears to be one of the other two fancied horses in the race. Leave it to me. I'll call Russ Gleeson in Chester and fill him in on the rather fishy details associated with some of O'Connor's recent actions. I'll let you know what happens.'

Chapter Seventeen

Jay thought about phoning Vicky Benson to ask if she was going to run Fateful Meeting, but decided it was probably best to leave her in peace to make up her own mind. He did, however, look at the horses due to run in the paper on the morning of the race. He was not really surprised to see that her horse was down to run, although, of course, she could withdraw it at the last moment if her nerve failed her. In her riding days she had always been as brave as any man on the circuit. Making a note of the time of the race, Jay organized himself so that he could watch it on television. He had told Jed about his conversation at Haydock, and the older man joined him as they watched the preliminaries. The betting was making Harry Solomons' horse favourite, although it was top weight, but it was clear from the way the prices had moved that there had been heavy money on O'Connor's horse during the course of the morning. It had moved from 7–1 third favourite behind Vicky's horse in the morning papers, to 7–2, with Harry's horse at 3–1. Her horse had gone out to 6–1 from 4 in the morning.

The race started, and a northern trainer called Neville Gethin had a runner which had obviously been primed to make the pace fast and furious. His horse normally ran over half a mile further than this race, so presumably they were hoping that it would outstay the other contenders. With three hurdles to jump, it still had a fifteen length lead, but by now O'Connor's horse had moved into second place, with Fateful Meeting trailing him a length and a half behind.

As they turned for home, it was clear that the early pace had been the undoing of Gethin's horse, and the rest of the field were closing on it rapidly. With two hurdles to jump, Paul Jenkins took O'Connor's horse easily past it, but Vicky's horse was still very much in contention. Jay was wondering whether or not its speed on the flat would prove decisive in the closing stages. Then Paul gave his mount two very hard cracks and the horse responded, opening up a six lengths advantage over Fateful Meeting. Vicky's jockey started to urge his horse to make up the distance, and as the winning post approached it was making steady headway. Jay and Jed were urging her horse to get there, but unhappily the winning post came too soon. O'Connor's horse won by three-quarters of a length.

Jed looked at Jay. 'I thought her jockey gave it a lot to do in the final stages. Do you think he was riding to orders?'

'I don't know,' said Jay, 'but it wouldn't be like her to run a horse without really trying. Either way, I suppose that she's safe as far as any criminal activity is concerned.'

'I guess so,' said Jed, and got up and walked back into the yard.

That evening Vicky rang.

'Hi,' said Jay. 'Rough luck today.'

'I wanted to let you know,' she said, 'in case you thought that was deliberate, it wasn't. I just think my jockey left it too late. I really wanted to win that race.'

'Well, have you heard anything else?' asked Jay. There was a pause.

'That's the extraordinary thing,' she said. 'When I got home there was an envelope through my door with £1,000 in it. What should I do?'

Jay thought for a moment. 'Well, you didn't do anything wrong, but I think you should tell both the police and the racing authorities. My suggestion is that you donate the money to the Injured Jockeys Fund. That way nobody can accuse you of anything.'

'Good thinking,' she replied. 'I'm really grateful for your help and support. I owe you.'

'Not at all,' said Jay. 'And you keep up the good work. I'm really impressed, and I hope you get a few more really decent horses.'

'Thank you, Jay. God bless, and goodnight.'

Percy finished his call to his Bermuda office with a satisfied sigh. His decision to open a branch on the island had paid dividends. There was now a considerable insurance market operating from the island. Although not yet challenging Lloyd's, it was still significant and growing.

As he reached for his coffee, his intercom rang. It was Moira. 'I've got Hansie on the other phone. He's insistent on speaking and seems very upset indeed.'

'Put him through,' said Percy, wondering what the normally rather cool young man was concerned about.

'Something terrible's happened,' Hansie burst out without even waiting to greet Percy. 'I'm really frightened.'

'What?'

'As I went to the underground garage to collect my car this morning, I was thinking about the morning meeting and not really concentrating. Not looking where I was going, I pressed the remote control to open the Ferrari's doors and almost ran into a concrete pillar. Thank God I did – it almost certainly saved my life.'

'How?' demanded Percy.

'The car exploded. It had a bomb in it. You can see the damage. There were a fair number of cars around it, which will never see the road again.'

'Are you all right?'

'Yes. I'm a bit shaken up. The police took me to hospital and they say I'm just suffering from a bit of bruising and shock.'

'Is there anything I can do?'

Hansie thought. 'No, but I wouldn't mind a chat.'

Percy flipped open his diary. 'Where are you?'

'I'm just about to go back to the flat.'

'I'll send Francis over. We'll have lunch and I suggest you have a stiff drink.'

'I'd already thought of that.' There was a hint of laughter in his voice, the first positive sign Percy had heard during their conversation.

Putting the phone down, he asked Moira to make the necessary arrangements and then phoned Jay who was appalled.

'Look, I know you're going to be really busy and I've got a fairly quiet day,' Percy told his friend. 'I'll phone Jackson and let the other board members know.'

His call to the policeman met with voice mail and he left a message for Harvey to phone him as soon as possible. He then phoned Howard and Roddy who were equally horrified. Both wanted to know if there was anything they could do. 'I'll let you know if there is,' Percy promised them.

He'd barely finished this call when Jay was back on the line. 'Can we keep this from Danny?' he asked. 'This is going to unnerve him even more.'

'I realize that but I don't see how we can. If Hansie's well enough to come down and ride at the weekend he's going to be in a different car and he's bound to tell of his experience. Even if he's not well enough he'll probably want to visit County View just to get out of London.

'By the way,' Percy added, 'as soon as I've seen him I'll call his father. I imagine that Hansie's already done that but Jan would probably like to hear an outside view of how his son is.'

For the next half-hour he was able to concentrate on his paperwork before Moira buzzed him again to say Jackson was on the line. Percy updated him quickly.

'I'd heard there had been an incident,' Jackson said, 'but there was no mention of the young man's name so I had no idea it was Hansie. Clearly this puts an entirely new angle on it. I'll talk to my colleagues in that section and let you know anything I can.' He paused. 'As I've said before, this is getting serious.'

174

'I know,' said Percy. 'Somebody really is going to get hurt soon.'

An hour later Hansie was sitting with Percy in the Carlton Tower Rib Room. The South African's appetite seemed none the worse for his experience as he demolished a T-bone steak.

'Dad wants me to go home but I'm not going. I'm staying here.'

'Are you sure that's wise?'

'Probably not but I'm not going. I like this job, I like my riding, and my social life, and I want to know what the hell is going on.'

Percy gave his next remark careful thought. 'Do you think you should stop seeing Pippa?'

'Hell, no. If she's involved she'll probably let something slip, and if not I don't want to give up a very satisfactory arrangement. I'll try and see her tonight and play the sympathy card,' he grinned.

'I thought you were suffering from shock.'

'A little of Pippa's special brand of TLC could do wonders. Thanks for lunch. I'm going back to the office to squash the exaggerated rumours that I'm sure are flying around.'

Percy laughed and waved him off as he stayed to pay the bill. It was a thoughtful and deeply troubled man who returned to Canada Square.

He had just settled at his desk when Roddy was on the phone.

'I don't know if you remember but I'm off to South Africa tomorrow for the stud managers' meeting. Would you like me to visit Jan Schmidt?'

Percy thought before replying. 'It's a nice idea but let's see how Jan reacts when I speak to him. It might worry him more than if we play it down. Anyway I'll call him and then speak to Hansie. I must say he's taking this very much in his stride, after the initial shock.'

By the time Percy rang Jan, Hansie had already spoken to his father so he had got over the horrific explosion and reluctantly accepted that his son was staying put. Jan was grateful for Roddy's offer but assured Percy that it was not necessary. However, he made Percy promise to keep an extra vigilant eye on his son and report back immediately if he felt it would be wisest to send him home.

Chapter Eighteen

As the passengers from the Paris flight moved slowly towards passport control, a man of medium height in his forties reached into his inside pocket and withdrew his passport. It showed his name as Thomas Patrick Daly, aged forty-two, a citizen of the Irish Republic. There was nothing particularly remarkable about his appearance. He had medium-length dark hair, was neither pale nor suntanned, and had brown eyes. He was well built and moved with a purpose. He was carrying only a holdall that looked to be about three-quarters full and was small enough to pass as cabin baggage.

He passed immigration and customs without any problems, stopped at a book stall to buy a *Racing Post*, and walked on towards the Gatwick Express. He bought a ticket and caught the next train to Victoria, concentrating most of his attention on his paper with an occasional glance at the scenery. He paid particular attention to the declared runners for the meeting at Newbury the following day. On arrival at Victoria, he took a taxi to one of the more comfortable hotels in Sussex Gardens near Paddington station. A booking had been made in his name. He signed the register and chatted amiably to the middle-aged receptionist. Explaining that he would be dining out and leaving early, he paid for the room in advance.

She nodded agreeably, and gave him the key to his room on the first floor.

Opening the door, he looked around with indifference. It was just somewhere to stay the night, it looked fairly clean and had its own bathroom with shower. He unpacked his bag, put his toilet kit in the bathroom and carefully took out a sparkling white shirt. He put this on a shelf in the small wardrobe and then hung up a pair of good quality grey trousers, a dark blue blazer with brass buttons, and a restrained striped tie.

He washed his face and hands and looked at his watch. It was just after six. He turned on the television and watched nothing in particular until shortly after seven.

Using the remote control he turned off the TV, got up and checked the money he had removed from his bag. There was a little over £500 in tens and twenties, and about 200 euros. He opened a carefully concealed false bottom in the holdall and, removing a leather-bound desk diary, put most of the money in the false bottom. He repacked the bag with a couple of pairs of clean socks, underwear, a handkerchief, three packets of Marlboro cigarettes, and a half-bottle of Irish whiskey.

Putting the holdall in the bottom of the wardrobe, he left the room and locked the door. He carefully checked the corridor, then took a roll of sellotape from his pocket and stuck a tiny piece from the very top of the door to the edge of the frame. It would take a sharp-eyed person to see it, and if it was tampered with it would be very difficult to stick it back precisely.

He left the hotel and hailed a taxi. It dropped him ten minutes later in Camden. He'd been told exactly where to go. He crossed the road and entered a large Irish bar called O'Mally's. He ordered a pint of Guinness. As it was served to him, he leant across and whispered, 'Would you tell Mr O'Sullivan that Thomas Daly is here.'

'And why would he be wanting to know that?' came the surly answer.

'Because he's expecting me,' snapped the customer, and picking up his glass he crossed to an unoccupied table facing the bar. The barman disappeared through a door and shortly after returned with a tall, very powerful but overweight man, his hair cut so short his head was almost shaven. The barman pointed in the direction of Daly. The big man helped himself to a large Irish whiskey and walked across.

'And how would I know you're Thomas Daly?' he demanded without even introducing himself.

Daly reached into his pocked, opened his passport and slid it across the table.

The big man looked at it and sat down. 'And what can I be doing for you?'

'You've got a parcel for me,' was the reply. 'It's a special model ordered from Dublin.'

The big man looked hard at him. 'And where's my payment?'

'I see you're still testing me,' snapped Daly. 'It was delivered to you last night exactly half in euros and half in pound notes, so would you bloody well stop wasting my time and give me the bloody package.'

The other man half smiled. 'All right,' he said, 'but you can't be too careful.'

'I know,' agreed Daly in a slightly softer tone.

'Go out of the front door, turn left, and at the end of the pub you'll see a little alley. Go down that, turn left, and you'll see a black door into the back of this place. Wait there and I'll give you the package in about three minutes.'

Thomas Daly drained what was left of his Guinness, got up and followed the instructions. Sure enough, a few minutes later the door opened and the big man thrust a brown paper parcel into his hands. It was clearly wrapped round a not very big and not very thick box.

'And don't do anything rash with it.' O'Sullivan smiled, turned on his heel and closed the door behind him.

Daly weighed the box in his hand and, grunting with a degree of satisfaction, placed it in a plastic supermarket bag he removed from his pocket, walked back into the street and hired a cab. He dismissed it in the Edgware Road and walked along until he found a small Italian restaurant. Going in, he ordered a large plate of spaghetti and a bottle of red wine. When the spaghetti arrived, he looked distastefully at it.

'It's a man you're feeding, not a bleeding mouse. Now go and get me a proper plate of spaghetti.' The little waiter didn't hesitate. Grabbing the dish, he rushed off. Two minutes later he returned with about three times the amount.

'That's more like it,' snapped the Irishman. 'Now, get the cork out of that bloody bottle. I'm dying of thirst.'

As the unfortunate waiter tried to put a small sample into the bottom of the wine glass, his customer grabbed the bottle, took a swig from the neck and nodded his grudging approval.

'That'll be doing me,' he said, and filled his glass almost to the brim.

He swiftly demolished both his spaghetti and wine, then followed this with a double helping of a particularly sickly-looking chocolate cake. Calling for the bill, he paid in cash, making sure he didn't show the size of his bank-roll. With a curt nod, he strode out of the restaurant and walked briskly back to his hotel. He said good evening to the young Asian who was now tending reception, and made his way up to his room. The sellotape was still intact and had clearly not been tampered with. He unlocked the door, entered the room and hung the Do Not Disturb sign outside.

A large slug of the Irish whiskey was poured into his bathroom glass and thrown back in one gulp. Then he opened the parcel. In it was a small revolver, a silencer and a plastic bag with six bullets. He checked the action, saw it was well oiled, and that the serial number had been filed off. He'd been promised a clean gun. He was confident that the man who'd ordered it for him would ensure that it had no history. After another slug of the whiskey, he undressed, got into bed and was soon sleeping as if dead.

At 6.30 a.m. the alarm on his wristwatch rang and he was instantly awake. Taking a moment to get his bearings, he was out of bed and into the shower. After a careful shave and cleaning his teeth, he dressed in the same clothes as the previous day but changed his socks and

180

underpants. He repacked the bag after removing the money and putting the gun in its place. There was also a neat light plastic document case into which he put the diary. This was zipped closed and placed down the side of his holdall. He double-checked the room. Nothing was left behind. He lit a Marlboro, walked down the stairs, nodded to the young Asian who was still on duty, and strolled round to Paddington station. There he bought a *Racing Post* before taking the escalator upstairs to the Beach Bar. He ordered a large coffee and two croissants.

Taking them outside to the almost deserted balcony area, he opened the *Racing Post* to the Newbury pages and checked the runners. He noted with satisfaction that County View had runners in the first, second and fourth races. This confirmed what he had read the previous day.

Paying particular attention to the fourth race, Daly circled the horse's number and the jockey's colours. He then folded the paper, slipped it into his side pocket, and went to the ticket office. Although trains were stopping at the racecourse, he booked himself through to the main Newbury station. Seated on the train, he read the rest of the *Racing Post* in a totally relaxed manner.

At Newbury station, he found a taxi and asked to be taken to the racecourse.

'You're early, aren't you?' commented the driver.

'Ah, I like to walk the course before racing starts,' was the response.

'Are you a trainer then?'

'No, I'm just a punter, but the going can affect the horses' performance so I like to know what I think it is before I start helping the bookmakers' holiday funds unnecessarily.'

The taxi driver chuckled.

'Anyway,' said the passenger, 'when we get to the race-course I want you to go down the back way as if we were going to the railway station. I'm going to go in where the horseboxes normally come out.'

'No problem,' promised the driver.

When they arrived the Irishman leant forward and passed the man £25. The driver looked pleased.

'If you pick me up here straight after the fourth race, there'll be another £50 for you,' he promised the cabby, who clearly thought that Christmas had come early.

'There's a pub over there.' The cabby pointed to the London Apprentice. 'I'll be in the car park.'

'Don't leave early. I might get delayed collecting my winnings,' Daly joked, 'but I'll be here before the fifth race starts.'

'As good as done, guv'nor,' was the cheery reply. And with a nod of his head he put his vehicle in gear and drove off.

The Irishman walked into the car park area. An observer would realize he was well acquainted with the layout of the course. At the main entrance, he bought himself a member's badge and presented his bag to the young lady on security. Putting it on the table, she opened it, had a quick look inside, and asked him to open the little document wallet. He did so cheerfully. She looked at the leather-bound diary, zipped the wallet up for him herself, and handed it back.

'Good luck today,' she said.

'Thanks. I hope I won't need it,' he replied with a broad smile, and walked into the racecourse.

Buying a copy of *Time Form*, he then went into the seafood bar, where he ordered a lobster salad and a small bottle of white wine. Engrossed in the booklet, he was apparently making up his mind which horses would carry his hopes that afternoon. He chose a table where he could watch the racing on television, carefully placed his holdall between his feet and slowly ate his lunch.

Before the first race Daly went to the Tote and bought three £5 winning tickets on the first three horses on the card. Sitting down, he watched the first race. Number one failed to win. Feigning annoyance, he crumpled up the one ticket he was holding and put it into the ashtray. After the second race, the same thing happened. The little charade was repeated again after the third. Any casual spectator of his behaviour would have assumed that he'd lost on all three races and was less than happy. As soon as the third race was over, he walked over and gave an apparently casual glance at the horses in the pre-parade ring for the fourth race. He had a good look at number nine, the County View runner, and knew he'd recognize it as it came towards him. He also made a note of the girl leading the horse. She was wearing a smart waterproof jacket in the well-known bright blue County View trademark colour. He watched with interest as the horse was led across to the saddling boxes and he saw that Jay Jessop and Danny Derkin, who he knew was his Head Man, were jointly doing the honours. He had made a point of attending three race meetings before today, including one at Newbury, to make sure he really knew what Danny looked like. He was praying that the horse wouldn't come in the first four so that it wouldn't be delayed by going into the winners' enclosure, and in particular he was keeping his fingers firmly crossed that it wouldn't win. This would necessitate a trip to the dope box which would completely throw out his planned timing.

He did not watch the race but listened to the commentary from near the parade ring. To his relief, he heard that the horse was not in the first four. He casually made his way towards the railed walkway which led from the stable block to the horses' entrance between the saddling boxes and the pre-parade ring. This was used by horses going to and from their races. He positioned himself a little way from the rails on the right-hand side going towards the stable block. He knew from his previous scouting that the groom was normally on the left of the horse and Danny walked up on the right. He was also very close to the point where the road letting traffic out on to the back road crossed the horses' walkway.

After a few moments, he saw horses beginning to come towards him. The first four were of no interest, but he then saw the bright blue of the stable girl's jacket. As expected, Danny was on his side. Daly kept well back till the horse was almost opposite him. He then walked briskly up to the

183

railings and followed the horse to where it reached the intersection with the road. Quickly pulling the silenced revolver from his pocket, he shot Danny twice in the back, returned the gun to his pocket, and walked not too quickly out on the roadway.

As he reached the pub, Daly was relieved to see the taxi waiting for him. He sat in the back and passed the taxi driver the promised £50. He gave a quick glance out of the rear window but could see nothing which indicated any pursuit. Seconds later he was startled to hear a siren and looked back again. He was reassured to see it was an ambulance with lights flashing, travelling at high speed. He very much hoped that it would be too late to be of any influence on the health of its occupant. He was pretty sure that his payday would be rather better if the shooting proved fatal rather than just very damaging. Arriving at the station, he thanked the driver, got out and walked casually on to the platform. He knew he had about a quarter of an hour to wait and the minutes seemed to drag past interminably. He sat down and read a local paper which he'd bought outside the station, and made a mighty effort to look casual and relaxed. With an inward sigh of relief, he saw the train approach. He boarded it in a leisurely fashion and sat in a corner seat. The train stopped at the racecourse station. A couple of young women got on and joined him in his carriage. They were full of excitement about some incident which had occurred at the racecourse. They didn't know what it was but were aware of a lot of police activity. Daly continued to appear engrossed in his paper while listening to see if anything useful emerged from their conversation. It didn't.

Alighting at Reading, he made his way to the ticket barrier and into the men's toilet. Here he quickly changed from his racecourse clothes to the grey flannels, the white shirt, the tie and the blazer. He replaced the gun in the secret pocket of the bag, removed the wallet with his diary and substituted the passport he was carrying for the one hidden in the cover. He then replaced the diary in the wallet and zipped up the holdall. Leaving the station, he deposited the bag in the privately run left luggage store nearby. He was quietly confident it would be a few days at least before anyone took any notice of it. Pocketing his receipt, he made his way to the boarding point for the express coaches to Heathrow and was soon sitting comfortably as the vehicle sped up the motorway before turning off. He was dropped at the Aer Lingus terminal, walked in and collected a ticket which had already been booked in his new name.

'You'll be boarding in forty-five minutes, Mr McGrath,' he was told by the pretty girl at check-in. 'I suggest you go straight through because of the security checks.'

He thanked her politely and was soon through security and sitting waiting for the Dublin flight to be called.

Less than half an hour later the plane was taxiing down the runway and he felt a real sense of relief as it became airborne.

When drinks were served, the stewardess regretted they had no Jameson on board so he settled for two miniature bottles of scotch. Declining any water, he sipped his drink with rather more restraint than was his normal habit, and started to read the *Evening Standard*. There was nothing particularly interesting from his point of view but at least it passed the time. Looking at his watch he saw that they would soon be landing, so he got up, went to the toilet, washed his face as well as his hands, and returned to his seat. On the way down the aisle one of his fellow passengers glanced up, looked at him casually, and then suddenly looked much more closely. He quickly averted his gaze to make sure that Daly, now calling himself Mr McGrath, had not noticed his reaction. As soon as the Irishman was settled in his seat, the other passenger walked to the rear of the aircraft. Here he attracted the attention of one of the stewardesses and beckoned her. She came up with a ready smile.

From the identity flashed in front of her, she saw that he was Detective Sergeant Wise from the Metropolitan Police. He leant forward and spoke quietly.

'There is a very dangerous criminal on this aircraft,' he

said. 'There's no need for alarm – he's not a hijacker or anything like that, but it's important that he's arrested as soon as we arrive in Dublin. If you fetch me some paper, I'll write my instructions and you can give them to the captain so that he can radio ahead.'

Seconds later she returned and he quickly wrote the name and telephone number of the head of security at Dublin airport. He added his name with a cryptic message, 'Key player in the Ahearne situation on this aircraft. Get me off first and I'll point him out to you.'

For additional authority he signed it with both his full name and rank and also his police identity card number. He gave it to the stewardess and returned to his seat. She quietly phoned through to the cockpit and said she had urgent information for the captain. Walking in a casual manner, she made her way forward, knocked on the door and identified herself. Once in the cockpit, she quickly explained the situation to the captain and gave him the slip of paper. Seconds later he was through to Dublin with the information.

In a matter of minutes the captain had a response. He was told that the airport police were expecting the London policeman in relation to something totally different but that they would have a reception committee waiting at the foot of the steps when Daly alighted. They asked the steward to ensure that Detective Sergeant Wise was first off the aircraft so he could be at immigration to point out his quarry.

The steward, pretending to serve the policeman a whisky, whispered that he would be escorted off first. A barely perceptible nod acknowledged this information.

Arriving at the airport, Wise was quickly ushered through immigration where he was introduced to a detective inspector who had three plain-clothes constables with him. As soon as Daly appeared, they fell in behind him. In a flash he was in their grip and handcuffs were put on him before he was led away to an office in the customs area which was normally kept for the interrogation of suspected smugglers. The Irish policeman turned to the Englishman.

'So what have we got here?' he said.

'We've got one of the men who helped Liam Ahearne escape. I was with the so-called Friend when he was handed over to what we now know were bogus policemen and he,' pointing at Daly, 'was one of them.'

'Well, that's most interesting, and can I ask what brings you here?'

'I'm over here to question a man you've got in custody who we believe may have been involved in a raid on a West London bank a few weeks ago.'

The Irish policeman made a couple of telephone calls and then turned to Wise. 'You already had a reception party waiting for you,' he informed him. 'One of my guys will take you down to where they're waiting and they'll take you off for your interview. We'll keep you informed on what happens with our man.'

With that they shook hands warmly and went off to pursue their separate enquiries.

Chapter Nineteen

At the racecourse the scene had been very different. Heather, the stable girl, hadn't realized that Danny was injured and had rushed off after the loose horse. However, the lad leading up the next horse about fifteen yards behind saw that Danny was lying in a pool of blood. He yelled to the steward who was on duty to prevent vehicles crossing the horses' walkway to and from the stable block. The man ran over, saw Danny's condition, and telephoned the office for an ambulance urgently. Paramedics arrived quickly on the scene and were deeply concerned about Danny's condition. He was just alive but had lost an enormous amount of blood. They weren't sure if one of the bullets had hit his spine.

Unaware of the drama, Jay was talking to his runner's owners. He was to become all too aware, however, when the public address system urged him to go to the stable block as quickly as possible. He rushed over to be met by the racecourse doctor who told him of Danny's life-threatening injuries and that he was on his way to the local hospital. Jay rushed back to his owners and explained the situation. Leaving them thunderstruck, he ran off to his car. He phoned the horsebox and made sure that Jack Doyle would find Heather, get the vet to check the horse out, and return to County View as soon as was sensible. He then phoned Eva to tell her the news. She was aghast.

'There's nothing more I can say at the moment. I'll call you when I arrive at the hospital.'

One of the racecourse security guards had been drafted

in to guide Jay to the hospital, where he pulled up outside Accident and Emergency. He rushed in, explaining who he was to the receptionist.

'Your man's gone straight into surgery,' she told him. 'There's nothing you can do at the moment but wait.'

He walked outside and thanked the security guard, giving him a £10 note to get a taxi back to the racecourse.

The next hour seemed interminable. Finally a youngish man in a white coat walked up to him. 'I'm the registrar,' he explained.

'What's the news?' demanded Jay.

'Well, he's in a critical condition, but at the moment he's holding his own.'

'Can I see him?'

'You can in a few moments, but he's unconscious and we intend to keep him that way, at least overnight.'

'What are the injuries?' Jay asked.

'One bullet was lodged in the lung but fortunately missed the spine by a fraction. The other has smashed a couple of ribs but that's not too serious. We've removed both bullets. The real danger is the amount of blood he's lost and the tremendous shock he's suffering from.'

'What are his chances?' Jay queried, dreading the answer.

'At the moment I would say fifty-fifty,' the doctor replied, 'but he's young and appears to be very fit, and these two factors are definitely on his side.'

Jay was about to ask again if he could go and see Danny when the doctor stopped him. 'I'll take you in to see him in a few minutes, Mr Jessop,' he said, 'but I need you to give me some details. We don't even know the young man's name or anything about the circumstances. Needless to say we've got to inform the police.'

'As soon as possible,' Jay agreed, 'but it's likely the racecourse has already done that.'

The doctor nodded. By this time they'd reached a door leading into a small, neat and very clinical office. The doctor sat down and took out a form. He filled in as much as he could and then passed it over to Jay to add details of name, address, next of kin, etc.

There was a knock at the door and two men stood in the entrance. With a smile of recognition Jay walked across, and shook Harvey Jackson by the hand.

'Golly, it's good to see you,' he said.

'Well, when I heard about the incident I phoned the racecourse. When they told me it was one of your men I decided to get involved myself. This, by the way, is Sergeant Brownlow,' he said, introducing the other policeman. Unlike his boss, he was in uniform.

'So, what can you tell me?' he asked Jay.

'Very little,' was the reply. He summed up what he knew about his and Danny's journey to Newbury, the normal procedures which took place, how the horse had run, and how Danny and Heather had taken it back to the stables after the race.

'Does Danny have any known enemies?'

'Well, to the best of my knowledge only our friend Liam Ahearne.'

'Ah, the infamous Friend,' commented Jackson.

'Well, you already know about the marquee being burnt. Danny was convinced this was the work of someone in The Friend's circle. Also we have this strange situation of our horses being hijacked on the way to Ayr, and large bets seemed to emanate from Ireland. On the other hand, if The Friend was involved in that I don't think he'd have had any scruples about killing the two horses.'

'Perhaps not,' replied the policeman, 'but a lot of even the toughest men would have scruples about shooting horses in cold blood. Perhaps he has animal-loving friends?'

Jay looked doubtful. Turning to the doctor he asked, 'When will we able to see Danny?'

'Well, you can see him now but I doubt if you'll be able to talk to him before tomorrow night at the earliest.'

'Let's go anyway,' said Jay.

Danny was in a private room, surrounded by machinery

and tubes. An oxygen mask was on his face. 'May I make a call?' Jackson asked.

The registrar nodded.

Jackson dialled a number and snapped out orders to have a uniformed policeman with a flak jacket and a sidearm in the hospital as soon as possible.

'We won't take any chances,' he told Jay. 'I hope you don't mind, but I intend to put him under twenty-four-hour guard,' he informed the registrar.

'Not an ideal situation,' was the reply, 'but I suppose it's sensible under the circumstances.'

Jay looked at Danny with a deep-felt concern. Walking over to the bed he held the stricken man's hand and whispered 'Danny', not expecting any response. He was right. Turning to the registrar, he indicated he was ready to go. The three of them left the room. Sergeant Brownlow was waiting outside.

'You stay here until you're relieved by the armed guard,' ordered Jackson.

Walking down the corridor, the registrar put his hand on Jay's arm. 'Don't bother to keep calling the hospital. I promise I'll give you a report at lunchtime tomorrow, or sooner if anything dramatic happens between now and then, but I very much doubt it will. We'll keep him sedated, and you know we're doing everything we can for him.'

Jay nodded his gratitude and, shaking hands, walked out of the hospital side by side with his policeman friend.

'I'll get this incident out to the national papers, the television stations, and in particular the local radio and television stations,' he informed Jay. 'I'll also have every member of the racecourse staff interviewed along with waiters, bar staff et cetera. You never know what we'll turn up. As soon as something breaks I'll be on the phone. Sorry to ask this, but he's not into drugs or gambling, is he?'

'I'd bet my life on it, Harvey. He's too happy in his work, and Jed and I would have noticed any change in his behaviour.'

191

'Sorry, but I had to ask,' the policeman explained sympathetically. Patting Jay's shoulder, he moved briskly to the waiting police car.

Jay walked thoughtfully over to his car and started his drive back to County View. Although evening stables were well over, a large number of the staff had stayed behind in the canteen in a hushed and clearly worried state. Having updated Eva on the situation, he walked in with Jed and briefly told the staff all he could.

'As soon as I get any news I'll make sure you know,' he promised them. 'Let's all pray that Danny pulls through. Goodnight, everybody,' and he turned quickly to hide the emotion which was now beginning to swamp him as the reality of the situation kicked in.

He and Eva had a very gloomy evening, and Max was unusually quiet, knowing what had happened and realizing that this was not a time for jollity in any sense. Jay gave him a hug and Eva took him upstairs.

'What would you like to eat?' she asked her husband when she rejoined him.

'I'm really not in the mood for anything.'

'Well, you must have something,' she said. 'How about a couple of poached eggs and some baked beans?'

'That takes me back to my student days,' he told her with a smile. 'It'll be fine.' He went over to the bar and poured himself a very large whisky. Holding the bottle towards Eva, she shook her head and said, 'I'll have a glass of wine when we sit down.'

Jay finished his whisky in two large gulps and poured himself another.

'Steady,' said Eva. 'You've got a long night ahead of you. You'd better start getting on the phone and letting the other directors know what's happened. You can be sure that before too long the press will start phoning you too.'

Before he had a chance to do anything, the phone rang and it was the managing director of Newbury asking what news there was. He was a long-standing friend of Jay's and was obviously deeply upset. Jay told him of Danny's condition and asked if there was any news on his front.

'No, but the police have got the details of everyone working at the racecourse this afternoon, and so far everyone's been really co-operative.'

'Thanks a lot,' Jay responded. 'If there is any news I'll certainly let you know.'

Before the phone could ring again, he rang Howard and Percy. Roddy was on his way back from Africa. The conversations were brief. His friends were horrified. Not even Percy was prepared to speculate on who could be behind it.

'Well, you couldn't have a better policeman on your side than Harvey Jackson,' was his encouraging comment.

'I know,' Jay agreed. 'Let's hope he gets the bastard.'

As Eva had expected, for the next hour the phone rang constantly from the media, and without being rude Jay explained that he really didn't have anything to add to the details they'd already got from the police.

'Frankly,' he said to them, 'you'd be better off talking to the police. They'll know of any developments before I will.'

Having managed to eat his simple supper between calls, he now sat down and the emotion of the afternoon and evening really hit home. Eva sat on the settee beside him and put her arm round his neck.

'He's a tough fellow,' she said. 'He was nearly killed in Ireland, and I'm sure he'll pull through. I know it's hard for you to put it out of your mind but it's after midnight now and you've got to get some rest.'

Somewhat reluctantly Jay agreed, and finished his third large whisky but rather more slowly than he'd sunk the first two. Giving his wife a wan smile, he followed her up the stairs.

The next morning, after a restless night, he went into the yard. It seemed strange without Danny's bubbling presence but he and Jed got things organized in their normal efficient way. As he went round he told everybody that there was no more news but promised to let them know as soon as he heard anything.

Work went on as normal but there was none of the usual banter. At the end of the morning Jay walked into the office with Jed. 'There's been no news,' Eva told him, but passed on one or two messages from the press and owners. Jed went back to his cottage and Jay sat down to look at the papers before lunch. The story had missed most of the early editions but Jay wasn't going to take much pleasure from reading about the terrible event of the previous afternoon. The telephone rang and he rushed to it, hoping it was the registrar with good news.

In fact it was Harvey Jackson.

'We've had a breakthrough,' he enthused. 'A taxi driver heard our message on the radio and came in to see us. He picked up a man after the fourth race who left by the back entrance of the racecourse and went straight to the railway station. What is interesting is that he had an Irish accent and was carrying a holdall. Apparently, one of the barmaids in the Barry Copes Fish Bar noticed this man with a bag kept firmly between his feet while he ate, and he even carried it to the counter when he collected a drink. She remembered thinking there must be something valuable in that bag. What's more, she corroborates that he had an Irish accent.

'As soon I heard this I phoned my friend, Terry Mullings, who's number two in the Dublin police force. Pat McKenna, his boss, is away for a couple of days and we are even closer. We play golf at least a couple of times a year. Terry just called me back to say that it looks as if a man who was arrested coming in from Heathrow last night may well be our man. What's more, one of our London policemen, Derek Wise, was the one who spotted him. He had been involved in the handover of Ahearne to the bogus Irish policemen. This man was evidently one of them. If he is, this could well lead us to the whereabouts of The Friend.'

'Well, that's great news,' said Jay. 'Now let's hope we get equally good news about Danny.'

He sat down at the table feeling distinctly more like eating the grilled chop which Eva had put in front of him than he had a few minutes earlier. Almost immediately the phone rang again and Eva passed it to him. It was the registrar.

'I haven't got any great news for you,' he reported, 'but Danny is still holding his own and there's certainly been no deterioration. It's just a matter of wait and see. I'm going off duty at seven tonight and I'll call you then. I would say that the fact that there's no deterioration is definitely encouraging.'

'Thank you so much,' said Jay.

As soon as he had finished his lunch he walked over and brought Jed up to date.

'Well,' suggested the older man, 'it looks as if Danny might have been right about the marquee fire and perhaps he was right about the Ayr incident too.'

The afternoon passed quietly, although Howard and Percy rang to see if there was any news. Jay briefed them on the most recent developments. He also phoned Freddy Kelly in Ireland to tell him. There had been no coverage of the Newbury incident and at that stage the police had made no announcement about the detention of the passenger from Heathrow.

Just as they started to watch the seven o'clock news, the registrar rang as promised.

'I have some more encouraging news for you,' he said. 'Danny is definitely showing signs of improvement but we're going to keep him sedated overnight and then take a view in the morning. Don't get too excited because relapses do happen, but at the moment he looks as if he's turned the corner. I'll call you again in the morning.'

Chapter Twenty

Jay was in the Turf Club on Friday night. He had had an excellent dinner along with a full carafe of the Club claret. Before that he'd had a couple of glasses of champagne with two of his friends but had politely declined their invitation to join them for dinner at Scalini's.

Now he was sitting by himself in the deserted bar, steadily and deliberately getting drunk.

He didn't know why he was doing it but he knew he was. He was depressed and felt lonely. He'd tried to reason with himself that it was ridiculous, but all the strange events of the last few weeks kept hammering away at him: O'Connor's raiding of his best horses, the drugs incident at O'Connor's with Billy Dean trying to discredit him, the fire at County View, the deliberate killing of the horses in New Zealand, Ayr, and now Danny. He felt he was cursed and wanted to get out of racing. Although Danny was on the mend, all the excitement and triumphs of Jay's last season as a jockey and the early days of County View seemed to have faded into an almost meaningless past.

He knew he still loved the satisfaction of bringing on young horses to their full potential. He enjoyed the company of most of his owners and the excellent relationship he had with his staff. He liked encouraging young people, but where'd that got him with Paul Jenkins? Were there any really new, exciting challenges, or was it all going to turn into the same routine that his publishing company had eventually become? He loved Eva and Max and he knew he had great friends in Howard, Percy, and more recently Roddy and Hamish, but he'd thought that Victor was a real friend and what had happened there? Finishing his champagne, he got up, said goodnight to the barman and the night porter, who asked if he wanted a cab. He refused, saying he felt like a walk. The porter thought to himself, I hope it does you good, Mr Jessop. He was very fond of this member and hoped that he wasn't going to get himself into trouble.

Walking purposefully and still steadily, Jay made his way to Annabel's. Greeting the doorman and then the cloakroom attendant, he signed the book and entered the club. At half past ten Annabel's was already full, so Jay sat at the bar. 'Champagne or brandy, Mr Jessop?' the barman enquired.

'Champagne.' A glass was put in front of him.

'No, I don't want a glass,' he snapped. 'Bring me a bottle.' The barman did as he was told but a slightly concerned look crossed his face as he turned away.

'And a Monte Cristo No. 3,' he added as the barman turned to serve another member.

'I'll be right with you,' came the reply. 'I'll just serve this gentleman first.'

The gentleman in question was late middle-aged, over-weight and balding. Jay watched as he carried a glass of champagne and a large brandy to one of the tables very close to the bar and sat down with a stunning woman in her mid-thirties. With long, slightly wavy chestnut hair, she had a flawless complexion that looked like alabaster. Her eye make-up was restrained but still highlighted her dark green eyes. Her lips had a pale rose blush to them which was so subtle he wasn't sure if it was natural or not. She looked up, caught his eye and smiled. He raised his glass to her and she returned the gesture.

'Who's that?' he asked Jacky, the barman, in a more friendly tone than his previous snarl.

'I don't know, Mr Jessop. I've seen her in here once or twice but that's the first time she's been here with Mr Johnson.'

'So she's not his wife?'

'Goodness me, no,' was the reply. 'She's a very different kettle of fish to Mrs Johnson, I can assure you.'

Jay drew appreciatively on his cigar and drank another glass of his champagne. The couple who had been sitting next to him got up and left. Jay was concentrating on his champagne but he became aware of somebody moving on to one of the vacated bar stools. Turning, he saw the stunning lady was now sitting next to him. He smiled.

'Good evening,' he said.

'Good evening to you,' she replied. 'Could a lady beg your indulgence for a glass of that delicious Krug?'

'Of course,' he replied, and beckoning Jacky asked for another glass. 'Won't the gentleman you're with object?'

'Probably,' she replied, 'but he's boring me.'

Jay laughed. 'Well, you're frank if nothing else, and how do you know I won't bore you?'

'I just have a feeling,' she said, 'though I'll be interested to find out.'

'And what do you do?' was Jay's rather mundane question.

She paused, and with an enigmatic smile replied, 'I'm in the entertainment business.'

'What aspect?'

'Glamour and relaxation,' she said, 'and I'm very much my own boss, before you ask me what company I work for.'

'That sounds intriguing.' He smiled, taking another sip from his glass. She emptied hers and looked enquiringly at him. 'I think we're ready for another one,' he advised Jacky. The remains of the existing bottle were shared between them and another was instantly produced.

'I love dancing,' she announced. 'Would you join me?'

'Only if they have a polka,' he joked. She looked at him questioningly. 'I have a limp,' he said, 'so I'd probably have to hop.'

'Well, it didn't show as you came in,' she said.

'Ah well,' he said, 'it's only when I try to do anything energetic it becomes more obvious.'

'I'll take a chance,' she said. 'Perhaps we can just have a

slow amble around the floor.' Taking a gulp from his glass, he got up and followed her to the dance floor, which was studded with little lights. She turned and slid into his arms in a movement both graceful and extremely sensuous.

Jay could feel an electricity he hadn't experienced since his early days with Eva. He quickly pushed the thought from his mind. By the time they'd been in each other's arms for fifteen minutes, Jay was completely captivated and agreed when she suggested they might take a little more refreshment. Returning to the bar, he saw that one of the small tables was now free and he guided her to it while he went over and asked Jacky to bring the bottle. She enquired about Jay's occupation and somewhat obliquely he informed her he was in the livestock industry.

'Where?' she queried.

'Oh, mainly abroad,' he said and changed the subject. She was bright enough to know he didn't want to pursue it. Their discussion turned to the forthcoming election and he found they both had a jaundiced view of politics in general. From that they moved on to their favourite places and cities, and he discovered that New York, Paris and somewhat surprisingly Verona were her favourites.

'I can understand New York and Paris, they're both exciting and sophisticated, and in their own ways very beautiful, but Verona surprises me.'

'Ah, but it's so romantic,' she replied.

'I suppose it is,' he agreed, 'but I guess I'm not a particularly romantic person.'

'I doubt that,' she smiled at him. 'In the right circumstances I'm sure you could be very romantic.'

Emptying his glass, he asked her if she'd like to share another bottle.

'Not here,' she said. 'I don't know about you, but I'm getting very hot. I live just around the corner. Why don't we go there?'

He paused for a moment. 'Well, at least let's finish what we've got in front of us,' he said. 'I hate wasting good champagne, particularly at this price.'

At that moment Jacky came over and said to him quietly,

'Mr Jessop, there's a gentleman outside who needs to speak to you urgently.'

Jay was somewhat startled but, nodding apologetically to the young lady whose name he still didn't know, he got up and walked out into the entrance hall. To his amazement there was Benny.

'God, has something bad happened?' he asked.

'No, but it bloody well might,' responded Benny. 'What the hell d'you think you're doing, Jay?'

'What are you talking about?' said Jay.

'D'you know who you're with?' Benny challenged him. 'I can't believe you do.'

Jay shook his head.

'Well, you're only with Vanda Green,' he replied. 'She's one of the best known top-class whores in London, although she prefers to call herself an escort. It was she who helped us catch that bloody South African who was doing all Victor's dirty work.'

'I don't believe you,' said Jay, 'and anyway I can look after myself.'

'No, you bloody can't,' said Benny. 'You're coming with me.' Turning to the doorman, he said, 'Go and tell the lady that Mr Jessop's been called away urgently and then help me get him up to my car if he gives me any trouble.' Jay actually went without giving any trouble, although very reluctantly.

'I don't need your car,' he said. 'I only live around the corner.'

'I'm not letting you out of my sight,' the East Ender announced. 'You're coming back to my place where I can keep an eye on you.' With that a car drew up driven by Angel. None too gently Benny pushed Jay into the back and got in beside him.

'Back to my place,' he instructed his brother. 'Well, let's pray that none of the bloody gossip columnists were in there tonight.'

'Do you think they'd know who she was?'

'Quite likely,' replied Benny. 'The barman did, that's why he phoned me. How do you think it would look in tomorrow's paper if it was announced that Jay Jessop, the famous racehorse trainer, was seen leaving Annabel's with a glamorous lady, known or unknown?'

'He didn't tell me who she was,' sulked Jay.

'Well, he bloody well wouldn't, would he? He's far too tactful to say any member is with a tart.'

Jay was stunned enough by recent revelations to have partly sobered up and to take the situation on board. By this time they were drawing up outside Benny's small, well-cared for house. Helping Jay out, he let himself into an empty downstairs. Angel locked the car and gave Benny the keys.

'Right,' he instructed Jay. 'Be quiet, I don't want to wake the old girl up. She'll have enough of a shock at breakfast as it is.' He led Jay upstairs and opened a door. The room was more spacious than Jay would have expected, and he noticed an open door leading to an en suite bathroom.

'I'll let you sleep it off,' Benny announced. 'You'll find a towelling robe behind the bathroom door. Goodnight, and keep your fingers crossed for the papers in the morning.'

The next morning Jay woke up with a strong suspicion of a hangover, though he was reluctant to admit it to himself. Looking at his watch, he nearly had a fit. It was a quarter to eight. He leapt out of bed, threw on the towelling robe, and rushed downstairs to be met in the kitchen by an amused Benny and a somewhat startled lady. Benny introduced him to his wife Sonia, explaining, 'As I told you, Jay had a bit of a problem last night, so I brought him back.'

Jay apologized for the inconvenience but was hopping from foot to foot waiting to get a word in edgeways about his main concern.

'What the hell do you imagine County View will be thinking?' he snapped at Benny. The question was greeted by a huge grin.

'Don't worry, I phoned at six o'clock to say you'd had a touch of an upset tummy last night so I brought you home and you were still sleeping like a baby. The things I do for you!'

His wife chuckled. 'You men are all the bloody same,' she said. 'Here's the phone. You'd better phone that poor wife of yours.'

Jay dialled his home number and felt distinctly uncomfortable when Eva was clearly concerned about his well-being.

'I'm absolutely fine,' he assured her. 'I'm going to have some coffee and be on my way home in about twenty minutes.'

'Fine,' she said. 'I'll make sure we've got something light for lunch.'

Sonia gave him a hard look. 'I don't think she'd be giving you coffee if you'd had an upset tummy,' she scolded him. 'Anyway, you're not leaving here with just that after last night's activities.' Much against his will, she sat him down with a cafetière of coffee, and was soon frying egg and bacon and making toast. Benny was also drinking coffee and watching Jay's face with considerable amusement. Knowing Jay's normal frugal routine which went back to his years as an amateur jockey, he watched his friend wilt under his wife's strong maternal instinct and equally strong personality.

Half an hour later, showered and shaved, he was ready to leave. As he went, Benny whispered, 'Don't bother to stop for the papers. I'll get all of them and check if you've managed to stay out of them. I'll call you when you're on your way down the motorway.'

With that he bundled Jay into his car and drove him back through the relatively deserted streets to Hays Mews. Minutes later Jay was in his Jaguar and on his way down Cromwell Road heading for the M4.

As he approached the Newbury junction, his mobile phone rang.

'Well, you've been damn lucky,' Benny told him. 'There's nothing at all. I'll do the same with the Sunday papers and I'll phone you one way or the other.'

'You're a pal,' Jay said with feeling.

'I know,' said Benny, 'and don't you forget it. Talk to you soon, and let's hope I don't read anything in the morning.

Drive carefully, and for God's sake don't eat too much at lunch and give the game away.'

As soon as Jay arrived home, Roddy rang to report that the meeting had gone well. The three stud managers knew and liked each other. The policy for the coming year had been agreed. Without picking on France, Roddy had suggested that next season a quarter of the mares should be covered by young, well-bred, but as yet unproven stallions. This change of policy had been well received and hopefully would go a long way towards rectifying the rather conservative policy that had been pursued in France.

Jay congratulated his co-director and guaranteed that funds would be available if the right animal came on the market.

Jay went round evening stables with Jed. He found the gentle munching of hay and soft snuffles from contented animals both tranquil and soothing.

Chapter Twenty-One

Eva was putting an omelette in front of Jay who was going to have a quick lunch prior to taking the afternoon off to play one of his infrequent rounds of golf.

Inevitably the phone rang. Eva took the call. Obviously the caller was somebody she knew well. She asked solicitously about his and his family's health before handing the phone to Jay.

'It's Freddy Kelly,' she explained.

'Hi, Freddy. How's life?' he asked his long-time friend and ex-stable jockey.

'Great,' the retired champion replied. 'What do you think about the news?'

'What news?' Jay questioned.

'About the reward for The Friend. Don't you know about it?'

'Nothing at all.'

'Well,' continued Freddy, 'it's all over our papers and radio and television today. Somebody has put up £100,000 for information leading to the arrest of The Friend. The money has been deposited with a top Dublin firm of solicitors and it is guaranteed that information leading to the arrest of Liam Ahearne will result in the money being handed over to the informant in cash with no questions asked and with no contact with the police.'

'Well, let's hope it works. I'd love to see that bastard behind bars again.'

'Come on, Jay,' Freddy interrupted. 'I'm sure you know something about this. In fact I'd have good money on it that you put the reward money up.'

'You'd lose your bet, Freddy. I must confess I did think about it and even discussed it with Howard and Percy, but somehow we just haven't got around to doing anything. I suppose we've been more worried about Danny's health and we're still trying to fathom out what's behind all these incidents which have plagued us. Before the attack Danny was convinced that it was all down to The Friend, but the more I think about it the more I can't see it. He may well have been able to mastermind some of the goings-on before the escape and obviously it would be even easier now he's on the run. But I just can't see that he would have the sort of money required to bankroll O'Connor.'

'Yes, I can see that,' Freddy agreed. 'I know the police never got any real money when they arrested him and I'm sure he has a million or two stacked away, but not the sort of money that we're talking about with O'Connor. And anyway I can't believe he's got a Far East connection. That is, of course, assuming that these rumours we have heard about the Far East are true.'

'Well, we've nothing proved yet. One of Percy's top men has information which certainly indicates that the money is coming from Singapore, but whether or not that's where it originated is still open to question.'

'It will be interesting to see if the reward brings any results,' Freddy mused. 'If there's any other news, you can be sure I'll call you, Jay.'

'Thanks. By the way, isn't it time you came over and spent a few days with us?'

Freddy paused before continuing. 'Look, you are going to be short-handed until Danny's mended. Why don't I come over, do a bit of schooling for you and even take horses to the races if you or Jed are tied up at other courses?'

'Hell, that would be fantastic!'

'Right. Fill in the forms and send them to me. I'll sign them and send them back to you with the photos for the stable pass. That shouldn't take long – the licensing committee will probably chase it through in view of Danny. When do you want me to start?'

'As soon as possible. What about your business?'

'Maureen can look after the few horses we have here and I can keep in contact with everyone by phone. I'll let you know definitely but next Monday should be fine.'

'You're a real pal,' Jay replied.

'I'll be in touch, and keep saddling those winners, Jay.'

As he drove to the golf course outside Cheltenham, Jay gave further thought to the Dublin news and phoned Harvey Jackson to update him.

'I'll give McKenna, my Dublin friend, a call later today,' Harvey told him, 'and see if there are any developments. I'll let you know what happens.'

Jay then rang Howard. His fellow director was enthusiastic about the Dublin development and thrilled about Freddy. Jay of course promised to keep him informed of any news he received.

He then phoned Percy, who staggered Jay by saying he already knew about the reward.

'How the hell did you learn so quickly?'

There was a pause at the other end and then a chuckle. 'I put up the money.'

Jay was genuinely taken aback. 'I know we talked about it in principle but we never made a decision.'

'I know,' said Percy, 'but I decided to do it off my own bat. I checked with my lawyers and accountants and they guaranteed that we can reclaim it on tax – I won't bore you with the details.'

'Well, I'd like to make a contribution,' Jay insisted.

'Sorry, no,' Percy replied. 'I've told you, it's not costing the company anything, and it's not just a matter of personal interest. The Irish police have been very helpful on a number of occasions and I see this as a way of perhaps helping them. By the way, if you want to tell Eva, do, but otherwise I'd like you to keep this to yourself. You'd better include Harvey,' he added.

For the next three and a half hours Jay concentrated entirely on his game. He had been a 6 handicap player years before but struggled in the low teens now. Still, he loved golf and it kept his mind off racing and its related problems. By half past six he had showered, changed and was on his way home. He phoned Eva as soon as he was outside the town. Forty minutes later he was pulling up in front of his house and wandered into the kitchen where the table was already laid for dinner. Opening a bottle of wine, he poured himself and Eva a glass and related his conversations with Harvey, Howard and the particularly surprising one with Percy.

'He's a damn good friend, isn't he?' she commented.

'He most certainly is. You can see why I've made a point of keeping close to him for so many years. And I don't mean for financial reasons.'

'I know you don't, darling. He's just a really good friend, and I know that you trust him implicitly.'

They then settled down to a delicious beef stroganoff – one of Eva's specialities. Jay more than did justice to it and had just finished some excellent Double Gloucester, poured himself a brandy and lit up a Monte Cristo when the phone rang again. This time it was Harvey.

'Well, the ad has certainly caused a flurry of activity in Dublin,' he announced. 'I've spoken to McKenna who has made the recapture of Ahearne a top priority. It seems the lawyers have been inundated with offers but so far most of them appear to be totally useless. However, there are three which have a ring of authenticity about them and the police are looking into these carefully but very low key. They're responding to all media questions by saying that although there have been several responses from the public none of them have proved to be of any interest to date. The last thing they want is for Ahearne to get really concerned if he's still in Ireland and move to a new hiding place if one of these leads is genuine.'

'I can see that, so I suppose there's nothing we can do except wait and see what develops.'

'Afraid so,' the policeman replied. 'By the way, how's Danny?'

'Oh, so much better. Eva went to see him this morning and he was out of bed and taking a few steps. They even allowed him to sit outside in the fresh air yesterday afternoon as it was such a gorgeous day, and he was very much hoping they'd do the same today. The one thing we're all worried about is that he'll try and push himself too soon. You know what he's like.'

'I certainly do,' agreed Harvey, 'but I'm sure the staff there will keep a good eye on him. I think it's going to be a bit more difficult for all of you when he returns to County View.'

Just as they were sitting down to watch some TV, the phone rang.

'Hi, it's Hal,' the cheery American announced. 'I'll be over next week if that suits you?'

'Absolutely,' was the response. 'And we expect to see you here.'

'You will. Try and keep me away. Must rush. Will be in touch.' With no more chat, the line went dead.

Without Danny Jay found himself spending more time in the yard with Jed and going to race meetings he would normally have left to his Head Man. He was having to do his paperwork in the evenings and was seeing less of Max and Eva. He couldn't wait for Freddy to arrive. Jed was as pleased as Jay when their old colleague pulled up in his new Mercedes station wagon.

'You never know what I may need to have in the back,' he retorted to Jed's caustic comment.

Hal phoned to say he was in London and after two days' work there he would be driven down to County View. True to his word he arrived in the early evening.

Hal Bancroft looked every inch what he was – a successful businessman in his early fifties, self-assured but not arrogant, with a friendly but extremely alert manner. He was six foot two and had the physique and complexion of a man who took exercise on a regular basis, much of it in the sun. As he walked towards Jay with a broad smile, Jay remembered the word he'd used to sum Hal up when he'd first met him – the man had 'presence'.

Following Jay into the house, he was enthusiastically

greeted by Eva, who received a big hug and a fatherly kiss on each cheek.

'Well, I guess it's martini time for you?' Jay suggested, and the big American gave an assenting nod. Eva sat him down and chatted away while Jay mixed Hal's cocktail. He and Eva settled for a glass of white wine.

'Come on, I want to know everything that's going on,' Hal announced. 'Let's get the problems out of the way first and then I want to see the horses and talk to you about their prospects. I very much hope there's a worthwhile meeting somewhere near London in the next few days where I confidently expect to see County View saddle at least one winner.'

Jay smiled and proceeded to outline the various events of the previous few weeks. Hal listened thoughtfully. Much of it was not new as Jay had kept him up to date on the phone, but this gave a much better opportunity for more detailed consideration.

'Right,' said the American. 'Let me give it some thought. Now what about the racing?'

Jay recapped on the results over the last few weeks and the prospects coming up. He singled out one or two horses for special mention and told Hal that he would be running My Seeker at Sandown four days later and thought that it would take a very good horse to beat her.

'Well, you know it's one of my favourite courses,' the American reminded him, 'so I'll make sure to be there. Now let's go and walk round. How are Jed and Danny?'

'Danny's much better and should be home soon, but he's even more worried about this Friend situation now, as you can imagine. Jed's on top form. I'll give him a buzz. I'm sure he'd like to walk round with us. Freddy is over here and helping, but he's at Lambourn at the moment doing some business connected with his bloodstock operation. He'll be here in the morning and it's great to have him.'

Out in the yard they met Jed who greeted Hal with genuine pleasure. They walked in a leisurely way round the yard and Hal was particularly pleased to see The Conker and Pewter Queen in such good form. They'd been stable stars in the early days when Hal first met Jay and later became involved in County View.

'Now let me have a look at this fellow who's going to run so well at Sandown.'

'Of course,' Jay agreed, 'but this fellow happens to be a mare. She's won two stayers' novice hurdles and looks set for the third.'

They walked across to My Seeker's box and Hal admired the thoroughbred who looked a gleaming picture and couldn't have been more friendly. They finished the tour and said goodnight to Jed.

Over supper they changed the subject. Hal brought Jay up to date with what was going on in his publishing empire. 'The English titles are a real asset,' he enthused, 'and my policy of switching editors across the Atlantic from time to time has worked wonderfully. Not only has it broadened their outlook but we have a remarkably low turnover amongst our senior staff. Those we do lose are normally head-hunted to go to jobs at a level which we don't have open for them at the time, but interestingly enough three have spent two years abroad and have come straight back to us when a suitably senior post has become available.'

This news was a real pleasure to Jay who had always taken great care of his staff, and the fact that he had trusted Hal to do the same was a major factor in his eventual agreement to the sale.

'Right,' said Hal. 'I'm ready for my bed. I'm going to mull over what we've discussed as far as O'Connor is concerned and I may have an idea that could be helpful in the morning.'

At breakfast Hal insisted he wanted to watch the exercise and he viewed the first two lots including some schooling. Seeing Freddy at work was like old times. Just before midday he suggested that he and Jay went to the Shepherd's Rest for a quick lunch. Eva was going over to Cirencester to pick up Amanda and they were going to have a girlie afternoon in Cheltenham.

When the men were settled in the pub with plates of the

famous shepherd's pie in front of them and glasses of real ale to wash it down, Hal started. 'I've got a golfing friend near Boston. He's what you'd call a venture capitalist and he's made one or two investments in my operation when I've been acquiring other businesses. His name is Fergus Brady and he has many influential contacts in the financial world of Ireland. I'd like to put your situation to him and see if he can dig out anything for us. The fact that he's American with an Irish background and has no contact at all with racing might be very helpful.'

Jay was enthusiastic. 'The other thing,' Hal went on, 'is that I'd like to talk to Marvin and of course Benny. They might well be able to fill in a few relevant details which may have escaped your memory, or at least put their own slant on events which could be useful before I talk to Fergus.'

When they returned to County View, Hal's chauffeur-driven car was waiting for him with his luggage already in the boot. With a broad grin, he got in the car. 'See you at Sandown,' he promised.

Three days later Jay and Eva were waiting for Hal to join them in the Fish Bar on the ground floor of the stand at Sandown Park. They had arrived in plenty of time and Jay was quietly confident that My Seeker would run a big race. It was a competitive field but she was one of their horses that had consistently improved as the season went by. Jay was hoping she would show as much improvement on the racecourse as she had at home. With a little luck she would develop into a Cheltenham Festival horse.

Sipping their wine, they were really looking forward to Hal's company. Because they wanted to have a good lunch and enjoy a glass or two, they'd arranged for Jack Doyle to drive them. He was one of the few people whom Jay allowed to drive his precious, and now fairly ancient, Jaguar. The American came striding across the restaurant in his normal confident way and, ignoring Jay for a moment, greeted Eva with a hug and kiss on both cheeks.

Turning to Jay he demanded, 'And how's this mare going to run?'

Jay lowered his voice. 'I really think she'll win,' he said confidentially. 'For once I've had a decent bet on her but I don't want to announce it to the world.' Hal nodded understandingly.

They sat down to enjoy cold salmon salads and their chat. When it was time for My Seeker to be saddled, Hal went with Jay to the weighing room to collect the saddle and then walked with him across the lawns to the saddling boxes. The mare was a particularly tranquil animal who took racing in her stride. It was only a matter of minutes before she was ready and being led across to the parade ring. My Seeker was a County View horse so they were the only members of the party. For once Percy, Howard and even Roddy had other business to attend to.

David Sparrow walked into the ring with a confidence that had grown since he first joined County View. He'd met Hal before but this was the first time the American had seen him ride. More for Hal's benefit than the jockey's, Jay leant down and quietly gave Sparrow his instructions.

'Keep her handy. If anything goes mad, let it. I want you in the first three or four the whole way round. When you come up the hill the last time, move up to second but if the pace is slowing down go for it.' Moments later the bell rang and the fifteen runners were quickly mounted and on their way to the start.

'I gather you think quite a lot of this young man, as well as the mare,' Hal said. Jay nodded his assent. 'Well, I can tell you there's a fair bit of money going on her. I notice she was 5–1 in the papers this morning but she's down to 2–1 now. I got 3 on her.'

'Let's keep our fingers crossed,' said Eva, taking his arm and leading him up to the grandstand. 'We'll let Jay watch this in his normal solitary splendour,' she added with a mischievous grin. Jay crossed the lawn in front of the stand

212

and found himself a good vantage point. The field set off at a strong but not unreasonable gallop and were well bunched as they passed the winning post for the first time. My Seeker was lying third immediately behind Fearless Fred who'd been the hot favourite ever since the morning. Having won three of his last four races at Ascot, Haydock and Doncaster, he deserved his favourite's mantle. Almost as soon as they reached the back straight the field started to become far more spread out. The leader soon gave way to Fearless Fred who injected a significant increase into the pace. Young David Sparrow covered the move and very rapidly the two of them left the rest of the field struggling behind them. The positions remained unchanged as they swung round the bend and entered the stiff uphill climb to the winning post. Fearless Fred showed no sign of weakening and still had a length and a half lead on My Seeker as they jumped the last. Now her young jockey gave her a slap down the shoulder and she produced the acceleration which she'd shown in her previous races as well as at home. The one slap was enough, and within a few strides she'd got up to gain a length lead. Resisting the temptation to look round, Sparrow kept riding her out with hands and heels to win by a comfortable three lengths. Fearless Fred was a good ten lengths ahead of the third.

Jay was delighted and was soon joined by his equally thrilled wife and Hal. 'Well, both of them lived up to your billing,' the American, who had managed to pick up a few hundred pounds, chortled. 'I'll take you to dinner. I realize that you won't want to go all the way into London but how about if we go to that nice restaurant, The Riverside, at Maidenhead. I've got nothing else on tonight, so I'm very happy for my driver to take me down there and then back to London later.'

This invitation was enthusiastically accepted and an agreeable two hours were spent. As they parted to go their separate ways, Hal looked at Jay and quietly said, 'I'll let you know the minute I have any information.'

Repeating his traditional kiss on each of Eva's cheeks, he shook Jay warmly by the hand and jumped into the back of his car. Jay and Eva were driven back to County View by Jack Doyle in as cheerful a mood as they'd been in for a long while.

Chapter Twenty-Two

Ross Hogan had watched Jay's horse win at Sandown Park. He put his tape recorder into his side pocket along with his notebook, and went across to the bookmaker where he'd had his customary single bet. He collected a little under £200, put it into his wallet, and walked slowly but purposefully out of the racecourse and into the car park.

Two rather scruffy young men in stonewashed jeans and camouflage jackets followed him. As they approached the far side of the park where Hogan had left his car, they increased their speed and closed in on him. Two or three yards behind, he flashed around and took them by surprise. One immediately produced a flick knife, and the other, taking his hand from a side pocket, revealed he was wearing a knuckle duster.

'Your wallet,' snarled the youth with the knuckle duster. Reaching into his inside pocket in a resigned manner, Hogan suddenly moved like lightning. A perfectly aimed kick with one of his highly polished brogues hit his potential assailant beneath the knee. With a scream, he dropped to the ground clasping his leg. This had so surprised the knife-wielder that before he knew it his arm was in the grip of his intended victim. With a wrench and a twist his shoulder was dislocated. He too shrieked in pain. Bending and picking up the knife, Hogan put it in his pocket.

'If I ever see either of you again I'll kill you,' he said. His manner and tone of voice left both of them in little doubt that this was no idle threat. Turning his back on the two still agonized louts, he made his way unhurriedly to his car, opened it with his remote control, and got in. As he passed one of the car park attendants, he opened his window and handed him the now closed knife.

'Someone seems to have dropped this,' he said. 'I suggest you give it to the police. It looks as if it could be lethal.' With a broad grin at the stunned official, he closed his window and drove out of the racecourse. Thirty-five minutes later he pulled into an underground car park below a block of luxury flats just off the Edgware Road. Unlocking the door, he strode to the lift. A few moments later he was letting himself into a rented apartment on the sixth floor. He removed his jacket and went into the kitchen where he made himself a pot of tea. He retrieved his mobile phone from the jacket he'd worn to the racecourse and sat down to enjoy a cup of his brew. He thought for a moment, then dialled a number.

'Good afternoon, Johnny,' he said. 'Have you any news?'

'I've found out a fair amount about Michael Coleman. He was a trainer in Newmarket and enjoyed some success in a small way before turning to the bloodstock industry. Again he was successful, but fell foul of the authorities and left for Singapore. He has a number of clients over here and in Hong Kong and seems to do very well. Actually rather better than I would have thought these few clients could have financed. I have a shrewd suspicion that he has another much more lucrative source of income and that's what I'm digging into. What news on your front?'

Hogan briefly mentioned the incident at Sandown but dismissed it as being irrelevant to his reason for being in the UK.

'Well, as we know, there's a lot of strange activity around County View. There seems no doubt that the escaped Ahearne is involved in some way but I'm sure there's something much more significant than that going on. Jessop has a group of East Enders led by a man called Benny who is both investigating on his behalf and giving him a fair degree of protection. He is working with a man called Marvin Jones who is an international investigator for

216

a very large insurance operation. He seems to be highly regarded.'

'I've heard of him,' said Johnny Tang. 'You're right, he's very good.'

'Well, this Benny is no idiot,' Hogan resumed. 'He's also been watching Gavin Tang, and what's more I'm pretty sure he knows I'm watching Gavin too. So far we haven't trodden on each other's toes.'

'What have you told the boss?' Tang asked.

'Very little so far. There's something here that's really puzzling me. There's a lot more going on than meets the eye. Any news from New Zealand?'

'Yes, there's one very significant piece of information. The Australian vet who signed that insurance form is known to be bent. He's never been convicted of anything, but the racing authorities have made a number of enquiries, so far without coming up with anything which has allowed them to take action. He also seems to have a long association with Coleman. By the way, Angus Stewart appears to be totally honest, and there's no question of any of his staff being bent.'

'Anything else?' asked the Australian.

'No,' was the reply. 'When do you think you're coming back?'

'I've no idea at the moment, but I think it'll be a week or two. Talk to you soon, Johnny,' and he hung up.

He was lost in thought for a while, then made a call. 'Hi, darling,' he greeted the female voice that answered the phone. 'How about dinner tonight?'

'I'd love to. Where shall we meet, Dad?'

'How about the Greenhouse?'

'Done,' she said. 'Would eight o'clock be OK?'

Her father agreed.

A couple of hours later, Hogan stood up as a stunning brunette walked in and glided across the restaurant to his table. With a big kiss, she seated herself and smiled as he poured her a glass of chilled white wine. 'I see you're still supporting the New Zealand wine industry,' she commented, sipping her glass of Cloudy Bay.

217

'You know I'm a creature of habit,' he reminded her. They both ordered Parma ham, followed by lobster thermidor for her and a grilled Dover sole for him.

Ross Hogan had an élite and powerful network of investigators. He was represented in nearly all the capital cities of the industrial world, as well as some of the developing countries. In most locations he had a maximum of two agents, all of them either ex-policemen like himself, or ex-members of a secret service.

Zara was responsible for their worldwide communication network. After obtaining a first class honours degree in mathematics at Warwick University, she had returned to Australia where she had joined the police force. She gravitated towards IT and rapidly gained a reputation for hard work and technical ability, coupled with creative thinking. Much to the police force's disappointment, she left and joined Microsoft where she soon attracted the attention of the top management and was drafted to their US headquarters. After six months there she was sent to Europe, where she headed a development team based in Frankfurt. A year later she left to join her father's operation. She was based in London with four highly skilled and totally trustworthy women working for her. She had left good friends wherever she worked and her network often proved most useful to her father. Unkind people would describe her as a top-class hacker.

Nothing went on in her father's operation that she didn't know, and there were very few organizations in the world where she couldn't access their most secret files, with or without their knowledge and approval.

She was already aware of Ross's current project. She was working busily on trying to trace where O'Connor's money was coming from, and also who was behind the mysterious syndicate which had bought the ill-fated quartet of horses in New Zealand. She had also checked on the company Gavin had negotiated to buy and the financial organizations he was working with. So far they all seemed to be above board, though neither she nor her father had understood why Gavin was being so secretive with Hamish.

When they'd finished reviewing the situation and speculating on a number of possible explanations for the strange events surrounding the County View operations, her father paused and gave her a hard look.

'I know that look,' she said. 'You're going to ask me to do something really difficult or unpleasant.'

'Quite the contrary,' he said. 'Difficult, possibly. Unpleasant, almost certainly not. There's a young Afro-Caribbean called Marvin Jones. He's a highly successful international investigator working for a man called Percy Cartwright. Johnny Tang speaks highly of him.'

'I don't know Cartwright, but I know of him,' his daughter replied. 'He has a massive insurance company and a reputation to go with it.'

'True,' agreed her father. 'Now I want you to get very close to this Marvin.'

'How close?' she questioned her parent, rather archly.

'That's entirely up to you,' he smiled.

'And what do you want from him?'

He explained Cartwright's involvement with County View, the death of the horses, the possible involvement of The Friend, the growing rumours about Singapore money financing O'Connor, and now the recent news that the Irish trainer was betting very heavily and not very successfully.

'And where does this come in my list of priorities?' she asked.

'Top,' was his immediate response.

'And how do you suggest I get to know him? I suppose I just phone him up and ask him to dinner?'

'That seems as good a way as any,' her father replied with a totally straight face, 'but I suggest lunch at first.'

'You have to be joking!'

'Not at all,' was the reply. 'Tell him you're writing a document on insurance scams and I'll bet he'll jump at it. He'll probably think that you might even have some useful information for him. I suggest you use your Microsoft

219

background. Clearly we don't want our operation mentioned, but find out as much as you can about Cartwright's involvement with County View and Hamish Tang.'

'Ah, we're back to your famous Tang Dynasty again, are we?' she quipped.

'Well, they do pay us extremely handsomely, and it's seldom they give us something which isn't interesting.'

'Agreed,' she said. 'Now, come on. Let's talk about rugby.'

Like her father she was a fanatic and they reviewed the various serious contenders for the following year's World Cup. He promised to take her to Twickenham for the forthcoming Six Nations matches as long as he was still in the UK or Europe.

Shortly afterwards they grabbed a cab in Berkeley Square, which dropped him off in the Edgware Road and took her on to her flat overlooking Regent's Park.

Driving back from Uttoxeter alone, Jay was wondering why Online Boy had run so badly. The horse had been working really well at home and more than holding his own with some of the other young horses that had already been placed or won that season. As he explained to Norman Barnes, there was no excusing the horse's jumping, which had been abysmal. David Sparrow had just said that he'd run without any real life, and Jay had the sinking feeling that perhaps he'd been hit again by some sort of virus. On the other hand, the three horses that had been affected before now had clean bills of health, and all the blood tests, including the most recent on today's runner, had proved negative. All he could suggest was that the horse had just had an off day which does happen from time to time. The owner was sanguine if disappointed. Jay promised he would have his horse thoroughly tested in a couple of days' time once he'd recovered from the exertions of the race and travel. He would report back as soon as he had any news. Jay was so used to this stretch of motorway that he was almost on automatic pilot by the time he'd passed Spaghetti Junction, and was on his way down the M5 to the Cheltenham turn-off – his normal route back to County View.

The ring on his mobile phone jerked him out of his reverie, and pressing the connect button of his remote control equipment he heard a rather pleasant female voice. 'Is that Jay Jessop?' she asked.

'It is,' he replied, not recognizing the voice.

'My name is Vanda,' the voice continued. 'You may remember, we met in Annabel's a few weeks' ago.' Jay was instantly alert and warning bells were ringing. 'Don't worry,' the voice continued. 'I knew who you were that night. You're far too well known to get away with the rather evasive tactics you used to avoid revealing your identity. To be perfectly honest, I don't really blame you. I imagine being seen leaving with me could have caused a bit of scandal if the wrong person had noticed us. In fact I enjoyed your company. Although you'd obviously drunk a fair amount, you were both entertaining and courteous – that is until you did your disappearing act.

'However, I'm not phoning about that particular evening, but about a piece of information which came to my ears yesterday. You know what I am, and you probably realize I mix with quite a lot of girls in the same line of business. Very few of them are friends but we tend to let each other know if any of our clients have idiosyncrasies which might be dangerous or annoying. You'd be amazed how many pillars of society can become violent or try to avoid paying us.

'One of the girls I know quite well is from Singapore and is called Mae Chung. She works for a particularly unpleasant pimp called Jimmy Yong who has a reputation for being associated with some pretty nasty members of the Chinese community, and though never convicted is widely believed to be involved in both drugs and illegal immigrant trafficking. Mae had a drink with me last night and was concerned but intrigued. Jimmy had instructed her to phone you and say she had some information about some of your horses which had died in New Zealand. She was

221

to refuse to give any more information over the phone, and to insist, if you wanted it, for you to meet her at her flat in Maida Vale. When you arrived she was to keep you as long as possible, and if she couldn't seduce you, to ensure you were there long enough for it to appear you had time. Mae would hand you an envelope she had been given. As soon as you left she was instructed to phone a particular journalist from one of the gossip columns and tell him you'd spent an amorous interlude with her. It's not that she's particularly moral, but she just feels that this is part of something which may well be out of her league. She doesn't want to go through with it but she's terrified of Jimmy.'

Jay paused so long before replying that she asked in a slightly louder voice, 'Are you still there?'

'Yes,' he replied.

'What are you going to do?'

'I've no idea at the moment. Thank you for the information, and I'll call you if it seems useful. I'm sure you realize I need to think about this carefully.'

'Of course,' she replied. 'You can usually get me on this number. I haven't withheld it from you. Good luck, and be careful. Jimmy's a very nasty piece of work and mixes with equally nasty and dangerous people.'

'I really do appreciate your call,' said Jay.

'Well, good luck, whatever happens, and I hope you sort it out. By the way, Mae's a very nice girl – very pretty but not very bright.'

'I understand,' he replied, 'and thanks again.'

Not surprisingly, the conversation wiped Online Boy's poor showing completely from his mind. Jay was worried. Clearly there was something seriously threatening behind this situation if the conversation with Vanda could be taken at face value. He had a sinking feeling that in essence it was probably reliable. Needless to say, he had refrained from telling Eva what had really happened on the night of his 'upset tummy'. The fact that there had never been a whisper about the meeting in the press suggested that if

222

anybody at Annabel's recognized either of them, they were too discreet to try and make anything out of it.

Waiting until he got off the motorway, he pulled into the side of the road and dialled Benny, hoping that the East Ender would be there. To his great relief, he was.

Without any unnecessary preamble, Jay related the conversation with Vanda in as much detail as he could recall. 'Bloody hell,' was Benny's instant reaction. 'This Jimmy Yong is a right nasty bastard, I can tell you.'

Benny was clearly thinking. 'You've got no option but to let Harvey Jackson know. Frankly this is probably way out of my league. You know I'll give you any help I can, but I think the least you need is his advice.'

Jay could see the sense behind this. 'I'll speak to him as soon as I can and get back to you when I've got some news.'

'You do that, and don't talk to anyone else,' Benny advised him. 'Not even Howard or Percy, and certainly not Eva.'

'Don't worry, I won't. That's the last thing I have in mind at the moment,' Jay promised. 'I'll call you as soon as I can.'

Deciding there was no point in delaying, Jay phoned his policeman ally and told him everything. Jackson was clearly thinking before he replied. 'Well Vanda has been an informer for a long while and she's been very helpful from time to time. This friend of hers, Mae, isn't known to me but I'm sure she will be to some of our Vice Squad boys. However, Jimmy Yong is and, as she told you, he's a thoroughly nasty piece of work. There's no doubt he's deeply into the drugs trade, and we're almost certain that he's involved in shipping in illegal immigrants. A number of them finish up working for him in the sex trade. What's more, he most certainly has regular contact with the Far East, and I wouldn't be at all surprised if he actually works for one of the large criminal organizations over there. He's somebody to be very careful of, Jay. Under no circumstances are you to contact this Mae, but I'll make sure she is discreetly questioned by one of our undercover officers.

'The only positive thing that comes out of this is that we now seem to have a direct link to the Far East and this would seem to confirm that there is some sort of conspiracy out there aimed at you or County View, or both. Leave it with me, but keep this under your hat. There's no need for you to air your night of indiscretion to any of your colleagues, and I am sure you can trust Benny to keep his mouth shut.'

'I can count on that,' Jay agreed.

'Right. As soon as I've any news from you on the Mae front I'll be in touch,' Jackson promised. 'I'll not waste any more time and get on it now.'

Eva was sitting opposite her husband in the Shepherd's Rest where they'd gone for a light lunch and a break from their normal routine. She put down her wine glass and looked at him seriously.

'I'm worried about Danny. He's only been back five days and he's bored and trying to do too much. I'm sure he's still worried that the police don't seem to know who's really responsible for the attack on him, even though they've arrested this Daly.'

'I do take your point,' replied Jay, 'but what can we do about it?'

'Send him somewhere well away from County View, somewhere he's never been before, somewhere we could be sure he was being well cared for. I'm sure it would do him good.'

'I agree, but that's a tall order, isn't it?'

'No. Why don't we send him over to Mother's? They've always got on well and he respects her. He's never been to South Africa, the climate would do him good, and she'd make sure he didn't overexert himself. There would be enough new sights to take his mind off his problems, he'd be able to go racing with her, and he'd be able to start exercising gently. We could find out exactly what his regime should be from his doctors but I'd have thought some gentle swimming in Mother's pool wouldn't do him any harm.'

'That's a brilliant idea. You'd better check with Fiona first.'

'I have and she's all for it. All we need do now is check with his doctors and persuade him it's for the best.'

'Good luck,' her husband responded with a broad smile. 'I'm going to leave this one to you.'

'Coward, but you're probably right. He won't argue with me as much as he would you.'

'Right, you might as well start this afternoon, and I suggest the first thing to do is to make sure his doctors think that he's capable of the flight to Cape Town and also what he's allowed to do when he gets there. Obviously we'll pay for it.'

'Of course, and he's travelling club class. He'll need plenty of room if he's not going to stiffen up, and he's worked hard enough for us to deserve it even before someone tried to kill him.'

Jay nodded and changed the subject back to Max's activities at school and in particular his growing prowess at badminton – anything to take his mind off Vanda's call.

By the end of the day Eva had confirmed with her mother the most suitable dates, had obtained a list of dos and don'ts from Danny's doctors, and had found a seat on a flight early the next week. All that remained was to persuade Danny.

The next morning Jay saw Danny wandering around the yard trying to be useful without doing anything heavy. He called him over. 'Eva would like a quick word with you, Danny. It's an idea that she and I talked about yesterday, and I very much hope you'll like it. We all want you back in the saddle as quickly as possible, and I'm sure that Eva's idea will give your convalescence a boost.'

Danny gave him a questioning look, but nodded and strolled over to the house.

Twenty minutes later he reappeared grinning from ear to ear. 'I can't imagine why you thought I wouldn't accept

225

that deal, guv'nor,' he positively chortled. 'I've always wanted to see big game, and I know that Fiona will look after me like my own mother. I've already told Eva that I'm more than happy to go next week, and at this very moment she's confirming the booking.'

Jay put his arm round Danny's shoulders and gave him a friendly hug, making sure that it wasn't too energetic in view of the still healing wounds.

'I'm delighted. Just make sure you listen to Fiona and don't go trying to run before you can walk.'

'I promise to be a good boy,' Danny replied, trying hard to keep a straight face.

'Well, you'd better be off and tell Jed what's happening. I'm sure he'll be delighted to have you out from under his feet until you're really well again.'

Danny smiled again and trotted off to break the news to his long-standing friend and colleague.

Jay hurried to the house to let Eva know how enthusiastic Danny had been. 'I know,' she replied. 'It was no hard sell at all.'

'This means Danny will be away for Christmas,' Jay suddenly said, thinking aloud. 'Won't your mother be here?'

'Oh, I forgot to tell you. It seems that Mother has a new boyfriend and she's already told me she expects to spend Christmas at his farm and has confirmed that Danny will be more than welcome.'

'This seems a bit sudden,' her husband said, somewhat primly.

'She's been keeping it to herself. She only told me when I raised the subject of Danny with her a couple of days ago. She's worried that we'll be upset, but I assured her that with everything else going on at Christmas and the New Year, we'd probably enjoy her company even more when the festivities are over and the frantic racing programme slows down a bit. She's half promised to come for the latter part of February and to stay through the Cheltenham Festival. She also hinted she might have this new man with her.'

'How do you feel about it?'

'Well, as I never knew my father it doesn't really seem any sort of intrusion. If it makes Mother happy it's fine by me. By the way, I've booked Danny's flight for next Tuesday. I've also told him I'll help with his packing to make sure he doesn't go with either too much or the wrong things.'

'What would I do without you?' Jay wondered aloud, and taking her in his arms gave her a long and lingering kiss.

Chapter Twenty-Three

Zara was sitting opposite Marvin, still slightly surprised that her father's subterfuge had worked so smoothly. They were sitting in the Oxo Tower looking across London, enjoying a delicious light lunch of wild mushroom soup followed by grilled trout. The conversation had been easy and interesting. Zara had done her homework and asked him informed questions about the way in which large insurance companies became suspicious about fraud, how they exchanged information, why they pursued the perpetrators, often without recovering what they had paid out. He explained it was to discourage would-be cheats who operated on a truly mind-blowing scale. He also pointed out that spotting potential fraud was probably more important than remedial action.

While concentrating on her trout, she pondered about the man sitting opposite her. She found him enormously attractive, both conversation-wise and physically. She could not help wondering what he would look like without his immaculate but rather severe suit, and his sparkling white shirt. She was aroused from her reverie by a shocking question.

'Now that we've got over the chat, why did you really want to meet me?'

She was so taken aback that for once she was at a loss for words before replying, 'Well, I told you.'

'What you told me and what you really want bear little relation to each other. Zara, you're a rather enigmatic figure. You work for an unnamed company with a small group of extremely well-qualified IT experts. You've worked for Microsoft, the Australian police, and now no one seems to know exactly what you do. You do, however, live in an exclusive address in Regent's Park, your phone is ex-directory, and if you have a social life other than going to the gym nearly every day and flying around Europe, you disguise it extremely well.'

Zara was almost speechless. 'Where on earth did you get all this from?' she demanded.

Smiling, Marvin replied, 'I would have thought you'd know by now. I'm an investigator. When I got a mysterious telephone call from out of the blue I made my enquiries. I have a very good network as I'm sure do you. So come on, what's all this about?'

Zara had recovered her poise and decided that at least some of the truth was necessary to retain his confidence and to get the information she was seeking.

'Well, I'm an investigator of sorts as well,' she said, 'and one of my clients has lost some very valuable young thoroughbreds in suspicious circumstances. I'm trying to find out a little more about it.'

Marvin laughed. 'Well, what a coincidence, so am I, but I'm sure you already know that.' She smiled and nodded rather self-consciously. 'Well,' he said, 'let me think about it. I'll give you a call and next time you can buy. I'm sure your company or your client can afford it.' With that he called for the bill, not even suggesting coffee, picked up her hand in an extravagantly courteous manner, and kissed it briefly. 'I look forward to our next meeting,' he said, in what was a polite but firm dismissal. She smiled sweetly, thanked him for lunch, and beat a somewhat hasty and confused retreat.

As soon as she got back to her office she phoned her father and reported the extraordinary encounter. Rather than being concerned, he roared with laughter and said, 'Well, perhaps we've found a useful ally. Let's meet for a drink tonight and consider our options.'

In view of the sensitive nature of their impending conversation, they planned to meet at Ross's flat. At 6.45 she was ringing the bell. Her father opened the door, greeted her cheerfully, and led her into his sitting room.

'We have to assume that your attractive Marvin will have reported your conversation to Percy Cartwright by now,' he began. 'To a degree our cover is blown, but on the other hand at this stage he can only associate you with the bloodstock activity rather than the broader issue of what's going on at County View. In fact it may well be that he's not involved in that, although I doubt it as his boss is a director of the company.

'I think you should meet him, tell him all we know about what happened in New Zealand, the Australian vet and the not very savoury Michael Coleman. We may not be adding much to his knowledge, but at least it will show that we're putting our cards on the table, even if we're not revealing our whole hand at the moment.'

She looked hard at him as he made the last remark. 'Are you suggesting that we should?'

'I haven't made up my mind yet. I think I want to speak to Johnny Tang and then to our client. At that stage the two of us might seek a meeting with Percy Cartwright as well as your Marvin.'

This really surprised his daughter. It was very seldom that her father revealed his identity to anyone, and even more seldom to anyone who wasn't a client at the highest level.

'What are you doing this evening?' he asked.

'I'm going to go to the gym now, and then I'm going to eat in. I've got quite a backlog of routine work to get done as a result of spending most of the last four days trying, but obviously failing, to convince Marvin that I was a simple researcher trying to write a learned paper about fraud in the insurance industry.'

Her father chuckled. 'OK, off you go, and let's make sure we keep in touch if anything relevant occurs.'

Ross put his mobile phone and his pocket dictating machine on to the big table in front of the window. He then placed a notepad with blue and red pens beside it. He was carrying a glass and bottle of water across to the table, prior to making a number of calls to his agents around the world, when his mobile rang. He picked it up and saw the caller was Johnny Tang. 'Johnny?'

'I've got a real problem.' The concern in Johnny's voice immediately alerted Ross – this was something serious.

'Give.'

'I've had a package delivered to me by special messenger. The contents are appalling.'

'What the hell are they?' Hogan demanded.

'A human tongue.'

'God almighty. Are you sure?'

'Not only am I sure. I now know whose it is, or I should say whose it was,' the investigator replied. 'As soon as I'd got over the shock I phoned one of my friends in the police force. He told me they'd found a dead body in a stolen car in the car park near Raffles Hotel. It had clearly been parked there sometime overnight.'

'Do you know whose body it is?'

'Unfortunately, yes,' was the reply. 'It belonged to one of my informants, called Sammy Cox. He works at the racecourse and runs messages for a number of small-time criminals. He also collects, in a very minor way, for some of the smaller illegal bookmakers. He was definitely not big-time, but it's amazing how often he could let me have useful information. I've used him from time to time for over four years. What is really ominous is that yesterday afternoon he phoned me to say he'd got some hot information, and claimed that one of the big and very respectable local businessmen was deeply into the drug business. He insisted that it was somebody above reproach and this would be worth serious money. Normally I'd pay him anything between two and five hundred dollars. When he asked for twenty thousand I knew he considered it something seriously big. We agreed to meet at ten o'clock last night in one of the bars used by hookers where he was well known and so nobody would be surprised that he was there. I went, but he didn't turn up. After half an hour, I was starting to attract some attention, so I decided to leave.

'What's really worrying,' he continued, 'is that not only has the poor devil been killed, but I'm told he was tortured before he died. It's quite clear that he revealed my identity, hence the warning represented by the tongue.'

Ross Hogan snapped, 'AT immediately! I mean, immediately! And phone me as soon as you're safe. I mean that, Johnny. Immediately,' and he hung up.

AT was their code for 'about turn'. It meant that any agent in danger was to immediately leave where he was and go to somewhere he knew he would be safe. Not even Ross Hogan would know that destination until the agent called him.

'Damn and blast,' he cursed. Ignoring the bottle of water, he poured himself a neat brandy. He drank this slowly while he considered his next action. Picking up his phone again, he typed in the word 'instant' and sent the one word text to Zara. He didn't expect an instant response as she would probably still be at the gym, but was sure she would check her voice mail either just before leaving or as soon as she was alone. Sure enough, twenty minutes later his daughter was on the phone. 'Forget your other plans,' he instructed her. 'The St John's Wood Hilton in fifteen minutes.'

'Agreed,' and her line went dead.

Leaving his flat, he hailed a black cab and was sitting in a corner of the busy bar when his daughter joined him. He quickly related Johnny's news. 'My first instinct was to phone the client,' he told her, 'but we really haven't anything concrete to tell him. I'm tempted to expedite our proposed meeting with Cartwright. It's only a hunch, but I've got a feeling that the rumours about O'Connor's money, the violent incidents surrounding County View, the deaths in New Zealand, and now this murder, are all related. I also think that Cartwright and your friend Marvin might be useful allies in this situation.'

She nodded in agreement. 'I'll make the calls in the morning,' he said, 'so be sure you're ready to join me as soon as we can fix this up, hopefully tomorrow or the next day at the latest.'

She smiled, and breaking the tension announced that any new opportunity to meet the gorgeous Mr Jones would be more than welcome. Joining the light-hearted moment, her father gave her an affectionate punch and said, 'Well, we might as well eat together again tonight.'

They returned to his flat. He checked his voice mail. There was nothing urgent.

'Where shall we eat?'

'Here,' replied Zara. 'There are plenty of shops in the Edgware Road. You sit where you are. Open a decent bottle of wine. I'll get something and I'll rustle you up one of my exotic dishes.'

'Oh lord, no,' her father exclaimed, rolling his eyes in mock horror, knowing he would be more than well fed.

At the same time the phone rang at County View. Eva answered.

'Hi, Harvey. Jay's on his way back from Bangor. You should get him on his mobile.'

'I'll try, but if I don't succeed there's some great news. I've just heard Ahearne has been captured at Haydock Park. That's all I know at the moment.'

Eva whooped with delight. 'You try him immediately. He'll be over the moon.'

'Right.'

Ten minutes later an ecstatic Jay was on the line. 'Isn't that fantastic? It looks as if our troubles are over. What a boost for Danny.'

Eva joined in his jubilation and restrained herself from reminding him that O'Connor was still very much in their lives. There were still huge question marks over his motives and where his financing was coming from.

The proposed meeting between Ross Hogan and Percy couldn't take place for three days as Percy was in South Africa negotiating the premium on a large shipment of diamonds to Amsterdam. It was unusual for him to become personally involved at this level but the sums involved were so huge and the client such a long-standing one that he felt obliged to attend the meeting.

When Moira told Marvin that Ross had suggested a meeting, although slightly surprised, he was enthusiastic about the idea. Percy asked her to set it up as soon as possible on his return. As was normal County View practice, he kept the other directors informed of the latest development. Howard was his usual enthusiastic self, Jay was interested but, after various disappointments, was not getting too excited or counting any chickens. He was still worried about the outcome of Vanda's call. Roddy was much more interested – after all, the stud side of the County View operations, and hence the loss of the four horses in New Zealand, was his major concern.

Percy was a little puzzled by Hamish's reaction which had been unusually low key, even for him. He admitted to having heard of Ross Hogan but implied it was only very much second-hand, and he seemed anxious to change the subject. He was almost as evasive when Percy asked what news there was from Johnny Tang, but eventually admitted he'd heard nothing for several days but was sure that the investigator was working hard on trying to discover who was behind the mystery purchase and subsequent deaths.

As soon as he politely could, he ended the call and Percy put it down to the fact that he probably had much more pressing business matters on his mind.

On his return to England, Percy arranged to have breakfast at Simpson's with Marvin before going on to Canary Wharf where the meeting with Ross and Zara was scheduled for 9.30 that morning. Peter, the head waiter, had reserved one of the discreet boxes that the County View directors traditionally used for their breakfast meetings. After the normal greetings and Marvin asking how the negotiations had gone in South Africa, Percy brought the conversation back to the two Hogans.

Marvin reported on his meeting with Zara in rather more detail than had been the case in their brief telephone conversation, occasionally bringing an amused smile to Percy's otherwise serious expression. At the end of his report Marvin looked enquiringly at his boss. 'How much should we tell them about what's gone on and what we know?'

'I don't see what we have to lose by being totally frank,' Percy replied. 'After all, we've nothing to hide and what they don't know would hardly be difficult to find out. The one exception is, we should probably not mention Johnny Tang's involvement. Hamish seemed somewhat reticent on this subject when I spoke to him, and the fact that we've got an extra person digging into the Singapore situation other than ourselves is hardly relevant to them. From what you tell me Zara was rather more cagey than we have any reason to be, so it'll be interesting to see how open they are with us at the meeting.'

Marvin thought for a moment before agreeing to the wisdom of this course of action. They finished their coffees, got up and found Francis waiting just across the Strand in Exeter Street.

They were in Canary Wharf in time for Percy to glance at any emails which Moira felt were particularly important, before the two of them settled themselves and awaited the Hogans' arrival. Bang on time, the two of them arrived in reception and were shown into Percy's office by the welcoming Moira. Handshakes were exchanged and Hogan got straight to the point. He explained that one of his clients was particularly concerned about the mysterious death of the four horses and he was totally frank about his knowledge of both the dubious Australian vet and Michael Coleman, the suspect bloodstock agent. He told them what he knew of the events surrounding County View, but omitted to mention The Friend. Marvin was slightly surprised when Percy volunteered all their knowledge on this front and also the history of Danny and The Friend, although he didn't say that Danny was a reformed drug addict.

Hogan reciprocated by revealing that there was growing doubt that Coleman's bloodstock-generated income was sufficient to finance his luxurious lifestyle. There was always the possibility that he was doing deals for an unknown major player. However, there were rumours circulating that he might well be involved in some aspect of the drug trade. This was news to Percy and Marvin. There was a lull in the conversation which was broken by Zara.

'From what you've told us and from what we've learned,' she said, 'I can't believe that the death of these four horses is a completely isolated incident and was just a way of making a quick three or four hundred thousand dollars. It seems to me that it's much more likely to be part of an overall plan to damage County View, but does anyone have any idea why this should be?'

Both Percy and Marvin looked at her with some respect. 'We agree with you on both counts,' said Marvin. 'That is one of the areas which really mystifies us. We're equally puzzled about any possible relationship between those incidents which look as if they might be directly connected with our friend in Dublin and those where any link is far less clear. Likewise, is there any connection with O'Connor?'

Percy picked up the theme. 'There have always been jealousies and tense rivalries between owners and trainers in racing. Indeed County View has been involved in some of them. But none has been as obscure as this or with possible international ramifications. May I make a suggestion? One of the people who has been particularly helpful in investigating the County View problems is a senior police officer called Harvey Jackson. I believe it would be helpful if you met him and had an equally frank conversation with him. You'll find him incisive, but he is also the soul of discretion.' Ross Hogan nodded in agreement. 'I'll also phone Hamish Tang, our Far Eastern director, and see if he feels a meeting with you would be useful. I'm sure you've heard of him and his huge international trading conglomerate.'

Hogan nodded. 'It would be difficult to spend any time in Singapore or Hong Kong business circles without coming across his reputation and his various businesses,' agreed Hogan, without revealing his relationship.

Chapter Twenty-Four

A few weeks after Frank Malone's string had arrived, Jay gave the bookmaker a call. 'Frank, I've been looking at your new horses on the gallops this morning. They all seem to be settled and working really well. We know they were all fit when they arrived so I think the time is approaching when we see how they do in a race.'

The bookmaker was enthusiastic. 'Anything in mind?'

'Well, next week there's a meeting at Cheltenham, and although it's obviously not the same calibre as the Festival, it will be good competitive racing and there are suitable races for all three of them. The weather's been kind to us so far, and as all of them appear to like going somewhere between soft and good there's a fair chance that we'll have conditions to suit them all. I thought we might make an afternoon of it and run the trio, if that fits in with you.'

'What a bloody great idea! Let's go for it.'

'OK, so I'll make the entries and let's keep our fingers crossed that we don't get a lot of rain or, worse still, a really cold snap.'

'I'll get my prayer mat out,' joked the owner. 'Keep me in the loop.'

Over the following days the three horses worked really well at home. The weather had been kind, and two days before the meeting the going at Cheltenham was good to soft. Jay phoned Frank, who confirmed he'd certainly be there, and the horses were duly declared.

This was clearly a very important day for Jay, Frank, and of course the horses themselves. On arrival at Cheltenham Jay went through his normal checking procedure before meeting Frank and his son Lance at the Barry Copes Fish Bar. Jed had come with him and had offered to do the saddling so that Jay could pay particular attention to Frank. Jay noticed to his surprise that O'Connor had no runners that day. He mentioned this to Frank when they met, and Lance replied, 'he probably just doesn't want to be around if they run well, particularly as these are definitely the most competitive races they've run in since they came over from Ireland.'

His father nodded, before pointing to the Cheltenham page of the *Racing Post*. 'I see they're all well fancied,' he commented. 'Rampant Raider's even money, Double or Quits is 2–1, and the filly is 5–1.'

'Well, they deserve to be short priced,' Jay replied. 'They all had good form in Ireland and they've all won since crossing over here, although not in the company they've got today. Now, come on and let's have something to eat. We've got a busy afternoon ahead of us.'

The afternoon was hectic as there was only one race between each of the three runners' contests. Double or Quits came second, being well beaten by the runner-up to Cool Customer in the previous year's Champion Chase. On the other hand, Frank's horse was two lengths ahead of the third with the field well strung out behind in what had been a blindingly fast two mile chase. Jay thought it odd that Cool Customer had not been entered in the race, which did have very decent prize money. On paper it should easily have won.

In the three mile chase, the highlight of the afternoon, Rampant Raider proved his outstanding class. Although only winning by a length, he had been cleverly ridden by David Sparrow who had moved up steadily in the finishing straight to win more easily than the distance suggested. Frank and Lance were ecstatic.

Their afternoon finished on a high note when My Sweet Colleen came second in a thrilling two and a half mile novice handicap hurdle, being beaten only by a short head in a photo finish.

Frank was thrilled as they had their end of afternoon

post-mortem. Jay summed up. 'I think we can run Rampant Raider in whatever we want. I honestly believe the filly is going to improve and I can see no reason why we can't run her in top novice handicaps, although we'll have to see what happens to her weight after today's performance. We may have to bide our time and run her in level weight races. I'd like to think a bit about Double or Quits. We've got to accept that apart from the winner the rest of the field was not really the best of the two mile chasers in the country. We may have to be a bit more modest in our aspirations.'

Frank and Lance both accepted this assessment quite cheerfully and asked Jay if they could visit their three horses in the stable block. 'Absolutely,' said Jay. 'Let's walk over and I'll sign you in. It'll be at least another half-hour before they leave anyway as Jed will want them to cool off and settle down before they're boxed home.'

All three horses were duly made a great fuss of by the father and son before they returned to the grandstand to watch the final race. Although they had no specific interest in it, one of Frank's big clients had a runner and he wanted to be around when it ran to have a word with the owner after the race. The horse duly won, and with a wry grin Frank told Jay that he'd be paying out a decent lump as a result. 'But not as much as I picked up this afternoon,' he chortled.

After meeting his client, Frank insisted on another celebratory drink, though Jay settled for a cup of coffee.

On their way back to the car park, Frank took Jay to one side and spoke quietly. 'Look, old sport,' he said, 'I've heard a bit more news from Ireland. It seems that O'Connor's been over there two or three times recently and has been having some pretty serious meetings with one or two bookmakers. He owes a lot of money and they're beginning to lose patience with him. This would seem to tie in with what we've heard this side of the Irish Sea.'

Jay said nothing for a moment. 'Look, I really appreciate

this, Frank. Every little thing you can tell me helps and I'll make sure the right people hear this. Thanks a bundle.'

Then with a cheery smile and patting the bookmaker on the back, he changed the subject. 'Well, you've had a good day and I think we're all going to have a lot of fun with these new horses of yours. I'll talk to you soon,' and breaking away from his newfound friend and ally, he walked to his car. He immediately relayed the latest intelligence to Percy, asking him to make sure that Marvin and Benny knew. He then phoned Howard who took it in his stride, before leaving a message for Jackson to give him a call as soon as possible.

Before he got back to County View, the policeman had rung and listened to Frank's news.

'Well, it does seem that your Irish competitor is beginning to have some serious financial difficulties. I'll let McKenna in Dublin know, and perhaps you'll make sure that Benny keeps his ears to the ground as well.' He changed the subject. 'By the way, Mae is proving very helpful and we are building up a good case against Jimmy Yong. I want to ensure it's watertight before we bring him in and we're not far short of that. You can start relaxing on that score at least.'

Harvey Jackson had a long conversation with his Dublin friend Pat McKenna. When he put the phone down, he walked across his office and closed the door. This was a signal that he was only to be disturbed in a real emergency. He looked at the notes he'd made during the conversation, then stood up and prowled around the office. A few moments later he picked up the phone and got through to Moira in Percy's office.

'Is Mr Cartwright available?'

'I'll just check.'

He was put straight through. Percy knew that Harvey was not a man to make telephone calls after six o'clock at night unless there was something he really wanted to discuss.

241

'If I came round straight away could you spare me anything up to an hour?' he enquired.

Percy looked at his desk diary. 'There's nothing I can't change. See you as soon as you like.'

'I'm on my way. By the way, see if Jay's around. We may want to have a conference call after I've talked to you.' With that he put the phone down, leaving Percy mystified and intrigued.

Using his direct line, Percy rang County View where Eva answered. He told her he needed to speak to Jay urgently. He said that Harvey Jackson had phoned, with something clearly pressing on his mind.

'He's over at Max's school at the moment. Max has been playing in a badminton match. It should be over any minute now and I imagine he'll be back within the hour.'

'Get him to call me when he gets in,' Percy requested.

Twenty minutes later Moira was showing Harvey into Percy's office. 'It sounds as if you've had a hard day,' Percy commented. 'I'm going to have a drink. What about you?'

'A large scotch with a little water would hit the spot,' replied the policeman. Two of these were rapidly dispensed, and the two men sat down in the comfortable chairs around the small meeting table.

'I've had the most extraordinary telephone call from Pat McKenna in Dublin,' Jackson started. 'Ahearne's come out with a story so bizarre that McKenna said he's inclined to believe it. Having thought about it, I must confess perhaps I do as well.'

Percy looked at him seriously over the rim of his glass and let him continue.

'Ahearne denies all knowledge of any of the incidents with which we've been connecting him, but the real bombshell is that he said he had no idea he was going to be rescued. As he was put into the police car he thought that the three men were genuine policemen and was completely staggered at the subsequent events. They said almost nothing to him and drove him south of Dublin for about half an hour. They then left the car and got into a beaten-up van where one of them sat in the back with our friend. His companion was completely uncommunicative. When the vehicle stopped, a hood was put over his head and he was taken into a house and up some stairs. He was put into a room which he subsequently found was one of two connecting with its own bathroom. One was a small bedroom and the other a not particularly big sitting area. There was a television but no phone.

'After a few moments another man came in with a mobile phone in his hand. He dialled a number, made a connection and then handed the phone to The Friend. A heavily accented voice told him that he would be kept where he was for two or three weeks, at least until the initial heat had died down. He'd be fed, given an exercise bike, but not allowed out of the room he was in. If he tried to escape he would be seriously hurt. At the end of this period he would be smuggled out of Ireland and given enough money to survive on for a few weeks. He'd be put somewhere where he should be able to make contact with some of his previous associates. The telephone call was terminated, the phone taken from his hand, and the big man left the room. Ahearne heard not only the door being locked, but bolts being slid across as well.

'According to him, the next three weeks consisted of three meals a day, magazines but no newspapers, DVDs, but it turned out that the television was not connected to either satellite or terrestrial channels. In other words, he had no idea what was going on in the outside world.

'After nearly a month, he was collected, taken downstairs with a hood on, and again put into a van. He had no idea where he was. The next thing he knew he was decanted at a small fishing harbour in the dark and put on to a fishing boat manned, as far as he could tell, by Eastern Europeans. He was escorted to a cabin where he was fed but not allowed outside. Twenty-four hours later under cover of darkness he was put ashore via a rowing boat, again not knowing where he was. He was given a package and left there. Opening the package he found £1,000 in it, approximately half in euros and half in sterling.

'Making his way off the beach, he eventually found a road and discovered he was not very far from Southport. He found himself a B and B and stayed the night. The next day he phoned friends in Liverpool who collected him and took him to a house on the outskirts of Manchester. He's been there ever since. He managed to get more money from one of his ex-contacts on the clear understanding that as soon as he could get access to the cash which he had hidden he would repay the loan with lavish interest. After two or three weeks of this life he became bored and took what turned out to be the disastrous decision to go to the races. By this time he'd grown a beard and thought he'd be safe. He was, however, unlucky. One of the bookmakers had an old Irishman helping him who recognized The Friend from his days in Dublin. The old man still regularly received papers from home so knew about the reward, and the rest is history.'

'Bloody hell,' was Percy's reaction. 'If it's true where does that leave us?'

'God knows,' was the reply. 'Let me finish. He swears he's never heard of Billy Dean, he'd never met O'Connor, although he did see him at the races from time to time before he was in prison. According to him it was before O'Connor was working for himself, in the early days when he helped his father and later when he went to the big yard. He denies having any possible motive to burn down a marquee at County View, and does not seem to have connected Danny or Jay with his incarceration. He is convinced that it was a rival gang setting him up to get him out of the way.'

Percy got up, took both their glasses and refilled them.

'Shall we see if Jay's back?' he asked Jackson, who nodded. Percy had a quick word with Moira and in a few moments she put Jay through. He was told he was talking to both Percy and Harvey. Briefly but comprehensively, Jackson related The Friend's story.

'Well, what do you suggest we do next?' Jay's voice

clearly betrayed that he was both amazed and concerned. It was Jackson who replied.

'I think that we ought to have another word with our new Australian friend, Mr Hogan, and his daughter. I've been making some enquiries since we met. There's a lot more to that gentleman and the lovely Zara than would appear at first glance. My information is that he actually runs a highly recommended, very discreet, and very high-powered international security and investigation agency. To be honest, I'd be surprised if he would take on anything quite as simple and small as the New Zealand horses episode but I'd lay good odds that this is only part of what he's really concerned about.'

Jay was silent, but Percy was his usual positive self.

'From what I've seen from my brief interlude with the man, I'd agree with you. What's more, according to Marvin, his daughter is highly qualified and well thought of, and is not there just as a result of nepotism. I don't really see that we've got anything to lose by involving them more.'

'I agree,' was Jackson's response.

'I think we need to let Howard, Hamish and Roddy know of these developments,' Jay insisted down the phone, 'and is there any reason why we shouldn't bring Benny in as well?'

'I certainly agree that you've got to let the other directors know,' was Jackson's reply, 'and from what I've seen of Benny he's always been completely reliable and loyal to all connections at County View. Just to be on the safe side I'd let Howard make the call on that, after all he's known him longer than any of us.'

Percy nodded before remembering that Jay was at the other end of the phone. 'I'm quite happy to talk to Roddy and Hamish,' he volunteered, 'but I think, Jay, you ought to speak to Howard. As soon as we've got their reactions I think that we should set up a quick briefing meeting with Marvin and Benny. Unless anyone can think of an objection, we should contact the Hogans and bring them into the picture as well.'

'I'll get on to Howard straight away,' said Jay, 'and be in touch as soon as I can.'

Jackson and Percy finished their drinks and Jackson promised to be in touch early the next morning. He was shown out by Moira.

Percy phoned Roddy to let him know the latest developments. The young man was clearly taken aback and somewhat cautiously agreed that the Hogans should be in on the act. His reluctance stemmed not from any prejudice but because he hadn't met either of them.

Roddy suggested he should call his father-in-law but Percy pointed out that as he'd received the information first hand it was probably better coming from him. He was quite sure that Hamish would want to talk to his son-in-law when both of them had had a chance to digest this latest chapter in what was developing into more of a puzzle as well as a saga.

By the time all this had finished Moira buzzed him to say that she was off and that Francis was waiting to drive him to his dinner engagement with two other major players in the London insurance market.

After his recent overseas trip and the events of the afternoon, it was a function he could well have done without. Reluctantly, he reminded himself that at this late notice it would be extremely rude not to meet as agreed, particularly as the dinner had been set up at his suggestion. At least it would take his mind off County View for a couple of hours.

Howard's reaction to the news was frankly incredulous. So much evidence pointed in the direction of The Friend that he'd taken it for granted that it was indeed the Irishman who was behind all the incidents. He agreed with the course of action which was outlined and also that Benny should be brought into the circle. 'After all,' he pointed out, 'he's been involved and included in most of our discussions up until now – I can't see any good reason why we should exclude him at this stage. It may be that he brings nothing new to the party but he and his brothers are very good at keeping their ears close to the ground, and frankly the more brains that are working on the case the better.'

Jay agreed with him and promised that he would contact Benny as soon as he could. This he did, without going into details over the phone, and explained to Benny that there was going to be an urgent meeting.

He'd no sooner finished his conversation with Benny when Howard called him back. 'What about Danny?' he asked. 'How the hell's he going to feel? He thought the attack on him was the work of The Friend, who as far as Danny was concerned is now out of harm's way, but now it's suggested that some totally different and unknown person is behind it. It's hardly going to make him sleep better in his bed.'

Jay paused before answering. 'You're right, of course,' he said. 'My instinct is to say nothing to Danny, and leave him in blissful ignorance for the time being. After all, he is in South Africa.'

Howard agreed, but reminded Jay that all the directors must know to ensure that it didn't slip out. Jay said he would do that, and warn Eva to alert her mother to their agreement.

Meanwhile, Roddy had been speaking to his father-in-law explaining in as much detail as he could what had happened. He also promised that he or one of the other directors would update Hamish after the forthcoming meeting with Hogan.

'What do you know about him?' he asked his father-in-law.

'Oh, I've heard that he has a well-respected organization,' was Hamish's response before changing the subject and asking about his daughter's health and what the two of them were up to. Roddy was surprised that his father-in-law didn't seem particularly au fait with Hogan's activities. He'd always thought that there was very little that went on in his area that Hamish did not know about, or influential people he wasn't acquainted with or informed about. The more he thought about it all, the more he was intrigued. He decided he would like to be personally involved in the discussions which were due to take place in the next day or two.

To this end he asked Jay if there was any reason why he couldn't attend. Jay, who was already concerned that the meeting might be getting rather unwieldy, could think of no acceptable way of excluding him. He was, after all, a director of the company and the New Zealand operation was very much under his direct area of control. So he agreed in principle to Roddy's attendance, though he did suggest that as Percy and Jackson knew Hogan they should have the final say.

Jay rang Howard again and asked if he too would like to be at the meeting. To his delight Howard made exactly that same point about numbers and made an alternative suggestion.

'I don't think there's any need for me to be there but I would have thought that perhaps it was best to let Jackson and Percy have an initial meeting with the Hogans and Marvin and Benny. Then you and Roddy could join them after they've had a chance to chew the fat for a bit and perhaps come up with a few ideas. If you're not there for the first meeting, Roddy can hardly feel that he's been excluded,' the older man concluded.

Jay could see the wisdom of this plan, and phoned Roddy with the suggestion. The young man hardly hesitated before agreeing the moment he knew Jay too was going to join the meeting later. Percy was more than a little relieved at the news. He too had had misgivings about the size of the group.

Chapter Twenty-Five

The following morning Percy arranged a meeting with the Hogans, Marvin and Benny at his own offices. They were convenient, secure, and boasted as good a communication resource as anywhere in the City of London. The initial meeting would take place at 5.30 that evening. Jay and Roddy would join them at seven and hopefully the second meeting would be over by 8.30, allowing all to have dinner at a reasonable hour. Percy's first inclination had been to invite everybody for a simple meal in his main boardroom, but on second thoughts he felt it would be better if the County View directors ate by themselves, possibly joined by Jackson if he was both available and agreeable.

By 5.40 everyone scheduled for the first meeting was gathered in one of Percy's meeting rooms. The two Hogans were introduced to Benny, whom they'd not met before, and were told briefly why he was there. Marvin smiled to himself as he saw Zara glancing with a slightly puzzled expression in the direction of Benny. Hogan clearly took the East Ender's presence in his stride and seemed relaxed but certainly interested in what was going to be revealed.

Without beating about the bush, Jackson launched into a summary of Ahearne's story. As had already been agreed, Danny's previous drug addiction was omitted. The group was told that, in view of the near fatal experience which Danny had endured, they were not going to let him know that there was now some serious doubt if it was The Friend behind the attack.

When Jackson had finished, Percy took up the narrative.

He said there was a growing conviction amongst those who had been involved with County View that these various attacks were being financed from somewhere in the Far East. Although it seemed unlikely that Ahearne was the source of this, there was little doubt that there was an Irish involvement. There were clearly some big question marks over O'Connor's integrity to say the least, and perhaps even his innocence of criminal activity. These rumours about Far Eastern money, in conjunction with the death of the four thoroughbreds in New Zealand, also pointed to the possibility of there being a Singapore or Hong Kong criminal organization behind the string of incidents. It was significant that, with the exception of Billy Dean's clumsy attempt to implicate Jay with planted drugs at O'Connor's, all the other acts had been efficiently planned and executed. Percy looked at Hogan.

'Now you can see why we thought it would be useful to involve you in our discussions, Mr Hogan. And,' he added hurriedly, 'that of course includes Zara.'

Before Hogan could answer, Marvin broke in.

'I know that you have explained your interest in the insurance claim against the bloodstock, but, as you realize, Mr Cartwright here is the main potential loser. But I also know from my contacts that you are well respected in the Far East as a diligent and successful investigator. That's why I'm happy to have you here.'

'I agree,' joined in Jackson, 'and I've also learned that your activities normally involve rather larger scale events than a stud farm in New Zealand, even if it is the subject of an attempted major fraud. I suspect, Mr Hogan, that you have bigger fish to fry. Although I have no doubt that the bloodstock is part of what you are investigating, I have a distinct feeling some of the broader concerns that we have are likely to fall within your realm of interest as well as ours.'

The Australian paused, and Percy could not help thinking he would probably be a pretty awesome opponent sitting across a poker table. 'All right,' he said. 'I am indeed the head of an organization along the lines you have described. It is also true that the bloodstock incident is not the sole area of our interest. We have reason to believe that it was undertaken by an organization which is impinging on a number of aspects of one of our client's businesses. On the other hand I can honestly say that at the outset we had no knowledge of The Friend or indeed the possibility that his activities and the attacks on County View were in any way related to our investigations. The possibility emerged after I arrived in England and following some research by Zara.

'Although not as close to the various attacks on County View as you all are, I am coming to the conclusion that there is a strong link. Even if this Mr Ahearne is involved I can't believe that he is a significant factor. In fact I can't help agreeing with you that he's probably telling the truth.'

Marvin rejoined the discussion. 'I'm becoming more and more convinced that there is a close connection. Mr Cartwright knows I have extremely good information which indicates that money has flowed from the Far East to Switzerland and then on to O'Connor.' At this Benny, who'd sat surprisingly quietly for him, interrupted.

'One of the interesting things that seems to be emerging is that O'Connor has been gambling very heavily over the last couple of months and has mainly been losing.'

Percy supported this view. 'It's not only Benny who has given us that information,' he told Hogan. 'One of County View's owners is a major bookmaker who has recently purchased an Irish bookmaking company and consequently has good information about significant players and major gambles in that country. From different sources he has heard the same, and also that the main bets on the winning horse at Ayr came from that side of the Irish Sea.'

It was now Jackson's turn to intervene. 'With my old-fashioned policeman's hat on, what I can't come to terms with is the motive behind all these various activities. I can't help feeling that if we could figure that out we'd be well on the way to thinking of a more direct avenue to explore.

251

At the moment we have a lot of supposition and very little evidence. What we do have is strictly circumstantial.'

It was clear that they all felt the same. At that moment Moira opened the door and in came Roddy and Jay.

Jay recognized Ross as the man with the recorder and notebook. He said nothing but was aware of Hogan's slight smile as their eyes met.

Introductions were made and Percy summarized the conversation that had taken place so far. It was Roddy who spoke first of the two newcomers.

'Well, it seems to me that there are still two courses of action open to us. Clearly we need to confirm as soon as possible that Ahearne's story is true. If it is, we need to find out as much as we can about the source of O'Connor's money which may in itself lead us to some idea of what's behind all this.'

Marvin interrupted him. 'I know that Percy touched on it briefly, but there is no doubt at all that the money in Switzerland is arriving from Singapore. So far we've been unable to trace the mysterious syndicate that appears to be behind this, but there's every reason to believe that it's probably the same source which was responsible for buying the four young horses in New Zealand.' Both Jackson and Hogan nodded in agreement.

'The other point,' continued Roddy, 'is that we should now make a real effort to find out as much as we can on the ground in Hong Kong and Singapore. I'm sure my father-in-law will put his resources behind it. Mr Cartwright has already said Marvin can spend as much time in the area as seems sensible, and hopefully, Mr Hogan, you'll be able to help us as well.'

Percy assured the group that as far as he was concerned Marvin had no other more pressing responsibilities at the moment, and they all looked at Hogan.

'Well, I think I need just another two or three days to clear up some areas of interest I have here, but then I'm very happy to move over to Singapore. Zara will stay here and let us know anything she finds out. By us, I'm including everyone round this table, although I think it would

252

be more sensible if she channelled any news to you, Mr Cartwright, and you as well naturally,' he said addressing Jackson.

So far Jay had been sitting quietly listening. 'I've no argument with anything that's been suggested,' he finally said, 'but from my own point of view the priority should be to discover who's behind the attack on Danny. Although we have no reason to believe it would happen again, unless we know what's behind it, and more importantly who's behind it, we can hardly count on that. It would also give a clue as to whether any of the rest of us are in danger.'

Jackson nodded vigorously. 'I'm visiting Pat McKenna in Dublin tomorrow. I know he's deeply concerned about the whole situation, even though the attack on Danny took place in England. He is, after all, a citizen of his country.'

Jay continued. 'My other question is, do you feel it's necessary for us to increase security at County View – or indeed for any of us to take additional measures to ensure our own safety?'

Jackson spoke again. 'There's little doubt that the activities and the violence have escalated. Under the circumstances I believe there should be more full-time security at County View and I think there should also be a properly trained security guard on your horseboxes, particularly if they're travelling any distance.'

It was then Benny's turn. 'I can guarantee that my brothers and some of my contacts can look after Jay and his family plus Roddy and Howard,' he said, 'and I assume that you're pretty well protected anyway, Mr Cartwright.'

'Well, not to this extent,' Percy admitted, smiling wryly. 'Francis always drives me everywhere but he's not exactly a full-blown bodyguard. As you know, Marvin's in charge of our security and I'm confident that he can ensure that I'm not left unduly exposed.' He paused and looked round the table. 'Do you think that perhaps we're overreacting?'

Jackson spoke firmly. 'No. Definitely not. There's been one attempted murder, and we don't know what else this particular gang is capable of or, indeed, may have already been responsible for. We're constantly reminded, as far as terrorists are concerned, that vigilance is essential. I can assure you, gentlemen, the same is true for all of you here.' Turning to Hogan, he said, 'If you don't mind me saying so, sir, I think you should ensure that your daughter is protected as well.'

Zara started to protest, but her father silenced her. 'It will be done,' he said simply.

Percy looked round the table. 'Is there anything else you feel we should discuss this evening?'

No one spoke. 'In that case, I suggest that you, Mr Hogan, and Zara of course, might like to be Marvin's guests at dinner. Over a meal, I suggest you plan what you feel would be the most sensible course of action when you all get to the Far East. Can you make it?' he asked Benny, who immediately agreed.

'I'd like to be included in that dinner,' Roddy chipped in.

'You'd be more than welcome,' replied the Australian.

Turning to Jackson, Percy said, 'Would you like to join Jay and myself for dinner?'

'I would, but I think I ought to get back to the office and arrange to see McKenna tomorrow. Well, gentlemen and madam,' he said, smiling to Zara, 'I think that's all that I can add to this evening. Does everyone have my direct line here?' Everybody nodded with the exception of Benny who looked slightly uncomfortable. 'Of course you haven't, Benny,' said Jackson. 'Well, I think this might be an occasion where we both turn a blind eye to which side of the fence we normally sit.' With a broad grin he took out a card, wrote his direct line on the back of it and gave it to Benny. With a cheery wave, he walked across to the door followed by Percy. 'Don't worry, I can find my own way out.'

'I'm sure you can, but you won't get through our security doors without my card.' Jackson laughed and bid everyone farewell.

As he got to the door, Percy turned and said, 'Jay, I think you might give everybody a well-earned drink,' and handed him a key. 'Believe it or not I'm miserable enough to lock the drinks cabinet if I'm not here.'

There was a round of chuckles as he walked out and Jay, with Benny's help, dispensed drinks from Percy's lavishly stocked cabinet. Their host rejoined them and after a few minutes of relatively light-hearted conversation they all left for their separate meals. The conversation would almost certainly centre on the intriguing but worrying events which had been discussed in the previous two hours.

Marvin took his little group to Rules in Maiden Lane, one of his favourite haunts. They were given a corner table, although the restaurant was always so noisy it would be very difficult for anybody to overhear their conversation. The food was ordered. Benny and Hogan opted for lager, and Marvin chose a bottle of good Chilean red wine.

Interestingly enough, it was Benny who opened the conversation. 'I might be called cynical,' he said, 'but what if The Friend is lying? That means our concentration mainly on the Far East connection could be well off target.'

'I'd thought of that too,' agreed Hogan, 'but of course I don't know this character. On the other hand he seems to have convinced some fairly cynical senior policemen. Although I don't think we should close our minds to that possibility, I still have a feeling that we should concentrate on the Far Eastern link but at the same time try to dig out this apparent Irish connection to both the Swiss bank and O'Connor.'

Roddy spoke. 'There's merit in what both of you say, but there's another consideration which we haven't really looked at. What if O'Connor's not really involved in this? It would appear that he hasn't been directly involved in any of the incidents and he certainly doesn't have a criminal or even shady reputation. It seems to me that he's probably a pawn in somebody else's game.'

Marvin agreed. 'It seems to me that it's really important to try and discover if there is someone in Ireland who is channelling the money to the Swiss account and if so where he's getting it from in the Far East. All our enquiries so far would indicate it comes from Singapore. I believe this, plus the pretty clear connection between the New Zealand incident and Hong Kong, would indicate that the money is coming from there and that for some unknown reason County View has been targeted. So far none of us can think what that reason could be. If it was simple revenge by The Friend on Danny in particular and County View in general it would be understandable, but I think we all agree that Ahearne doesn't have the financial resources to back what's been going on. Even though he's got a lot of criminal contacts it would have been difficult for him to mastermind this plot from behind bars.'

Somewhat reluctantly, Benny agreed before making another interesting point. 'We now have a number of indications that things are wrong in the O'Connor set-up. He is uncharacteristically bad-tempered, and even more telling is that he's suddenly started to gamble and lose in a way that seems also to be out of character. I think it's all bloody odd and my instinct says that he's having money problems.'

Marvin nodded. 'I think that looks a real runner. Give me a couple of days and I'm sure I can find out if there's been any interruption in the money flow from Switzerland to Lambourn.'

For the first time Zara spoke. 'I haven't said anything before but I've been working with two of my colleagues on tracing the money back from the account in Switzerland to Singapore. I think we're very close to cracking it.'

They all looked at her with attention. 'That could well be the key to unlock a number of these closed doors,' Roddy said.

'It would be a great step forward,' Ross agreed, 'but it's almost bound to be in some fictitious name. That's why I think that Marvin and I need to get there and do as much digging as we can on the spot.'

They could all see the wisdom of this proposal. For the next half-hour they took stock of the situation from every angle but didn't really come up with any new ideas.

By 10.30 they were all pretty tired and split up. Hogan and Zara shared a cab, and he asked the driver to go directly to his flat. 'I'd like you to stay over with me,' he told his daughter. 'There's a couple of things I want to talk to you about, including making sure that not only you but your offices are well protected until this investigation is completed.'

Somewhat reluctantly she agreed, but she knew her father well enough to realize there were occasions when you simply didn't argue with him.

Getting back to his flat, he opened the door which had three locks on it, one of which had been added when he took possession. As they'd all been very modest in what they'd drunk at dinner, he suggested they might have a nightcap. She slightly surprised him by asking for a malt whisky on ice as he was known to disapprove of diluting single malts in any way. He opted for a brandy. When they were relaxed with their drinks, he reminded her of the Johnny Tang situation and said that, against his normal policy, he felt like calling him. He then threw a question at her which took her completely by surprise.

'Do you think that Gavin Tang was using his acquisition of this boat-building company to screen his real reason for being over here? It looks entirely genuine and seems to have satisfied his father, but if you look at some of the factors they could all make young master Tang a prime suspect.'

'Explain.'

'First of all, he's interested in horse racing. Next, we know he gambles and sometimes quite recklessly, although never to our knowledge on this scale. As I said, he's always been interested in racing but this interest seems to have grown of late. He's also recently developed an interest in bloodstock. Next, he almost certainly has the clout to finance this sort of operation if he's been clever enough to siphon off some of the profits from the many companies he now runs. Last, and in some ways from my point of view the most telling, is that I find it extraordinary that he didn't tell his father and his brother about this impending UK deal. It's always been a very tightly knit family, and to my knowledge there's never been a secret between any of them. This of course includes Jerline, who we understand was shattered to find that Gavin had been operating in the UK without at least calling her. I know I'm repeating myself, but although his explanation sounded really plausible, I'm beginning to have my doubts.'

'OK,' his daughter replied, 'but we've all been saying that the motive is probably critical to understanding why these incidents have taken place. What possible motive could Gavin have for financing a little-known Irish trainer and then following this up with a number of attacks, including one attempted murder?'

Her father stood up. 'I'm damned if I can work it out,' he said, as he restlessly walked up and down the room. 'There's one other thing that worries me.'

'What's that?'

'Johnny Tang said Sammy Cox had confided that some important businessman was somehow involved in a big drugs operation. That just doesn't ring true with any of the Tangs. I know from time to time they've been ruthless in their dealings, but there's never been a whiff of anything illegal, let alone connected with narcotics. Sometimes I wonder if there are a number of entirely separate strands which we're trying to weave together but which in reality have no connection whatsoever.'

'I can follow your thinking, but on the other hand there are so many coincidences if that were true. God, if only we knew what that poor man Cox was going to tell Johnny. That might have been a huge help.'

'I agree. Come on, we're not going to get any further tonight. Let's sleep on it and make some plans over breakfast.' He got up, kissed his daughter goodnight, double-locked his front door and put the two chains on it as well. He was quietly laughing at himself as he made his way to his bedroom. 'I must be getting soft in my old age.'

Meanwhile, at the Turf Club, Percy and Jay were also reviewing the situation.

They had really found little to add to the conclusions that had been reached at the meeting, although Percy was becoming more and more adamant about the need for security for all of them, and in particular at County View.

'What do you think of Hogan?' he enquired.

'He doesn't say a lot,' Jay replied, 'but I suspect that he and his daughter are extremely good at what they do, and Harvey certainly seems to have a high regard for their reputation.'

'Yes,' Percy agreed, 'but two things slightly puzzle me. Hamish has been surprisingly quiet about the whole issue and seemed reluctant to discuss it, and in particular Johnny Tang, when I spoke to him. Similarly, I was surprised that somebody in Hogan's position seemed to know so little about Hamish and his business empire.'

'Neither of those two points had occurred to me, but on the other hand I guess I haven't been as close to some of these developments as you have,' Jay commented. 'Clearly the whole thing is most worrying, but as I said earlier my overwhelming concern is the possibility of another attack on Danny, plus the effect it's going to have on him when he learns there's doubt about The Friend's involvement.'

'You're right, but I don't see there's anything else we can do.'

He noticed that Jay was yawning. 'Come on, young man,' he said, getting up. 'We'd both better get to our beds. I guess you'll be up at the crack of dawn to get back to County View, and I don't suppose that I'm going to be in the office much after 7.30 tomorrow morning. I've got Francis outside so we'll drop you off at Hays Mews.'

In the companionable silence which comes from years of friendship, they sat in the back of the car until they reached Hays Mews. Percy told Francis to stay where he was until they saw Jay safely into his front door. Francis then drove his exhausted boss back to his home.

As Percy had forecast, Jay was up early and back at County View just before seven. Supervising the horses' routine with Jed took his mind off the conversations and the problems posed the night before. He was fully relaxed by the time he went in for lunch. On the way his phone buzzed showing there was a text awaiting him. It was a message from Jackson. 'Have news. Call me when alone. Harvey.'

Although anxious to learn what the policeman had to say, he had a quiet lunch with Eva, taking the opportunity to bring her up to date with the discussions of the previous evening. She was still worried, but glad that real action was being taken. Percy's operation at this end had her full confidence, as did Hamish Tang's in Hong Kong and Singapore.

Desperately trying to avoid any sign of anxiety, Jay shared a pot of coffee with her after lunch, before making an excuse to wander out into the yard. He jumped into the Land Rover and drove up the gallops as if checking the going, before coming to a halt and calling Jackson. The policeman answered immediately.

'Vanda's little friend, Mae, has spilt the beans. As soon as we offered her protection she admitted that Jimmy had tried to set you up, and also revealed that a number of the girls working for Jimmy were indeed illegal immigrants. She named them and was able to tell us where several were actually living and working. His attempt to frame you was already enough to arrest him, but along with the five illegal immigrants we can now pin on him we've got him well and truly nailed. He's already under arrest, and I'm sure we'll get one or two of his smaller fish in our net too. I have a feeling that Mr Yong may not be made of particularly stern stuff when we get him under heavy interrogation. I'm very hopeful he'll be able to help us with Hogan's and Marvin's investigation in Singapore and Hong Kong.'

'Wow, that really is good news,' Jay enthused.

'I'm going to let everybody know but I'm clearly not going to say how we got the lead on to Jimmy Yong. We'll make sure young Mae is well protected. Evidently she has relations in Italy and we're going to see whether we can get the Italian authorities to agree to her taking cover there. Mind you, it may not be too easy for a call girl! We've told Vanda that her friend will be looked after, but we haven't let her into any other secrets. You might like to call and thank her. That at least won't do any harm.'

Jay thanked Harvey for his prompt and helpful actions and rang off. He phoned Vanda, not quite sure if she'd be available at this time in the afternoon. Almost immediately he heard her distinctive but attractive voice on the line. He explained as much of what had happened as Harvey had agreed, and thanked her sincerely for her help.

'I'd invite you to have a drink with me to celebrate,' she giggled, 'but that might be misconstrued in more than one quarter and I'd hate to compromise your good name.'

'I'd love to meet you again but I think that perhaps discretion is the better part of valour,' Jay agreed. 'Thank you again, Vanda. You've been a huge help.'

Turning the Land Rover round, he drove back to the house and told Eva the good news he'd received from Harvey, with the suitable editing he'd agreed with the policeman. Naturally Eva was delighted.

She was still beaming as he phoned Roddy, Howard and Benny.

'He's a good bloke, that Jackson,' announced Benny rather reluctantly, 'even if he is a bloody copper.'

Jay laughed. 'Well, he's better on our side than against us.'

'I'll agree there,' the East Ender replied in a more generous tone. 'Happy Christmas. I may see you at Kempton.'

'Let me know and I'll have badges for you.'

'Thanks, boss. Love to Max and Eva.'

For a change Jay actually felt better and realized that he was looking forward to Christmas with his family and the exciting racing in the days immediately afterwards.

Chapter Twenty-Six

Every year it was the same. One day it was November and the next Christmas. A council of war considered all options and opted for two Kempton runners. Rampant Raider would run in the King George. This had got Frank Malone in a state of great excitement. Pewter Queen was going to run in the two mile five furlong handicap hurdle. Her last run had been at Newbury four weeks earlier and she finished fourth. This resulted in the handicapper being rather lenient and dropping her five pounds. At the time of making the entries Jed, who had known her since she was a foal, was not his usually enthusiastic self. However, two days before declarations were to be made he told Jay that he hadn't seen 'the Queen' as well for over a year. Needless to say Howard was extremely excited about the prospect of one of his two favourite horses running at Kempton on Boxing Day.

The staff were going to be well spread around the country. Jed was going to Wincanton where Wild Sultan was running in a £15,000 two and a half mile handicap hurdle, and Freddy was off to Wetherby with Percy and Understated, who was entered in a £20,000 novice handicap steeplechase.

On the 28th Jack the Lad was going to run in the Welsh Grand National, My Sweet Colleen was entered in the juvenile hurdle which, with £30,000 to the winner, was bound to be extremely competitive. Frank's and Lance's horses would both be there.

As always on Christmas Day, a few of the stable staff with strong family commitments would have the day off, but all of them bar two would be back for Boxing Day. On Christmas Day everybody worked flat out to be finished by half past twelve so that they could set off for the now traditional Christmas lunch at the Shepherd's Rest.

The horses running on Boxing Day and the 28th received special attention, but the rest were given quick, light work. Hansie, who had decided not to go back to South Africa for the holiday, had volunteered to help out on Christmas Day and Boxing Day and moved into the Shepherd's Rest for the whole holiday. On Boxing Day Chris and Amanda had also volunteered their services. Amanda was now past any heavy work but insisted that she was more than capable of grooming the horses before they left for the races. The horsebox would be leaving directly after the Christmas lunch as driving to Wetherby on a bank holiday was not in the best interests of the horses. Freddy would be there to ensure all was well.

Lunch was a happy occasion, with spirits all high following a good run of winners and placed horses in the previous few weeks. Harry Solomons had done even better and was now £150,000 ahead of Jay in the Trainers Championship. Percy, who seemed rather fixated on O'Connor's results, would keep Jay and Jed up to date with his position in the Trainers League Table, almost as if neither of them ever looked at the racing pages themselves. He had a reasonable number of winners, but so far any real big prize money had eluded him. There was no likelihood of him challenging for one of the top places. The nearest contender to Harry and Jay was Neville Gethin who had a very high win to runner strike rate and was now only £120,000 behind Jay. These three knew that it only needed a few winners over the Christmas/New Year period for the picture to change significantly, and the likelihood was that the Cheltenham Festival and the meeting at Aintree at the end of the season would seal the contest.

On Boxing Day Jed and Cathy left early for Wincanton, driven by Hansie, who insisted he would be more helpful doing this than going to Kempton. Jay gratefully accepted. Although not far away, it was not an easy journey, and the horsebox had left before them. Freddy had phoned from Wetherby to say that all was fine and that Wild Sultan had eaten up well and the going looked just about perfect. Eva, Jay, Chris and Amanda took the helicopter to Kempton. On their arrival Jay, as usual, went first to the stables to check on his runners, and then to the weighing room for a final precautionary look at the declarations. His mind set at rest on both counts, he joined his wife, Chris and Amanda in the restaurant, along with Howard and his wife Bubbles. The last arrivals were Frank Malone and Lance. Both owners were keen to know Jay's view of their horses' chances.

Jay again said that Pewter Queen was probably in the best form she'd been for over a year, and that the handicapper had been kind to her. On the other hand, like the rest of the card it would be a competitive race.

Turning to Frank and Lance, he attempted to play down the bookmaker's enthusiasm. 'Rampant Raider is a very good horse, of that there's no doubt, and he's certainly very well, but remember we're up against Classie Vintage, last year's Cheltenham Gold Cup winner, and Rolling Rock, who was a very close runner-up. The going will suit all three horses, and as you know the other two are three and four to one, and your horse is five. The odds reflect how open the race is.'

'I see that O'Connor's got a horse in it. What are its chances?' Lance asked Jay.

'Well, to be honest I'm rather surprised it's running. It's a good handicapper but it's hardly in this class and perhaps he's running it for the prize money which is still good for fourth or fifth. Incidentally, I notice he's brought a jockey over from Ireland who rode for him quite a bit over there.'

They turned their attention to the food. Everyone, except Jay, tucked in heartily. On these big occasions, he had no great appetite. He also settled for sparkling water, although he didn't have to drive home. 'I'll join you in something stronger,' he promised the party, 'if we've got something to celebrate at the end of the afternoon.'

They watched the preliminary races, which included a very high class novice chase and an equally competitive hurdle. Harry Solomons won the chase and the £40,000 going to the winner, while Neville Gethin picked up the £60,000 novice hurdle with a horse that showed real class. Jay smiled to himself, wondering what Danny's comments would have been if he'd been there with them. He was probably following everything from South Africa and was cursing County View's two chief rivals.

The time came for Jay to go and saddle Rampant Raider and he was accompanied by Frank, Lance and Chris. The rest of the party made their way to the owners' and trainers' section of the grandstand.

Frank's horse was a real professional, and although interested in his surroundings was showing no signs of pre-race nerves. He was soon saddled and strolling to the parade ring. He walked around on his toes but showed no sign of sweating up or being fazed by the vast crowd. Understandably Frank was getting very excited. Jay, of course, was familiar with his two Gold Cup rivals, but took a bit more interest in O'Connor's horse as he had not seen him run before. He was undoubtedly a good-looking animal, and, as always with O'Connor's horses, he looked in the peak of condition and was well turned out. Jay glanced at the trainer and his Irish jockey and felt there was a good deal of tension in both of them. Their conversation was very brief and there was no sign of the owner.

The bell rang and Jay legged David Sparrow up, wishing him good luck. There was no need to remind him that the plan was to be in the middle of the field on the first circuit and to move up to third place as they turned for home. With three fences to jump in the home straight, finishing speed was of the essence particularly as the Kempton course was one of the flattest in the country.

The race started at a fast but sensible pace, which was to be expected of such a high class field. The runner-up in the previous year's Gold Cup was in the lead leaving the back straight, and the reigning champion had moved into second a length behind. To Jay's surprise, O'Connor's horse was on the rails inside the Raider and was being urged to make an effort a surprisingly long way out. As they were about to leave the final bend, O'Connor's horse started to swerve to the left, carrying Rampant Raider with him. The action clearly took Sparrow by surprise and he found himself travelling at almost 45 degrees to his line while the leading pair gained a good seven or eight lengths. Keeping his head, Sparrow checked his horse while O'Connor's horse continued careering across the track. Instantly Sparrow moved up on the other side and gave Frank's horse two firm cracks behind the saddle. Approaching the second last he'd made up a lot of the ground but Jay was wondering if the additional effort so soon in the race was going to prove costly. Rampant Raider continued to make progress and was now behind Rolling Rock, the Cheltenham Gold Cup runner-up. However, Classie Vintage had gained a good length and a half as he jumped the last. Sparrow sat patiently on the Raider as he jumped the final fence and moved into second place. He hit his horse twice behind the saddle but to no avail. The champion won by a length and a half, with Frank's horse coming second, three-quarters of a length in front of the third. After the erratic running in the closing stages, O'Connor's horse finished a rather tame seventh. Frank looked at Jay. 'Well, what the hell do you think about that?' he asked.

'I'm not at all sure,' said Jay, 'but there's bound to be an enquiry.' No sooner had he said this than an announcement to that effect came over the public address system.

'Come on,' said Jay. 'Even though we may have lost the race unluckily, your horse ran a blinder so let's go and enjoy that.' Reaching the unsaddling enclosure, a really crestfallen Sparrow was off the horse and undoing the girths.

'I really couldn't do anything, guv'nor,' he explained. 'I'm really sorry, Frank.'

'Hell, it's not your fault,' Frank replied before Jay could say a word. 'It was that bloody jockey, or do you think the horse just did something odd of its own volition?'

'I really couldn't tell,' was the answer. 'I was concentrating so much on the horses in front and getting into the right position, that the move took me completely by surprise.'

'I'd be amazed if it didn't,' Jay said sympathetically. 'It really wasn't your fault, David,' he said. 'Now go off and weigh in.'

'What do you think's going to happen?'

'Well, obviously, whatever the stewards decide can't affect the placings, and I guess when they review the video they'll have to decide whether or not it was deliberate or accidental.'

'What do you think?' Lance asked him.

'I wouldn't like to guess, but we know enough about O'Connor to suspect that he wouldn't take losing the race lying down if he could do anything about it.' Almost immediately the expected announcement was made that places remained unchanged. Jay walked across to the weighing room where he was met by the stewards' secretary.

'Tough luck,' he said quietly, 'but the incident has been referred to the Jockey Club.'

'Thanks for the information, but it doesn't help us a lot, does it?' Jay said wryly but with a smile.

'I know,' said the secretary, 'but I'd better not say anything else.'

Needless to say, when Jay got back to the party his group was agog with the incident. Frank and Lance were getting very sympathetic reactions from the rest. Howard was bursting with indignation and was sounding off about O'Connor. Jay grasped his arm firmly. 'Quiet, Howard,' he said. 'I don't want you getting into any trouble by making completely unsubstantiated accusations.' Howard looked at him and nodded. 'Come on, relax for ten minutes, and let's concentrate on what we hope will be a successful run by Pewter Queen.'

Frank bought a couple of bottles of champagne. 'OK, we came second,' he said, 'but that's not too bad in the King George, is it?'

Jay refused the proffered glass but added, 'I promise

you I'll join you after the last,' he said, 'irrespective of what happens.'

Twenty minutes before Pewter Queen's race, Jay collected the saddle and went to the saddling boxes. Howard was now in a state of considerable agitation, but Pewter Queen showed her experience and behaved in her usual relaxed and interested manner. By the time she was saddled and in the parade ring, the whole party had gathered to see the beautiful grey mare. Bubbles had injesisted that Frank and Lance join them. The instructions had been simple. 'If the pace is good until the crown of the final bend, you can wait till you're between the last two hurdles if you want to,' Jay reminded Sparrow. 'As you know, she's got a hell of a good finish. On the other hand, if it's a dawdle don't be frightened of going up and making it as you go down the back straight the second time. She's one of these rare horses that has stamina and a kick at the end.' Sparrow nodded. Then he was legged up and on his way to the start with the fifteen other runners in this valuable handicap.

'Well, she'll be easy to see,' Howard pointed out as they watched the field canter past the stands. Pewter Queen was the only grey.

Passing the stands with a circuit to go, the whole field was intact, which was not surprising as they were all seasoned handicappers. The fifteen of them had won thirty-seven races between them, and Pewter Queen was joint top with seven wins to her credit, plus she was the only Cheltenham Festival winner in the field. Entering the back straight the final time, it was clear that the pace had steadied. Jay was willing Sparrow to make a forward move, and almost as if by telepathy the lad gave the mare a slap on the shoulder to which she immediately responded. As she moved into the lead, the horse which had been lying fourth accelerated and passed her. This suited Jay's plans admirably. Pewter Queen was able to drop in a length and a half behind. She and the leader started to draw away from the rest of the field. Howard was getting seriously excited. Entering the finishing straight, the two of them had drawn away from the rest except for one big chestnut who had emerged from the pack and was now setting off in hot pursuit of the leading pair. Jay studied the horse carefully and realized it was the top weight. Without saying anything to Howard, he was fairly confident that if all went well Pewter Queen would see off his challenge. The big question was how much had the leader got left in its tank?

Jumping the second last, Sparrow still had Pewter Queen a length behind the leader, but the chestnut was now only two lengths behind the grey and was closing. Going into the last, all three jumped well in the same order but with only a length between first and third. Here Sparrow got lower in the saddle and gave Pewter Queen one crack. She responded immediately with the acceleration which she'd shown so often in her heyday. She forged clear of her rivals who were left fighting it out for second place. Howard was beside himself with joy, and Jay could hear Bubbles screaming on the step behind him. As soon as Pewter Queen passed the winning post, they all left the stand as fast as they could, ready to greet their star. David Sparrow was grinning from ear to ear as he was led in by Holly, Pewter Queen's groom. Her grin was equally expansive. Howard enthusiastically patted Sparrow's boot and gave the girl a big kiss on the cheek as they pulled up in front of the winner's sign. Bubbles embarrassed the young jockey by kissing him on both cheeks as soon as he dismounted. Very quickly they were surrounded by press photographers who took photographs of Howard and Bubbles with the mare, David with the mare, and then David and Jay with the mare. 'Off you go,' Jay instructed the young lad, 'and don't forget to weigh in properly.'

'Honest, I won't,' he replied, and trotted off.

Turning to Howard, he said, 'Right, I'll have that glass of champagne now,' as he watched the mare being led off to the dope box. On their way to the bar, both he and Howard received numerous congratulations. Jay watched Howard and Frank work their way up to the bar arguing about who was going to buy the champagne. Jay glanced past them and was met by a ferocious scowl from Quentin O'Connor. If looks could kill they certainly would have then. Jay ignored him and turned back to chat to his very happy group. The two owners returned armed with handfuls of glasses and two bottles of champagne. The corks were quickly popped and glasses filled. Cheerful toasts were drunk to the two horses and a somewhat embarrassed Jay. Frank was the first to say, 'And let's not forget the rest of the staff behind this great afternoon.' As the initial excitement died down, Howard looked at Jay.

'What do we do with her now?' he enquired. Jay thought for a moment.

'Well, Howard, you've always wanted to breed from her. She's won a really good race on a really big day. If you're going to breed from her this year, she needs to be covered within the next couple of months. Frankly, she's been such a fantastic mare for you, my instinct would be to retire her now. Let her relax and then send her off to stud in a week's time. All being well, in three or four years' time we'll be toasting her offspring.'

Howard turned to Bubbles. 'What do you think, babe?' he asked.

'I think that's the right thing to do. If she got hurt in the next race we'd never forgive ourselves.'

Howard turned back to Jay. 'Deal done,' he said. 'What's the next step?'

'Well,' said Jay, 'you'd better come down sometime in the next week or two and we'll have fun deciding which stallion to send her to.'

Howard smiled broadly. The conversation drifted on for a while before he, Frank and Lance made their farewells, and Jay, Eva, Chris and Amanda walked back to the helicopter. Turning on his mobile, Jay found a message from a very excited Freddy who said that Understated had won with great ease. There was also a recorded message from Jed which said that unfortunately Wild Sultan had fallen at the last when disputing the lead. Happily both he and the jockey had emerged unscathed.

Although they were all disappointed about the Sultan,

the rest of the afternoon had been so successful that spirits were bubbling on the way back to County View. Eva had prepared in advance a simple supper in the kitchen so they'd all be there to greet the runners and staff when they returned.

Later that evening Frank phoned but not to talk about Rampant Raider as Jay had assumed.

'O'Connor had a lot of money on us not winning. That must be the reason for that bastard jockey's antics.'

'Steady. You may well be right but let the authorities deal with it.'

'OK,' was the reluctant reply. 'But I could have both of them hurt.'

'Come on, Frank. Let's not drop to their level. We've got a great horse and will have much more fun enjoying him in the future. O'Connor's a rather sad person at the moment.'

'I suppose you're right. Anyway, thanks for a great day.'

'Any time. It's dead easy.' Both laughed knowing it was far from the case.

The next morning spirits were high. Wild Sultan was none the worse for his fall and Percy was on cloud nine with Understated's win.

Crossing to the yard, Jay was surprised to see there had been a really hard frost. A cold night had been forecast but not this bad. Jed saw him and hurried across. 'We won't be able to use the grass. It's like concrete up there.' He pointed to the gallops. 'I've got the chain harrows on the all weathers. It's the best we can do.'

Jay reluctantly agreed. At lunchtime he called Chepstow. The report was gloomy. 'It's unraceable now,' he was told, 'and unless there's a thaw tonight we won't race. The chances are very slim, Jay.' The groundsman was not happy at the prospect of his top jumping fixture being lost.

Jay thanked him, told Jed and phoned Frank. 'The result of the inspection should be on Radio 5 Live before 8 a.m. but don't expect miracles,' he told the bookmaker. They chatted for a while about Rampant Raider and Jay promised to report if he heard anything earlier about racing being on or off.

Jay and Jed sat in the kitchen at 7.45. As feared, the racing at Chepstow and at all the turf courses was abandoned.

Max had a great day playing with his new toys, and in particular watching a DVD of the previous month's World Badminton Championships.

'Well, at least we had a decent Boxing Day,' Eva consoled him.

Chapter Twenty-Seven

Jackson had a call from Pat McKenna in Dublin.

'We've had another interesting development,' he announced. 'A young woman called Maureen O'Casey has been to see us. It appears that she's been Daly's girlfriend for the last two years and is concerned about how she's going to live now that he's behind bars. She's looking for a deal. She claims that she has heard Daly discussing various criminal activities over the last eighteen months, including agreeing to undertake the hit on Danny, and she's prepared to give us information which will lead to the man who she claims has been paying Daly for these activities. As you know, we've got modest sums of money we can pay to informers but she's looking for something substantial. I wondered if your racing friends might be prepared to fund this on the clear understanding that it's no arrest, no cash.'

'How much is she looking for?'

'A hundred thousand euros,' was the reply.

Jackson paused before answering. 'I'll speak to them and see what they say. Do you think she's genuine?'

'I think she's both worried and avaricious,' McKenna replied, 'and she's also talking of selling her story to the papers if this man is successfully captured and convicted. I didn't think it was up to me to point out that this might be a very dangerous course of action if he's already responsible for at least one attempted murder.'

'I agree,' said Jackson, 'but at this stage that's up to her. Right, I'll call you back as soon as I've got some news.'

He phoned Percy with the information. His response

was positive. 'My company would do this. It's all part of our genuine investigation into the New Zealand crime and could obviously have much wider implications than that. Go ahead.'

Jackson rang McKenna with the news. 'I'll get her in today if I can and come back to you as soon as I've finished speaking to her,' he promised.

Jackson had barely got through his front door that evening when the phone rang and an excited McKenna was on the line. 'She's spilt the beans in a big way,' he announced. 'Evidently, Daly has been acting as a heavy, including some serious physical violence other than that to Danny. She doesn't know the man's name but she took the precaution of writing his telephone number down which Daly had been silly enough not to clear from his mobile. She did this on three occasions so knows that it's been the same man. More importantly, she heard Daly negotiating the actual figure for the Newbury attack. He was obviously very excited when the call was concluded, left his phone on the table and went round the corner to buy himself a bottle of Jameson's whiskey. Two days later he left Ireland, and two days after that the attack took place at Newbury. We've traced these calls and they all go to one subscriber. Guess who?'

Jackson thought before answering. 'My money would be on Ahearne or O'Connor.' There was a chuckle at the other end.

'I wish I'd had a bet with you. It's a man called Kieran Hanagan. We know he's a big-time financier and we've been deeply suspicious that some of his activities are not legal. We've never been able to pin anything on him.'

'What are you going to do next?'

'We're going to check this information very carefully and then we'll bring him in for questioning. We'll do that after we've got both a written statement and a videoed statement from Miss O'Casey. We don't want her backtracking.'

'Can I tell the County View team?'

275

'Let's wait until we've got it sewn up,' replied McKenna, 'and then I can see no reason why you shouldn't.'

The following morning Jay left Jed to supervise a schooling session and returned to the house. Hal had phoned from New York and needed Jay to call back as soon as possible. The subsequent conversation was short and to the point.

'My friend Fergus Brady has spoken to a number of his contacts in Ireland and several came up with the same name. It's a guy who has operated in the financial area for many years and is very well connected but has a few question marks hanging over him. His name is Kieran Hanagan and it seems that he may well be involved in money laundering at a very high level. One of Fergus's contacts has done business with the man and it was always above board, but he too has heard questionable rumours. He gave Fergus an introduction and the man's telephone number.

'The day before yesterday Fergus phoned Hanagan and explained that he had a large sum of money which he would like turned into a readily transported and internationally accepted commodity of some sort. The money was in Ireland which was the reason Fergus was contacting him. At first he was very wary and said he'd call Fergus back. Evidently he phoned Fergus's friend who vouched for him and implied that Fergus had been known to sail close to the wind. Yesterday Fergus got a call and was asked whether or not diamonds would be a suitable medium for him. He also asked how much Fergus was looking to invest. He was not at all fazed when told it was in the region of half a million dollars. He promised to come back to Fergus within the next few days.

'I don't know whether that's of any help, Jay, but it occurs to me it's worth some of your investigator friends looking into it.'

'You're an absolute star,' Jay told him. 'I'll let you know as soon as I have any news.'

He passed the information on to Percy and Jackson and left them to use it as they each thought fit.

Jackson considered for a moment and then rang McKenna.

'That gives her story more credibility. Thanks a million.'

'Can I let my lot know?'

'Hell, Harvey. They've given us all they know all the time. This latest from the States helps us. As long as they keep it to themselves, and not a word to the press, it's fine by me.'

'Thanks. It does seem the jigsaw is beginning to fall into place.'

In London, Hogan had a call from Johnny Tang.

'I'm completely safe,' his colleague assured him, 'and not even you would guess where I am. I do, however, have some news for you. I phoned Ralph Murray, my police friend, in Singapore and asked him if there had been any further developments in tracing the murderer or murderers. He feigned no knowledge of what I was talking about and hung up. A few minutes later he called me back on what he assured me was his personal secure line. There has been a very significant development indeed. One of his informers is a man called Tim Horner, who he assures me has proved to be completely reliable in he past. Horner phoned him with some fascinating information.

'Apparently, the night when Sammy Cox disappeared and was due to meet me, he'd met Sammy in a bar that they both frequented. Sammy was rather drunk and confided to Horner that he'd got some important information about drug trafficking and that he was going to meet me later to tell me. He added in a knowing manner that I wouldn't be at all happy when I found out it related to my family. By this I can only assume it's some member of the Tang family.'

Hogan thought carefully before he replied. 'That doesn't come as a total surprise to me.' He quickly brought Johnny up to date, and told him of his suspicions that Gavin's negotiations in London with the boat-building company were quite possibly a cover for some other activity. He added that he and Marvin were about to fly to Singapore and Hong Kong.

'Would you like me to give you an introduction to Ralph Murray?' Johnny asked. 'He's completely reliable and has been a close friend of mine for many years. He's an extremely effective and loyal policeman but he knows when to be discreet. The two of you might find him very useful.'

'That would be great,' Hogan replied with enthusiasm.

'Right, have you got a pen handy? Start any conversation by saying that you're calling on behalf of the Tang Dynasty. I'll advise him of that and to expect either you or Marvin to call him.'

'Fantastic. I assume that I can contact you on this line any time from now on?'

'Absolutely,' replied Johnny. 'Would you like me to return and help you there?'

'Definitely not. You stay where you are. Keep a very low profile, but let me know if you hear anything new.'

'Sure thing,' Johnny responded, 'and I'll let Ralph know you'll be calling him. Anything else?'

'No. Just stay safe,' Hogan instructed him. 'I'll be in touch. Marvin and I are leaving the day after tomorrow.'

Chapter Twenty-Eight

They were approaching Changi Airport, and Marvin looked down in amazement at what appeared to be a huge car park. On his only previous visit to Singapore he had landed and departed at night. As the plane prepared to land he realized he was gazing at an armada of gigantic vessels. He was reminded that Singapore had, for hundreds of years, owed its success to its strategic location. Originally its importance was based on military and trading considerations. Now its enviable prosperity was the result of meticulous exploitation of Singapore's unique geographical position, making it a pivotally important trading port.

As they waited to disembark, Hogan gave him a playful nudge in the ribs.

'I hope you don't chew gum,' the Australian remarked.

Marvin was slightly surprised as he'd shown no evidence of this particular habit for well over twenty hours in the company of the Australian. 'No, but why do you ask?'

'Well, you can get arrested for throwing chewing gum on the streets in this city,' Hogan replied. He then looked a little more serious. 'I know you've only been here once before, Marvin, and very briefly. There are a few points you should be aware of. This is a very well-organized city, with strict codes of behaviour. If we have any meetings with a number of people at the same time you'll find that even very senior executives will not speak. Only the top man and a very few close associates will comment, but don't be misled. The rest will be listening attentively and will be making both written and mental notes. It's just the custom here, and often misunderstood by Europeans.'

Ross had already insisted that Marvin stayed with him at his company flat. It had three bedrooms and the two guest bedrooms were also fitted out as sitting rooms. Anyone staying there could work in peace and quiet.

'The flat is totally secure, and as we're going to work together we might as well live together,' Ross suggested. Marvin protested, not wanting to impinge on someone he barely knew, but Ross was adamant.

'It's going to be useful for both of us to be able to talk whenever anything crops up on either front. I've always felt that two heads were better than one. By the way,' he advised Marvin, 'when we arrive we will go to the Grand Hyatt where I'm well known. We'll appear to check in. The manager is an old friend. He will arrange for a car with a trusted driver to collect us from the service entrance. From there we'll go to the apartment. It's probably an unnecessary precaution at this stage but you can never be too sure. We're almost certain to be noticed by someone who recognizes one of us, so we might as well let them think we're staying there. It will give us a little more freedom for a day or two, with any luck.'

Marvin was impressed at the thoroughness of his new colleague's preparations, and nodded his acceptance.

They arrived at Scotts Road and entered the hotel as planned. The manager was on hand to greet them, having been alerted of their impending arrival by Zara in London. Events went exactly as Ross had forecast. After a warm greeting they were asked to fill in registration forms which the manager took from them. He then rather loudly suggested they went to the bar at the back of the lobby and had a drink while their luggage was taken to their rooms.

Hogan led the way to the dark and almost London club-like bar. At this time of day it was almost empty, and they sat sipping beers, recovering from the long flight. A few minutes later Ross's phone rang.

'Great,' he responded, and, finishing his beer, he beckoned Marvin to follow him.

They took the lift to the basement and Ross led Marvin to an unloading bay off the street where a black Lexus with tinted windows was waiting for them. The driver drew up outside a newish but far from ostentatious apartment block. Ross pressed the combination to enter, and they took the lift to the tenth floor. Opening the front door, he quickly switched off the various security devices which included a far from standard burglar alarm and closed circuit television. A few moments later there was a ring at the door and the driver was there with their luggage. Ross thanked him, tipped him generously, shook his hand, and he left with a broad smile.

'I can see you're well organized in this city,' observed Marvin.

'Well, I've been operating here on and off for the last fifteen years so it would be a bad show if I wasn't,' the Australian remarked. 'Now, make yourself comfortable,' he instructed Marvin, showing him to one of the two guest bedrooms. 'I'm going to have a shower and change, and then I suggest we have dinner on the waterfront.'

Refreshed, they left the apartment, jumped into a taxi and arrived at an area overlooking the harbour. Row upon row of very simple and sometimes even dilapidated restaurants nestled side by side. It was obvious that Hogan knew one of them. He walked in, spoke to the waiter, and they were led to a table. The Australian smiled at Marvin.

'Let me do the ordering,' he suggested. When the food arrived it was unlike any Chinese food that Marvin had eaten before. He was somewhat diffident about trying it but was not prepared to lose face in front of his new colleague. Much of the food was surprisingly spicy, and some of it in his eyes was not particularly visually appealing. As he tasted it, his misgivings were rapidly overcome. They both ate slowly while Hogan, without in any way pontificating, tried to brief Marvin on the way in which the Singapore culture worked.

'You'll need to realize that Hamish Tang is in many ways almost an emperor. He is at the top of a hierarchy, and in front of strangers or even other businessmen who are known to him, it would be very unusual for anybody to make a comment, and unheard of for him to be challenged in an opinion.

'We're unlikely to have problems in our dealings with Hamish and his two sons, but that may not be the case when it comes to the police force. We understand that Murray is very high up but he is not the boss. If ever he makes a decision it will be with the clear understanding that it is subject to the approval of the Chief of Police.'

The following day they were both up shortly after six o'clock and after a light breakfast they sat down at a dining table which also served as a work surface. Finding two pads, Hogan pushed one across to Marvin and produced his normal blue and red pens. 'Right, let's make a list of the contacts we want to make plus our main objectives, then we can start phoning. I suggest you leave the bedroom door open so that we can shout to each other if there's any reason we need to speak before then.'

At the top of Ross's list was Ralph Murray and hopefully his informant. Marvin was making Lewis Rees, Jeremy Glover's contact in Singapore, his priority, and then Hamish. 'I think I ought to let him know I'm here as soon as possible,' he said to Hogan. 'Percy let him know I was coming but if he found out I was here and hadn't told him he'd probably be miffed and might even think that we were working behind his back.'

Marvin then walked into his bedroom and started making his calls. An hour and a half later they compared notes over a cup of coffee.

Hogan began. 'Ralph Murray was expecting me and is pretty confident he can get both of us to meet the informant early this evening. He suggests we meet at the Hyatt where we appeared to check in. He'll arrive shortly after us and his informant should join us soon after that. The manager will guarantee that we have a private room. I've also done some checking on Michael Coleman. He's made a couple of trips to Hong Kong and back in the last ten days. What news on your front?'

'Pretty positive,' responded Marvin. 'Lewis Rees and Jeremy were not only articled at the same major accountants at the same time, but were friends at university. They've always been close, and Jeremy guarantees that Rees is totally trustworthy. Also, Percy phoned with some news. Hal Bancroft, the American, has a contact who has produced a fascinating piece of information. The man responsible for the money flowing from here to Switzerland and then on to O'Connor appears to be an Irishman called Hanagan. Jackson has passed this information on to Dublin who have long had suspicions about this man.'

'Interesting. The plot thickens.'

'Next, I had a friendly chat with Hamish and told him you and I were working together.'

'And how did he take that?'

'Very much in his stride, but Percy still has a feeling that Hamish is being rather reticent and even wonders if he knows something which he hasn't let on yet.'

'I wonder why he'd do that? There haven't been any boardroom problems, have there?'

'None that I'm aware of, and I'm sure Percy would have told me if there had been. As far as I know Hamish has always been extremely positive and very helpful on the business side of both County View and the stud operation. After all, his son-in-law is responsible for the whole of the bloodstock side.'

The Australian was thoughtful. 'If Hamish Tang lives up to his reputation it's highly unlikely he'd be involved in anything dubious, so it would be interesting to know why he's being reticent, if he is, or whether Percy's just being oversensitive.'

Marvin agreed.

'I know a man called Alex Hilton,' Hogan announced. 'He was a successful merchant banker but he made one or two, shall we say, indiscreet transactions and his reputation suffered irreparably. Although he's never been involved in drugs himself, he has hinted to me in the past that he moves money for a number of Chinese business-men who he is convinced are involved in narcotics. I helped with a few contacts when he was out of work, and he's repaid me with good inside information on some of the more shady financial activities in this part of the world. I'll give him a call and see if he can meet us this afternoon. Now, I don't know about you but I'm starving. Let's go and have an early lunch.'

Hilton agreed to come round later, so after a light and delicious meal eaten in a local restaurant, the pair returned to Hogan's apartment. A remarkably well-dressed man in his forties arrived. Marvin was introduced as an insurance investigator but the name of his company was not dis-closed by Hogan. Refusing coffee but accepting a glass of sparkling water, Hilton sat down and clearly felt at ease. Hogan launched into the story which he and Marvin had already agreed.

They were investigating the theft of a valuable package of uncut diamonds which had been flown from Amster-dam to Singapore. Their investigations had indicated that the stones were going to be used as a form of currency to launder a substantial amount of drug money. They won-dered if Hilton had heard of any significant sums of money which might be relevant. Their visitor looked hard at each of them in turn. 'That's very strange,' he said. 'I've heard of a similar sum of money looking for a safe home but I've heard nothing about the diamonds.'

'That's not surprising,' said Marvin. 'It's an extremely well-known company that's lost them and they're con-cerned about their reputation if this gets out. So far the police have not been informed and hence my company has been engaged to locate them. We are well aware of Hogan's reputation and contacts in this part of the world, hence my presence here with him today.'

Hilton smiled at Marvin. 'And if I was able to help you, what would be in it for me?' He let the question hang in the air.

'Well, I'd have to check back but my guess is something between $50,000 and $100,000 if we recover them, and

$25,000 if we believe the information is genuine but we fail to utilize it successfully.'

Hilton stood up. 'I'll see what I can do,' he said. 'I'll have to talk to a couple of people and it may take a day or two. Clearly, I'll have to be very discreet. If it's the people I think it might be, they're extremely dangerous but on the other hand they've done well by me.' With a knowing smile he shook hands with each of them and walked across to the door where Hogan let him out.

'What do you think?' Marvin asked.

'I think he's taken the bait. We'll just have to wait and see what happens.' Hogan looked at his watch. 'Come on, we'd better be on our way. I certainly want to be at the hotel before Ralph Murray or his contact arrives.'

Half an hour later they were sitting in a comfortable meeting room which had been made available to them by the hotel manager. Hogan phoned Murray to say which room they were in, and told him to come straight there. The policeman in turn promised to alert his informant. 'You do realize he'll expect a significant sum of money and also total discretion?'

'Naturally,' replied Hogan. 'How much are we talking about?'

'He might ask for more but ten thousand sterling would probably do the trick. Apart from anything else he does want to keep on the right side of me.'

Fifteen minutes later there was a knock on the door and an Oriental-looking man in his forties was ushered in by Hogan. He had previously mentioned to Marvin that the policeman's mother was Chinese. Smiling broadly, Murray explained his casual dress. 'I felt that my uniform would draw unnecessary attention to me and that wouldn't really suit any of us, would it?'

Hogan introduced Marvin with the same story that they had told earlier. The policeman looked dubious but obviously decided that they were not anxious to reveal Marvin's real identity and background. Hogan didn't let on that the late Sammy Cox had been asking for a great deal more money than Murray had mentioned on the

285

phone. They listened attentively while Murray explained that although drugs had always been a big problem in the area it was only recently that a number of major local corporations had added this as an extra string to their bow. 'I'm not suggesting it's rife,' he added hastily, 'but there are at least three or four where we have strong suspicions. So far we haven't been able to nail any of them. This might be the sort of breakthrough that we're really looking for, and if it turned out to be valuable for you as well so much the better.'

There followed another knock at the door and the policeman ushered in a sunburnt, very wrinkled and painfully thin man. 'This is Tim Horner,' he announced. He was clearly of European descent and looked as if he had abused himself with alcohol, drugs, or both. But his eyes were piercingly blue and, to Marvin's surprise, there was a frankness about them rather than the shiftiness he'd expected.

'Tell us what we want to know,' Murray demanded. 'Let's not waste our time.'

'How much do I get?' was the instant reply, and again the eyes looked frankly into each of the other three men's in a way that was almost challenging but certainly not insolent.

'We're offering ten thousand sterling,' Murray told Horner, 'but only if we're convinced it's genuine information. If it proves to be both genuine and something which leads to the sort of conviction we're hoping for, we'll double it. And that doesn't mean just nailing two or three petty street dealers,' he added.

The other man nodded. 'Not generous, but I'll accept. However, if it turns out to be as valuable as Sammy thought, I'd expect you to top the whole lot up to thirty thousand and you'd still be getting a bargain.'

The policeman looked at the other two. Both nodded their acceptance.

'Right, so what have you got to tell us?'

'It won't take long,' was the reply. 'Sammy phoned to say he had some amazing information. It wasn't like him to share it but on the other hand he was right more often than not. I agreed to meet him but when I got there he was half-drunk and very cagey. He'd changed his mind about telling me who he thought was in the frame but he did say that he was meeting Johnny Tang that night. "It'll shake him rigid," he said, "and he won't like it because it's very close to home."'

The three men absorbed this information before Hogan spoke again. 'Have you any idea what he meant by that?'

'None whatsoever, but I can't help wondering if he was referring to one of the Tangs. After all, you couldn't get much closer to home than that, could you?'

The three remained non-committal, but their minds were working in overdrive. It was Marvin who asked the next question. 'If you're right, have you any idea who might have been responsible for the murder or organizing it?'

There was long pause before the other man answered. 'I've only heard of a tongue being cut out once before. You may remember it was another informer called Little Jake,' he addressed Murray. 'It was never proved, but the rumour on the street was that it was Tommy Lang and I know he's worked for some big drug dealers in the past. He's an evil bastard and not someone you'd want to cross.' All three men were silent until Ross spoke.

'And who might have paid him for that? Are there any rumours on that front?'

'Yes, but rather vague. The word is that it was an international businessman who only recently entered the drugs business. Why he should do that nobody knows, if he's as rich as the rumours suggest. But further than that, I have no idea.'

The policeman looked at Marvin and Ross. 'Any more questions?' Both shook their heads. 'Right, Tim, we'll think this over. If we've got any more questions I'll call you and if our other checks bear out what you say you'll get your first payment within a week. If you have anything, phone me. However small it is, it may help us and that would help you.'

Horner looked him straight in the eye. 'That's fine,' he replied. 'I know I can trust you.' He got up and walked over to the door waiting for it to be opened. The policeman obliged and gave him a friendly pat on the back, with a warning. 'Keep this to yourself. We don't want another corpse on our hands.'

'Don't worry about that. Just make sure that you're as discreet as I'll be,' and with that he walked out and made his way to the lift without looking back. Murray closed the door.

'What next?' asked Hogan.

'Well, I think you'd better get on to your man Johnny Tang,' Murray replied, 'and see if he can shed any further light on it.'

With some difficulty, Marvin kept a poker face. Hogan had not told him of any relationship with this particular Tang but from Murray's comment it sounded as if Johnny Tang was on Hogan's payroll.

The Australian's normally impassive face showed a brief sign of irritation. 'Let me think about it,' he said. 'I really appreciate what you've done and we'll come back to you in the next day or two. If this guy is as reliable as you say I think we ought to pay him the first whack of the reward as you promised.' The policeman nodded, got up and shook both of them by the hand, opened the door and let himself out.

Marvin looked impassively at Hogan, who eventually broke the silence. 'OK, he's one of my agents,' he admitted, and relayed the incident of the tongue and how he'd instructed Johnny Tang to disappear as quickly as possible. 'I admit I should probably have told you earlier, but at that stage I didn't know how discreet you were and I was worried for Johnny's safety. I promise you, I'm not hiding anything else from you, with one exception. It's an important one. As you know, I was watching Gavin in London. This was on Hamish Tang's instructions. I've worked for him on and off for many years. Gavin seems to have been spending more money than Hamish can account for him making, and he became concerned that

288

this, along with Gavin's newfound fondness for gambling, might indicate that he was involved in something distinctly worrying.'

Marvin gave Hogan a very hard look. 'I believe you, but no more surprises or I go it alone.'

The Australian smiled understandingly. 'You have my word on it.' They shook hands.

'Let's have a quick drink in the bar,' suggested Marvin. 'We've got time before we meet Hamish and it will help keep up the pretence we are hotel guests.'

'Done,' was the instant response.

Chapter Twenty-Nine

At exactly five thirty Ross and Marvin were ushered into Hamish's huge office. The need for these proportions was partly explained by one item – a massive glass table which easily and regularly sat twelve. In addition to this and Hamish's large but tasteful desk, there was ample space for a huge television screen plus a sitting area with two settees and four comfortable chairs. They were all uphol-stered in exquisite tan leather. With a warm smile, he greeted the two of them and led them to the sitting area.

Knowing Hogan's taste, Hamish poured him a single malt whisky and looked enquiringly at Marvin. 'I'll have the same please, Mr Tang.'

'Please, call me Hamish,' he invited the young man. 'Now, cheers, and tell me the news. Before you begin, I can tell you that Percy has phoned me several times and I know the main points of the conversation you all had with Harvey Jackson. However, I'd still like to hear your version – and of course of any new developments.'

Hamish seemed to take everything they told him in his stride, but when Hogan related the latest information from Jackson he looked genuinely surprised.

'I find it quite extraordinary,' he said, 'but it does look increasingly as if there is indeed a strong connection with this part of the world and the various occurrences sur-rounding County View. Like you, I'm completely at a loss to imagine what the motive can be.' At that moment his phone rang, and with a look of annoyance he picked it up. His expression changed as he told his PA, 'Put Mr

Cartwright through.' He listened and his normal impassive countenance changed to one of alert interest.

'I've heard of him,' he told Percy, 'but frankly have never had any dealings with him. As I think you know, both Ross and Marvin are with me, and I'll let them know now. Do you wish to speak to either of them?' It was clear that Percy had no wish to interrupt the meeting but sent his good wishes via their host.

Ross and Marvin sat expectantly. 'Well, there's another development. Hal Bancroft – you probably know he's a small shareholder in County View but a close friend of Jay's,' he explained to Ross, 'has phoned with some more information on the Irish situation. He's discovered that an Irish financier called Hanagan is trying to move money from Ireland to Singapore and apparently in exchange for a number of probably stolen diamonds. This clearly again links Ireland to this territory and may be further evidence that whoever is backing O'Connor and is responsible for the County View problems may well be operating on my doorstep.'

The two investigators exchanged meaningful glances, but failed to say they were already aware of this. 'I think that we've probably discussed all that we usefully can this evening,' Hamish announced, rising and clearly bringing the meeting to an end. Turning to Marvin, he said, 'I hope you'll indulge me if I ask my Head of Security, Alan Bell, to show you our systems and get any comments you may have.' Turning to Ross, 'You've seen them often enough. I suggest you might like to use one of our empty offices to tell Murray the latest news, and perhaps have a direct chat with Percy and/or Harvey Jackson. I'll get Mary Cheng to find you an empty office.'

The two men left the room, and moments later Marvin was being led away by Alan Bell. Mary found Ross an empty meeting room and a few moments later Hamish entered, closed the door and motioned Hogan to sit down opposite him. 'What was it you wanted to see me about in private?' he asked.

'The one thing I haven't told you,' Ross informed him,

'is that I've had two alarming conversations with Johnny Tang. I know you've used him from time to time but you may not be aware that he's my main agent in Singapore. In fact he supervises my whole operation in this area when I'm not here.' From his expression it seemed clear that Hamish was unaware of the extent of his cousin's involvement with Hogan.

Hogan related what had happened to the unfortunate Sammy Cox, his subsequent conversations with Murray and Hilton and then Tim Horner. He left his bombshell to the end. 'It seems, Hamish, there is a real possibility that a member of your family is deeply involved in the drugs business and may well be implicated in what has been going on in and around County View. Indeed it would also seem that the insurance scam in New Zealand is part of the whole picture.'

Hogan had never seen Hamish Tang at a loss for words before. He was clearly a deeply troubled man. 'Who can it be?' he wondered aloud. 'You're surely not considering either of my sons, but I do of course have four cousins and a number of nephews apart from Johnny.'

'I'm not going to mince my words, Hamish,' the Australian replied. 'I'm not ruling anyone out.'

Hamish looked even more concerned. 'Well, what do you want me to do? How can I help?'

'We need to see if we can trace any dubious transfers of large sums of money from any of your companies to an unusual person or organization and we need to do it quickly.'

The initial shock was clearly over when Hamish spoke. 'I have a team of top-class forensic accountants at my disposal. I'll get them here immediately under the pretext that we are considering a major acquisition. This would require our finances to be one hundred per cent waterproof, however deeply they are examined by the most aggressive of accountants who would certainly be employed if we embarked on such an attempted takeover.'

The Australian had become used to the power, contacts and rapid decision-making of Hamish Tang but even he was impressed with the speed at which the man was going to move.

'You've brought me desperately worrying news,' Hamish informed the Australian, looking him straight in the eye, 'but I believe in you enough to be sure there is something here which could be seriously dangerous to my family and my companies. I appreciate your diligence and your honesty, and you can rely on my support in every way. Now I suggest we go back to my office and have another stiff drink and I'll let Mary know that it's time to bring Marvin back. But first I suggest you speak briefly to both Percy and Jackson so that you've got something to discuss with the striking Mr Jones when you're alone later.'

With a surprisingly broad grin for a man who'd just received such staggering news, he left the room. Hogan took him at his word and quickly spoke to both Percy Cartwright and Harvey Jackson. He only revealed his private conversation with Hamish to the latter, asking Jackson to keep it to himself. He explained that this was nothing to do with lack of confidence in Marvin but because he didn't want Marvin to think that one of the Tangs was directly involved in their problems.

When he returned to Hamish's office the other two men were already sipping their single malt whiskies. Hamish pointed to a glass waiting for him and asked whether he'd successfully spoken to Percy and Jackson. Hogan confirmed that he had, and with a broad wink indicated to Marvin he'd fill him in on his conversations later.

On the way back to Hogan's flat, the two men sat in the back of the taxi deep in thought. Marvin had a distinctly uncomfortable feeling about Hamish but couldn't put his finger on it. He was well aware of the Oriental's reputation for being impassive but he was beginning to wonder if this was a big act.

Beside him, Hogan was thinking along different lines. He too was amazed at the man's reaction and the speed at which he had moved to bring in forensic accountants. The more he mulled over the situation the more he decided he

293

had to take Marvin into his confidence. Turning to his companion, he spoke seriously.

'There's something I want to talk to you about. I'll wait until we are alone at the apartment.'

Marvin looked curious but said nothing.

The Australian continued: 'I think we'd better arrange to see Murray again. Let's see if he's free for dinner tonight. I'm sure we can find a private room somewhere.' He dialled the number and the policeman answered immediately. Hogan told him they had fresh news and felt a meeting would be valuable. He listened to Murray for a moment or two. 'That'll be fine,' he said.

Turning to Marvin, he said, 'Ralph has a friend with a restaurant just off Scotts Road. It has a few private rooms and evidently our policeman friend has used it many times in the past. We're to meet him there at nine o'clock unless he calls to say the room's not available.'

Back in the apartment Hogan looked straight at Marvin. He'd decided to tell him everything except that he had planned to meet Hamish alone.

'When you were being taken on your tour, which I think had been deliberately orchestrated by Hamish, I was put in a small meeting room where I could phone London. Almost immediately Hamish came in and questioned me further. He was clearly deeply concerned about something so I decided to tell him everything about Johnny Tang, Sammy Cox and the suspicion that a member of the Tang family might be involved.

'His immediate reaction was to bring in a team of top forensic accountants to go through his companies' books to see if money has been improperly transferred. He's doing this under the guise of a supposed major acquisition of a competitor. I just have a feeling that Hamish may not be telling us everything he knows.'

Marvin looked at him before replying. 'I have the same feeling. He's almost too inscrutable in the circumstances, and he's always been rather evasive about his relationship with Johnny Tang.'

Hogan agreed. 'It'll be interesting to see if Murray has

discovered anything else and also just what he knows, if anything, about the mysterious Kieran Hanagan. Lewis Rees may well be helpful on that front,' he added.

Marvin nodded. 'I think I'll give him a call. Hopefully, if we alert him now he'll be able to let us have something by lunchtime tomorrow.'

While Hogan poured each of them a glass of chilled white wine, Marvin phoned Lewis who said, 'I've told you all I know, but I've heard one of my colleagues, Barnaby Cullen, mention Hanagan recently. I'll call him tonight.'

At 8.45 Hogan's driver called for them and soon they were being ushered through the busy restaurant into a small, air-conditioned room at the back. The lighting gave it a warm but businesslike atmosphere. Rising to greet them, Ralph grinned. 'He has two other rooms like this which are more romantic and have convenient large chaise longues,' he informed his two visitors. They laughed and sat down.

'Let's get the food ordered and then we can be undisturbed.' He pressed a bell on the table and a very pretty Chinese waitress entered. She took their orders and paused. 'Beer or wine?' Murray enquired. Both of them opted for beer. 'You'd better bring six bottles,' he told the waitress, 'and perhaps you'd be kind enough to put three of them in an ice bucket.'

'Of course, sir,' she said, and glided out of the room.

They made small talk until the food was served, the beer poured, and the ice bucket put in easy reach. The waitress turned to Murray. 'You'll be undisturbed now, but please call if you need anything more.'

Hogan took the lead and recounted the conversation he and Marvin had had with Hamish and then the subsequent one he had had alone. Marvin filled in the information about Hanagan.

Murray looked thoughtful. 'Never heard of this Hanagan,' he told them, 'but I have got Tommy Lang under arrest. Jackson tells me that Jimmy Yong is now in splendid isolation in one of the police safe houses outside London. He's under constant guard and isn't going to get away. I'm sending over two of my men to interview him and if necessary he can be flown over here to act as a witness. We're not going to be charging him with anything in this country so won't have to go through the problems of extradition.'

At that moment Marvin's phone rang. He listened for a few moments and said, 'That'll be fine. I'll have one colleague with me and perhaps two, is that OK?' It clearly was, and Marvin bade the caller goodnight.

'That was Lewis,' he explained. 'Friend Barnaby evidently knows quite a lot about our Mr Hanagan and he's agreed to meet us for breakfast at the Hyatt at 7.30 tomorrow morning.' Looking at his two dining companions, he smiled. 'I'm sure one of you can arrange a private room.' It was Murray who assured him it would be no problem.

'What do you think you can do now?' Hogan asked the policeman.

'Well, we'll have to take a close look at Hamish Tang. I suspect there's not much we don't know about him but if he is hiding anything it'll probably be very difficult to uncover from outside. I'll certainly see if we have any information on Kieran Hanagan and will continue to interrogate Lang and those members of his organization we've already arrested with him. I don't think there's very much more we can do tonight, so let's enjoy the rest of the food and be ready for an early start tomorrow.'

Marvin and Hogan took a taxi from the restaurant back to the apartment. Half a mile or so away Hogan turned to Marvin. 'I don't know about you but I'd like a bit of a walk.'

'I agree,' said Marvin. They asked the driver to stop. He pulled into the side, Hogan paid, and they set off. It was a bit like walking in a sauna. It was about as hot and as humid as Singapore could get, and soon they were both beginning to regret their decision. Just then an elderly car drew up alongside them. Two men jumped out, while a third remained behind the wheel. They both had knives. Hogan reacted immediately and kicked the man coming towards him with a vicious blow to his solar plexus. Marvin was slower, and his assailant stabbed straight for his chest. Marvin parried the blow but in so doing received a nasty cut in his forearm. Hogan's attacker was writhing on the ground and the Australian moved quickly to help his colleague. At that moment the driver got out of the car with a gun in his hand. 'Stand back or I'll shoot,' he snarled. Both men did as they were told while their attackers got themselves back into the car. The driver kept them both covered, then dashed round to the other side of the car, jumped in and drove off.

Hogan looked at Marvin's arm. 'You need some treatment,' he said. Taking out his mobile phone, he called Murray, who told them to stay where they were and he'd have help there within seconds. He was true to his word. A few moments later a police car arrived, and out jumped two armed men plus a man dressed in civilian clothes. He had a small bag with him, and explained that he was the police doctor on duty that night. He looked at Marvin's arm, bandaged it tightly, and instructed the police to take them to the nearest hospital with all speed. The five of them squeezed into the car and they sped off. Ordering Hogan to wait, the young doctor ushered Marvin quickly through into the accident and emergency area. The wound was cleaned and stitched by one of the duty doctors and Marvin was given an antibiotic injection. In a little over an hour they were outside Hogan's apartment, and the two policemen watched them as they entered the building.

They had barely sat down, Marvin with a large glass of brandy in his hand poured for him by Hogan, when the telephone rang. It was Murray enquiring about their health.

'I'll have you collected in the morning,' he said. 'I think this is some sort of warning. If they'd really wanted to get rid of you I guess the guy with the gun would have shot you both.'

'That's very comforting,' laughed Hogan, and thanked the policeman for his help. 'We'll see you in the morning.'

'Are you sure Marvin's going to be all right?'

Hogan looked at his companion. 'I think he'll be fine. Sore, but I can't see him wanting to miss tomorrow's meeting. Goodnight, and thanks again for your help.'

Sitting down, he looked at Marvin. 'It's pretty obvious we're being watched. The only person other than ourselves who knew we were going to that restaurant was Murray, and I can't imagine that he'd broadcast the fact.'

'I guess you're right,' said Marvin. 'I think I'm ready for bed.'

'I'm sure you are. Get a decent night's sleep. See you in the morning.'

The following morning Murray, Marvin and Ross were sitting in a small private room in the Hyatt. Spot on 7.30 Lewis and his colleague, Barnaby, entered. Barnaby was short, somewhat overweight, and was already looking warm even at this time of day. He had a cheerful presence but a very shrewd look about his eyes. They ordered various juices, coffee and toast with the exception of Barnaby who unselfconsciously ordered a full cooked English breakfast.

Once the food was served and they were alone, Barnaby launched into a rapid but succinct outline of what he knew. He did this while voraciously demolishing his food, seeming to have the knack of talking and eating at the same time.

'Well, I've come across your Mr Hanagan a few times. We've put money into two of his ventures, one a hotel development in Ireland, the other as a co-funder of an acquisition of a marina in Thailand. Both of them have proved good investments and there never was, or has been, anything dubious about either of them.

'However, he has presented us with three other possibilities, all of which we rejected. One was the acquisition of a casino, another was a small cargo shipping company

298

operating in this area and then onwards to North Africa, and the third a small private air cargo company which needed finance to lease further aircraft. They all looked financially sound businesses but we were suspicious of both the people owning them and the type of use to which they'd be put. To be honest, they smelt uncomfortably like smuggling-related enterprises.'

There was a look of intense interest on both the investigators' and the policeman's faces.

Barnaby continued. 'What I find interesting is that we understand he's been involved in moving money in and out of Switzerland more recently, and I know the financial authorities both here and in Switzerland have him under close scrutiny. We also know he was here briefly ten days ago, and we've now got an alert out to be informed any time he enters.'

Murray smiled. 'It seems that I might be able to use your network,' he chuckled. 'However, I've got a bit of additional news. Mr Hanagan arrived in Singapore yesterday lunchtime. Interestingly enough he came via Bangkok.'

There was a pause while the others absorbed this information. This time it was Lewis who spoke. 'We'll let you know the minute we hear anything, if we do, won't we, Barnaby?'

'Of course,' agreed Barnaby.

As soon as breakfast was over the two bankers left together, followed by Murray.

'Now what?' wondered Hogan as he and Marvin waited for the lift.

'God knows, but it will probably surprise us,' Marvin replied with feeling.

Chapter Thirty

Meanwhile, back at County View there had been a sense of anticlimax after the excitement of Boxing Day at Kempton and the disappointment of Chepstow being called off. This atmosphere did not last long when Jay announced that he intended to run Understated at Ascot the following week. The young horse had come out of his Boxing Day run full of himself. There was a new £100,000 race on the card and Jay was reasonably confident that Percy's horse would turn in a performance which would show that he was probably the most improved and exciting young chaser in the country. Needless to say Percy was over the moon at this prospect. When he learned that O'Connor had entered his unbeaten Black Angel for the race, he was even more excited. As the tension between the two yards had grown, Percy had taken this even more personally than Jay had; he was backed up by Eva who was showing an aggressive streak which was new even to Jay.

The racing columns highlighted the clash of these two first class horses and noted that Neville Gethin's horse was also a real contender. However, their real interest centred on the potential clash between Jay and O'Connor.

On the morning of the race Jay had a number of telephone calls wishing him good luck, and in particular from Howard and Frank Malone, both of whom said they would be there to give support. For once Jay was beginning to show some pre-race nerves, something that even in his race riding days he seldom let come to the surface. There was such an atmosphere of expectation and excitement in the yard it was almost as if they'd gone back to the days when Splendid Warrior was the country's leader chaser, having successfully defended his Cheltenham Gold Cup crown on two occasions.

Arriving at the racecourse, Jay went through his normal procedure of checking that Understated was fine and that the declaration had been completed properly. He then made his way to the owners' and trainers' bar where Eva was already in animated conversation with Percy, Frank, Lance and Howard. They were soon joined by Roddy and Jerline. Jay was finding the whole atmosphere rather over-powering and quietly excused himself, saying he wanted to go to the stables and ensure that all was well. On the way back he was delighted to run into Harry Solomons. His rival commented on the forthcoming big clash and assured Jay that his own runner, Shooting Starlet, was only there in the hope of picking up some of the place money which went right down to the sixth.

'You never know with steeplechases,' he commented, 'but I think the chance of any of us beating you and O'Connor is pretty remote. Come on, I'll buy you a drink. I've got some news for you.'

Rather than going into the owners' and trainers' bar, they made their way to one of the public bars where Harry, rather to Jay's surprise, came back with two glasses and a bottle of champagne.

'This is not common knowledge,' he said, 'but I just wanted to let you know that I'm retiring at the end of this season. Now obviously, it's not my final decision, but if you're interested I'd be very happy to recommend you to some of the owners with really good horses in my yard. I know they'd get the best possible attention at County View, and frankly you deserve a bit of good luck after all the aggravation you've gone through in the last few months.' With that he passed Jay a glass of champagne and said, 'I've really enjoyed our competition and I'm hell-bent on beating you this year.'

'Well, at the moment it looks as if you will,' replied Jay, 'but I'm not going to roll over.'

'I hardly thought you would,' Harry grinned. 'Anyway,

I'd be pleased if you'd keep that to yourself for a bit. As I start to tell my owners I'll let you know if any of them are interested in talking to you.'

Jay gave the older man a squeeze on his arm. 'You'll be missed, you know.'

'Oh no, I won't,' said Harry. 'I've no intention of walking away from racing altogether. You lot can't get rid of me that easily.' He drained his glass, filled it again, and topped up Jay's.

'I don't normally drink before races,' said Jay.

'I know,' said Harry, 'but this is a special occasion.'

When Jay rejoined his crowd, it was only Eva who noticed he'd been away longer than usual.

'Any problems?' she enquired.

'No, none at all,' he said. 'I've just been having a chat with Harry Solomons. I'll tell you about it later.'

Interrupting the animated conversation that was going on, Jay pointed out that it was time to saddle the runner. Needless to say, Percy wanted to go with him. On the way to the saddling enclosure, Jay noticed that O'Connor was ahead of him and beckoned to Pete Corbett, Understated's groom, to take their horse into a box well away from O'Connor. As always, the horse was as good as gold and they were soon on their way to the parade ring.

They were standing watching the horses circle when somebody tapped Jay on the shoulder. He turned round to see O'Connor standing in front of him with a far from friendly look on his face.

'I suppose you think you're going to beat my horse today. Well, you've got another think coming,' the Irishman snarled at him.

Jay looked at him coolly. This seemed to infuriate O'Connor even more.

'I know you think you're a big guy,' he said, 'but why don't you put your money where your mouth is? I've got £50,000 which says my horse will beat yours, irrespective of where they come.'

Jay could hardly believe his ears. Nobody had ever made a proposition like that to him. He returned the

Irishman's gaze. 'I'd have thought by now you'd know that I don't bet,' he replied.

'Ah. I knew you wouldn't have the guts to take me on.'

'I will,' said a voice behind Jay. He turned to see Percy standing there. 'I'd take you on with pleasure, but from what I hear it's unlikely I'd be paid if my horse beat yours.'

There was a gasp from those who'd heard Percy affront the man so openly, and it wasn't just Jay's friends who had heard the remark.

O'Connor paused. 'Right, if that's what you think, I'll bet my horse against yours. Whoever wins takes the other horse.'

Before Jay could say anything, Percy stretched out his hand. 'Shake on it,' he said. The two men glowered at each other, shook hands, and O'Connor turned on his heel.

Jay was aghast. 'What the hell do you think you're doing?' he said.

'I'm going to teach that bastard a lesson,' Percy replied.

Jay thought for a moment. 'Whatever you do don't mention this to David Sparrow. He's got enough responsibility in trying to win the race without knowing that if he loses we might lose the horse as well.'

Percy saw the wisdom of this, and Jay turned to the rest of his group and reiterated what he'd just said to his friend. They all agreed. It was Frank who spoke first.

'I wonder what the hell set him off on that. The guy must be getting fairly desperate.'

Jay made no further comment and quickly said, 'Here comes David. Now change the subject.'

Sparrow needed no instructions on how to ride the horse. Having touched his cap to everyone in the little group, he walked across the ring to where Understated was now standing ready to be mounted. Percy walked with Jay. As soon as the lad was astride his horse, he patted his boot and wished him good luck.

'Thanks, Mr Cartwright,' replied David. 'This is going to be a tough one and we'll need all the luck we can get.'

After a couple of circuits of the parade ring, the horses

were on their way to the start. Apart from O'Connor's and Jay's horses, Harry Solomons was running Shooting Starlet and Gethin was running Walk the Line.

The preliminaries at the start went without incident as all the runners were now seasoned campaigners.

As Jay had expected, Gethin's horse made the pace, which was a generous one as they passed the stands with the full circuit of the Ascot course still in front of them. Harry Solomons' horse moved into second place, and O'Connor's horse was now tracking him, with Paul Jenkins glancing over his shoulder from time to time to see where Understated was sitting. Sparrow had him just behind O'Connor's horse running alongside one of the outsiders. The position remained unchanged until they turned for the long run up to the finishing post. At this stage Paul asked Black Angel to improve its position. Jumping the third last fence fluently, it made rapid headway on the two horses in front of it. Approaching the penultimate fence, Jenkins had now overtaken Harry's horse and was closing rapidly on the leader. Sparrow had covered every move that Paul had made and was now sitting half a length behind O'Connor's horse as they approached the last. Percy was going mad, and the rest of the County View supporters' team were equally vocal. Jumping the last, Paul got seriously to work on O'Connor's horse and soon he was in the lead and going away from Walk the Line. David Sparrow kept his cool and encouraged Percy's horse with two slaps on the shoulder. Understated crept alongside and the two of them fought out stride for stride as they approached the winning post. The crowd was roaring, and the big screen was showing no perceptible difference between the two horses as they flashed passed the winning post.

Percy looked questioningly at Jay. 'Did we do it?'

'I really couldn't tell from here. Looking at the screen, I think we did.'

Almost immediately it was announced that there was a photograph. There was hubbub from the crowd and the bookmakers were clearly undecided as to the result. Some were betting against O'Connor's horse winning, and some against Jay's. Presumably this was dependent, not on any knowledge of who had won, but on how much money they had on each horse to win. Moments later the result was announced. 'First, number three, Understated, second number two, Black Angel. The third was Shooting Starlet.'

Even amid the jubilation of knowing they'd won, Jay still heard that Harry's horse had got up to grab third place. Percy and Jay made their way hurriedly to the winners' enclosure and got there just before Sparrow was led in to enthusiastic applause. O'Connor, scowling with a face like thunder, walked over to Percy. 'Take the bloody animal home with you,' he said, and turned away.

'I wouldn't dream of it,' said Percy. 'I've had more than enough satisfaction in beating you, and the sooner you go back to Ireland where you came from the happier most people in racing will be.' Turning to Jay he said, 'Under no circumstances is that horse to come to your yard.' Jay nodded with quiet relief.

They were surrounded by the press who were asking questions about the horse, but a number had already heard of the wager between O'Connor and Percy. Percy refused to comment, as did Jay. Once the feverish excitement had died down, the County View contingent returned to the owners' and trainers' bar where Percy bought the group champagne. It was Frank Malone who drew their chatter back to O'Connor's extraordinary performance.

'I'm beginning to wonder if he's really losing it,' said Frank. 'That was not the behaviour of a rational man.' Howard agreed, but Jay decided to keep his own counsel. In one sense he felt sorry for the man, but on the other hand reasoned to himself that the problems facing O'Connor were very largely self-inflicted.

Chapter Thirty-One

Two days after his conversation with Ross and Marvin, Hamish Tang was sitting in his office when his private phone rang and a furious Gavin was at the other end.

'What the hell's going on? My finance director has just told me that a gang of outside accountants have moved in with written authority from you and are going through all our books with a fine-tooth comb.'

'That's right,' his father replied.

'What's it about and why the hell didn't you tell me?'

Hamish had expected this response from both his sons, particularly Gavin who was far more volatile than Fraser. He was ready with his reply. 'Three days ago, while you were in China, I got a telephone call from Jack Taylor at International Consolidation and Systems. He's interested in a merger, with us being the dominant partner. I could hardly discuss this over the phone but I moved quickly to ensure that all our books could pass scrutiny in the event of the conversation going further and due diligence being set in motion.'

A slightly mollified Gavin replied, 'Well, I can see that's very exciting but it would have been nice if you had given me some notice.'

'I can understand that,' his father replied, 'but you haven't got anything to hide, have you?'

'Good God, no!' was the swift reply. 'What on earth do you mean?'

'Only joking,' his father replied. 'We'll talk about it over lunch if you're free.'

'Looks like I am. I'll confirm it later.'

'I'll be running around myself,' said Hamish, 'so let Mary know. I suggest that we have lunch here so we can talk completely openly.' Gavin agreed and hung up.

Gavin was distinctly uncomfortable. The thought of his books being under such scrutiny made him very nervous. He had always been so careful but had he made a major error? Had he overlooked something? If he had, he knew his father would be far from understanding or forgiving.

Back in London Jackson received another call from an excited McKenna.

'We've got everything that we need from Miss O'Casey but there's been another development. We went to arrest Hanagan and found out he's on his way to Singapore. Fortunately we sent plain-clothes men to his home. They just asked to have a word with him, so hopefully his housekeeper, who answered the door, won't alert him to the fact that the police called. Obviously we could alert the Singapore police but with your contacts and with your Jones and Hogan on the ground, I thought it would be best if it came from you.'

Jackson agreed and promised that he would relay the information to Singapore. He added that he would give them McKenna's telephone number as it was highly likely they'd want to check some of the details before they made any move. McKenna agreed to this. Apart from 11 p.m. to 6 a.m. local time he would be available with his private number switched on to receive any calls from Singapore. During those hours he hoped to grab a little sleep, he chuckled to Jackson.

Jackson phoned Ross Hogan and gave him the news. Hogan promised to let Murray know and to keep Jackson advised of any developments. He also made a note of McKenna's telephone number.

In Singapore Hanagan was already settled in a private apartment and talking to his Oriental client and paymaster.

'As I mentioned to you on the phone, O'Connor is getting very twitchy. He's complaining bitterly that he can't go on without substantial additional funds. Evidently his bank has been sympathetic because of the regular payments that have been going in, but now that we have reduced the flow, and stopped it entirely this month, he's started to create. He's told me that if he doesn't receive at least £100,000 by the end of this week he'll have to start laying off staff.'

'Is he still gambling heavily?' asked the Oriental.

'No,' was the reply, 'but not through lack of trying. He owes the bookmakers so much money they're refusing to accept the sort of substantial bets which he's been making.'

For once the Oriental looked worried. 'Look, Kieran.' It was unusual for him to address the Irishman by his first name. 'I've really got a cash flow problem and there's no way I can raise that sort of money on the quiet for several weeks at least.'

It was the Irishman's turn to look worried. 'What's wrong?'

The Oriental paused and thought carefully before answering.

'I'll be frank with you. I've been playing the stock market and I've made a major error. At the same time a substantial drug shipment was discovered by the customs in Marseilles and I've lost that income but my supplier is insisting that I pay him. Even that's going to be difficult but the man is just too bloody dangerous for me to refuse.'

The seriousness of the Oriental's position became apparent to Hanagan. He'd never heard him swear before and he'd never seen him remotely agitated.

'There's another problem,' he went on. 'A team of forensic accountants are going through the books of all my companies and Gustav my finance director and I have not had a chance to make any adjustments to ensure that these experts don't uncover our recent activities.'

'Christ,' said Hanagan. 'If Gustav Brandt can't hide them, nobody can. What are you going to do?'

The Oriental looked at him. 'I honestly don't know. If my father knew he would not only be furious, he'd also refuse to help me. The thought of the precious Tang family name being tarnished would infuriate him. I was hoping you'd be able to bail me out for a few weeks.'

Hanagan looked amazed. 'You can't be serious. I've already paid out £160,000 in cash to keep O'Connor going, and have you forgotten the quarter of a million you still owe me from the last drug transaction?'

The Oriental shook his head. 'I know but I'm sure this is only a temporary situation. Let me have another half million and I'll pay you ten per cent in three months' time. Christ, that's forty per cent at an annualized basic rate.'

The Irishman shook his head. 'I'm really sorry, I can't,' he said. 'Even if I had the money, I'm not sure that I would. I thought you were a sound investment but I'm clearly losing my judgement.'

The Oriental's expression changed dramatically. It was now vicious. 'You let me down now and I'll make sure you go with me.'

'You do that and you're a dead man,' the Irishman said as he stood up. 'Now I suggest you go home and give this some serious thought. I'll stay here tonight and then I've got other fish to fry.' With that, he opened the door and indicated that the still fuming Oriental should leave. It was particularly humiliating as the apartment belonged to the man who was being almost physically evicted.

On the other side of the city, Hogan, Murray and Marvin were sitting down digesting and discussing the most recent news from Jackson and Murray's subsequent conversation with McKenna.

The policeman spoke. 'There's little doubt that Hanagan is the key link in our chain but at the moment we've got no reason to arrest him here. What's more I'm not sure that McKenna has evidence which would result in him being extradited quickly if at all. On the other hand McKenna has good information and a key witness in Ireland, and once Hanagan is behind bars there it would probably be surprising how many other criminals would suddenly be prepared to be helpful in stitching him up for good. The so-called honour among thieves tends to be true of the lower echelons, but in my experience it's less so when big hitters are involved, particularly if their criminal activities are of a financial nature. Also, strangely enough, there are even hardened criminals who are very uncomfortable with the drug trade.'

'So what do we do now?' asked Marvin.

'I'm allocating a team to find out where Hanagan is and who he's meeting. We know he arrived yesterday but we don't know where he went and there's no record of him checking into a hotel. We've started a check on airport taxis but so far none of them have turned up trumps. It may well be that he had a private car waiting for him.'

'If he is behind the various activities in England and New Zealand, that would be my theory too,' Hogan agreed. 'Everything has been so well planned and executed, it's hardly likely he'd leave such an obvious trail as a taxi from the airport, even though he probably has no idea he's under suspicion.'

Marvin thought for a moment before turning to Murray. 'Presumably you can find out where he's flying to when he gets to the airport. If it's not direct to Ireland, would you be able to apprehend him and just deport him as an undesirable visitor?'

'That is a possibility,' replied the policeman, 'but the only problem is that it would alert him to the fact that he's under suspicion. I think we need to keep our fingers crossed and hope that he decides to go straight back to his home country. I'll check with my boss and see if he would be agreeable to your suggested action, if necessary. It might be difficult. He does play by the book.' He gave a rather tired smile. 'God, a lot's happened in the last few days. You guys have certainly made sure that a policeman's life is not a simple or even a dull one.' He stood up. 'I don't think there's very much more we can do for the time being. If we find Hanagan, or anything else emerges, I'll be in touch straight away.'

Chapter Thirty-Two

Hanagan was collected from the apartment by Emil, his usual driver when he was in Singapore. The drive to the terminal building was uneventful and Hanagan politely refused the offer of help with his luggage. He always travelled with very little – a small holdall and his laptop. He checked in and went through security with no problems.

Unbeknown to him he had finally been traced by Murray's men and was now under surveillance by three police officers. Their job was to confirm that he did indeed board the British Airways flight to London. The police at that end knew he was due to catch an onward flight to Dublin two hours after his arrival. Both Jackson and McKenna had been alerted to this. Jackson would have plain-clothes police at Heathrow to confirm that he caught the connection, and McKenna would have members of his staff in readiness to apprehend Hanagan the minute he landed in Dublin.

Hanagan bought a cold beer and the *Financial Times* and sat down to while away the hour or so he had ahead of him before departure. He did not concentrate on the paper with his usual single-mindedness. He was mulling over the events of the last twenty-four hours, and in particular the telephone call he had received that morning. It was neither constructive nor friendly, and the Irishman was beginning to regret that he'd ever got involved with horse racing. It was not that he had any qualms about the original plans, or indeed what had happened since. In fact all the events had been orchestrated by him and executed by members of his small, highly efficient, and in many cases violent, organization. He was much more concerned about the potential loss of very large sums of money, and he had an uneasy feeling that the Oriental was not going to let the matter rest after their altercation the night before and an equally heated telephone conversation that morning before he left the apartment.

He was still musing on the implications of this when his mobile rang.

'Are you all right, sir?' questioned Emil.

'Absolutely,' was the Irishman's reply. 'Why shouldn't I be?'

'Well, sir, I've just heard that a few minutes after we left your apartment it was bombed. There's no doubt that if you'd still been there you would be dead. You must be very careful until you get on the aircraft.'

'Mother of God!' exclaimed the Irishman. 'I've only a few minutes to go. Thanks for telling me.'

'You'll let me know when you get to Dublin, won't you, sir?'

'Of course I will, and thank you again, Emil.'

The driver had worked for Hanagan for over seven years, and not only was he completely reliable in that role, but he and members of his family had been particularly useful in providing Hanagan with information and valuable contacts in the criminal world of Hong Kong and Singapore.

Seated in the first class compartment of his London flight, he could feel his concern being replaced by anger as he considered the implication of his driver's call. It was clear that the Oriental was intent on carrying out the threat from the previous evening.

Hanagan was puzzled. Obviously the man was desperate for money. The Irishman was surprised that he'd given up trying to enlist Hanagan's help as quickly as he had.

He passed the rest of the journey drinking far more than he normally did, sleeping with the help of a Dalmane, watching a video without any great attention, and planning his actions when he got to Ireland. He was certainly not going to take this lying down.

Arriving at Heathrow, he turned on his phone and saw a text from O'Connor. 'Phone me urgently, and I mean urgently.'

Hanagan ignored the message, deciding it could wait till the following day. He was quite sure it was just another insistent demand for funds. He was completely unaware that he was being carefully watched by two of Jackson's men who phoned their boss to confirm that their quarry had indeed boarded the flight to Dublin. Jackson called McKenna who assured him that Hanagan would be detained the moment he landed on Irish soil, initially for his involvement in the Daly attack on Danny. Subsequently a number of his other activities would merit charges in their own right.

On arrival at Dublin, Hanagan passed through customs and walked towards the driver who was waiting for him. Before he got there he was grabbed by two men in plain clothes. They were joined by two uniformed policemen and he was formally arrested and taken to the police station where McKenna was waiting for him.

In spite of vehement protests, he was put in a cell and left to cool his heels. Meanwhile, McKenna received a call from Jackson who told him of the narrow escape that his prisoner had had in Singapore. This, he felt, might well be relevant to the impending interrogation.

Deciding that the man's resistance might be quite low after the long flight, McKenna had him taken into an interview room and conducted the questioning himself.

Hanagan denied all knowledge of Daly or indeed of County View or any of its employees. He looked completely blank at the suggestion that he had arranged for the attack on Danny Derkin. McKenna let him continue along this line for a while. He suddenly interrupted him. 'You're wasting your time and mine,' he said. 'We have a witness who heard you and Daly discussing the attack. We've also got your mobile phone calls logged which confirm both our witness's story and the fact that you have had a number of conversations with Daly. We also know that you've been involved with various activities in the Far East

314

and are directly responsible for an attempted insurance scam by the poisoning of four extremely valuable race-horses in New Zealand.'

'That was absolutely nothing to do with me. I wasn't involved in any way.' Hanagan cut himself off in mid-sentence, realizing he had admitted knowledge.

'So are you telling us that the money that's been going to Switzerland into Quentin O'Connor's bank account has nothing to do with you? I've got to tell you all our infor-mation indicates that you transferred it. We've traced it all the way from Singapore to Switzerland via your bank account, and we also know that you set up the account in Switzerland which provides O'Connor with the bulk of his income. The banks in both Switzerland and Singapore have now traced the QBQ bank account dealings to you and it's only a matter of time before they uncover the source of these funds.'

Hanagan was beginning to look decidedly nervous.

McKenna left what he thought might be his ace until the end. He then played his card. 'We also know that an attempt was made on your life in an apartment which is owned by the Tang empire. It's not unreasonable for us to assume that you've fallen out with somebody very high up in that organization. There's no way you'd be staying there unless you had such a contact and the porter has said that one of the top directors left after seeing you last night – and he was clearly in a very bad mood. I'll leave you now, Mr Hanagan. You can sleep on it and we'll talk again in the morning.'

In Singapore, Ross and Marvin were sitting down catching their mental breath. They had just been told by Harvey of the latest staggering developments.

'I suppose we'd better bring Murray up to date,' Marvin suggested.

'No, we don't have a problem there,' Ross informed him. 'Jackson's taking care of that too.'

315

'Then what the hell do we do?' the Londoner wondered aloud.

'I'm going to have a bloody good dinner,' replied the Australian. 'I don't think there's anything we can do at the moment but wait and see what happens next.'

Marvin agreed, although he was clearly reluctant to be doing nothing.

They were halfway through dinner at the Hyatt Hotel when Marvin's phone rang. It was Hamish Tang. 'I need to see you and your policeman friend Murray immediately,' he said. 'I mean immediately. Get to my office now.' There was no mistaking the tone of his voice. Ross phoned Ralph Murray.

'I'm actually having dinner with my family for a change,' he complained, 'but I guess this does sound pretty important.'

At the Tang headquarters Ross and Marvin were shown into Hamish's office by a rather subdued Mary. There was none of the normal polite welcome by Hamish. 'Please sit down, gentlemen. You'd better both have a drink. I'll say nothing until Murray arrives. I don't want to go over the same ground twice.'

Without asking, he poured all three of them generous measures of malt whisky and placed another in front of the empty chair. Shortly afterwards Mary showed Murray in. Gesturing to him to sit down, Hamish passed him his drink and sat down himself.

'I'm afraid your suspicions that money financing this operation was coming from Singapore are entirely correct. What's more, so is your instinct that it was in some way connected with the Tang business conglomerate and that it was somebody high up in my family.' He paused and took a large swig of his whisky. 'It's more than somebody high up,' he announced, and paused again. The three of them were tingling with anticipation. 'It's one of my sons,' he continued in a voice that was now charged with emotion. 'I'm afraid to tell you it's Fraser.'

None of them knew what to say. Eventually it was

Murray who spoke. 'Are you certain of this, and how do you know?'

'I'm quite certain,' replied Hamish. 'One of the accountants I put in to go through the books came across some totally fictitious purchases which had been made by Tang Argent, the silver dealing company which Fraser controls. Huge payments were being made against invoices for metal that was never delivered. Fraser and his finance director, Gustav Brandt, were covering these transactions very cleverly and from time to time repayments were being made, some of them very substantial, which made things look legitimate. Nobody was going to challenge the chief executive and the finance director, even if they had thought anything was suspicious.

'The rest of Fraser's companies were making good money and, although not nearly as profitable as Gavin's, were giving me no cause for concern. As you know, we've been in a strongly acquisitive mode for the last two years and I've spent the greater part of my time working on these acquisitions rather than enquiring too closely into what either Fraser or Gavin have been doing. They both appeared to be performing extremely well.'

All three men maintained their silence. Hamish took another drink. 'Although we have no definite proof yet, it would appear that Fraser was also dealing in drugs at a very high level. Quite why he went down this avenue is a mystery to me, as indeed is the fact that he was clearly financing the attacks on County View. I've no idea what his relationship was with O'Connor.'

'What's he got to say?' asked Murray.

Hamish paused and looked at him very unhappily. 'Fraser and Brandt have disappeared. It seems that they got wind of it and vanished without a word. Not even his wife knew that he was no longer in the city.'

Again it was the policeman who spoke. 'If you're absolutely sure of this, I'm afraid I have no other course of action but to issue instructions for both of them to be immediately apprehended. We'll also cover the airport and the docks.'

'Of course you've got to do that,' said Hamish, 'but I have a shrewd suspicion they're already well out of the country. Remember, Fraser has always been fascinated by the sea and sailing, and I'm sure he would know how to leave the country very quickly and quietly.'

It was Ross's turn to speak. 'Hamish, I can't tell you how sorry I am. As you know, I was beginning to get concerned about a family involvement but I was hoping that it was nobody as close to you as this. It must be devastating for you.'

'It is,' replied the father, 'and I really can't think why he would possibly have wanted to do this.'

'I'm sorry to be practical, Mr Tang,' Marvin interrupted, 'but how much of this can we let the County View directors know?'

'I think we've got no alternative but to let them know everything,' Hamish replied, 'but do you mind if I tell Roddy and Jerline? She's going to be as devastated as I am. Gavin is on one of his regular trips to China, but I've already phoned him and instructed him to return immediately.

'Well, gentlemen,' he said, looking round. 'That, I'm afraid, is the sad reality. I suggest we all finish our drinks and meet tomorrow to discuss how this should be handled from a publicity point of view. Clearly you can't keep it quiet,' he said to Murray, 'but obviously I want it to be announced in the least damaging way possible as far as the family and the company are concerned. Heaven knows its going to need fiendishly clever PR to achieve anything other than pandemonium on the stock market and waves of total disbelief and horror throughout my family.'

The three men left the tycoon with genuine sympathy for him as a father with a terrible dilemma.

Murray rushed off to report to his boss and set the necessary wheels in motion.

318

A subdued Ross and Marvin returned to the apartment. 'We'd better let London know,' said Marvin.

Ross agreed. 'What a bloody mess! What happens now?'

'We sit tight and see what they say. Knowing Percy, he'll think it all through very carefully.'

Chapter Thirty-Three

Shortly before the breakfast break, a black Mercedes with tinted windows drew into O'Connor's yard. Two smartly dressed young men approached him. One was carrying a slim and expensive-looking suitcase. They looked as if they could be bankers, and indeed that's what they were. They worked for a small Swiss private bank. The one without the briefcase spoke.

'I suggest we go somewhere we can speak privately.' His manner was authoritative and O'Connor had no inclination to be difficult as he had no idea who they were or what they wanted. He led them into his study and closed the door. They both sat down without being invited. He followed suit behind his desk.

'Mr O'Connor,' the first said while the other put the briefcase carefully on his knees. 'I'm afraid that you're going to close this enterprise down.'

O'Connor opened his mouth to protest. The young man with the very slight French accent held up his hand to silence him. 'Hear me out. Your funds have dried up, you're heavily in debt to bookmakers, you're in danger of your feed merchants ceasing to supply you, and you already have had to lay off staff. We represent the source from which your monthly funds have been derived. I'm afraid this source is now dry as far as you're concerned.'

O'Connor tried to interrupt. The young man silenced him again with a wave of his hand. 'All is not completely disastrous from your point of view. You are to transfer all the passports and ownership documents of the horses owned by your racing establishment to James Dixon, the

Newmarket bloodstock agent. You are to inform all your outside owners that you've ceased training and ask them to remove their horses within a week. You're to choose six of your better staff to remain here to look after the horses. Dixon will be responsible for their wages. All your debts, including your gambling debts, will be paid. Before we go we need a list of all your creditors and how much you owe them. This is to include estimates of any bills which you are expecting by the end of this month.'

O'Connor was thunderstruck. The young man continued. 'We have here ן cheque for 100,000 euros. When you have signed the various documents which we have with us today, we will give it to you. In four weeks' time, assuming you have complied with all we have asked and any other requests we may make, a similar sum will be transferred to whichever bank account you nominate. Do you have any questions?'

'Why?' stammered O'Connor. 'Why now? The horses have been running well and we've probably had fewer disappointments than would normally be true of any training establishment.'

The young man with the briefcase spoke for the first time. 'In that case why have you lost so much money?' he asked. 'But this is irrelevant. The decision to close down your operation has nothing to do with your success or failure. In fact it has nothing to do with you, it is entirely a matter of business. The money raised by the sale of the horses running in your stable's name is needed for another more urgent investment.'

He did not add that Dixon had already done a deal and had paid a substantial sum for all the O'Connor-owned horses which was already sitting in their Swiss bank before onward transmission to a nominee account in the Cayman Islands.

'I suggest you phone Mr Dixon to make the necessary arrangements but he has asked us to instruct you not to run any horses unless he specifically authorizes it. Are there any other questions?'

O'Connor was silent. He was almost relieved that the

last few months of financial disaster were behind him. The prospect of his debts disappearing and him having 200,000 euros with which to start life again was not without appeal. He was beaten and for once he knew it. 'Can I offer you gentlemen a drink?' he enquired.

'That's very kind of you,' replied the first, 'but we are in a hurry. We must be on our way.' His companion now opened the briefcase and put some documents in front of O'Connor.

'You can take as long as you want to read them,' he said, 'but I can assure you they are just a legal form of what we have already outlined to you.' He passed the documents over to O'Connor and closed his briefcase. 'We'll go and have a walk round your yard,' he said, 'and get some fresh air. We'll be back in ten minutes to see if you have any queries.' They got up, let themselves out and walked swiftly and purposefully into the yard. Ignoring the no smoking signs, they casually lit up and leant over a gate leading into a small paddock and watched three horses grazing contentedly. They said nothing to each other. Finishing their cigarettes, they dropped them, ground them out with their heels and, nodding to each other, walked purposefully back into O'Connor's house. He was still signing pages as they walked in.

'You've initialled every page as well as signed where marked?' the document carrier enquired. O'Connor nodded and passed the documents across his desk. The briefcase was opened, an envelope passed to O'Connor, the documents put in, the briefcase closed. The two men got up and walked out. Pausing, the spokesman turned to O'Connor. 'It was nice doing business with you, Mr O'Connor. Be lucky,' and he walked out.

O'Connor sat in a daze. He tried to phone Hanagan but there was no answer. He then rang his father, who was largely sympathetic but did remind his son he had thought it was too good to be true from the outset. 'What are you going to do?' he asked.

'Go somewhere quiet,' was the reply. 'The media will be

in a frenzy when they learn what's happened, and I can really do without that crap.'

'Any idea where you're going?'

'Probably to Paris,' was the reply. 'I've got a girlfriend there who will put me up. I'm hardly known in France and there's plenty to keep me occupied. What's more, I imagine my Swiss friends will be happier if I'm somewhere not too far away. They gave me a telephone number where I could leave messages letting them know my whereabouts until the second payment has been made.'

'I'm sorry, my boy,' his father said with feeling.

'Thanks for not criticizing me. It would have been justified.'

'I know,' the older man said. 'Now keep in touch and don't go drinking too much.'

At County View, Jay was sitting down after morning exercises had finished and was reading the *Racing Post*. There was nothing particularly relevant to him in it, but he did take the opportunity to glance at the previous day's results which indicated that Neville Gethin, the northern trainer, had had three wins.

His phone rang and it was a very excited Harry Solomons. 'Have you heard the news?'

'What news?'

'About O'Connor.'

'No.'

'Well, I've just had James Dixon, the bloodstock agent, on to me. O'Connor has put all his horses on the market, asked his outside owners to remove their horses, fired most of his stable staff, and has just left a skeleton to gently exercise those that are left. I understand that all they're doing is being put on the horse walker.'

Jay was thunderstruck. 'What the hell can that be about?'

'Well, we know there have been rumours about him having financial problems. It sounds as if they've just caught up with him in a big way. I've already had a couple of my previous owners phoning to ask if I'll take the

323

horses back and I imagine you'll be in the same situation before the day's out. Do you think you'll accept them?'

'I'll have to think about that. I suppose I can hardly blame the owners for accepting the extraordinary prices that were paid and there are obviously one or two such as Cool Customer that I'd love to have back. To be perfectly honest, a couple of owners showed not very nice sides to their characters and I'd probably tell them to get lost, but Bill Smith, Cool Customer's owner, was extremely embarrassed, and he has bought and sent me a promising youngster.'

'I'm in much the same position,' Harry explained. 'Well let's keep in touch and see what happens.'

Minutes later the phone was ringing from the racing press. Jay asked Eva to take the calls and to say that he was out but would ring back as soon as he was free.

He phoned Howard, Percy and Roddy (who had not yet heard from Hamish). They were all ecstatic. Jay promised to let them know of further developments.

As expected, three of the owners who'd taken horses away from County View phoned to say that the bloodstock agent had contacted them and the horses were on the market. He was sure they would be available at a less inflated price than had been the case when O'Connor had bought them, and they also told Jay that Dixon was pressing for a quick sale.

Jay had barely had a chance to take all this in when Harvey Jackson phoned. 'I've had a long conversation with McKenna,' he started. He proceeded to advise Jay of the various developments which had occurred from the time that Hanagan had left Singapore, narrowly escaping being blown up in an apartment that belonged to the Tang business empire, to his arrest in Dublin. But now there was even more dramatic news.

Early in the morning Hanagan had been taken ill. The police doctor diagnosed that he was suffering from severe stress and high blood pressure and advised that it was imperative he was given time to recover. He was in serious danger of a heart attack. He had been transferred to the local prison and put in their hospital. He had a round the clock guard by his bedside with a tape recorder to make sure that anything he said was not lost in the event of the prisoner's death.

Chapter Thirty-Four

McKenna had just finished being briefed on a bad hit and run case when his telephone rang. It was the police surgeon responsible for Hanagan.

'Look, this prisoner of yours is pretty poorly. I want him moved to a hospital where there's specialist knowledge and equipment on hand. I don't suppose you want to lose him before you've got the chance to question him further?'

'Dead right,' was the reply. 'You make the arrangements but I want him under twenty-four hour guard by two officers at all times. One of them is always to be with him and I don't care what the doctors or nurses say. There's been one attempt on his life and I wouldn't be surprised if there's another. Somebody probably wants him silenced, and I don't.'

'Right,' agreed the surgeon. 'I'll let you know where he is. I'll make sure your men accompany him in the ambulance.'

McKenna called in his deputy and explained the position. 'I want experienced officers we trust and I want to talk to them myself. I want them armed and I want another officer in reception at all times checking on anybody making enquiries about Hanagan's health or location.'

Within the hour, twelve policemen had been briefed who would take it in turns to ensure a twenty-four hour watch not only on the patient, but also on the hospital reception.

Shortly after eight o'clock the next morning the police surgeon was on the phone again. 'Hanagan has deteriorated during the night. He's been insistent that he wants to make a statement to the police but he wants to do it in front of a priest and his own lawyer. He wants to make his confession after he's finished the police statement.'

'Right,' said McKenna. 'Go ahead. See if there's any particular priest he wants. If not, we'll get Father Joseph who's always been helpful to us in the past.'

Just after midday there was a knock at the door and Sergeant O'Leary walked in. He had a tape recorder in his hands. 'I think you'll find this pretty interesting, sir,' he said. McKenna motioned for him to turn the machine on and they both sat down to listen. Hanagan's voice was low and clearly weak but he was audible, although pausing from time to time to take several breaths. His statement lasted for over fifteen minutes.

When it was finished, McKenna arranged for a transcript to be put in front of him as soon as possible, and had the tape copied twice. The original was put in his safe, one copy in another police station, and the third sent to Jackson by courier. Half an hour later he was on the phone to Jackson, giving him the information and promising to fax a hard copy through to him immediately as well as sending him the tape.

Hanagan had admitted to being behind not only the Danny attack but all the other incidents involving County View.

Many months earlier when he was in Hong Kong, Fraser Tang had asked for a meeting. Hanagan had done business with Fraser before, and although some of it was of a dubious nature this was the first time that it had become clear that Tang was heavily involved in the narcotics trade.

When they'd finished their conversation on this matter and Hanagan had promised to launder a very substantial sum of money for Fraser, Tang then changed the subject completely. He told Hanagan that he wanted to undermine a major English training yard. When Hanagan realized which one it was, he was genuinely amazed. Fraser explained that money was no object and asked Hanagan to go away, think about it, and come back with a plan.

Hanagan was familiar with Irish racing and had one very good contact who had been a racing journalist but was now the deputy editor of a major newspaper. He was in Hanagan's pay. Not only was he an excellent source of information, but from time to time he placed helpful and positive comments about certain of Hanagan's investments. He could be equally negative about those of some of his competitors.

Hanagan had put his problem to the journalist and between them they had come up with the solution of finding an Irish trainer with proven ability but as yet no great success. His ambition had to exceed his scruples. After a few discreet enquiries O'Connor became the prime candidate and very quickly the vehicle of their plan. Hanagan met O'Connor himself and kept him in the dark about who was really financing the enterprise, apart from saying that the money originated from the Far East where it was known he had many contacts.

O'Connor wanted to know the motive behind this, and Hanagan at that stage could say with all honesty that he had no idea as he had never been told. It was clear that O'Connor had his doubts about the veracity of this, but as long as he was being financed to achieve his objective he wasn't too worried. It was some months later, on one of the very rare occasions when Hanagan and Tang met in the evening, that Tang drank too much and admitted why he had undertaken this expensive and dangerous project. He confessed to Hanagan that he had always felt that his father preferred Gavin and Jerline to himself. His jealousy had exploded into simmering rage when Hamish had backed Roddy's involvement in County View and then subsequently Gavin's growing love of racing, his frequent visits to racecourses with his father, and his developing friendship with both Roddy and Jay. When he heard that Gavin was considering having horses at County View it was the final straw.

He set out to damage County View and the bloodstock

operation in such a way that his father and brother would lose face and Roddy probably his job.

Right at the outset of their plans to build up O'Connor's operation and damage County View, they had a dossier prepared on the racing yard and all those connected with it. Strangely enough, Danny's suspicion that Ahearne was passing on information from prison was right in an oblique way. In fact, one of Hanagan's criminal associates was doing time in the same jail as Ahearne. He became friendly and started to pass what he knew on to Daly, and through Daly to Hanagan.

Hanagan saw this as a stroke of luck. By constructing the incidents in a certain way he could throw suspicion on The Friend and cause confusion among both the police and those involved with County View.

Through the same associate he heard of Ahearne's impending transfer to Ireland and this was an absolute godsend for him. He seized the opportunity, and the rest was history. However, he was completely thrown by the Billy Dean incident, and although it caused confusion it actually had nothing to do with his plans. He had arranged for Daly to set fire to the marquee at County View hoping it would encourage owners to move horses to O'Connor.

The Ayr incident was also conceived as a way of throwing suspicion on The Friend, but had the added advantage of giving them a golden opportunity to make a significant financial killing, even though it was relatively small in terms of the big picture.

The attack on Hansie came when O'Connor was beginning to get really nervous and then heard through Pippa that the South African was apparently making enquiries into his activities which were getting a bit close to home. This was set up by Hanagan without O'Connor's knowledge.

A number of these incidents, although planned and executed via Hanagan, were in fact at Fraser's behest. He was beginning to get desperate as his own financial predicament worsened, and he was trying to bring the County

View and O'Connor situation to as quick a conclusion as possible. The decision to withdraw funds and sell the horses was entirely as a result of the problems he was facing through his stock market losses and the very severe pressure from his drug supplier.

When Hanagan learned of the extent of Fraser's problem, he decided to withdraw his support which led to the bomb attack in Singapore.

'That in essence was the whole story according to Hanagan.' McKenna paused for breath.

'The more I see of people, the more I see the truth in the old saying that God gives you your friends and the Devil your relations,' joked Jackson. 'Well I guess that wraps the whole thing up, doesn't it?'

'Well, it does at my end,' agreed McKenna, 'although whether Hanagan will survive seems very doubtful. He's going down so fast that he's asked for the Last Rites.'

'As soon as I've got your fax, I'll talk to Jay and Percy,' Jackson informed him. 'Clearly we've got to let Hamish Tang know all this as soon as possible. It's going to be a terrible blow to the man.'

'I can see that,' agreed McKenna. 'It's bad enough that one of his sons is behind it, but the fact that everything stems from jealousy of his brother and sister and the perceived favouritism of his father will make it even harder.'

'I know,' said Jackson. 'I'm glad it's not my job to tell him.'

Minutes later there was a knock at his door and several sheets of faxed paper were put in front of him. Once he'd read them he phoned Jay and then Percy and summarized to each the essence of Hanagan's confession. He then faxed the transcript from Ireland to each of them. The next few hours saw frantic telephoning between the various directors of County View. Jay had decided to tell Roddy. Roddy had already heard from Hamish and both he and Jerline were in a state of shock. He asked Jay to tell his father-in-law the contents of Hanagan's confession. He felt he could not face it himself.

Jackson had already agreed that both Ross and Marvin should be told of the latest developments. They were to advise Murray, but not until they knew that Hamish had been told himself and had had a chance to talk to his son and daughter.

That night Howard and Percy both drove to County View for a quiet supper with Jay and Eva and to review the dramatic events of the last few days. Roddy felt it better for him and Jerline to be alone.

'God knows how poor Hamish is going to take this,' a very sympathetic Howard commented. 'He'll be devastated.'

'I wonder how he'll feel about his involvement with County View now. He may be sick of the whole thing,' sighed Percy.

'Well, there's nothing we can do about that. The ball's in his court,' was Jay's reaction.

'Changing the subject, has there been any news of Fraser?' asked Eva.

'The last we heard was that he and Gustav Brandt, his finance director, had disappeared and so far there's been no sight or sound of them, I gather. Needless to say the Singapore police are extremely anxious to talk to both of them.'

'Well,' said Jay, 'I think that all we can do now is to get on with running County View. You'd better phone your mother and she can give Danny the good news. At last we know who his attackers were and their motives. Finally he can rest easy in his bed.'

It was a relieved quartet that made their farewells shortly after midnight. Francis drove Percy and Howard to London, dropping Howard off on his way and taking an emotionally and physically exhausted Percy back to his home. 'Thank God I'm not married,' he mused as he dropped into bed shortly before 2 a.m.

It turned out that Hamish took the news of Fraser's motives surprisingly calmly. The sheer horror of discovering that his son was a criminal on so many levels had apparently taken him beyond this further shock. He was

331

deeply saddened by Fraser's motives, but searching his heart he knew that he had never favoured the two younger siblings. He'd always encouraged, and indeed in the early days financed, Fraser's marine interests. Fraser had been given a flying start with the businesses he'd been entrusted to run, and Gavin had got where he had not only by working just as hard as Fraser but probably by exhibiting a little more flair. Jerline had never been involved in the business and only had special treatment to the extent that most fathers give their daughters.

Hamish knew he could never forgive his son. He had brought dishonour to those closest to him. It was a betrayal he could hardly comprehend.

After giving a lot of thought to his involvement in County View, he decided to keep his shareholding for the time being but to withdraw from any of the management activities including resigning his directorship and assigning Roddy a permanent proxy to vote on his behalf. The other directors completely understood this and accepted it.

Jay was insistent that Hamish was still always welcome at County View. Indeed, he and Eva would be hurt if he didn't visit them from time to time when he was in England. He made it plain that he understood and respected Hamish's feelings, but that everyone connected with County View would miss his involvement.

Hamish was clearly touched and promised that he was certainly not going to become a hermit.

Hogan and Marvin returned to London feeling that they'd not made a particularly significant contribution towards finally solving the problem. The directors of County View were adamant that through their contacts the pair had been instrumental in setting in motion the chain reaction which eventually led to the dramatic conclusion to the mystery. Unhappily it had also left a deep well of sadness for a family they'd come to like and admire.

As a token of their esteem, Eva arranged a dinner party. It took place at the end of an afternoon's racing at Newbury where for once County View didn't have a runner. It was odd for everyone involved to be attending a meeting without a specific interest in at least one of the races. In many ways it was even more enjoyable as there was no likelihood of disappointment, although there clearly wouldn't be the joy of leading in a winner. All the directors were there, along with Jed, Jerline, Danny and Fiona, who'd flown over a few days before with a thoroughly healthy and cheerful Head Man. Roddy and Jerline were both putting on a brave face and were definitely pleased to have a diversion. Marvin, Ross, Benny and Zara made up the complement. Jackson had been invited but declined because of a previous engagement. Little was said about the events which had preoccupied them all for so long. Benny was at his most mischievous when he whispered to Jay he was surprised that Vanda was not there. Jay studiously ignored the remark.

The conversation centred on the key horses at County View and their chances at the rapidly approaching Cheltenham Festival. It was a happy, confident and rather inebriated group that eventually made their various ways home.

Epilogue

The two men sat in commodious, well-cushioned rattan chairs under a huge sun umbrella made of palm leaves. They were positioned a few yards from the edge of the sea on a tiny, almost unknown island in the Maldives. On the table between them were two glasses of cold German beer, and close at hand was a cooler filled with an ample supply of the same brew.

Behind them was a small, simple bungalow. The outside belied the luxury and comfort of the interior. It had been built some years ago specifically for the two men sitting there. A group of Filipino builders, under the direction of a skilled Thai architect, had constructed it to the most demanding of specifications. The builders knew nothing about the project other than that they were highly paid, and had no real idea of the exact location of the island. Similarly, the architect had contacts only with an Irishman who paid him generously and largely left him to his own devices. From time to time he visited the project to ensure that not a corner was cut and that the minutest detail faithfully followed the agreed plan. As soon as the bungalow was completed, another simpler but still comfortable second bungalow was built a hundred yards from the main residence. This housed an elderly Chinese couple who acted as caretakers when the main property was unoccupied. They became cooks, servants and house-keepers when the two men were in residence and when they entertained the young Filipino or Thai girls who were their frequent visitors, normally two for each man. The third inhabitant of the bungalow was another Chinese man in his thirties. His main job was to maintain the small but highly powerful motor launch tied to the wooden jetty in front of the men. This was used to provision the island for both the three permanent residents and the owners and their guests when required.

The Chinese was also responsible for servicing the powerful ocean-going cruiser that was hidden in a large and discreetly positioned boathouse. This was used by the two owners to visit their island and to return to their base. It was invariably driven by the Oriental now sipping his beer.

The young employee was content in the knowledge that he was safe from the Hong Kong police force who wanted him for a particularly nasty murder. Quite what his employers' relationship was he neither knew nor cared, although it was clear the German was deferential to the Oriental. When girls were required on the island he was dispatched to a specific place where they were waiting. They were brought to the island and no conversation took place between him and the four girls, although inevitably they chatted excitedly amongst themselves.

The three servants sat calmly outside their bungalow with an air of expectancy which could easily have been mistaken for anticipation of an order from one of the two men. Otherwise they sat in silence gazing impassively out to sea.

It was the German who first noticed the small dot at sea which gradually increased in size as it approached the island. It was not unknown, but rare, for a passing boat to call in, and no visitors were expected. In a few minutes it was clear that the island was indeed the destination of the fast-approaching craft. The watchers had already determined that there were only two occupants. One was steering while the other lolled nonchalantly in a comfortable seat in front of the quite large cabin. The boat throttled down and inched its way towards the beach until it was expertly brought to a halt.

The passenger, dressed in a smart khaki uniform with immaculately pressed shorts, jumped over the side and walked purposefully but casually up to the two men. His reflective sunglasses and the shade from his peaked cap made it difficult to distinguish his features. He did, however, appear to be Oriental.

The German looked at his Chinese companion and said one word: 'Official.'

'Tax?' suggested his companion.

'That or some other attempt to extract money,' the German replied.

The visitor drew to a halt two paces in front of the seated men and removed his sunglasses.

It was difficult to tell if their expressions were those of amazement or fear. They soon turned to terror as the man they knew all too well removed his revolver from its holster and, before they could move, shot both of them dead – one bullet in each head. He paused and looked at the three still impassive figures sitting outside the servants' bungalow. He beckoned. The elderly couple shuffled quickly towards him and, without a word, he pointed to the boat. The young man just looked at him, nodded, and followed them. Not looking back, the assassin made his way to the edge of the sea and watched the three servants scramble into the boat. He clambered over the side and motioned them into the cabin. He nodded to the driver, who reversed the launch and then turned it and headed out to sea at full throttle. The assassin did not even glance back at the island. He walked to the side of the boat, undid his belt and dropped it, the holster and the gun, over the side. He walked to the bow, withdrew his mobile phone and dialled a number in Singapore.

'It is done.'

'Thank you.'

Johnny Tang took out a Marlboro cigarette from the packet in his breast pocket, lit it, and, leaning on the boat rail, watched the sun set into the ocean.